D0049018

ALSO BY KAREN AKINS

LOOP

TWIST

KAREN AKINS

ST. MARTIN'S GRIFFIN
NEW YORK

TWIST. Copyright © 2015 by Karen Akins. All rights reserved. Printed in the United States of America. For information, address St. Martin's Press, 175 Fifth Avenue, New York, N.Y. 10010.

www.stmartins.com

Library of Congress Cataloging-in-Publication Data

Akins, Karen, author.
    Twist / Karen Akins. — First edition.
        pages cm
    ISBN 978-1-250-03100-6 (hardcover)
    ISBN 978-1-250-03101-3 (e-book)
    [1. Adventure and adventurers—Fiction.   2. Time travel—Fiction.   3. Kidnapping—Fiction.   4. Dating (Social customs)—Fiction.   5. Science fiction.]   I. Title.
    PZ7.1.A39Twi 2015
    [Fic]—dc23

                                                                    2014040845

St. Martin's Griffin books may be purchased for educational, business, or promotional use. For information on bulk purchases, please contact the Macmillan Corporate and Premium Sales Department at 1-800-221-7945, extension 5442, or write to specialmarkets@macmillan.com.

First Edition: April 2015

10   9   8   7   6   5   4   3   2   1

To my parents, Carl and Connie Hoffman, for letting me read books instead of making me play sports—good call

acknowledgments

FIRST, I WANT TO SAY a HUGE thanks to all of my readers. I have been blown away by your response to this twisty story that popped into my head. If I could give every one of you a pega-moo, I would.

There's no way to adequately thank everyone at St. Martin's Press for their support of *Loop* and *Twist*. I've had the most won-derful, enthusiastic team behind me: Holly Ingraham, Jeanne-Marie Hudson, Marie Estrada, Karen Masnica, Kerry McMahon, Michelle Cashman, Susan Andrews, Elizabeth Curione, and ev-eryone else on the SMP team. You're all blarking fabulous. And thank you to Lisa Marie Pompilio and Shane Rebenschield for gorgeous covers.

I'm so grateful for my agent Victoria Marini's guidance and encouragement along the way—thank you.

My circle of writing friends keeps growing and growing, and I'm so blessed by all of you. Elizabeth Briggs, Kristin Gray, I.W. Gregorio, Andrea Hannah, Kate Hart, Stacey Lee, Kim Loth, Cortney Pearson, Rachel Searles, Morgan Shamy, Mandy Sil-berstein, Evelyn Skye, you are the best!

Big, huge tackle hugs to: Authoress and the MSFV Sort-of-Secret Society, The Lucky 13s (especially to Kelly Fiore, a.k.a. my little gif Padawan, and Justina Ireland for all the fun gif wars), Arkansas SCBWIers, the YA Binders, and Bill and Becky Babler at the White River Lodge for putting up with some serious writ-ing retreat shenanigans year after year.

I have been bowled over by the support from librarians, teachers, and bookstore owners near and far. Thank you so much for introducing *Loop* to your readers!

This is the part I dread, where I know I'm going to have forgotten a sweet friend who has been an amazing supporter and cheerleader for me. So rather than name everyone, I will just say, "You know who you are. And you know that I love you. *Thank you.*"

Thank you again to my family! Carl and Connie Hoffman, Bill and Betty Akins, Carolyn Wagnon, Ellen Matkowski, Sara Hoffman, Mark and Julie King, Anna and Noah, Owen and Myles, and all the Hoffmans and Wings.

Henry and Oliver, you are my funny little muses, and I couldn't love you more.

Finally, Bill, thank you for being there every step of the way on this wild journey. You've waited a really long time for this (-dary).

*Any intelligent fool can make things bigger, more complex,
and more violent. It takes a touch of genius—and a lot of courage—to
move in the opposite direction.*

—ALBERT EINSTEIN

chapter 1

THERE ARE FORTY-SEVEN RULES every Shifter must obey. I'd broken all but two of them. And I didn't know it yet, but I'd end up blowing one that hadn't even been created to bits.

My feet sank to the ankle in mud. Eau de manure mixed with the smell of meat roasting on a spit. My stomach simultaneously turned in revulsion and grumbled with hunger. I really needed to remember to keep energy bars in my pocket. Oh, well. Nothing I could do about it in . . . I glanced down at my Quant-Com . . . ahh, September 3rd, 1666. That date rang a bell.

I hate bell-ringing dates.

A haze of smoke haloed the thatched roofs like a blanket. Angry voices erupted out of a tavern up the street when the keep kicked some drunkards from his establishment. They joined a throng of people pushing carts and carrying sacks, all headed the same direction. As the drunkards passed, their slurred Cockney tones were unmistakable.

I was somewhere in England. That matched the bells for some reason. But didn't make me feel better. I tinkered with my Com. It was practically useless since it didn't control or manipulate my Shifts through my microchip anymore, not that I missed being controlled or manipulated. At all. My Com pretty much acted as the world's fanciest pocketwatch now, telling me the date and location of where I landed when I naturally Shifted. Well, and it had a nifty stunner feature. But sometimes the Com took a while to pull info up. I was flicking the edge of the Com when a set of feet clomped down beside me on a wooden board.

"Ugh. That was close. Almost landed in the—" That's when the person who had landed next to me noticed my presence. Finn stifled a laugh at my muddy predicament. "Here."

He lent me an elbow to pull myself out of the muck.

"Fancy meeting you here, gov'nuh." I wiped a patch of mud off my hands so I could reach up and give him a smooch without mussing up his wavy auburn hair.

"Here being . . . ?"

"1666. Somewhere in London, I think."

"Yep. Aldersgate District." Finn pointed at a sign for an apothecary across the road, barely visible through the smoky haze.

"You're like a walking QuantCom," I said.

"Nah. I've been here around this time with Dad on mercy missions. Bubonic plague. It's one of his hobbies."

Finn's dad was a surgeon as well as a Shifter. Like Finn and me, he traveled through time and space. It was a hereditary ability. Finn's little sister had also gotten the gene. I'd inherited it from my mom's side.

"Your family is so weird," I said. Although more normal than my family, I guess, if you could even call us that. But Finn knew I didn't like talking about my father, so he didn't say anything in response. Besides, he was too busy coughing.

"Why does this date seem so familiar?" I asked. Quigley would kill me for not knowing my history.

"Uhh, Great Fire of London," Finn choked out.

"Blark." He was right. The fire had consumed most of the city over the course of four days. This was only the second day, though. The flames were still confined to an area closer to the Thames, near the bakery where the fire had started on Pudding Lane. It explained why everyone was rushing out of the city like herded cattle, though.

"Aldersgate." Finn peered around looking for landmarks. "I remember there's a Haven near here. By Saint Ann's."

"After you." I gestured for him to lead the way.

Finn started down an alley then stopped short and spun around. "Wait." He stared at me expectantly. "You almost forgot."

Good grief. "Do we really have to do this?"

He nodded.

It was kind of ridiculous, a plan that Finn had come up with for my benefit—to help me establish whether I was with Past Finn versus Present Finn (Well, not Present Finn. More like, Not-Quite-As-Distant-Past Finn). *My* Finn. Whatever. I was supposed to ask him a question that only the him that was dating Present Me would know.

Our relationship is going through what you might call a challenging stage right now. And by "right now," I mean "since the moment I met him."

"By virtue of the fact that you're asking me to ask, doesn't it establish that you are you?" I pointed out.

"Ask."

"Umm . . . what song do you sing every time we're in the Institute greenhouse?"

" 'It's Not Easy Being—' "

"Sing it." The right side of my mouth twitched up. If he was going to be a stickler, so was I.

He belted it out, froggy voice and all. I reached up and kissed him on the cheek, but he reeled me in closer. When I pulled away, he'd placed something in my open hand.

A chocolate energy bar.

"You look hungry," he said.

"What would I do without you?"

"Probably starve." He tucked the wrapper away in his canvas rucksack. His dad had trained Finn well over the last six months since he'd discovered he was a Shifter. Finn had once likened it to backpacking—whatever you carry into a time period, you carry out. Turns out most of the Rules of Shifting developed through common sense, long before Shifters came out of hiding.

I straightened Finn's rumpled T-shirt. That was one of the things I had taught him, to wear as plain clothes as possible. Even if he stuck out, he wouldn't be memorable.

Then again, I didn't see how it would be possible to forget someone as gorgeous as Finn.

He pulled a knit cap out of the sack, and I took one out of my pocket. Another little trick of mine. You could pass as a sailor in almost any time period with one. I tucked my long, light-brown ponytail up in the hat. I wished I could say I'd grown my hair out because I liked the way it looked. Nope. I'd just been too busy the last six months to bother with cutting it.

"Now, what do you think we're doing here?" Finn asked as I finished my snack.

"No clue." It was still hard for me to get used to, this Shifting back without a predetermined goal. As a chipped Shifter, every mission had had a reason behind it. Study something. Deliver something. Test something. Most of my trips as a free Shifter so far had been visiting Finn and his family or tagging along with my mom on art investigations. Finn and I also sometimes turned up at the same place in the past together, like now. But we usually ended up just poking around. Interesting, yes, but purposeless.

Well, that wasn't counting my trips back using the reverter. Ahh, the reverter. I pulled the device out of my front pocket. I never let it out of my sight—even for a moment.

Such a nightmare I'd gone through for such a small object. It looked a bit like a writing pen from Finn's time—long, thin, and cylindrical. Only this was no writing pen. When it went off— glowing green and vibrating like a ticked-off tea kettle—it meant that a nonShifter had made a change to the timeline in my present. Those changes in my time were only detectable by unchipped Shifters like myself. This device was the only thing that would put it back to normal. Unfortunately, the ability to detect those changes had the side effect of making us unchipped Shifters come across as a bit confused . . . muddled . . . fine, catpoop crazy. I didn't care though. I'd rather seem confused to the rest of the world than live a lie.

"This feels different from when we usually meet up," said Finn. I had to agree. Our typical meet-ups felt like a breath of fresh air. These smoke-filled surroundings were anything but.

"Maybe we're supposed to deliver a message between Haven members," I said. We turned back down the alley. The Haven Society was a meeting place for free Shifters, past and future. I'd never delivered any messages before, but I knew some of the Resthaven residents had friends in the past.

At the mouth of the alley someone slammed into my shoulder as he passed.

"Excuse me," I said before looking up to see who had bumped me. Whoever it was wore a suit made of a shiny, silver material. His entire head was covered with a hood and protective mask. Finn and I may have looked a little out of place in our non-descript clothes, but this guy looked like a space alien.

And last I checked, there were no seventeenth-century space aliens.

When the person looked back and saw me, he visibly startled. Then took off in a dead run. It looked like whoever it was had recognized me.

"Come on." I tugged on Finn's sleeve to follow.

The silver-clad person took off through the serpentine, narrow alley. As he ran, he knocked objects down behind him to block our path. I parted a dingy line of clothes strung between two soot-covered brick walls. The smoke grew thicker, clawing at my eyes and making it hard to see, which didn't make sense as we weren't that close to the initial outbreak of fires.

We reached the end of the alley. It ended in a T shape at the back of another set of buildings. The smoke had grown so profuse, I could taste it down the back of my throat. I squinted in both directions, not sure which way the silver-suited guy had gone. A cat hissed to my right, like he'd just been frightened. I took off that way, Finn close at my heels. It was easier to see this direction anyway. Someone had lit a bunch of lanterns in the street up ahead.

"Wait." Finn caught me by the shoulder.

"We're going to lose him," I said, trying to wiggle away from Finn. But then I realized why he had held me back.

Those weren't lanterns.

Something was burning. Something big. I tugged at Finn's hand and raced forward, my other hand clutching my Com, stunner out and ready. Ash fell from the sky like snowflakes. I skidded as we turned a sharp corner into the next street. My boot slammed hard into a puddle, and mud splattered my front up to my chest. I caught myself against a metal grate on the wall. It sliced my arm, and blood oozed out the gash. Dang it. Finn helped me steady myself. Flames licked out and greeted us from the storefront blazing across the street.

"Those poor people," I said quietly as I wiped mud and who knows what festering germs away from the wound. "Are we supposed to stop the fire?"

"How?" He had a point. It wasn't like they had instantaneous soakswitches from my time or even fire hydrants from Finn's. There was nothing we could do but stand there and watch it burn.

It went hot and fast, which actually appeared to be a good thing. The fire was so intense that it consumed the wood of the storefront before the blaze had the chance to spread too far.

Neighbors and shopkeepers poured out into the street and formed a sad attempt at a bucket brigade. They used hooks to pull down walls to protect bordering buildings. I thought over my Great Fire history and realized their efforts were a moot point. This area would be gone within a few days anyway.

My eyes sifted through the crowd searching for flashes of silver, but I didn't see any. I now recognized the silver suit for what it was—protective fire gear from my time, from the twenty-third century. That thing could easily withstand temperatures upwards of 2,000 degrees. Swarms of rats scurried away from the growing flames. Chaos flared up as quickly as the fire.

"I don't think anyone could survive that," said Finn.

I gulped. So why were we here?

"Bree." Finn shook his head slowly from side to side.

"Maybe, umm. . . ." Ugh. I couldn't think straight. It was so hot. I removed my cap and fanned myself. The breeze didn't cool me off, but it gave me a much-needed waft of oxygen.

"Bree, look." Gently, Finn turned my face so I was staring directly at what remained of the doorway.

There in a puddle by the already crumbling rafters floated three pools of wax with wicks barely sticking out, each still flickering a faint green.

This was the Haven.

So what had happened to everyone inside?

>—◆—

"Whoever it was, I think he's long faded." Finn scraped his boot through a pile of still-sparking ash. Only a couple hours had passed, but the street was almost deserted. The few people who hadn't already fled the city were busy grabbing belongings so they could.

"I know." I'd held out as long as possible, hoping the silver-suited person would return, but was clearly deluding myself.

"Hey, Bree." Finn stooped to pick up a piece of paper from the cinders. He waved his fingers, and it stuck to them. "It's compufilm."

"What?" I snatched it away from him. Compufilm was a twenty-third-century invention.

"What does it say?" He peered over my shoulder as I unfolded it.

"To save his, destroy yours," I read. "And then random letters and numbers and stuff with a bunch of blanks."

"Huh," he said. "Wonder what that means. To save his what?"

"Finn."

"And then who is the 'he' referring to?"

"Finn." I held the film for him to examine more closely.

"And destroy what?"

"Finn!"

He finally glanced up. "What?"

"I wrote this. It's in my handwriting."

He snatched it back. "Was that Future You in the silver suit?"

"Couldn't be. That person towered over me. They were, like, six feet tall."

"Could that have been me?"

"I doubt it. That was twenty-third-century gear. Besides, I don't think that person was here to fight the fire. I think they started it."

"Why would they do that?" asked Finn. "This area is going to be destroyed by fire anyway in a matter of days. It all sounds so . . ."

"Ominous." Blark. I hated ominous. I started to run my fingers through my hair, but my hand went limp.

Finn stared at me with a look of horror on his face. "Bree, your arm."

I looked at it and gasped. The arm that I'd cut had suddenly blown up three times its normal size and turned a gruesome orange. I knew these symptoms.

No. It couldn't be.

"Capuchin fever," I said. "It was eradicated thirty years ago. I mean, thirty years ago in my time."

"What's capuchin fever?"

"You don't have it back in the twenty-first century." I tried to wave the question off, but my arm had grown so swollen, it resembled an orange watermelon. "It's a dormant virus, but if exposed to the right germs . . ."

"Make it stop!" said Finn.

"But I don't know why—" And that's when I felt it. *Whir.* The reverter was going off in my pocket. Son of a germ-infested monkey. Some nonShifter from my time had changed their past. As a result, a long-extinct disease had returned. "Come on."

Shifting while using the reverter felt different than when I was naturally called to a place. It resembled the sensation of when my chip used to dump me somewhere. Kind of like being shoved rather than pulled.

I held the glowing green device out and wrapped my good arm around Finn before clicking the end of it.

Shifters, chipped or otherwise, normally weren't able to Shift forward into their future. Only backward. I possessed the rare ability to Shift other people, namely Finn, into my own time because I was a chronogenetic mish mash. My father was born at the turn of the twentieth century. My mom gave birth to me at the turn of the twenty-third century. Apparently, that made me the temporal equivalent of double-sided sticky tape.

Finn squeezed me close to his side. He needed to be touching me for my quantum tendrils to latch on to him. As I took one final gaze over the streets of London, I couldn't tell if the dull, red haze in the distance was the sun coming up or another building burning down.

chapter 2

"AHH, A SHIFTER. Welcome to Jamaica, mon." A Rastafarian tossed a handful of dreads over his shoulder and held out his hand until he saw the state of my arm. "Is that the capuchin?" His tone changed from laid-back and friendly to business-like in an instant. "We need a quarantine procedure over here!"

I ignored the man and peered over his shoulder. We were in a hoverport, somewhere in Jamaica. I didn't bother checking my Com for details. I didn't care what year it was. Clearly it was some point after Shifters had come out in the open, but before the cure to capuchin fever had been discovered. All I cared about was stopping someone from making a blarking stupid decision.

Finn had never been on a reversion mission with me. He stood at my side, biting his nails, staring at my arm. I didn't need a quarantine. I needed to find the idiot who had caused this change.

And there he was.

A man in his mid-twenties fidgeted in the line to board the next hovercraft, destination Atlanta. I'd seen a picture of him before. Somewhere. And suddenly, a lesson from Contemporary Developments in Biology clicked in my head and I knew exactly who I was looking at. It was a young James Canavan, one of the most brilliant minds to ever work for the Centers for Disease Control. Over the last thirty-five years, he had single-handedly created vaccines for more than a dozen infectious diseases. Including capuchin fever.

Canavan stepped out of the line, then back into it. He glanced at his watch, the boarding gate, his watch again. He stepped back out of line. Back in. Back out. Yep. One of the most brilliant minds of modern medicine.

Who apparently had once considered quitting med school to live on a beach in Jamaica.

But it wasn't him that I needed to find. My eyes scanned through the waiting passengers. There. By the windows. The older Dr. Canavan watched his younger self, only prying his eyes away to steal glances at the sapphire blue waves that crashed onto the sand outside. A tear trickled down his cheek, and for a millisecond, I felt sorry for him.

Then my arm started to throb, and that millisecond ended.

I marched toward him just as he parted his way through the waiting passengers toward his younger self.

"Dr. Canavan," I called. They both looked up, but I ignored the younger one. "You can't do this."

"Do . . . what?" The older man looked around nervously. He winced and gripped his neck. Shifting was painful for nonShifters. Probably because they, oh, I don't know, weren't meant to be doing it.

There was a rumble behind me as the Rastafarian who had greeted me pointed two guards in my direction. The capuchin actually worked in my favor. I could tell neither guard wanted to get too close to me. Still, I hurried. The reverter had already started to slow its whirring. If I didn't hurry, Dr. Canavan's change could be permanent.

"You can't stop your past self from boarding that hovercraft." I pointed at the young Canavan who looked completely perplexed by what was going on around him.

"How did you know—?"

"It doesn't matter." I lifted up my balloon of an arm. "You can't abandon your work to stay here."

"Attention"—the reggae song playing over the loudspeakers halted—"the young lady with capuchin fever needs to proceed to medical quarantine immediately."

The reaction was immediate and explosive. Everyone scattered in a panic with an outcry of "Capuchin! Where is she?"

Crapcakes. A woman jostled into me and then saw my arm and screamed. I flinched and dropped the reverter. Another woman kicked it across the room. Blark!

Finn saw what had happened and joined me to rush after it as it rolled. My arm had gone numb by the time I reached the reverter. If I remembered my capuchin symptoms correctly, I had about three minutes before it rapidly shriveled and fell off. But I doubted I had even that much time before the reverter's window closed. I had to get to the doctor. Finn cleared a path for me.

"You can't do this," I said when I reached the elder Canavan.

"I'm afraid it might be too late." He gestured at the public hysteria surrounding us. His touch held genuine compassion as he prodded my arm. "I'm sorry."

"It's never too late." This was going to be one of the simpler ones. He wasn't going to fight me or try to stop me like some of them did. I held the reverter against the bare skin on the back of his neck and, without a single word of protest from him, clicked the trigger.

The older Dr. Canavan instantly vanished. My arm was back to normal. The hysterical crowd turned back into patiently waiting passengers, and the younger Dr. Canavan was again standing in line for the hovercraft, acting as if nothing had happened. I watched him until he had boarded, which he did with only a tiny backward glance.

Finn, who was now diligently guarding a patch of thin air, wandered over to me. He wrapped his arms around me and rested his chin on the top of my head.

"That was . . . amazing," he said.

"That was an easy one." I flexed my arm at the elbow, thankful to have an elbow. "And I lied to him."

"What do you mean?"

"I told him it was never too late, but that's not true." I held up the reverter. The green light faded slowly. The whirring noise quieted to a hum. And then the device turned dark and silent. "If I don't stop a change before the reverter switches off, it's permanent."

"You could have lost your arm."

"Along with about a million other people." Not to mention the other hideous diseases Dr. Canavan had helped eradicate over the past few decades.

"What was he thinking?" Finn looked at the departing hovercraft in disgust.

"He wasn't thinking. He was feeling." I said it like a dirty word.

"The horror," said Finn, laughing.

I laughed, too, but if there was one thing I'd learned over the last six months, it's that it takes a rare, rare person to willingly sacrifice the things he loves for the greater good. Nine times out of ten in these reversions, I had to wrestle the nonShifters to the ground and jab them against their will in order to fix their changes.

But easy or no, each assault of the timeline felt like a personal attack against me.

"Do you want to stay here and enjoy the beach for a little while?" asked Finn.

"I just want to go home."

⊶

"I vote we pitch a tent and stay here forever." Finn had stretched out on his usual cool, mossy boulder in a hidden corner of the greenhouse at the Institute. He said that every time he came to the twenty-third century.

"Forever's a long time." I scratched at a patch of lichen on the base of the rock. I loved this place. My school really was my second home.

"Well, I'm glad I get to share it with you." He grinned. He

had this amazing blind faith that everything would work out, even as I constantly discovered ways to disprove him.

I didn't deserve him.

Hush. I silenced the nagging fear that cropped up every time I thought about Finn's and my future. It was difficult enough keeping up with our past.

"How's your arm?" he asked.

"Fine," I said. "Like it never happened."

Because, technically, it hadn't.

I didn't understand how the reverter worked or why, but it completely erased Dr. Canavan's change to the timeline. Well, not *completely*.

Canavan would be haunted by a vague patchwork of memories of what he had done and what his life would have been like if he'd succeeded in making that change. For lack of a better word, I had started calling those false memories "flashes." I didn't understand that part either, but I knew they would torment him.

"So I don't get it," said Finn.

"Get what?"

"I thought they were going to be careful, screen all the people who wanted to make changes, to make sure something like this didn't happen. How could they approve a leading immunologist to play fast and loose with the space-time continuum?"

They, of course, referred to the Initiative for Chronogeological Equality. ICE. And the answer to Finn's question was . . .

"I don't know."

"If you hadn't stopped him, a lot of people could have gotten sick, right?"

"And died."

"Why would ICE allow that? I don't get it."

"Maybe they're not in as much control as they think they are," I said. "Maybe I'm not either."

I brushed my finger against the fading gash that had almost

altered my life forever, but that I'd been able to seal in a matter of seconds when I got back to the twenty-third century. Finn tried to understand the weight of responsibility that now pressed on me every second of every day with this reverter, but he couldn't really.

"Do you have plans later?" he asked.

"I don't think so," I said after having to give it some thought. It was hard to say. Trying to keep up with my schedule had become a full-contact sport. It's not that I was a social butterfly like my best friend, Mimi, and it was Spring Break, so almost all the students were gone from the Institute, but I felt like there was something I had wanted to do.

"Not planning on seeing someone, are you?" Finn sounded the teensiest bit suspicious.

"Who would I be seeing?" He couldn't be thinking about my ex-friend Wyck. It had been six months since Wyck's future self had tried to kill me by throwing me off the Washington Monument. His *future self,* not the Wyck that I had been friends with— the Wyck that had stuck by me when I was a pariah because of my mother's coma last year or helped me with my class assignments or laughed through stupid movies with me. But I still couldn't wrap my head around the fact that he could become that person.

I'd only seen Wyck once in the last six months, and that was when the reverter went off and I had caught him trying to change his past, just a couple weeks after our encounter at the Monument. He went back and tried to talk the admissions council at the Institute into letting him back into the Transport Program after he was expelled for pushing Mimi down the stairs. Again, the guilty party was actually his future self, but Mimi hadn't been able to tell the difference, and I certainly wasn't going to stick up for him. I jabbed that reverter into Wyck so fast he never saw it coming.

Part of me wanted to go talk to him. I had so many questions I still needed answered.

But there was no way I'd do that behind Finn's back.

"Oh, I remember what I wanted to go do," I said. It was a movie I thought Finn would like. "*Death Rumpus IV* is out today. You'll like it. All you need to know is the main character always gets killed off at least twelve times in each movie. He has a revivapaddle strapped to his chest, and it brings him back, and he keeps going."

"Sounds horrible . . . ly awesome!"

"We can grab dinner beforehand."

"As long as you don't Shift away in the middle." The hint of jealousy was back.

"What are you talking about? Who am I going to go see?" I started to laugh.

"Me," he said glumly.

Oh. This again? I snapped my mouth shut but had to stifle a giggle.

Thankfully, my trips back to spend time with his past self had grown less and less frequent. In fact, as far as I knew, there was only one trip back that I hadn't taken. My final one. The one where I asked him to protect me, the one where I lied to him and told him I'd never see him again.

"You do remember that he's *you*," I said.

"I know. I just wasn't expecting this to be so hard. To know that you spend time with him, that you kiss him. That you . . . love him, too."

"But he. Is. You."

"I realize it makes no sense," he said.

"Well"—I wrapped my arms around his waist—"today I'm all yours."

"Okay." He returned the embrace and gestured to my pocket. "Now let's just pray we can make it through a whole meal without that stupid green thing going off again."

And there it was. That stab in my gut, wondering what life would be like for him if he wasn't with a girl who was so chronologically complicated.

"Let me go change," I said. I reeked of smoke.

We crawled through the old abandoned air ducts and emerged in the dorm room I shared with Mimi. Finn lowered me to the ground before hopping down after me. I grabbed a change of clothes and was about to step into the bathroom when the door whished open. Mimi and I both let out a shriek of surprise.

"What are you doing here?" I asked. "I thought you went skiing with your family."

"We got back yesterday. My brothers are still in town so I decided to get some peace and quiet. Oh, hey, Finn." She gave him a little wave. I was thankful that Mimi knew of Finn's existence. It made things easier not having to hide him. Of course, she just thought he was my loving boyfriend (true) from the archaic but picturesque area of Old New Mexico (which I completely made up in a moment of panic). Finn and I had made up a bogus internship that kept him traveling a lot. Mimi didn't know he was from the past or that he was a Shifter, much less an unchipped Shifter. Then again, I also hadn't figured out how to break the news to her that *I* was an unchipped Shifter.

"I love skiing," said Finn. "Where did you go?"

Oh, no no no. This always happened when Finn tried to have a pleasant conversation with anyone from the twenty-third century, which I tried to keep at a minimum. His definition of skiing would be something bizarre like going to a snow-covered mountain and hurtling himself down it with slabs of wood strapped to his feet.

"Did Charlie have a good time?" I asked. He'd gone with them. Charlie was also the one topic of conversation sure to steer Mimi off course.

"Yes." Mimi got that blissful vacant look she reserved for her shmoopiepants, then snapped back with it. "Did you end up staying in town?"

"Pretty much." That had been my original plan. I really needed to catch up in some classes. Between spontaneously Shifting somewhere almost every day and keeping up with reversions to the timeline, my grades had slipped. It wasn't like Mom could ground me; however, she could make my free time miserable. But I hated lying to Mimi. And I felt like that was all I ever did anymore. I decided to dip my toe in the truth. "Finn and I took a quick jaunt to London."

"Ooh! Fun. Did you do anything exciting?"

"Not really," I said while Finn mumbled, "Nothing much."

I twisted the compufilm clue around in my pocket nervously. So much for the truth.

As Finn and I were leaving the Institute, we passed Headmaster Bergin in the hall. Finn stiffened by my side, but I nodded politely and kept walking. Bergin smiled at me from underneath his thick white moustache.

When we reached the sidewalk, Finn said, "How can you stand to be in the same building with that man?"

"He doesn't remember what he did."

Right after I'd gotten back from having my chip removed, I'd gone to Bergin's office to confront him. One minute he was there talking to me, packing up, ready to resign. The next minute, the office was empty. Turned out ICE had sent someone back to change the past and vote him off their advisory board before he ever got tangled up in all this. It was my first mission with the reverter, and I had no idea what I was doing. Needless to say, I failed to change things back to the way they were. But this was one change I wasn't all that sorry about.

"Why do you think ICE did that?" asked Finn. "I mean, wouldn't it make more sense to keep Bergin in the loop so he could spy on you?"

"I bet they thought they were killing two birds with one pebble."

"Stone," said Finn. "How would you kill a bird with one pebble, much less two?"

"Stone, whatever. Why would someone kill birds, period?" I had a habit of picking up obsolete sayings from the past, especially from the twentieth century. Maybe it was because half of my genes were from that time that I had such an affinity to that period's truisms, even if I didn't grasp the full meaning. Finn thought it was hilarious when I mangled them.

"Touché," he said, stifling a snort.

"I think they thought that by taking Bergin out, the change would take me out of the know as well. They didn't understand how activating the reverter back in your time must have made it impervious to their timeline changes. And as far as I know, they still don't realize that I've deactivated my chip and am aware of the changes at all."

"Are *they* aware of the changes?" Finn asked.

"You remember what Bergin said in his office. NonShifters' quantum tendrils adjust seamlessly to the timeline, so in theory, they shouldn't be. I mean, it's not like there are any Shifters working for ICE."

"And yet, somehow they are aware of the fact that it's possible to make changes. I thought only unchipped Shifters could detect the alterations."

"I did, too. But maybe they retain the knowledge that they can make changes even if they can't detect the changes themselves?"

"That makes my brain hurt."

"Me, too." I leaned in toward him. "Maybe we need something to take our minds off it."

"What did you have in mind?"

I ran my hand around his waist and pulled him in close. He

lifted me up so he could kiss me properly. And then . . . not so properly.

"That's better," I murmured.

And as Finn put me down and wrapped his arm around my shoulder in one of those simple, sweet ways, I realized that, changes or not, this timeline was pretty dang good.

chapter 3

"SPEAKING OF PEGAMOOS," said Finn.

"No one was speaking of pegamoos." We'd been looking over the menu, which was kind of pointless as Finn always ordered the same thing—chocolate chip waffles with bananas on top and a side of endive—and I had the whole thing memorized. We sat at our usual table out on the terrace of the sidewalk café just around the corner from my house in Old Georgetown.

"No one?" Finn held the endive up in the air. And sure enough, Ed, the tiny, winged cow, flitted down the street toward us. Mom had gotten him a couple of months ago, swearing up and down he was just a new family pet, but we both knew who she really got him for. I mean, I'd begged for a pegamoo every day for an entire year when I was eight. Nothing. Finn mentions once how cute he thinks they are. Welcome to the family, Ed.

The miniature bovine munched on the endive contentedly, mooing every so often for Finn to scratch his ears. I checked Ed's collar. Mom had left it on roam for some reason.

"Oh, my gosh, look at him." A tall girl with beautiful brown corkscrew curls cascading down her back cooed at Ed as she passed. At first, I thought she would keep walking. Ed gets that a lot because, annoying as he can be, he really is adorable.

She paused, though. Ed flitted over to her and lifted his chin for her to scratch it.

"Ed!" I started to shoo him away from her, but when I looked

Karen Akins

back over at the girl, she wasn't looking at him. She was looking at me.

"Do you remember me?" she asked.

Umm. "I'm sorry. Should I?" I took a closer look at her. The girl did look vaguely familiar. She was right around my age. Her skin was the shade of velvety cocoa. She wore a short skirt that flaunted her longer-than-should-be-legal legs. But nope. I didn't recognize her.

"It's okay," she said, but her countenance betrayed her disappointment. "It was a long shot. It's been years, and I was only there one semester, and—"

"Jafney," I said. The name burst in my head like a first kernel of popcorn, then—*pop, pop, pop*—the memories came back. I did recognize her. She was my friend Pennedy's roommate from our first year at the Institute. And she held the dubious honor of being the only student other than me to ever have been force faded from a mission. She'd been odd, and kind of overly friendly for my taste, if memory served me well.

"I haven't seen you since you got kicked out of school," I said.

"I didn't get kicked out." She twirled a strand of wooden beads between her fingers and glanced up and down the street nervously. "My family pulled me out."

"Oh. Sorry. I assumed you were expelled." No use sugarcoating it. The entire student body had assumed the same thing. "What did you do to get yourself force faded?"

She bit her lip.

"Sorry," I said again. "I'm being nosy."

"No, it's not that," she said. "It's . . . I didn't just happen to be walking by. I've been hoping to meet you."

"Meet me?"

"Yes, I've"—she bit her lip again—"I've kind of been following you."

22

"What?" I stiffened. Finn scooted into a defensive posture between Jafney and me. I squeezed his hand. He was here. I was safe.

"I can explain." She handed me a tattered photograph. It was a close-up shot of a younger version of Jafney standing next to a man in his early forties. He had his arm around her shoulder and wore the same beaded necklace that Jafney now wore. That wasn't the exceptional part, though. The photo was on compufilm, which was modern. The setting was clearly not. 1960s or '70s, if I had to guess, some kind of hippy commune. I handed it back to her.

"That's my father." She tucked the photo away. "I took it myself while I was at the Institute. Three missions in a row I snuck off to see him. They finally caught on by the third trip."

Apparently, we had more in common than a penchant for disobeying orders at the Institute. She was a child of two different eras, like me. We were both genetically linked to two times, our quantum tendrils clinging to both. Which meant she also had the unique ability, like me, to Shift people to our time. But that didn't calm my nerves or answer any questions as to why she was tailing me or telling me any of this.

"Why were you following me?" I asked.

"Because you're going to help me," she said.

"Says who?"

Finn nudged me under the table and shot me a *Be nice* look, but I ignored it. I was in constant danger of being found out as a secret unchipped Shifter, not to mention the reverter I toted around with me everywhere. ICE had already proved to what lengths they'd go to get it. I didn't need to get caught helping this girl on top of everything else.

"Says my future self," said Jafney with a new muster of confidence in her voice.

"I barely trust my own future self. Why would I trust yours?"

"Because there's . . ." Jafney squinched up her nose and pronounced her next words precisely, like she was rehearsing a password to get into a Prohibition bar. "There's no time like the past."

That got my attention. It was part of the clue my own future self had left me on the midterm when I first met Finn.

"How did you know—?" Finn started to ask, but I cut him off.

"If your future self really told you I'd help you, then she also would have mentioned I don't personally have the ability to do that."

"Well, not you. She said you'd take me to someone named John and he'd disable my chip."

"He's my dad," said Finn. "There's an injection that helps your body fight off the chip like a vaccine. He does the procedure back in the twenty-first century. Just to keep it on the down-low."

It was my turn to kick him under the table. He made it sound like we were running a home for time-traveling invalids, turning chips off left and right. Four. Finn's dad had disabled four chips. Mine, Mom's, Quigley's, and Nurse Granderson's. Besides, I hadn't decided if I even wanted to help this girl. Except . . . chicken-blarking-egg. Apparently, I would whether I wanted to or not.

"Fine," I said.

"You'll do it?" Jafney twisted one of those perfect, bouncy curls behind her ear.

"Yeah." I dug a fork into my omelet.

"Can we go now?" she said.

A pushy thing, wasn't she?

"Feel any urge to synch?" I asked Finn.

It wasn't like I could just Shift at will. My quantum tendrils still had to pull me somewhere. And they weren't budging.

"Nope," said Finn.

"Sorry," I said to Jafney. Her face plummeted.

"Look," I said, "are you sure you really want to do this? I don't know what all your future self told you, but there are consequences to turning off your chip."

"You mean the Madness?" said Jafney.

"Yes." I glanced around. It made me nervous having this conversation in public. "Only the Madness isn't real. Unchipped Shifters aren't insane. They're just the only ones who are able to perceive changes in the timeline."

I left out the details about ICE, that they were allowing non-Shifters to make those changes to the timeline. Instead, I made it sound like the timeline just changed itself on a whim. I didn't think Jafney bought it, but it wasn't my decision to make.

Only Haven members knew about ICE's involvement. It was up to Quigley and the others at Resthaven to decide if Jafney was trustworthy. I highly doubted they would. After all, she'd admitted to spying on me.

"Does it hurt?" asked Jafney.

"The injection?"

"No. The . . . changing reality?"

I couldn't really answer that one. I'd been able to revert most of the changes that had been made since my chip had been disabled. The ones I hadn't caught in time either didn't affect me personally or, in the case of Headmaster Bergin, worked in my favor.

"Not painful, but confusing." I wiped my spoon off with my napkin and stirred my drink. "Sometimes, I wonder what it would be like to go back and not know all this. Ignorance is bliss and all that."

"Hey," Finn said, "clearly being ostracized by your entire society is worth it so you can date me.

"Obviously." I poked Finn in the ribs, and he tickled me.

When I looked over at Jafney, she had a wistful expression on her face. I realized how insensitive I was being, flaunting my cross-century relationship with Finn when she hadn't been able to have that connection with her dad. I understood. I'd watched my mom suffer for almost two decades, missing my father. I scooted away from Finn. He laced his fingers through mine.

"You're absolutely sure this is what you want?" I asked Jafney one last time. "There's no undoing it."

"I'm positive," she said and looked between Finn and me. "I want what you have."

A tingle worked its way up my extremities as if my quantum tendrils agreed with her decision. I stood up and wrapped my arm around Jafney, but Finn laid his hand on my shoulder.

"I should probably Shift her home to Chincoteague. My pull will be stronger since it's a synch for me, and she's still chipped."

"Good point." I backed away so he could circle his arms around Jafney. She was only an inch or so shorter than he was. Right before they disappeared, it occurred to me that they looked like one of those Ken and Barbie fashion doll sets from his time.

The pulling sensation built and boiled within my veins. I closed my eyes, and a briny whiff of sea air bit at my nose before I opened them.

I smiled and dug my heels into a mound of sand.

Chincoteague.

chapter 4

"BREE!" A WHIRL OF HAIR and squeals came flying at me, and I didn't have time to react before I was knocked to the beach by Finn's kid sister, Georgie. She was tall, like Finn and her dad. With my visits back to Past Finn spaced out over weeks and months as they were, it was like I'd witnessed the world's fastest growth spurt in Georgie, and now we were almost the same age.

"Mom'll have kittens," she said. "She wasn't expecting you for dinner. Where's Finn?"

"I must have gone back further than him." Huh. That was a first. We'd always arrived at the same time before. Finn had to maintain contact with me in order to Shift into the twenty-third century, and I'd gotten into the habit of doing it every Shift we took together. "I'm sure he'll be here soon. I like the color, by the way."

I pulled a few strands of Georgie's brown and electric pink hair—her shade du jour—out of my mouth. She plopped down next to me in the sand, and I tugged my knees up to my chest. Aside from Mimi, Georgie was one of my best friends now. She always had some kind of sixth sense about my arrival. She'd come running from a mile away or sometimes pop up out of nowhere if she'd been on a Shift herself. Bugged the crap out of Finn when we were mid-kiss.

"You don't think your mom will really mind, do you?" I asked. It still sometimes felt a little intrusive, showing up out of the blue as I did. But it wasn't like I could call ahead. And I had to remind myself, from Charlotte's perspective, my visits had been spaced out over the last few years. It was only from my point of view that I'd seen the Mastersons every few days.

"Are you kidding?" snorted Georgie. "You know Mom. The more, the merrier."

"That's good. Because Finn's bringing Jafney." I glanced down the beach. Where were they?

"Gesundheit!" said Georgie.

"You're such a dort."

"Nope." Georgie shook her head. She was also used to my mauling of the twenty-first-century vernacular. "That is, in fact, not a word. And you're the dork."

"Anyway." I tossed a handful of sand at her. "Jafney's a Shifter. She's here to—"

Splash

A giant fish broke through the water about fifty feet out in the ocean then sank back down. The ripples danced across the surface in hypnotic circles. Finn's head popped out of the water, then Jafney's did, too. They both let out a yelp before they went back under.

I stared out at the water. Were they caught in some kind of rip tide? We had to do something to help them.

"Come on, Georgie!" I kicked off my shoes as I ran toward the water.

"What are you doing?" Georgie took a few steps after me. "Bree, you can't swim."

"I can swim." Okay, not really. Finn had been teaching me a little bit, in their pool. I could still barely propel myself forward, much less drag a girl almost a foot taller than me through the high tide. But I dashed out into the surf anyway. Before I went farther in than my knees, though, Finn and Jafney popped up yet again, this time much closer to the shore. Jafney flipped over onto her back and spouted a mouthful of saltwater into the air.

The smooth strokes of her long limbs were nothing like my floundering dog paddle. She and Finn took turns imitating each other. Finn let out a whoop of fun as he did a backflip thing into a little wave that cropped up.

"Hey, Bree," Jafney said, splashing through the lapping waves to give me a sopping hug. She trudged up the sand and gazed around in awe like she'd never been out of the twenty-third century.

"Hey." I looked down at my soaked pants. Finn noticed them, too, and cocked one of his eyebrows up in a what-the-heck-are-you-doing look.

I pretended I didn't see it. He'd freak out if he knew I had rushed out into the ocean without him there to make sure I didn't drown. I bent down and picked up a shell instead. It probably didn't fool him for a second. But he let it drop.

"Welcome to Chincoteague," he said to Jafney.

"Yeeee!" She jumped up and down, shrieking and clapping her hands.

Georgie, who was standing a mere foot away, put her fingers in her ears and mouthed, *What the blark?* at me.

"Jafney's here about her chip," I said. "Is your dad around?"

"No," said Georgie, "but I'm sure he'll be back soon if that's the reason she's here."

I still didn't understand it, how unchipped Shifters were naturally called to where they were supposed to be. Finn called it fate. Charlotte called it providence. Whatever it was, I didn't like to overanalyze it.

Talking about time with a Shifter is a bit like discussing water with a fish. It's so woven into our being that it's simultaneously everything and nothing to us.

"This is just soooooo amazing. I can't believe I'm really doing this." Jafney let out another squeak as she pulled her shirt up around her chest to wring some of the water out, revealing a taut tummy and curvy hips. She stretched her arms in a catlike pose above her head, tugging the shirt even higher, before smoothing it back down.

I wrapped my arms around my own torso. Charlotte's scrumptious cooking and my mom's renewed love language of Rocky Road brownies had packed on their share of a few extra pounds. Oh, and those Girl Scout cookies that Georgie kept stashed in her closet weren't doing my butt any favors either. (How have those gone extinct and we still have kelp nuggets?) Finn claimed that he liked me with some meat on my bones, especially since I'd been confined to such a restrictive diet at the Institute for so long. I liked my body, but that didn't stop me from feeling self-conscious next to this Grecian goddess.

Jafney dawdled back and forth through the sand as we headed up the beach. The way she zigzagged, she looked like she was in a drunken stupor or sleepwalking.

"What a Fruit Loop," whispered Georgie in my ear.

"Cut her some slack," I said.

It sounded like Jafney's life had been anything but easy so far. I could relate to that. And for all I knew, we'd become close. It's not like there were a lot of unchipped Shifters my age running around. I could use all the friendly faces I could get.

We made our way up to the house. It was about five times the size of my own and filled with pricey furniture. They could afford it—Finn's dad had had uncommonly lucky hunches in all his investments over the years. Their Haven beacon glimmered green in the foyer, casting its light on the Mastersons' art collection that crossed the line from pricey to priceless. The Beacon was an old tradition to welcome Shifters into the safety of their home. The Mastersons, however, chose to stretch the purpose of the Haven Society to open their doors to anyone in need.

In true Charlotte fashion, Finn's mom squawked for a minute, then tossed three more plates on the table and wrapped bacon around random leftovers from the refrigerator. Somehow, it came out a gourmet feast.

We bobbed our heads as Charlotte led us in grace, and a tenor voice that wasn't Finn's added a final, "Amen."

"Welcome home, John." Charlotte tossed Finn's dad a cloth napkin and hopped up to grab him a plate like he hadn't just appeared out of nothingness. Jafney was the only one who startled at his sudden appearance.

Finn bore a strong resemblance to his father, with their square jaws and tall, lean physiques. But as Charlotte shook her fiery auburn hair over her shoulder, there was no doubt that Finn had inherited an equal number of genes from her.

"Back from anywhere interesting?" I asked John.

"Best not to talk shop at the table," said John, his polite way of letting us know he'd been performing surgeries during a particularly gory battle from history. He adjusted his wire-rim glasses and finally noticed Jafney. "Oh, hello there. I don't think we've been introduced."

Jafney took that as her cue to begin talking about herself . . . and . . . didn't stop the entire dinner.

Turned out, her mother was a sociologist who'd written her dissertation on communal habitation choices, hence the hippy father. Jafney had lived with her grandparents after her mother died when she was five.

"Actually, not my grandparents." Jafney waved her fork in the air between bites. "My great-great-great-great-great-great-grandniece or something and her husband."

"Huh?" Georgie was the one who said it even though we were all clearly thinking it.

"Yeah, it's kind of confusing," said Jafney. "My mom lived on the commune off and on for years, where she met my father. She got pregnant with me and had me here—well, I mean, had me in the twenty-third century. She lied about the identity of my father so they wouldn't disrupt her research. Then she got pregnant again. With my brother. She gave birth on the commune back in the past, but she developed eclampsia during labor and died in childbirth."

The Mastersons and I all looked at each other, stunned, as Jafney continued.

"They had a hard time locating any suitable guardians in the twenty-third century. My mom was an only child, and her parents died when I was a baby. So once they figured out what had happened, they tracked down my brother's descendants and there you go."

"I'm so sorry for your loss," I managed to mumble through my shock.

"Oh, she's not dead," said Jafney cheerfully. "Not really."

Uhhhh . . .

"Don't get me wrong," Jafney went on. "I miss her. And Dad and my little brother. But once I turn off this chip, I can go back and see them. They're alive. Just not in my time."

I almost started to argue with her, but then I glanced over at Finn and realized that by my own logic, I was eating dinner with a corpse.

See, said the voice in my head I'd grown to loathe, *It will never work. It's too convoluted.*

No one at the table had a response, and I was pretty sure I wasn't the only one who was thankful when Charlotte sprang up from her seat and said, "Who wants plum tart?"

As I watched Charlotte bustle into the kitchen, I realized how uncomfortable life could be for her—constantly surrounded by people who had no concept of linear time. She had once told me that she thanked the Good Lord every day she wasn't born a Shifter because what if she floated away with the stove on and burnt the house down?

"But maybe your future self could go back and extinguish it," I pointed out.

"And maybe I'll let Finn bring that flying-cow poop machine back to the twenty-first century with him sometime."

And thus ended the deepest temporal theory conversation I ever had with Charlotte.

⤙

Jafney's chip reversal went smoothly. It was a simple injection that acted like a vaccine, allowing the brain to fight off the control of the chip. It could leave you weak and with a mean headache for a few hours, but otherwise, pretty non-traumatic. The traumatic part came later. When you realized the world you lived in wasn't the world you thought you lived in.

John sedated Jafney for the procedure. I wasn't sure if it was actually necessary or just to shut her up for more than three minutes.

"She'll be asleep for an hour or so." John patted her foot.

Finn came up behind me, his Labrador, Slug, trailing behind him, sniffing suspiciously at Finn's fingers. Slug could probably still smell Ed.

"Do we have time to catch that movie?" Finn asked.

"Should we leave?" I pointed at Jafney. I'd feel a little guilty abandoning her there. But she let out a snuffling roar of a snore, and I knew there was no point in staying. Besides, Charlotte wouldn't leave her side.

"If we synch now, we should make the ten o'clock," I said, looking at my Com. I wrapped my arms around Finn and gave in to the draw back to the twenty-third century.

Then I opened my eyes and saw where we'd landed.

Crapcakes.

chapter 5

"HUH-HO! YOU SNUCK US IN." Finn's whisper was practically a shout and earned him a few dirty looks from the moviegoers who streamed into the darkened theater around us.

"No. It was a snafu. There's a difference."

"You're a little sneak thief." He started to tickle me, but really, I wanted him to keep his voice down. It was true. I had just ripped off these poor movie theater owners. This was why there were Rules and entire classes on Temporal Ethics.

"I'll pay for the tickets on the way out. Let's just grab our seats before all the good ones are taken," I said. Several people around us had begun to stare. The last thing I needed was temporal theft on my record. I climbed into one of the sensory chambers and attached the bio-nodes to my scalp. Finn lurrrrved movies in the twenty-third century. Personally, I found movies back in his day quaint, but yeah. I missed the explosion of all my senses being engaged at the same time.

"You want anything to eat?" said Finn. "Popcorn?"

"That sounds good. I'll get some." I pulled off the node and hopped out of the chamber as Finn crawled in. When I got out to the lobby, I swiped my hair—my sole form of ID—across a scanner to pay for both our tickets and the snacks.

I joined the line for the popcorn (if one could call it that). Now that I'd had real popcorn—twenty-first-century popcorn with real butter that came from real cows—it was hard to go back to the purple stuff. I was just about to head back into the theater when I paused. Something was off. It felt like I was being watched. That's when I saw him, tucked into a dark corner, like a snake under a stone.

Leto Malone.

I marched over to him.

"What are you doing here?" I never bothered with pleasantries when it came to Leto—an unscrupulous chronosmuggler who had become a nagging yet necessary nuisance in my life. Technically, this was my own fault. I had agreed to work for him last year to pay my mom's hospital bills. I ended up not needing his dirty money, but had in turn recruited him to keep an eye out for Finn. And by "recruit," I mean bribe. I'd had Finn invest a good chunk of money back in his time, and it was worth a mint and a half by now. I'd then given Leto all but the last digit to access the bank account in which the fortune was held. In exchange, he'd agreed to keep his eyes and ears open for me.

But Leto had strict orders to keep his distance. Especially from Finn, who didn't approve of my association with the chronosmuggler. I'd never even disclosed Finn's full name to Leto.

"Hey, Dollface." Leto thrust his meaty hand into my popcorn bucket and pulled out a fistful. There went my appetite. He wore his usual tacky suit, and his hair was combed back so thick with grease, it looked like he had a helmet on. He crunched an unpopped kernel. "Heard a rumor you and Pretty Boy were having a little date night and thought it would be a good chance for us to catch up."

"How did you know I was here?" I asked. I didn't even know I'd be here.

"I pay well for up-to-date information on the whereabouts of my Shifter friends. Especially ones who are sitting on my fortune. Plus you always come to the movies on Saturday nights."

"It's not your fortune yet, Leto." I tapped my foot. "What do you want? Because if you came here to bug me for that last digit, it was a waste of your time and mine."

And Leto had become a master of wasting my time. The moment ICE had announced their new Shifting program a few months ago, he'd been first in line. He discovered the loophole of being able to change his own past almost immediately. Over and over again, I'd had to go back and revert his changes. Most had involved gambling or stealing someone's inventions. You'd think the idiot would learn.

Now here he was. I was starting to rue the day I'd ever dangled that bank account in front of his nose.

"You're not getting that digit, Leto. Finn is the only one who knows it," I said. Leto knew as well as I did that if he entered a wrong digit in an attempt to access the account, he'd be locked out of it. He wouldn't risk it by trying to guess.

"Well?" I said. But Leto was staring off into space, ignoring me.

"Huh?" He had this dazed look on his face that broadened into a knowing grin. I narrowed my eyes at him when he clicked his tongue and gave me an attagirl eye-squinch. "Sorry, Dollface. Just remembered something I gotta do later."

"Get out of here, Leto. If I need you, I'll contact you."

"Get your bloomers out of a bunch," he said. "Some interesting news came down my pipeline, and I thought you'd like to hear it."

"You thought wrong." Probably his newest get-rich-quick scheme. As far as I was concerned, anything that came down that man's pipeline was covered in slime. And I wanted as little to do with it as possible.

"Even if it has to do with a certain Finnigan Jonathan Masterson?"

I whirled around so fast, purple popcorn showered the little kid passing me.

"What did you just say?"

"It has to do with Finn—" But Leto didn't get to finish his sentence as I'd clamped my palm over his greasy lips.

"Where did you hear his last name? How?" I had never used Finn's full name around him. And Quigley had erased every trace of Finn and his family from the public record almost a year ago. I pulled my hand away.

"That's my news. His record's been reinstated. Including where and when he's from." Leto tsk-tsked. "But that's not the interesting part."

Leto grabbed one more handful of popcorn and slowly munched it. I whipped my Com out of my pocket and shoved the stunner prod against his neck. Enough games.

"Tell me everything you know."

"What's it worth to you?"

"You want the last digit?" I asked. "Fine. It's yours." It didn't do me much good now anyway. I had to get Finn back to his time pronto. And he could never come back.

"Y'know what?" said Leto. "This one's a freebie."

"You're turning down the last digit?" No blarking way. I didn't believe it. But I also didn't have time to ponder why Leto had had a sudden change of heart.

"I just want to see the look on your face when I deliver the last bit of news," he said. "That'll be payment enough."

"There's more?"

"Your friend Finn in there has been classified a chronofugitive."

"What?"

"Not just any chronofugitive. Level Five."

"What does that mean?"

"It means Finn is going to do some bad, bad things."

"*Going* to? As in he hasn't done them yet?"

Leto pinched the crease of his nose. "Do you know *nothing* about chronocrime?"

"Apparently not." And I would have preferred to never have the need to.

"Any crime that someone commits outside his present is considered a chronocrime. So if someone were—hypothetically speaking—to allegedly sell a stolen modern-day medicine to an individual in the past, that would be a Level Two chronocrime. This is all a hypothetical scenario, of course. Of which no one could prove my guilt. And which was done with the most benevolent of intentions. Hypothetically."

I rolled my eyes.

"But you said Finn's going to be accused of some crime, not that he's already committed it."

"Yeah. Retroactive reporting only happens at a certain level of offense. No one at the Office of Chronocrime Investigation's gonna bother to do that with a little harmless smuggling. Errr . . . alleged harmless smuggling."

"So what? The conviction is inevitable? Whatever happened to innocent until proven guilty?"

"No, they can't legally report back on the trial or the specifics or whatnots. Only the certainty that the crime will be committed and that he'll be accused."

"Sounds a lot like guilty until proven innocent."

Leto shrugged. "Obviously, the laws'd be a bit more lenient if I'd written 'em."

"So . . . Level Five. What does that mean?"

Finn was the kindest, most loving, least felonious person I knew.

"Means kidnapping, arson, maybe murder."

"Whah? There's no way he—oh my gosh." I had to get Finn out of here. I had to get him out of my time.

Leto managed to grab one more bite of popcorn as I turned and raced back into the theater.

"You're welcome," he called after me.

The chambers had already ascended twenty feet to viewing height as I rushed through the forest of stalk-like bases looking for Finn's and mine. When I reached our chamber, it lowered, and I climbed in next to Finn.

I tugged on his sleeve. "I have to tell you something."

"Shh. Movie's starting."

I'd debated between *Death Rumpus IV* and the *Spider-Man* re-

re-re-re-re-reboot for a while now, but Finn hadn't been ready to see what had happened to a franchise he loved so much.

Finn dipped his hand into our popcorn bucket. "I'm still not sure what the point is if he just dies over and ov—" His voice trailed off. Up on the screen, Horatio Melendez had already experienced his first death/revival, and Finn bit his fist because it was such a good one. "Never mind, never mind, never mind!"

"Finn, we need to get you home. Now."

"Huh?" He reached for a handful of popcorn, and his hand brushed mine. Finn lifted my wrist and mindlessly planted a kiss on my fingertips. It reminded me of the first time he'd done the same thing. On the roof of the Pentagon. I had thought he was in danger *then*. Ha.

I rubbed my hand against his cheek, and he pulled me in close, laid a kiss—gentle and satisfying—on my lips. One of those kisses that conveyed so much through so little.

I had no idea who would accuse Finn of doing something that would classify him as a chronofugitive or why. But if that person knew me at all, they'd know I'd do anything to protect him. And that protection started with getting him out of this century.

"Finn, I'm not kidding. You need to go. I'll meet up with you later and explain." I had to find out what he was charged with.

"Let's finish the movie first," he whispered and scooted back into his seat.

Suddenly, the screen changed. It was no longer showing *Death Rumpus*. It had switched to a stupid romantic comedy that I had specifically told Mimi she would have to make me the world's sparkliest friendship barrette if she ever wanted me to watch it with her.

"What the blark?" No one else in the theater seemed to be bothered by it. But at least Finn might be willing to go now.

I looked down at the popcorn bucket and realized that it was no longer purple. It was glowing green. Then I felt it, a beeping and whirring.

"Dang it. The reverter's going off." I didn't have time for some Richie McRicherson's whiny what-if right now.

"The what?" He leaned over and kissed me again.

It was only after I pulled my lips away from his that I realized those lips weren't Finn's.

They were Wyck's.

chapter 6

"AIGHH!" I HURLED MYSELF to the far edge of the viewing chamber. Away from him. Away from . . . Wyck. How was this possible?

"What's the matter, sweetie?" Wyck reached over and smoothed my hair back.

"Ummm . . . what are you . . . Aighh!" I yanked nodes off my head and body as fast as I could. What the blark had been changed? Where was Finn?

I clenched the reverter in my pocket. I had to fight the urge to click it right then and there. But if something went wrong on the reversion, I couldn't just disappear right in front of Wyck. He'd remember it, and the last thing I needed was for Wyck O'Banion to know I was an unchipped Shifter now.

The reverter was still going strong, and I pushed it down into my pocket. If Wyck saw it, I was a dead woman. The last time I'd had it in my possession around him, he'd tried to zap me and plunge me off the Washington Monument to get it back. Well, not him exactly. A future, evil version of him.

But this guy looked enough like that version of him to get me to push the emergency release button on the chamber and scramble down the ladder when it was still ten feet from the ground. I had to get somewhere private so I could revert this change.

"Bree, what are you doing?" he called after me.

I looked up at Wyck and shuddered. I couldn't believe I had just *kissed* him.

41

The path to the exit lit up step by step like luminescent lily pads as I pressed my way through the bases of the raised chambers.

"Bree!" Wyck had jumped from the chamber and was close behind me. I'm sure I was easy to spot, what with the way my pocket blazed green like it held a mutant asparagus.

"Wait up!" he said. "What's the matter?"

He caught up with me and grasped my shoulder. I flinched away as he touched me, remembering the way he had splintered my knee into bits six months before, the way he had crushed my windpipe with his bare hands.

Not him, I reminded myself again. Some twisted future version of him.

"Look, I don't know what's going on." I grasped my Quant-Com in my fist and flicked the stunner out just in case I needed it. "But you'd better leave me alone."

"What on earth are you talking about?" He stepped into a shaft of light from the exit, and I gasped. His appearance was so different from the last time I'd seen him. He looked . . . great. His usual messy hair was carefully combed and parted in a neat line, like a cement sidewalk crack that had been poured with precision.

"Why is your pocket glowing?" he asked. "Are you feeling okay? Do you want to go back to the Institute?"

"With you?" I almost choked. After he'd been expelled from the Institute, last I heard he was going to some reform program. I pulled my jacket over my pocket to cover it.

"Who else would you go with?" He looked around. His puzzlement was palpable.

Yeah, well, that made two of us, buddy.

"I need some air," I said, stumbling toward the lobby.

"Oh-okay." He followed close behind.

"No. You"—I backed away—"you stay here."

"All right." He pointed at the spot where he was standing, like he was claiming it. No argument. No fight.

There was no telling where this new compliance came from. But it didn't make me feel one whit better. As soon as I had cleared the exit, I turned and ran to the women's bathroom. Clutching the sides of the sink, I stared into the mirror, gasping. A mom with two daughters in tow walked in and flashed me a sympathetic look when she saw my stricken face.

"Boy problems?" she said.

A noise that might have been a laugh in more appropriate circumstances escaped as I nodded and fled to the farthest stall. I pulled out the reverter and stared at it. Clearly, Wyck had gone back and changed something in the past, something that made me end up with him instead of Finn.

The door opened. Wyck's voice filled the room timidly.

"I know you wanted me to wait in the theater, but I'm worried about you, Bree. Are you sure you're okay?"

"Fine," I said. "I'm fine. I think the popcorn disagreed with me."

"Popcorn? You were eating Blinky Beans."

"Blinky . . ." I hated those. But as I said it, I detected their aftertaste in my mouth. "Blinky Beans . . . yes. That's what I meant."

"Okay. Sorry. Let me know if you need anything," he said as the door slid shut.

What I needed.

I clenched the reverter, whirring merrily along.

What I needed was to stop this change from happening. ICE must have tasked Wyck with recovering the reverter again. In turn, Wyck must have decided it would be easier to pretend to be my boyfriend and go after it this way. And . . . then pretend that he didn't even know what it was when it was within easy reach. Yeah, that part didn't make any sense whatsoever.

The reverter's glow faded a tiny bit and snapped me back to the task at hand. It didn't matter why Wyck had done this. All that mattered was that I undo it. And quickly.

I brushed my thumb over the heart at the end of the reverter. BB+FM. The trigger was made from my old broken locket. Finn had scratched our initials in there himself. But they were so shallow, you couldn't even read them anymore.

I still wasn't entirely sure how everything worked with the Ice-Pick. It was the device that the Initiative for Chronogeological Equality had invented to enable nonShifters to Shift. But everything I knew about nonShifters' quantum tendrils pointed to the fact that the Pick *shouldn't* work. The reason Shifters were able to travel through time and space was that our tendrils—those bits in everyone's brains that rooted them to their present—were mutated. Shifters' tendrils flexed and clung to different locations and time periods. NonShifters' tendrils progressed in a consistently linear manner. Point *A* to Point *B*. Minute *Y* to Minute *Z*. Shifters weren't held by such constraints. We could go from Point *A* to Point *Q*. Minute *Y* to Minute *J*.

At first, I had thought that maybe the Picks were like temporary microchips, but Shifters' chips guided (well, forced) our tendrils to stretch to a certain point. The tendrils had to be stretchable first. Everything I had learned in Quantum Biology taught me that nons simply shouldn't be able to Shift. Their tendrils weren't like ours.

I clicked the end of the reverter and felt the familiar tug to the past.

Oww.

My feet hit the ground so hard that I stumbled forward, my knees slamming with a crack into a cold, marble floor. It only took me a moment to realize where I was, so familiar was this place to me. I'd landed inside the Institute, near the History department, down a scarcely used hallway I wouldn't have recognized if I hadn't spent so much time scouring my school earlier this year in search of a route to sneak Finn in. Large, metal storage cabinets lined the edges of the hall, and I slipped into a space between two of them while I gained my bearings.

My QuantCom beeped as the date popped up—about six months ago. I racked my brain to think of what Wyck could have changed around this date so that I'd end up with him rather than Finn. I wasn't left guessing for long, though. Wyck himself—the version I recognized and remembered, Wyck from six months ago—ducked into the hallway. He was followed closely by another version of himself, his hair grown out long and shaggy, spilling from the edges of a ball cap. This Wyck who was making the change didn't look like the Evil Wyck I remembered from the Washington Monument. This Wyck's eyes were clear and alert, and when he spoke, there wasn't a hint of hatred in his voice. Instead, pleading.

"Look," he said, "I know what I'm asking of you doesn't make sense, and I know you don't want to do it, but—"

"I'm still trying to figure out how you're even here." Past Wyck leaned against one of the cabinets with a clang.

"It will all make sense later. I promise. But you have to do this. It's important."

"She's my friend," said Past Wyck.

"And . . . this way, she'll become more than that."

I had my answer. He was doing this to force me to become his girlfriend. My fingernails bit into my flesh as I clasped the reverter, ready to jump out and shove it into his neck. But I also wanted to know *why* he was doing this. The device was still whirring steadily. I had a few minutes left.

"But it's a lie," said Past Wyck. "Bree's one of the best students at this school. I haven't seen any signs that would make me question her fitness to Shift."

"I know that." A fist landed against the cabinet next to his past self. There was the Wyck I knew and loathed. But he regained his composure quickly. "Look, just go into Quigley's office and report that you've witnessed some instability in Bree lately. She won't get in trouble. Bree won't even be angry at you."

Ha! I had to fight back the snort that built in my nose. I would show him angry.

"But it's her mid-term," said Past Wyck.

I'd heard enough. I knew the when, I knew the how, and I didn't give a hoot about the why at this point. Past Wyck was going to go and tell Quigley I wasn't fit to Shift, stop me from going on my midterm last year, which was when I'd met Finn. This shaggy-haired Wyck must still be acting as a puppet for the Initiative for Chronogeological Equality. ICE thought that they could stop me from acquiring the reverter this way. But they were wrong. The reverter was immune to their changes because I'd activated it in Finn's time—outside of all this loopy mess.

"If Bree finds out I did this . . ."

"I told you. Don't worry about that."

Wrong again, Wyck. You should definitely worry about that. I flicked the stunner out of the end of my Com, ready to pounce as soon as their backs turned. They walked to the end of the hall, turning the corner toward Quigley's office. I stepped out of the shadows in stealth mode. I didn't make it two steps, though, when someone pinned my arms to my side and slapped their hand over my mouth, trapping my scream. I struggled to get loose, but they held tight. For every move I made, my attacker had a counter-move already prepared.

I bit the hand.

"Ow!" The person released my arm long enough to smack it. "I forgot I did that."

I jerked away and spun around, my jaw dangling in disbelief. Because I knew that voice.

And I knew that face.

It was my own.

chapter 7

"WHAT DO YOU THINK you're doing?" I asked in a sandpaper whisper.

"Stopping you from reverting this change." Bree lifted her eyebrows in an unspoken challenge.

"Don't you realize what's about to happen?" I asked.

"More than you can comprehend."

"Well, explain it." I looked down at the reverter. The glow had grown weak—the whirring, feeble. "Never mind. There's no time."

I turned to chase down Wyck, but she grabbed my wrist, holding me back.

"Have you gone insane?" I whisper-yelled. "He's about to take everything from me."

Bree laughed—*laughed!*—at me.

"Don't be angry at him," she said. "He's just following orders."

"I. Know." ICE wasn't the greedy, unethical organization I had feared. They were absolutely evil.

The end-of-class buzzer sounded, and students poured out of classrooms in the main passage ahead. I struggled against Bree's grasp. If I hurried, I could still catch Wyck and stop him. But even as I had the thought, I felt the reverter quiet to a gentle hum in my clenched hand. It fell silent and went still.

It was too late.

The change was permanent.

"What have you done?" Tears filled my eyes as I spun around

to face my future self. I launched at her, a missile of self-loathing. This change had apparently prevented me from going on the mid-term when I first met Finn. The whole last six months of my life had been replaced with that of a stranger's. One who was Wyck O'Banion's girlfriend and ate Blinky Beans and . . . and . . . "How could you?"

She didn't answer, but instead wrapped her arms around me. At first I thought she was giving me some kind of I'm-sorry hug, but then her hold on me tightened. Tingles crept up my arms and legs.

"Where are you taking me?" I struggled against her, but I realized that she already remembered all this. Fighting was futile. Besides, there was nothing left I could do here. With a sigh, I gave in, and we Shifted away.

As a Shifter, one of the lessons that gets hammered into your skull over and over and over again is "Expect the Unexpected." Half the teachers at the Institute have a poster of the saying up on their wall (usually with a cutesie picture on it like a baby eating a lemon slice or a pegamoo calf getting sprayed in the face with milk).

But nothing—expected or not—could have prepared me for what awaited us where we landed.

It was a room unlike any I'd ever been in before. The space was a giant dome, maybe fifty feet in diameter. All metal with a slight sheen. My gaze drifted up and across the high, sloped ceiling looking for an escape route. There were two doors, on opposite ends of the room. Neither was marked with signage. Either of them could lead straight to freedom. Or a trap.

Rows and rows of three-foot circular, see-through bubbles lined the edge of the room. One of them was lit with a soft blue light. All the rest were dark. In the exact center of the room was a cylinder, eight feet high and the same width as all the bubbles. It appeared to be full of some kind of clear, jellylike fluid that sloshed sluggishly against the opaque sides of the container. It looked like the dunk tank at the carnival Finn had taken me to in Chincoteague, only taller and sealed at the top.

The whole place seemed to vibrate with pent-up energy. It gave me the sensation of being trapped in a metallic wasp's nest.

The thing that was most striking about the room was how friggin' cold it was. Frigid. My breath detonated in front of my face in icy plumes, and I rubbed my hands together to keep my fingers from stiffening.

"What is this place?" I asked my Future Self.

"The Cryostorage Room at ICE's headquarters."

It was the first straight answer Future Bree had offered. Unfortunately, it meant nothing to me. Well, other than the fact that we were in the belly of the beast. As I scraped my nail along the one glowing bubble along the edge of the wall, a layer of frost melted in its wake. Ice. How appropriate.

"Don't touch anything," snapped Bree.

I jerked my hand away from the glass.

"Then tell me what's going on," I said.

"No time." And, indeed, she had switched her full attention away from me and onto three interwoven tubes shooting out of the top of the center tank and into a hole in the ceiling above.

"We're time travelers," I said. "All we have is time."

She didn't respond, only pursed her lips and lowered her gaze to the tank. She reached out and pressed her palm against it, still not looking at me. I took the chance to really examine her. She looked crapawful, like she hadn't slept or eaten in days. Dark circles clung under her eyes, and her hair was scraggly and unwashed, but the same length and style as mine, so we appeared to still be close in age. Her clothes were stained with . . . was that blood?

"You sound like Finn," she finally said.

"Is he okay? When can I get back to see him?"

"You're with Wyck now."

"I'm not with—"

"Of course you're not." She snapped around to face me. "But Wyck doesn't realize that. And you won't let him."

"Do you have any concept what you just cost me back there?" I gestured over my shoulder as if those few precious minutes at the Institute could be reclaimed, as if I could reach out and clasp them. "What you cost us?"

Saying the words, the full weight of her actions settled over me like wet wool. The heaviness of my new—and now permanent—situation sank into my marrow and turned to sludge. I didn't know what I would face as I went home. I didn't know if my tendrils would draw me to Finn in the past like they always had if we didn't share a history. I didn't know if Finn would remember me even if I could.

As my eyes locked with my future self's, I could see that she remembered this moment. Remembered how lost and confused and angry I felt.

"I know none of this makes sense right now," she said. "And, honestly, it's still really . . . it's . . . it's not going to be an easy path, but I need you to trust me."

Did I have a choice?

I wandered back over to the bubble that was glowing blue and realized it was actually a window. There was a hollowed-out space behind it. And something inside.

"You said this place was ICE's Cryostorage? Storage for what?" I asked. But when I turned back around to look at Bree, she was staring at the tubes again. She'd told me where we were, but I still didn't know when. I checked my QuantCom. We were fifty years in the past.

This was a few years after Shifters came out of hiding. ICE had been around since almost the beginning. As soon as we'd gone public with our ability, it seemed they'd been right there alongside us, "helpful" at every turn. Can't find a job that thoroughly utilizes your Shifting ability? ICE career counselors can help. Can't afford a chip functionality check? Head to your local free ICE clinic. Cost of Buzztabs have you down? There's an ICE benevolence fund for that!

This period of history had been a hotbed of political and social upheaval. NonShifters had been scared of us initially—scared of our ability. It had all been one big scrambled chicken-egg in the beginning. Shifters had agreed to be microchipped because Future Shifters mistakenly claimed that it was the only way to escape a Madness that would develop down the line. The microchips, in turn, led to the Buzz when they kept Shifters from going where their tendrils wanted them to go.

The Madness ended up being nonexistent, or rather, misinterpreted. Technically *I* had the Madness—the ability to detect changes to the timeline. Like I said, one giant temporal omelet. And there was ICE the whole time, hovering over the skillet.

I tapped on the bubble, and soligraphic controls popped up. Even though they were a simulated hologram—nothing but bits and bytes—they felt solid to the touch. A series of words and numbers scrolled across the front. November Bravo Golf 1309874729. I waved my hand in front of the controls, trying to get them to disappear, but instead the bubble opened like a blossom. A long metal shelf began to extend. I turned my attention back to making the controls disappear.

"I said, leave her alone." Bree stomped over and put her thumb over a red button on the controls.

"Her?" I looked down and that's when I realized what ICE was storing here. Or rather, who. It was a woman, her skin a rippling map of wrinkles framed by snowy hair. She seemed familiar, but it was impossible to place her in such unusual circumstances.

Accident victims were sometimes placed in cryostasis until new organs could be designed and produced for them. But something told me ICE wasn't keeping this woman frozen while they made her a kidney.

Future Me brushed a wisp of the woman's hair back from the

age-etched face before pressing the red button, sending the woman back into the confines of the cryostorage unit.

"Who is she?" I asked. "I mean, is she . . . dead?"

"She's alive." Bree looked back and forth between the woman and the tank before shaking her head slightly and turning back to me. There was a new expression on her face, like something had clicked. She gave the central tank one last, long look before turning back to face me. "Oh my gosh. I know who . . . umm, I have to go."

"What? You mean synch?"

She shook her head and raced off to one of the entrances of the room. The door slid open. As if an afterthought, she turned back around and pointed at a metal screen propped up about ten feet from where I was standing. "You'll hide behind that."

"Huh?"

But she hadn't stuck around to explain. I didn't have much time to mull it over, though, because the opposite entrance began to unseal. I raced over to the metal screen and slid behind it. She hadn't said I'd get caught here, so that made me feel a smidge better.

Even through the screen, I could tell who one of the people was. Well, not who so much as what. His stiff, red scrub pants swished as he entered the room backward, dragging something heavy behind him. He was one of ICE's workers.

"Couldn't have picked a light one, ehh?" he said to another person following behind him.

I craned my neck as far out as I dared to get a glance at the other person, but the metal screen was grated, and I worried they'd detect the movement.

"I was following very specific orders." The voice was garbled with a grating rasp to it. I couldn't even tell if it was a man or a woman.

I risked a further peek to see why. My hand flew to my mouth before I could stop it. At least I prevented the cry of shock from escaping. It was the person I'd seen earlier. The person at the London Fire, dressed head-to-toe in the same silver protective suit as before. They *did* work for ICE.

"Well?" There was a harsh clip, even through the mask that distorted the voice. I stared at Raspy, willing him or her to pull the hood and mask away so I could get a look at the face, but no such luck.

"Well what?" said the red scrub.

"We had a deal," said Raspy. "She comes with me."

"It's gonna take a lot more than one. They got big plans."

"But we had a—"

"Take it to the higher-ups. Nothing I can do about it." The red scrub raised the soligraphic controls in front of the central tank. Willowy robotic arms descended from the ceiling and clamped onto the heavy object at his feet. They lifted their load above the tank and dumped the contents in with a *splosh*. The red scrub entered information into the controls, ignoring Raspy, who was pacing behind him.

"Fine," said Raspy. But his (her?) posture spoke defeat as she (he? . . . dang, it was really impossible to tell) headed to the far exit.

Blark. The exit that my future self had taken only a few minutes ago. I tried to think of a way to warn her, but then I realized that by virtue of the fact that I knew Raspy was going out there, so did she.

"Fine," the red scrub jeered at the sealed door. He finished up with whatever information he was entering and turned to leave himself.

As soon as he was gone, I crept out from behind the screen, moving with confidence since Future Bree surely would have warned me if this was folly. I had to know what was in that tank.

The fluid inside had turned a murky blue. The large mass inside floated lifelessly, completely obscured by the combination of thick, frothy, sloshing liquid and the layer of frost on the outside of the tank. A small, soligraphic model floated in the air where the controls had been. At first, it looked like a glowing, baby seahorse, but when I prodded it, I realized what it was. A hippocampus—the part of the human brain that contains the quantum tendrils. The part of the brain that enables Shifters to Shift. There was a number below the hippocampus, ticking up and down every few seconds. .01% . . . .03% . . . .04% 02%

Something twitched in the fluid. I flinched away. Scratch what I had said. I didn't care what was in that tank. I just wanted out of here. This place gave me the willies, and then some.

It was with a rush of relief that I felt my fingers begin to tingle. I was going home. What exactly I would face there, I still wasn't sure. But home.

The room around me began to fade. Right before I took my final breath of chilled air, I looked straight ahead at the tank.

A hand reached out of the darkness and pressed against the inner glass.

chapter 8

SQUISH.

My shoe slid into the unused sanislush of the otherwise empty toilet when I landed back in the movie theater in my time. A fitting return to my present situation.

I closed my eyes and could still picture the tank. There was a person in that thing. A person. But I didn't even know where ICE's headquarters were. And besides, that person was there fifty years ago.

I counted to ten, an unsuccessful attempt to slow my shallow breathing. When I opened my eyes, I could still picture that hand.

There was only one reason I could think of why my future self would allow this fake-girlfriend-with-Wyck-charade to go on. Whatever was happening at ICE had to be stopped. And now that Bergin had been cut out of their organization, Wyck was my only connection to them.

The fact that I wasn't really with Wyck provided mild comfort. No, "comfort" was too strong a word. Consolation.

A fresh wave of panic, anger, and sadness sent me reeling when I looked at the door to the bathroom and realized I had to go out there and face Wyck. I had no idea how to act around him. No idea what to say. All the memories I had of the last six months contained Finn. And now I had to somehow convince Wyck that I was his girlfriend. This was why unchipped Shifters had sequestered themselves at Resthaven. The repercussions of this change were staggering.

I was so alone.

No, not alone, I reminded myself. Finn wasn't here, true. And he could never come here again since he was a chronofugitive. But surely it was only a matter of time before I would Shift to Chincoteague to see him and explain what had happened. Plus, I still had Mom and Quigley and Granderson. They would help me piece together what had happened.

And, apparently, a *lot* had happened.

It couldn't have been more than twenty minutes that I'd been gone, but Wyck had likely worn a trench into the floor pacing outside. I splashed some water on my face and held my head directly under the revivamist jet. It wasn't quite as effective as a twenty-first-century triple espresso, but tasted a lot less like battery acid.

Deep breath. I opened the door.

Wyck sat about fifteen feet away in the theater lobby, on the corner of a massive fountain shooting globs of sparkly gunk that changed colors and scents depending on the number of people who were standing nearby and the moods they were in. His face was as pale as a washed-out snowman. He was staring at the bathroom door with an intensity that made me wonder if he'd blinked the whole time.

"Are you okay?" He jumped up the second he saw me.

"Yes. I just got a little . . . upset . . . from the movie." Forgetting for a moment that Wyck and I had been watching that dumb romantic comedy rather than *Death Rumpus.* "I mean, upset stomach . . . from the popcorn."

"Blinky Beans."

"Exactly. Upset that I didn't order popcorn instead."

His smile was equal parts relief and bewilderment as I pasted on a kajillion-watt smile.

"You could have had some of mine," he said, then made a half-hearted gesture toward the theater. "Do you want to go catch the end?"

"Nah. I should probably head home." A complete lie. I would

head straight to Resthaven. Quigley might have some insight into what the blark was going on. But I couldn't let him know that. "I'm feeling a little—I don't know—off tonight."

"Of course." He shrugged off his jacket, moving toward me. I skirted away until I realized he was only trying to wrap it around my shoulders.

He doesn't remember trying to kill me. He doesn't remember trying to kill me. Over and over, I repeated it to myself like a protective mantra.

The problem was, this Wyck might not remember, but there was no way I could ever forget.

Pressing our way through the throng loitering outside the theater, Wyck, without a word, took my hand. It was the sort of thing that Finn often did, a nothing that felt natural. But as Wyck did it, all I could think was, am I squeezing hard enough? Too hard? Can he tell I'd rather be holding a rotten squid than his hand?

He joined the queue for Publi-pods, and my mantra flew out the window. He might not remember what he'd done on a different timeline, but there was no way in the glittering bowels of Hades that I was going to be trapped in a Pod with him.

"Actually," I said, "I'm in the mood to walk." All the better to extract information from him. I needed to find out what I'd been doing for the last six months.

"I thought you weren't feeling well."

"The fresh air will do me good."

"Umm sure." He waved the next people in line ahead of us and followed me as I tore a path down the sidewalk.

I shoved my hands in my pockets so he wouldn't attempt another handhold, but we hadn't made it ten paces before his arm was around my shoulder.

Fake girlfriend.

Okay.

I could do this.

Even if I had no idea what *this* was. Were we a serious couple? Just hanging out?

"Hmm." I leaned my chin back and gazed at the stars. "It's nights like this that make me stop and think about . . . us."

That should get him talking.

But my wistful watching of the heavens seemed to have the opposite effect on Wyck. The silence between us stiffened. I didn't think I'd said something that would make him suspicious, but . . .

"Bree," he said quietly, "are you breaking up with me?"

"What? No!" How had he gotten that from "Hmm"?

"It's just that you've been acting so strangely all evening," he said, "and . . ."

"Oh, no. Wyck, that's not what I meant at all."

"And then with all the ICE stuff lately."

Oh, yes. Do keep talking.

"What ICE stuff would that be?" I asked in what I hoped would come across as nonchalance, but Wyck stopped walking and snorted.

"Very funny."

"Uhh." This conversation had not proceeded as planned. At all. I let out a halfhearted chuckle. "Ha. Gotcha."

"I know I've been busy with it. And I know I'm beating a dead pegamoo"—Wow. Did not need that imagery—"But this is exactly what I was worried about. The time factor taking me away from you. Dr. Lafferty said it's nerves. She said that it's understandable. Normal, even."

"Lafferty?" There was a Dr. Lafferty who had written my Quantum Bio textbook from last year, but he was a man.

"Lafferty. I told you about my interview with her three days ago. The medical director at ICE? Bree, are you sure you're feeling okay?"

"I . . . yes. Lafferty. I got her name mixed up in my mind with someone else . . . named . . . Dafferty."

"Dafferty?"

"So she said that nerves are normal." I tried to get us back on track.

"Yeah, and that there's nothing to be nervous about. 'It's only Shifting,' she said. 'People have been doing it for millennia.'"

"*Shifters* have been doing it for millennia," I said quietly, but Wyck didn't hear me.

"Besides, I told her I'd made you a promise." He reached out and grasped both my hands in his. "You want a Shifter boyfriend. You've got one."

What? I fought the urge to yank my hands away as I quickly replayed the conversation we'd just had. From the way Wyck was talking, I was the one who had pressured him into Shifting. But that was the opposite of what I wanted. I mean, yeah. I wanted a Shifter boyfriend. I wanted Finn. *My* Shifter boyfriend. I wanted Wyck to have never heard of the possibility. I wanted ICE to have never invented the IcePick and even *make* it a possibility.

No, a voice chimed in my head, *that's what Real Bree wants.* I couldn't act or think like Real Bree anymore. I had no idea what this Fake Bree wanted, what she needed, what she had been up to for the last six months. This was like waking up from a coma, only to find out that your comatose self had been not only living your life the whole time, but had been living it all wrong.

My solution: keep Wyck talking.

I maintained a steady stream of small talk all the way back to the Institute and managed to glean the following about the time I'd lost: I had still ended up Anchored, but for made-up health reasons, not for breaking the rules. Quigley wasn't a teacher at the Institute anymore. She had left to pursue humanitarian efforts, taking care of Shifters who had succumbed to the Madness, at Resthaven. Granderson had joined her there full-time as well, just as he had on my timeline.

When we reached the entrance to the Institute, where Wyck was still in the transporter program, I leaned forward to brush my hair against the scanner, but Wyck blocked it with his broad torso.

"Why the hurry?" He bent down, and at first I assumed he was picking something up but instead he whispered something into my ear that *really* made Real Bree want to slap him.

I closed my eyes and tried to pretend that somehow it was Finn standing in front of me, that somehow I wasn't betraying him or missing him or . . . I reached up, without opening my eyes and brushed my lips against Wyck's. They reciprocated with enthusiasm.

Okay, then.

I tried to return his kiss with an approximation of anything but revulsion. I kept my brain busy by coming up with a mental to-do list: Research this Lafferty woman, Infiltrate ICE, Strangle my future self when I caught up with her.

Wyck finally came up for air, and in the corner of my vision, I saw what looked like a photo flash from across the street. I glanced over, but I must have imagined it. There was nothing there.

"You seem distracted," Wyck said.

"I'm just tired."

He patted me on the shoulder. "You should go get some rest."

"I should."

Or.

I should plant another peck on Wyck's cheek, wait until he disappeared into his room, and run straight back out to catch a Pod to Resthaven.

Option two it was.

━━◆━━

"This had better be important." Quigley swept into her office and stared me down. Her furnishings and pictures—old-fashioned to the point of archaic—were much more suited to Resthaven than the Institute. We might be on the same side now, but I still avoided Quigley's office whenever I could. She had somehow managed to procure the most uncomfortable chairs made in the last three centuries, and every time I came to talk to her, I felt like an interrogation victim.

After she had her chip disabled, she knew it would be impossible to keep her position teaching history at the Institute. It would only be a matter of time before she couldn't hide the fact that, for her, history was changing. Still, I knew she missed it.

What I didn't know was why she, at midnight, was wearing a floor-length saffron velvet gown complete with ruched sleeves and a delicate lace veil instead of pajamas.

"Did I interrupt something?" I asked.

"A lovely lunch with Leo." She was referring to Leonardo da Vinci. Turned out the Quig was quite his little muse. She was the model for the *Mona Lisa*.

"Color study," she added. "He's having a bit of trouble capturing the exact shade of my irises."

"Brown," I said.

"Thank you for your expert analysis." She yanked the veil off and slid behind her desk.

"You look kind of ridicul—"

"I know how I look," she said. "Why are you here?"

Never one to mince words.

"Finn and I were on a date earlier, but then Wyck—"

"If you've come to me for boy advice—"

"Do you honestly think I'd come to you for boy advice?" Dr. Quigley and I had been on slightly friendlier terms now that she was my mentor and leader at the Haven Society rather than my teacher, but puh-lease.

"Well." Quigley tugged at the delicate embroidery at her neck. "If you ever do find yourself in need of guidance about behavior of the male persuasion, you know that you can always—"

"Go to my mom or Mimi. Never you. Never."

"Fair enough."

"But if I'm ever in need of a lecture on appropriate Renaissance etiquette, I know where to go."

"Again, why are you here?" she said.

I spent the next hour updating her on everything that had happened since I landed in London. When I stopped and considered that it was only one day—less than a full day at that—it didn't seem possible.

"You're positive Wyck was the one who made the change to the timeline?" she asked.

"Yep. I saw him do it."

Quigley pulled up my file.

"Ahh, here it is," she said. "Yes. 'Transporter O'Banion states that Ms. Bennis has expressed that she is overwhelmed by her workload and shows signs of debilitating fatigue.' I cancelled your mid-term assignment, and Nurse Granderson placed you on medical Anchorment soon after. Apparently all this occurred without any protest on your part. Granderson has been handling your care, and it looks like he's forged all the chip maintenance data to look normal."

She tucked the soligraphic file back into its data disk and tossed it to me.

"So there you go," she said. "It seems that even if nonShifters make these changes, there are still inevitabilities that drive our actions. You're still Anchored. Granderson and I still ended up here at Resthaven. Wyck is unfortunately still tangled up with ICE."

"Honestly," I said, "that doesn't shock me. You didn't see him last year at the Monument, Quigley. He was like a feral animal."

"And he was acting the same way when you saw him make the change?"

"No. That was the weird part. He was acting normal. Well, I mean, there were some flashes."

"Flashes?"

"That's what I've been calling them. I don't know the technical medical jargon. But you know those glimpses into the different timeline that nonShifters experience after I've reverted one of their changes? Well, they seem to be physically painful. It's like this *flash* of the other timelines seeps into his brain, and he gets confused and starts acting awful. Plus, after my future self stopped me from reverting Wyck's change, she told me he was acting on ICE's orders."

"Really? But then why did your future self stop you from using the reverter?"

"I have no idea. I guess this change ends up helping me to get a foot in the door at ICE. When I left Wyck just now, he really made it sound like I'm the one who talked him into joining their Shifting program on this timeline."

"Again, for what purpose?"

"The only explanation that makes sense is to give me a gateway into ICE's organization. It must have something to do with the frozen woman and whoever was in that tank."

"You said she looked familiar?"

I nodded. And for some reason, I could do so with more confidence now. Maybe it was just being here at Resthaven away from all the pressure of that situation, but I was almost certain now that I knew her.

"Did you recognize the hand?" asked Quigley.

"It was a hand."

"Male or female?"

"I couldn't tell. It all happened too fast." I held the reverter back up. "I don't even understand how I still have this thingamajig since Wyck stopped me from going back to Chincoteague where everything started. I just wish I could go back in time a few months and ask my past self what the blark is going on right now."

"You're thinking linearly, Bree."

"Shame on me."

"When Wyck made this change to the timeline," she said, "and convinced me that you were unfit to Shift for the mid-term, it set a different course of events into motion on this timeline. But your tendrils—and mine—are affixed to the true timeline. Or at least, our version of the Truth. And that reverter was activated in Finn's time, outside all these changes, reverted or not."

"Our version of the Truth? What do you mean by that?"

Quigley opened her mouth but then hesitated.

"It's like how you got that reverter in the first place . . ."

"Finn punched Bergin in the nose for it."

"No. Again. You're thinking linearly. How you *originally* got that reverter. Before it was even a reverter. When it was still an IcePick."

"Ohhh." Yeah, that one was a chicken-egg of particularly mind-scrambling proportions. It had actually happened about a week after my chip had been disabled—one of my first Free Shifts back in time. I had succumbed to the pull of the Shift and found myself smack-dab in the middle of Bergin's empty office. After a proper freak-out, I remembered that I was where I was supposed to be. I only needed to figure out why I had been called there.

And as I stood in his office, holding my precious reverter, thinking about the lengths I'd had to go to in order to obtain it and activate it, I realized that Future Me would eventually need to steal an IcePick to create said reverter. Then it occurred to me that maybe I *was* Future Me. Sometimes, the simplest path is the best. I checked Bergin's hidden drawer, and after trying out a few different combinations of his dead wife's name and birthday, it popped open. Yoink. I took his IcePick. Easy peasy.

So technically, I was now the proud owner of two reverters. Or rather, one reverter and one reverter-in-the-making.

Here's the mind-blowing part, though. It was only after I had hidden the IcePick in the Mastersons' safe that it occurred to me that I never should have been able to take it. It shouldn't have existed. ICE had already gone back and changed the past to vote out Bergin from their Advisory Board at that point. The time-line had already changed. But I guess my tendrils wouldn't cling to that false timeline. They'd only cling to the timeline I'd been on. Hence, I'd been able to Shift back and take the IcePick.

"So does that mean if I Shifted back to four months ago," I said, "I still wouldn't meet up with a Past Bree who was experiencing this timeline? Basically, there's no way for me to find out what she's been up to?"

"There's no way to test that theory," said Quigley. "The only way to force your tendrils back to a specific time is by activating your microchip. By reinstating your microchip, it would force your tendrils to cling to the current timeline. But it would also mean you would no longer be able to detect any of the changes. At least, like Granderson and me, it would appear that this version of Bree has still been acting in such a way as to live as a Free Shifter.

"There's another theory I've been working on as well." She brushed her hair against her desk to open a drawer. "But it's a bit complicated."

"Oh, thank heavens. Because so far this has all been so very simple."

It was a good thing that Quigley had grown as accustomed to my sarcasm as I had to her abrasiveness. She continued straight on as if I'd said nothing at all.

She pulled out another data disk and tapped it. A timeline, just like the one she used to teach with, erupted out of the button. As she flicked various points on the timeline—*bloop, bloop, bloop*—pictures bloomed out from it. It reminded me of an afternoon a few weeks ago that I'd spent with Georgie, sitting at the end of their dock blowing soap bubbles. I couldn't quite get the hang of it, and my bubbles never seemed to want to fully escape the wand that had created them.

"We're here." Quigley pointed to today's date on the line.

"Mm hmm."

"Finn's here." She pointed back to the early twenty-first century.

"And he'd better stay there."

Quigley gave a grim nod. She'd pointed out that if a single good thing had come of this change, it was that Finn, now a chronofugitive, was nowhere near the twenty-third century.

"Things have happened between then and now." She flicked various points and historical facts popped up. Presidents, stock prices, inventions, wars, game shows.

"Whyever did you give up teaching?"

She shot me a scathing look, but then I noticed something odd. None of the dates she had pulled up were within fifty years of our time.

"Ready for a headache?" she asked.

Always.

She tapped a date forty years back, and five bubbles bloomed from the same spot on the line. She tapped a date ten years back, and a dozen bubbles crowded the space above the line. Then she went to a spot near our present. Bubbles erupted from the line like a rolling boil until I lost count.

"What am I looking at?" I asked.

"Eventualities."

"What does that mean?"

"Each of these bubbles represents possible outcomes for each date in question. When nonShifters change an incident within their lifetime, it creates an alternate path."

"You mean an alternate reality?"

"No. Reality is still what is real, what's true. But perception of reality is what's changing."

"You lost me."

"Let's try another way of looking at it." She erased the bubbles, back to the original timeline. This time, when she tapped the date forty years back, a few separate timelines split off from the main one at that point. Ten years back, she touched one of the separate ones and four branched away from it. In the present, the splits resembled the tender, tiny roots of a sapling. But still the main timeline ticked away.

"I think I understand. My body might be here"—I pointed at a spot on one of the branching lines—"but my tendrils are here." The real timeline. Where Finn should be right now. With me.

"That's . . . the confusing part." For the first point in our conversation, Quigley looked uncomfortable. "You didn't turn off your chip on the real timeline."

She tapped a point six months back, and again multiple timelines shot from the main one.

"Your chip was causing you to cling to one of these other alternate paths when you turned it off. So you're not technically on the true timeline. None of us are."

"None?" I motioned around us. This house was full to the brim of unchipped Shifters.

"Well, very few. I only know of a handful of Shifters who were never chipped."

"So all of these people are running around on different timelines?"

"In a manner of speaking."

"Then why am I even bothering with this thing?" I held up the reverter. "I'll never be able to get us back to the real Truth. I'm wasting my time."

"You're not wasting your time," said Quigley. "You're pruning."

"Pruning?"

"Imagine each of these branches is an actual branch from a . . . a grapevine. What happens to a vine if it grows unchecked?"

"It takes over." Like that kudzu that was stupidly introduced to the southern United States from its native Japan in the late 1800s. It was marketed as a decorative plant to shade porches. It grew so rapidly, though, that it ate up acres of roadside forest and engulfed entire buildings. They had fought it with shears, herbicides, even fire, down to the roots. But if one tiny bit remained, it would just start growing again.

"Blar-r-rk," I said quietly. "Pruning isn't enough. We have to cut it down to the root somehow. Down to the true timeline."

"Exactly," said Quigley. "But all of this was information that you already knew, of course."

"It was?"

"Or, rather, should have been able to deduce. No. Here's where we slip into theory." She stretched out her palm expectantly. "May I?"

I realized she wanted the reverter. I handed it over with a cringe, loath to part with it even for a moment. When Quigley brushed it against the base of one of the alternative timelines, though, hope sparked in my chest. The line disappeared, along with all the other alternates branching from it.

The spark extinguished, though.

"That's what I've been doing," I said. "It's not enough. I can't stop them all."

It was like being sent off to battle and finding out the only weapon you had was a butter knife.

"I can't keep up with the pruning," I said.

"Exactly." She tapped the reverter against the original timeline—the True one—and all the other lines vanished.

"What did you just do?"

"The heart of my theory," she said. "Point Zero."

"Huh?"

"There is a moment on the original timeline that if we could figure out a way to revert it, we could stop the Initiative from carrying through with their plans. It would prevent all the other changes."

"Well . . ." I took the reverter back and started tapping points along the main line—farther and farther back—until no deviant lines existed. "Here. We just need to somehow get back to this point."

"No." She tapped the timeline again, and the tangle reappeared. "You're thinking three-dimensionally. Think *four*-dimensionally. Point Zero could be anywhere on the True timeline. It could be in the future."

"How?"

"It was a moment, a decision, that *triggered* the first change. Think about what you've just been through. It altered your time-line six months ago, but the change happened today."

"Then what could have triggered the first change? What happened at Point Zero?"

"No idea."

I waited for her to elaborate, but I knew she wouldn't. Quigley preferred to deal in fact, not speculation.

"So for now, I should just keep pruning?" I asked.

She nodded. "Whatever you do, don't do anything rash."

"Me?" I batted doe eyes at her. "When have I ever done anything like that?"

"Perhaps we should aim lower. Don't get *caught* doing anything rash. Which"—she drummed her fingers on her desk—"brings me to Finn. Promise me that if you do meet up with him in the past, you won't bring him back with you. It would be dangerous for Finn and put every member of the Haven at risk."

"I may be a bit reckless, Quigley. But I'm not an idiot."

I'd searched the public records on the Pod Ride over to Rest-haven. Sure enough, my boyfriend was a certified temporal bad boy. It would have been kind of hot if the crimes that consti-tuted Level Five Fugitive status weren't punishable by life in prison.

"Be careful, Bree," said Quigley. "You're the only hope for some of these Haven members."

No pressure or anything.

Quigley escorted me out. Resthaven was a refurbished Victo-rian mansion. It had served as everything from a boutique hotel to a brothel to a genuine sanatorium over the last four hundred years. Most of the newer residents, those whose chips had spontaneously malfunctioned, stuck to the common room. It was well past midnight but not unusual to find the space packed. Free Shifters kept odd hours, always coming and going. With all the changes over the last fifty years, many of them preferred to spend much of their time in the distant past, unsullied by fluctuating history.

Those who had been here the longest kept to themselves. I didn't blame them. Most of them hadn't been chipped in decades, if ever. With the jumbled knot that their timeline had become—being able to detect that something had changed without knowing what, when, who, or why—it was difficult for them to keep up a coherent conversation.

We passed a bedroom with the door ajar. Nurse Granderson was inside, checking on an elderly resident, one of the oldest ones here, if not the oldest. He smoothed out a tuft of her white hair before running a medical scanner down her stick-thin arm. I'd met her once, maybe twice. What was her name? Nava?

I paused and looked at the nameplate on the door.

Nava Schwartz. Yes. She was pretty feisty for being over one hundred years old. In her earlier years, before Shifters had come out of hiding, she'd worked as a cultural anthropologist. She'd gone back to Poland and worked as a postmistress in a small Polish village during World War II, taking samples of DNA from licked stamps, looking the future fallen in the face. One by one. Later, she used the DNA to identify the remains of Holocaust victims in a mass grave near Auschwitz and give them an appropriate burial. Something in her must have snapped, but in a good way.

Quigley had had Nava in to one of her history classes a few years ago to speak about the Holocaust. I remember Nava described the method the Nazis used to identify their victims in concentration camps—crude tattoos on their chests and arms. She said that their skin might have been marked with ink, but she made it her mission to mark their graves with flowers.

When the government offered Nava a microchip to help control her Shifting some fifty years ago, after Shifters went public, she had scoffed in their face. "Blue tattoos all over again."

Nava was one of the few of my kind who'd chosen to live with foresight and not fear. And what had it earned her? A diagnosis of the Madness and shunning from her fellow Shifters. Not around here, though. At Resthaven, she was something of a hero. Gutsy as all get-out with a wicked sharp sense of humor. Nurse Granderson cared for her as if she were his own mother.

And her body was the one I had seen frozen in ICE's cryounit fifty years ago.

chapter 9

"YOU'RE SURE IT was her?"

We were in Granderson's infirmary rather than Quigley's office now. He hadn't stopped pacing since I'd identified Nava and explained what was going on (or at least the little I understood of it). He took his role in the Haven seriously. He was there to help Shifters no matter where or when they needed him, be it 2:00 A.M. at Resthaven or 1870's Belgium. One time, I'd found him collapsed on the sofa in the common room. Cassa, another resident, told me not to wake him, that he'd spent the entire day Shifting from beacon house to beacon house throughout the past, treating Shifters for injuries and illness. He was always inoculating himself against some long-extinct disease he'd been exposed to.

"I'm positive," I said.

"But why her?" He flipped around, and I suddenly realized how tired he looked. Pale with exhaustion. In that moment, I felt a kinship to Granderson. If there was anyone else who had poured out every iota of energy for the last six months to help his fellow Shifters, it was him. "She can't prove a threat to them. The world sees her as mentally unhinged. She hasn't left Resthaven in years."

"Well, she's still here for now," I said.

"Someone must take her in the future then." Quigley's forehead scrunched, and it felt good to have someone else as confused as I was by all this. "I'll increase security here to be safe."

Quigley was fighting a losing battle, but I didn't bother pointing it out. I'd seen Nava myself on that cold slab. ICE *would* abduct her. It was inevitable.

"Maybe we're asking the wrong question," I said.

"What do you mean?" Granderson asked.

"Havens are a sure place to find Shifters in the past. Resthaven is a sure place to find Shifters in the present. There was nothing random about the abduction. I don't think the question is 'why her?'" I pointed at Nava. "It's 'why us?' Why kidnap Shifters at all?"

"Blackmail?" Quigley said. "A warning?"

"Maybe." I didn't quite feel the ring of truth to those theories.

It wasn't illegal to disable your microchip. Frowned upon, yes, seen as self-destructive as it was a sure way to land yourself in Resthaven, which to the outside world was perceived as a loony factory. But it wasn't against the law, so that ruled out blackmailing the Haven Society.

And a warning about what? Nava was no threat to anyone. Why would ICE target her? Whatever the reason, the person in that silver suit didn't seem particularly happy about being involved in it.

"There's only one way to find out," I said. "Wyck's signed up to Shift with ICE. I'll tag along with him and poke around their headquarters."

"Be careful," Granderson said.

"I always am."

Quigley snorted, and I had to bite my tongue to keep from smarting back.

I swear. Sometimes she acted more like my mother than my mom.

"My mom!" I hadn't even stopped to think how this change might have affected her.

At the time of my mid-term, six months ago, she had been in a coma. But she had been placed in that coma by none other than Headmaster Bergin in his desperate attempt to control the use of the reverter.

I'd won (if winning you could call it), but where did that leave my mom?

I pushed my way past the Quig and Granderson. They called out after me, but I ignored them, sprinting down the steps of Resthaven, out into the street. I took off for the nearest Metro station, pinging my mother's speakeazy as I ran. No answer.

Come on, come on. You have to be there. You have to answer. *You have to be alive.*

My brain was at war with itself. One side screamed, "There's no way your future self would have allowed that change if it meant Mom getting hurt." The other, "Can you really trust a future self who chooses Wyck over Finn? A future self who won't give you answers again?"

The ride home seemed to take twice as long as usual. With each passing minute, my imagination grew more deadly.

It was like walking in on a movie at the very end and having to guess the plot. No. Like walking in at the end and finding out you had starred in it without your knowledge.

Come on, you stupid slow train. I banged my fist against the ceiling of the cabin as it bulleted out of the station. Faster.

The moment we pulled into the Metro station, I took off toward the Publi-pods, thankful at least for efficient public transportation, and found a vacant one. I shouted my address and zoomed off. When the Pod reached my house, I jumped through the opening orb and rushed into the front foyer, straining to detect any hint of life. There was no sound but Tufty purring on the couch.

"Mom?" I clomped up the stairs two at a time. "Mom!"
Silence.

She had to be here. I couldn't have lost her again. I just . . . no.

"Mom?" I ran through every room, throwing open every closet, peeking behind every door.

She had to be here.

"Mom!"

I searched the last room.

She wasn't here.

It was too much. I didn't even know if she was alive. I was going to have to ask someone if my mother was clinging to life in a hospital bed or if she was . . . or if she was . . .

My shoulders began to shake. I couldn't do this again. I couldn't lose her again. And this time, I was alone. No Finn to lean on for support.

"Sugar booger?"

"Mom?" I looked up through tear-matted eyes.

She was here. She was fine.

I fell into her arms. She folded them over me, a shawl of protection.

"I couldn't find you," I said.

"I was with your, umm, your father."

I couldn't help it—I stiffened at the mention of him. She ignored it, if she even noticed.

"Sweetie, what's wrong?" She lifted my chin. "I thought you were going back to the Institute after your date with Finn. Is everything all right?"

Any semblance of strength melted away from me. She didn't even know about the change yet. And why should she? She had been back with my father, oblivious. There it was again, that bitterness. Sure, some ripples would spread out and hit other people in my life, but this change had been aimed squarely at me. Through coughing hiccups, I told Mom what had happened—what I knew, what I suspected, what I could only guess at.

One sunrise and three bowls of triple fudge ripple later, Mom tossed her spoon onto the floor next to my bed.

"Whoa."

"Yep."

After I'd recounted the whole day, we'd spent the next few hours scouring the news archives for any info we could find about, well, anything. Quigley's departure from the Institute was uneventful. Granderson's appointment as medical care coordinator at Resthaven was seen as benevolent but pointless. Mom's coma had never even happened.

"Which makes sense," she pointed out. "If you think about it in terms of Quigley's Zero Point—"

"Point Zero," I corrected.

"Point Zero theory. ICE may have put me in a coma a year ago, but the instigating events happened after Wyck's change."

One good thing to come of this, I guess.

"I just don't understand why my tendrils aren't calling me back to Chincoteague," I said. "I need to explain all this to Finn. He has to be worried sick."

"Mmm . . . hmmm." The way she said it (or rather, the way she didn't say it) made my stomach lurch.

"What?"

"Nothing."

"No. What?"

"Well, I just . . . perhaps we need to consider the possibility— however remote—that Finn might have changed with the timeline."

"But no one else did."

"No one else here in these bubbles or loops or whatever Lisa calls them. But, Bree, Finn is outside of this branched timeline that ICE has created. We don't know—"

"No." I wouldn't even let her finish that sentence, because to hear it aloud, even if I wasn't the one saying it, felt like it would make it true.

"I'm sure you're right." She smoothed my hair down. "And your father—he didn't seem changed."

Yippee. Still unwilling to meet his only child.

When I didn't say anything, she slid off the bed and picked up the ice cream bowls.

"Time for bed. You've lived a few lifetimes in the last twenty-four hours."

And yet none of them had been mine.

"Do you want something to help you sleep?" she asked.

"I'm okay."

"Are you sure? Just a little something to take the edge off."

I laughed. "You sound like a drug pusher."

Mom laughed, too. "I meant some warm milk. I know all these Shifts and timeline changes can mess with your inner clock."

"No thanks."

She was right, though. No matter what Wyck had done, no matter what my future self refused to do, no matter what the next step was, I was useless without clearing my head. I dozed off before Mom had even shut the door.

⊷

Hell hath no fury like a best friend kept out of the loop.

Mimi's tiny fists of fury almost hurt me as she woke me with a mock beating. I blinked into the darkness, the sun had already gone down. I'd slept the entire day away.

"Whah time izit?"

"Time to tell me about the scorcher date that you were supposed to fill me in on as soon as it was over. Nineteen hours ago."

Mm. The date. Blurry images reeled through my mind. Fire. Sand. Ice. Kiss.

"Was good." I yawned. "We went to the café. Saw, umm, Pennedy's . . . umm." No, that wasn't right. Ugh. Blurry. My dreams had been so vivid, sleeping all day.

"What? You saw Pennedy?"

"No." I propped myself up. "We saw—"

And that was when I remembered that there was no *we*. Nineteen hours, and I hadn't felt a single tug back to Finn. Mimi was talking about my date with Wyck. Mimi was still chipped. This Mimi had never even met Finn.

"Nothing. Sorry. I stayed up late talking to Mom, and I just woke up from a nightmare. Guess I'm a little disoriented."

"Well, Wyck's dropped by the room three times since noon to check on you. He said you weren't feeling good last night. But you were fine before you left for the movie. So what's going on?" She cocked her head to the side.

This was why free Shifters moved to Resthaven. I wasn't 100 percent sure who the president was at the moment. And now I needed to convince a girl who knew me better than almost anyone else in the world that everything was normal even though I had zero percent certainty what normal had been for the last six months.

I dodged.

"I was embarrassed." I lowered my voice. "Tummy troubles."

"Ahh." She sat down next to me. "Better now?"

I nodded.

"Probably just nervous about tomorrow," she said. "I'm sure that's why Wyck keeps swinging by."

"Nervous?"

"Well, I mean, nervous for him obviously."

"Obviously." I had to keep her talking. Mimi could catch me up on Wyck. "This has all happened so fast."

"Fast?"

Okay. Apparently not fast.

"I meant it's seemed fast at times, but in reality, so . . . slooow."

"It's definitely been a process." She squeezed my hand. "One thing's for sure. He never would have made it this far in the training without you. ICE should be paying you a salary."

"I don't know what you mean."

"Oh, come on. You've been his biggest cheerleader. Every time he's wavered or doubted, there you are with the Top Ten list of why Wyck will be the best Neo ever."

"Neo?"

"NeoShifter?" She laughed. "You really did just wake up, didn't you?"

"Yeah." The ironic part was that, for the first time since I'd found my lips locked on Wyck's, I felt alert and alive. It was like I lived on a desert island, and I'd found a map in a bottle that had washed to shore. But not the whole map.

My future self had torn off a tiny edge and left me that. Enough to take one step forward. But it was a big enough piece to know that that step led toward ICE. The sooner I figured out what ICE was doing and stopped it, the sooner I got my life back. The sooner I could get off this island. And Wyck held the rest of that map.

After Mom made us a late dinner, I went back to the Institute with Mimi even though it felt like landing on a foreign planet. My side of the room was mine. But . . . not. No pictures of Finn. The wall was plastered with shots of Wyck and me doing all kinds of extreme sports. I stared at them, searching for clues as to who this Fake Bree was. Apparently, I liked to stay busy with him. In the few shots with his arms around me, a careful observer—someone who really knew me—could see the strain in my smile. It was subtle, but it was there.

Somehow, this made me feel better.

Meems went into the bathroom to put her pajamas on. She had a French Revolution paper to write and was settling in for the night. When she came out of the bathroom, she was clutching the sides of her head.

"Do you have any extra Buzztabs?" she asked.

I hadn't had a single use for a Buzztab in six months, but I had continued to request my weekly allotment so as not to raise any red flags that my chip was nonfunctional. I pulled a full bottle out and tossed it to Mimi.

"Thanks," she said. "It's been a bad couple days for the Buzz for some reason."

The Buzz was a result of not being able to Shift to where you were naturally called. I guess it was the body's way of protesting the chip's intrusive control. That didn't explain why Mimi's Buzz was especially bad right now. But I still felt for her. The memory of that throbbing pain was all too fresh for me.

"Mimi, there's something you should know about—" No. I couldn't. I'd started to tell her the truth about her microchip more times than I could count, but I couldn't risk it. Things were already so screwed up. And Mimi was such a worrywart. If she turned me in—even with the best and most loving intentions in her heart—it would muss things even worse.

"What is it?" she said.

"Umm, something you should know about revolutionary France."

"Revolutionary France?"

"Yes. For your paper. Mom went there on a work trip . . . recently . . . and it was really, umm . . . scary."

"Yeah." Mimi stared at me like I'd sprouted a third ear. "I was actually about to start writing a section on the Reign of Terror, so that's really helpful."

"Well, you could quote her," I said.

"'Scary'? Yeah. I mean, that's insightful." Mimi fiddled with the edge of her compufilm. "Do you need to lie down again?"

I wasn't remotely tired after sleeping all day.

"Nah. I'm going to head to the—" I was about to say greenhouse, but that was Finn's and my spot. I couldn't go there. "I'm going to go for a walk."

"M'kay," murmured Mimi, but she was already neck-deep in descriptions of guillotines.

Real Bree would have headed down to the greenhouse. I meandered up, up, up to the least likely spot that I'd ever go, the roof. The tiniest twinkling of stars broke through the dull-glowing halo of the D.C. skyline. No one ever went up to the roof. I'd find privacy if not peace here. But as I found a nice precipice to lean against, I saw someone sitting against the opposite wall. Wyck.

He was nibbling at the edge of a high-density nutribar, perfectly balanced to optimize and conserve Shifter energy. I once accidentally took a bite of a piece of cardboard at a hamburger joint Finn and I ate at in the 1950s. The effect was quite similar.

Wyck patted the ground next to him.

"How ya feeling?" he asked.

"Better. Thanks." I sat down.

"Lafferty contacted me this morning," he said, without any other explanation.

"Good." That was good, right? Oh, for the love of Zeus's holey underpants, please tell me that was good.

"I'm officially approved." His face broke into that boyish grin that I knew, that I missed, that he used to reserve for harassing First Years and talking me into skipping class.

"That's wonderful."

"Pre-Shift diagnostics are tomorrow. ICE has to make sure I'm fit to time travel."

Okay, so that's what Mimi was talking about when she thought I was nervous about tomorrow.

Wyck looked away, like he was forming a question in his mind, of which he was afraid of the answer.

"You'll still come, won't you?" he said.

"Of course I will."

He brushed his arm against mine in a tentative attempt at affection, and my first instinct was repulsion. But then it was like my future self popped up in my brain, waving that sandy bottle. Keep him happy. Keep him interested. Keep him close. And only then would she give me the next torn piece of the map.

I leaned forward and found myself pondering each body movement. How would I act if he were Finn instead of himself? Okay. Put hand on his waist . . . here. And wrap my finger around his like . . . that. All right. That was as good as it was going to get.

"I knew they'd choose you," I said. "You'll be a . . ."

"Natural. Yeah. You've said that. A lot."

"That's because it's true," I said brightly.

"I guess." He picked off a corner of his nutribar and tossed it into a flock of pigeons at the roof's edge. One of them took a bite and gagged. The others scattered. Wyck folded up the rest of the bar and tucked it into his coat. "Bree, there's something I've never told you."

"What?"

"I . . . I've known for a long time that I'm going to be a Neo."

"Me, too. Like I said. You're a natural."

"No, I've *known*."

"What do you mean?"

"I had a visit from my future self. He told me I'd do this."

"Is that all he told you?" It was hard to hide my disdain, but I managed.

Wyck turned red and muttered, "Yeah."

Liar.

"You should get to bed," I said. "I'm sure you have a big day tomorrow."

"I'll ping you after lunch when it's time to leave." He stood up and held out his hand. "You headed in?"

"Not yet. I'm going to hang out up here for a while."

"See you tomorrow." As he stepped past me, his heel landed on my toe. Hard.

"Oww." I massaged the throbbing appendage.

"So sorry." There was a hardness to his voice that was eerily familiar. My gaze lifted slowly to his face, afraid of what I'd find there. For a flicker, I saw it. Evil Wyck. Pure malice. But it quickly melted to the opposite, and he stooped to touch my foot gently.

"Did I hurt you?" he said.

"It's nothing."

"No, I hurt you, I—"

"It's fine, Wyck. I'm fine." I wasn't fine. In fact, I had my finger poised over the stunner button of my Com in my pocket. But I wanted this conversation to end so he would leave. Now.

He nodded. I could tell he was bewildered at his own behavior. Wyck had no idea what had just happened to him, but I did. He didn't realize that his timeline had changed. From his perspective, he'd had a visit from his future self six months ago (which was enough of a shock on its own, I'm sure). But then the course of his personal history, and everyone it impacted, was altered. A new branch to the timeline had been born.

But a fragment of memory from a timeline that he had changed had flashed into this one. Wyck might have morphed into my adoring boyfriend on this particular timeline, but there were other branches where he'd been the opposite, where he had done ICE's bidding, no matter the cost to his sanity or his soul. Those branches could pop up at any time.

Wyck left, and I let loose a puff of breath I didn't even realize I'd been holding. I pulled my hand out of my pocket.

Something stuck to my fingers.

Something . . .

To save his, destroy yours.

The crumpled piece of compufilm from the London Fire. I stared at my future self's haphazard handwriting. I couldn't make bits or bytes of it. And then all those random numbers and letters. They looked vaguely familiar. They weren't dates, but what were they?

And then, to save his what? And who was *he*?

Thanks a lot, Future Bree. One change. That was all it had taken to crumble everything I'd fought so hard for.

Take me to Finn, I ordered my useless, mutated genes. *Now.*

Nothing.

I tamped down the anger that had started to build, the clench of my jaw sending shocks of pain down my neck.

I stayed there, seething, until the wind picked up and forced me inside. Mimi had fallen asleep at her desk, her hand clutched around my Buzztab bottle. I tucked a pillow under her head and wrapped a blanket around her shoulders. There were still things left to fight for, I reminded myself.

chapter 10

"THIS IS IT?" I didn't mean for it to come off as disappointed as it sounded, but I couldn't help it. I'd expected ICE Headquarters to look like some kind of fortress. Not a boring, dome-shaped building, indistinguishable from the other boring, dome-shaped buildings surrounding it. Seriously, architects had become a little obsessed with domes in the last century.

"It's bigger than it looks," said Wyck. "Most of it's underground."

Like moles.

Or snakes.

It creeped me out, though, to think that I had probably been underground in their Cryostorage Room.

There was no formal greeting desk as we walked in, but a scanner free-floated toward us and nudged Wyck in the arm. He brushed his hair against it, and it spit out two compufilm badges that stated "Wyck O'Banion" and "Guest." A swarm of ICE workers bustled past, all wearing their signature red surgical scrubs. Like Satan's medics, if you asked me. The last run-in I'd had with them, not counting the Cryo Room, had been in Bergin's office when two of them had tried to kill me. I bristled, but they didn't give us a second glance. I reminded myself that on this timeline, I wasn't an instigator, wasn't a rebel (that they knew of). To ICE, I was nothing but a Neo's doting girlfriend. I was nothing.

I wouldn't be nothing for long, though.

The aboveground portion of the building consisted of an enormous open space. Wyck hadn't been kidding when he said their headquarters were mostly subterranean. The only thing in this entry room was a massive sculpture. Floor to ceiling, about twenty hollow, translucent, colored tubes wended and weaved their way through the air. Each tube was approximately three feet in diameter. It looked like a jumble of giant rainbow spaghetti.

I startled as something shot through the tube above me. The humming aftereffect was almost musical. *Whoosh. Whish.* A man wearing a suit that cost more than my house landed at the base of the turquoise tube closest to us. He stepped out of it and straightened his sliver of a tie before marching across the lobby.

Ahh. The sculpture was their transportation system. I'd give ICE this: they had style.

Through the twisty maze of cylinders, a woman in five-inch crimson stilettos and a crisp skirt and lab coat, white as the driven snow, seemed to materialize out of nowhere. But then I realized— no, not out of nowhere, out of a black tube. It was off to the side and the only opaque one in the place.

"Wyck! Our newest Neo." Her teeth gleamed brighter than her outfit and were that kind of perfect-straight that could only be achieved by genetic meddling. Anything white always washed me out, but with her jet black hair that had one single silvery streak, her pale skin glowed. It was a fierce brand of attractiveness— impeccable. She struck me as the opposite of that Jafney girl, whose beauty was effortless and unaffected.

"Dr. Lafferty." Wyck ushered me forward. "This is my girl-friend, Bree."

"I didn't know you were bringing a visitor."

"I hope that's okay," I said.

"Of course." If this Lafferty woman recognized me, she kept it expertly to herself. And if she was upset that I was here, she kept that to herself as well. There was no reason why she would know me, though. They'd cut Bergin out of their organization. He had been my only link to ICE. Until Wyck.

"Today's procedures will be a bit boring," said Lafferty, "but as I told you before, the entire process is open to the public."

She gestured to the tubes around her as if their translucency held a pinky promise that ICE was a model of truth and light. Not all the tubes were transparent, though. Not, for example, the black one from which Lafferty had just emerged. It made me want to dive headfirst into that black tube the first chance I got.

I had more than a sneaking suspicion that I knew exactly where it led.

Lafferty led us to a hole at the base of the yellow tube. She stepped in it and was whisked away.

"It's really easy." Wyck gestured for me to go next. "Just get in and relax."

Relax. Yeah.

I stuck my toe in and nothing unsavory happened.

Oh, this was ridiculous. ICE wasn't going to kill me in a bustling lobby. I put my whole body in the tube. *Whoosh*. The sensation wasn't unpleasant. Kind of like what I always imagined flying must be like, only a lot less controlled. I was tempted to hold my breath even though I seemed to be encapsulated in some sort of air bubble that protected me from the wind rushing behind me. From inside the tube, takeoff felt and sounded like a cork exploding from a champagne bottle. The scariest moment was when the tube dipped and descended into a hole in the floor.

Down, down, around, around, there was no telling how far or how deep we'd gone. With vague unease, it occurred to me that ICE didn't need a security system as long as this was their sole form of transportation. It also occurred to me that I had no idea how I was going to stop. Then with an audible pop, my air bubble burst into an open space. It reminded me of a zero-grav chamber, only instead of a lack of air, the air felt soft somehow, as if I'd landed in a bowl of marshmallow fluff. I sucked in a deep breath to make sure I could. Lafferty had tucked the hems of her skirt primly against her body as she floated to one of seven port-holes in the side of the chamber. A yellow light blinked above me, and she motioned me over toward her. Wyck plummeted through the opening I'd just come through. Lafferty poked her arms through the porthole, superhero-style, and some invisible force sucked her the rest of the way through.

I felt like anything but a superhero as I made my way after her. Felt more like I was being sucked through a straw. With a *shlup*, Wyck followed suit.

The room we entered was tiny. Circular. Seemed to be a theme here. There wasn't much in it—a polymorphic chair that con-toured to Wyck's form as he walked toward it, a thin helmet that looked like it had cracked down the middle, some soligraphic con-trols that Lafferty had already pulled up. The lights in the room were dimmed, but the glow from the controls cast shadows across the ceiling.

"Did you enjoy the transportation system we've developed?" Lafferty asked, and I realized she was talking to me.

"Sure. I guess."

"It was designed to mimic the sensation of Shifting," she said.

I had to stifle a full-on laugh. She thought *that* was the sensa-tion of Shifting? Maybe if magical unicorns flew you to your destination. Forget about arriving into a weightless chamber. Half the time, I was lucky if I didn't fall from five feet high and get shin splints.

If they were this deluded about their training, what else were they turning a blind eye to?

"Whaddya think?" asked Wyck, and again I realized, he was talking to me. "Was it close to the real thing?"

Blark. Shut up, shut up, shut up. I nodded vaguely, hoping Laf-ferty wasn't really listening, but she vaulted herself into the con-versation.

"Oh! You're a Shifter?" she asked.

That did away with any doubt. I've seen many people feign

many emotions, but genuine surprise is a tough one. That shock? It was real.

"Go ahead and take a seat," she said to Wyck. "Today's final tests are perfunctory, yet important. But don't worry. There's no way you can fail, and really, there's no work on your part."

As she connected a series of sensors to his scalp, I decided to dig for a little more info about her.

"So you're not by any chance related to *the* Laffertys, are you? Charles and Xenthia?" I asked. The author of one of my Quantum Bio textbooks was Dr. Xander Lafferty, but when I'd entered the name Lafferty to read up on him, his parents were the first to pop up. Charles and Xenthia Lafferty, a husband-wife research team who were among the first to study tendril mutation—two of the most revered Shifters in their field before they died about ten years ago.

"I'm their daughter," she said.

"Oh," I said. "So it was your brother who wrote *Basic Principles of Quantum Biology*?"

She gave me a strange look. "My brother?"

"Xander Lafferty?" I said.

"You must be mistaken. I have a brother named Xander, but he certainly hasn't written any textbooks. He's a same-day chronocourier."

"Oh." Two Xander Laffertys running around? Doubtful. And a same-day chronocourier—the lowest of the low among Shifter jobs—in a family of celebrated Quantum Biologists?

I smelled a timeline change.

From the disdainful upturn of her nose, I could tell Lafferty didn't want to discuss it further, and I didn't want to push my luck.

She started to strap down Wyck's arms at the elbows. He bristled.

"Strictly precautionary," she said. "Don't want you to hurt yourself in case you have any involuntary muscle reflexes."

"What exactly are you doing?" I asked as she fixed the last of the sensors to his forehead and set the helmet in place.

"We're mapping his brain," she said.

"Mapping his brain?"

"So to speak. Actually, we're charting his quantum tendrils. Everyone's tendrils have a unique wavelength. Like a fingerprint, only instead of leaving a mark on a three-dimensional surface, they leave their mark on the fourth dimension of time."

Duh. Tell me something I didn't learn as a First Year. But this was also my one chance to keep her talking so I nodded along like it was fascinating.

"He's a nonShifter, though," I said. "His tendrils only cling to the present."

Technically, that was true for Shifters and Nons alike. A Shifter's *present* just happened to be wherever and whenever he or she was. That was key to the explanation Bergin had given me last year for how nonShifters were able to change their past. Unlike Shifters who were technically always in their present even at a distant point on the timeline, nonShifters were truly in their own past. Hence the introduction of their quantum tendrils could produce alterations to their own personal history. Still seemed bonks to me, but it didn't answer my question as to how these Neos could be anywhere but their present.

"It was a challenge." Lafferty had a fake cheeriness to her that reminded me of one of those creepy store mannequins back in Finn's time.

"We have to calibrate the Pick to keep his tendrils stable on his trip," she said. "The Pick has to be perfectly aligned to his biorhythms or else he could get hurt."

As she spoke, a soligraphic object appeared in front of her. She poked and prodded it, rotating it this way and that, looking for something. She expanded its size. Unlike the last time I'd been in this building, I recognized it immediately for what it was.

"So that's Wyck's hippocampus?" It wasn't until Shifters came forward about our abilities that the full role of the hippocampus was understood. Before that point, it was thought to simply be involved in the regulation of spatial memory, navigation, orientation . . . that sort of thing.

"You know your Quantum Biology," she said.

I couldn't tell whether she meant it as a compliment or not.

"Bree's studying it as her Specialization," said Wyck proudly.

"How will you force his tendrils to stay in another time?" I asked. "What keeps them there?"

I mean, in theory, any nonShifter could try to hitch a ride to whenever and wherever a Shifter was going, but their tendrils would keep them glued to their present. Or in the rare cases that a nonShifter's tendrils did spazz and get a little too elastic, they'd be snapped back home before they realized they had left. That was what déjà vu was.

"It's complicated," said Lafferty.

"I like complicated things." I knew I was pushing my luck, but quite frankly, I didn't really care. As far as I could see, the worst that could happen would be that this Lafferty woman would get angry at Wyck for bringing me along and dismiss him as a NeoShifter.

Boo-Blarking-Hoo.

She cocked her head to the side, not so much sizing up my question as sizing me up personally.

"Bree's plinky smart," said Wyck. "Top of our class."

"Thanks, Wyck." Now, really. Shut up.

But Lafferty must have deemed me worthy of an answer.

"It's always exciting to have a new generation show an interest in hippocampal biotheory." She didn't sound excited. At all. "Without boring you with the details, we temporarily trick his hippocampus, so to speak, into believing that his tendrils belong in a different time and place. Much like a natural-born Shifter."

"Except that's not true," I said. "A Shifter's tendrils are drawn to a specific time and place. Not tricked into going there."

"Perhaps 'tricked' was the wrong word choice. We *encourage* a NeoShifter's tendrils to safely adhere to an alternate spot on the space-time continuum." She sounded like she was quoting a brochure. "The technology is much like the microchip implanted in your own skull."

Right. The microchip that I didn't need and that no one knew had been deactivated. Still, I was the one who needed to shut up with all the where-I'm-drawn talk. Besides, as far as I could tell, that part of my brain was broken at the moment. If it were working, I'd be in Chincoteague right now. With Finn.

Lafferty drew a vial of blood from Wyck's arm. She opened a cabinet lined with row upon row of IcePicks and plucked one from the front. She inserted the vial of blood into a chamber on the side of the Pick. It looked just like my reverter only the end of the Pick consisted of a clear bulb, whereas the end of the reverter was a heart. The only functioning IcePick I'd seen up close was Bergin's. It had been full of some sort of blue fluid when it was activated, but it was empty now, as was this one.

"May I?" I asked.

There was that mannequin smile again as Lafferty placed it in my outstretched hand.

"Of course," she said.

"Is it an injection?" I asked.

"Mmmm." She made a noise that could have meant "yes," or could have meant, "ask one more question and I'll launch you down that black tube myself."

I gave her back the Pick. Nothing new to learn there. It was exactly like the deactivated one I'd stolen.

"That should do it." Lafferty detached the sensors and removed the helmet from Wyck's head.

"That's it?" he asked.

"I told you today would be easy. You'll hear back from us within seventy-two hours to coordinate a Launch date. I'll show you to the lobby." But then her speakeazy pinged. She looked down at it, and I could tell she really wanted to talk to whoever was on the other end.

Which meant I wanted to listen in.

"We can find our way out," I said confidently.

"Are you certain?"

"Sure." Wyck climbed first through the porthole, and I followed him. When we were both fully in the weightless chamber, I grabbed my pocket like I'd forgotten something. I gestured to Wyck that I was going to go back in the room, and he nodded. He pointed to the entrance port and waved. I gave him the thumbs-up.

As soon as he was out of the chamber, I drifted back over to the porthole and touched just the rim of my ear against the lowest part. Lafferty was deep in conversation on her speakeazy. I waited for a pause or hush in volume, anything to suggest she detected me, but nothing.

". . . no choice. It's a matter of compatibility. We have to go with the best match. This one's 97.2 percent." Gleeful. She sounded blarking gleeful. "You can't make those numbers up."

"Then why am I doing this? I thought the whole purpose of taking more Shifters was to avoid this very scenario." There was no mistaking that voice, scratched and artificial. Raspy, the person in the silver suit. I held my breath and pressed my ear closer against the port.

"What would you have me do? Go with a less-fitting subject? That's not safe."

"Safe?" Raspy's laugh had a harsh, metallic bite to it. "So relieved to hear you're concerned about safety. Do you realize the worldwide devastation that could have occurred by allowing James Canavan to Shift to a point within his lifetime?"

"But that didn't happen."

"Only because—" But Raspy stopped himself.

I held my breath. The finish of that thought was, only because

I had stopped him. But if Raspy knew that, then why didn't he tell her?

"Nowhere on his paperwork did Canavan indicate a desire to change his past," said Lafferty. "He said he simply wanted to re-visit a vacation spot he'd enjoyed in his younger years."

Raspy sighed, and with the voice-distorting apparatus, it came out almost like a growl.

"Are you second-guessing our deal?" said Lafferty after a pause.

"You know I don't have a choice."

"Yes, we wouldn't want to have to take her back for safekeep-ing, now would we? I know this last procurement must have been especially difficult for you, but—"

"Don't toy with me." Raspy cut her off with a slicing tone.

No, no, no. Let her talk.

But she'd gone into silent mode. At least I knew one thing. Well, two. Shifters were definitely being kidnapped. Nava and whoever was in that tank at the very least. And Raspy was the one doing it. I glanced at the light above the entrance to the cham-ber. Wyck would start wondering what was taking me so long.

"What do you want?" said Raspy.

"I want that cryolocker to stay empty just as much as you do, but we'll need your full cooperation. And a few more subjects. Strictly precautionary."

Oh, come on! Elaborate, people! But the only response was Raspy's ragged metallic breaths.

"There's one other thing you should know," he said. "That Shifter that was just here?"

"The girl with O'Banion?"

"She's not chipped."

"So?"

A pause. "She has . . . she could cause you trouble."

"Why are you telling me this?"

Yeah, why? If he knew who I was, if he knew what I was doing, why not tell Lafferty everything? I pushed my ear so hard against the port, half my head probably popped through. But I didn't care.

"She could cause me trouble."

"I think we can handle one nosy Shifter." I waited for Lafferty to elaborate, but nope. Her speakeazy beeped to indicate she'd terminated the connection.

I floated over to the entrance port and scooted through the hole.

Oh, I'd show them all trouble.

I would find out why Nava had been taken, and any other Shifter—past, present, or future.

I would free my friends.

And I would make ICE pay.

chapter 11

THE LANDING IN THE LOBBY was even gentler than in the anti-grav chamber, if that was possible. A thousand pillows on the soles of my feet.

Like Shifting, my arse.

Wyck sat on the ground with his back pressed to a chartreuse tube. When he saw me emerge, he hopped up, all smiles. I couldn't help but feel bad that in this version of the timeline where he could have been free of ICE, I'd been the one to drag him back in. But this was for a good cause. It was bigger than him. It was bigger than me. I had no idea why ICE was taking these Shifters, but it was up to me to stop them.

I latched onto the chance to explore the entryway a bit, brushing my hand against each of the colored tubes as I walked between them. They were all warm to the touch, to different degrees. When I got to the opaque black tube, I pressed my hand full against it.

Ice cold.

This had to lead to the cryostorage room. It had to. I stepped in front of the opening. A rush of cool air drew me in, frosty fingers beckoning me forward. My toe inched into the open cavity. There were answers down that tube.

"Careful." Wyck tugged on my forearm, and the spell was broken.

"Sorry." Not sorry. "Wasn't paying attention."

"Probably low blood sugar," he said. "I noticed you weren't at breakfast, and you left lunch so fast."

The meal-skipping had been to avoid him, but I couldn't say that. Like it or not, Wyck remained my one link to ICE, a link I couldn't afford to break, especially now as he was about to go on his first Shift. Well, his first Shift on this particular timeline.

"I bet you're right," I said. "Let's go grab an early dinner."

Wyck brushed his hair against a scanner next to the door to open it.

"You have scan access?" Good to know.

"They programmed it in when I was officially accepted."

We were halfway down the front steps when I bumped shoulders with a man heading up them.

"Excuse me," I said, then did a double-take.

"Leto?" I almost hadn't recognized him. His hair wasn't in its usual smarmy slicked-back style, and his suit was impeccable. Probably cost a small fortune, not to mention the ridiculous amount of man-jewelry he had on. He was tanned and looked like he'd just stepped off a yacht.

"What happened to you?" I whispered. "Where did you get all the money to buy this stuff?"

He wasn't hurting, I knew that. But this get-up was in a new class.

"Do I know you?" His voice still had his typical shady tang to it.

"You . . ." I thought back to the change. Mom had never been in a coma, so there wouldn't have been a reason to connect with Leto. That didn't answer where the money had come from, but . . . ha! I was free of him.

"No," I said. "I thought I recognized you, but I was thinking of someone else."

"But you said my name."

"Is your name Leto, too?" I prayed he was still more bluster than brains on this timeline. "What a coincidence."

"Heh," he said and turned back toward ICE's headquarters.

Ergh. He was going to try to make another change. I really didn't have time for this.

Before he walked through the entrance, though, Leto looked back at me with a boyish grin on his face.

"You look great today, sweetie," he said.

Leto shuddered and shook his head like he was thawing a brain freeze before skittering into the lobby.

Sweetie?

First he doesn't recognize me then *sweetie?*

Well, that was weird.

I stared after him as an ICE employee greeted him like an old pal. I rolled my eyes. Looked like I'd be doing another reversion of his soon.

Wyck took my hand. "Who was that?"

"No one."

He didn't question me, and I was thankful to get moving.

"Where do you want to eat?" he asked.

"The usual," I said before I could stop myself. It had come out automatically, like it would have if Finn had asked the question. I had no idea where or what the usual was with Wyck. "Or on second thought, I need to run by my house. We can grab something near there."

"Yeah. I've been wanting to try out that café around the corner from your—"

"No."

"No?"

That place *was* the usual. Finn's and mine. It belonged to us. It was like this was the spot where I'd arbitrarily drawn a line. Wyck couldn't have this memory, too. He couldn't have chocolate chip waffles with bananas on top. He couldn't have the corner table where Ed could come munch arugula.

He couldn't have the real me.

"It's kind of skinky, don't you think? I mean, they serve breakfast for dinner. What is that? Brinner? Dreakfast?" Blark, I loved that place. I mean, breakfast for dinner? It's the greatest thing ever.

"I was going to say retro. I thought you'd like it." The same look of confusion and hurt that I'd grown too used to over the last couple days crossed his face. "Y'know what? Maybe I should just head home."

"Wait." Maintain the link. I needed the next piece of the map. "That place sounds fine."

"You're sure?"

"Absolutely." Fake Bree would love to. But so help me, if he even looked at the chocolate chip waffles, I'd knock the table over so fast the ground wouldn't know what hit it.

When we got to the café, it was between meal crowds, practically deserted. Wyck spoke to the host and got us a spot on the street. I took a deep breath and followed him through the building.

We stepped onto the patio, and I couldn't stop from stealing a wistful glance to the corner where Finn and I usually sat, but someone was already settled there, his back to us. The periphery of my vision snatched at something in the way the guy moved as he turned his head to the side. I stumbled over the edge of a chair, and Wyck caught me, but it was like Wyck had disappeared. The chair had disappeared. Everyone and everything had disappeared but the guy in that seat.

Finn.

No. Not possible. He wasn't able to Shift here, or anywhere into his future, unless I brought him. My brain had conjured an illusion because Wyck and I had come to this place that I associated with Finn. It was someone else. With auburn curls that licked the nape of his neck. And a crevice at the top of his collarbone where you could brush your finger while he was napping, until he growled, "Stop it," without really waking up. The guy twisted around to face the street, and any doubt of his identity disappeared when I saw his profile. It was no illusion.

It was Finn.

I lurched toward him without thinking. There was no telling how he got here, but he couldn't stay. He was a Level Five Chronofugitive. He was in danger. I had to warn him. My leg rammed into the side of a table and sent it toppling.

"Are you okay?" Wyck reached over to steady me, oblivious to the fact that the guy who some alternate version of Wyck had tried to kill only six months ago was spearing a bite of banana three feet away.

"F-fine." Only I stumbled over the word, and it came out a bit like "Finn."

I edged toward Finn's seat. I didn't care that it was reckless. I needed to touch him, to check he was real. He lifted his eyes to meet mine. They stared past me, all expression drained from them. His complete lack of emotion gave me pause. Then he shook his head, a hard look settling onto his face—the movement was almost imperceptible—but it stopped me in my tracks. The message was clear: don't come near me.

How was he even here? It wasn't possible. He could only come to the twenty-third century by clinging to me, to *my* quantum tendrils. It wasn't like he could hitch a ride with just any Shifter. In order to bring him here, they'd have to be like me . . . born in this century but conceived in anoth—

Jafney.

I heard her before I saw her.

Actually, not true. I smelled her before I heard her before I saw her. Eau de I'm-Gonna-Kill-Her.

"Bree-ee?" Jafney stretched the word out like a wisp of salt-water taffy.

Every one of my body parts begged to betray my fury as I turned slowly to face her. We had the same time-crossed parentage, her tendrils as sticky as mine. She reached around me and wiped a squirt of syrup off Finn's chin with her finger then blarking licked it.

Looked like her tendrils weren't the only things that were sticky.

How could she? The danger she was putting Finn in by bringing him here, not to mention the danger she was putting me in. All of us, every member of the Haven.

And that's when I got Tufty-hissing-spitting-mad.

I ticked off the days it had been since the timeline had changed. Two. Two days. As in, forty-eight hours. Had Jafney just stayed in Chincoteague this whole time and thrown herself at Finn the moment he'd left the theater?

Jafney jostled past me and tossed a grape into Finn's mouth with a giggle. He chomped on it with an open-mouth smile, and I knew Charlotte would swipe him in the face with a napkin if she saw him do that. He lifted his eyebrows at Jafney in that flirty way that was supposed to be reserved for me. I held back a grimace. At least I was faking my attraction to Wyck.

Wyck.

I turned around, worried that he'd finally seen Finn and was ready to cause a scene. I mean, he'd tried to kill Finn six months ago (again, on a different timeline, but it still seemed like something that might nestle in your noggin). Quite the opposite of rankled, Wyck was oblivious, poring over the menu.

"I'm so glad we ran into you, Bree." Jafney leaned over and squeezed my hand. I yanked it away like she'd smeared something nasty on it. "How long has it been?"

Was she serious?

"Two days. It's been two days."

"Has it really?" She raised her eyebrows in mock surprise. "I've kind of lost track of time. A lot can happen in two days."

Obviously.

A river of lava bubbled and brewed on the tip of my tongue, waiting for the tiniest provocation to erupt.

"Were you going to introduce us?" She pointed at Wyck.

No. No, I was not.

"Umm . . ." Before I could stop myself, I turned to Finn for guidance, for some indication how he thought I should handle this. But apparently, he didn't have a pegamoo at this party.

"Hi, I'm Finn." He half-stood and took Wyck's hand warmly in his own. Unlike the last time they met, there was nothing aggressive in the action. Nothing forced or artificial.

This was Finn, wasn't it?

Jafney leaned forward. "And I'm—"

"Jafney," said Wyck. "I'm afraid I don't recall your last name. I remember you were Pennedy's roommate our first year at the Institute, though."

She clutched her cheek in a show of faux humility. "I can't believe you remember that."

It's not like you had a face transplant, sweetheart.

Okay. I had to get my emotions under control or I'd blow this thing. My main objective was still to remain Wyck's devoted girlfriend so I could stop ICE from doing whatever heinous thing they were doing. And now, I also needed to get Finn the heck out of Dodge.

"Not sure if you remember me," said Wyck to Jafney. "Wyck O'Banion. I'm in the transporter program."

He then turned to Finn and wrapped a possessive arm around my shoulders. "And how do you know Bree?"

I looked to Finn to gauge his reaction.

Fine, I kind of wanted him to blast out of his chair in a jealous rage.

Nothing. He just sat there.

"Oh, Finn and Bree are friends from ages and ages ago," said Jafney in an annoyingly chipper voice. "Aren't you now?"

Finn nodded without any show of emotion. I bobbed my neck and backed away. Forget ICE. Jafney's blabbermouth was currently my greatest threat.

"We should check if our table is ready," I said to Wyck.

"Oh, no, join us." Jafney yanked a chair next to hers and gestured to it.

"We wouldn't want to intrude," I said.

"Pish. No intrusion." Jafney patted the seat, and I fought an overwhelming urge to rip her arm out of its socket.

"I always love to meet your friends, sweetie. You know that." Wyck made to rub his nose against mine, and I dropped to the seat simply to avoid contact.

"Looks like we're joining you," I said.

Jafney beamed, and now I wanted to rip the lips right off her face.

Wyck and I ordered.

"I hear the waffles here are killer," he said.

"Yeah." Finn looked over the edge of his fork at me. "Killer."

Oh, this was a bad idea.

The atmosphere at the table thickened with silence. At one point, I twirled a knife in front of me in lazy circles to see if I could slice some of the tension, but all I did was almost cut off my thumb.

Wyck jumped at the wound with the edge of his shirt, even though it was nothing more than a nick.

"You're always injuring yourself," he said in a mock-chiding voice.

Finn almost fell off his chair in a massive choke-cough. I reached a glass of water out to him, but he brushed it aside. He took a sip from the one Jafney offered him instead.

"Where's the restroom?" Finn asked.

It would take all my fingers to count the number of times he'd taken a pee in this establishment, but he made a good show of letting Jafney point the way, and then walked down the wrong hall at first.

Once he disappeared, I counted slowly to twenty then excused myself as well. I caught him coming out of the bathroom and pulled him into the shadows so we were out of eyeshot.

"What the blark do you think you're doing here?" I kept my voice low but forceful.

"Keep your voice down." He peeked over my shoulder.

"What the——?" The volcano was back. He actually had the nerve to give me cheek over what could very well be the most perilous thing he'd ever done. And I knew for a fact he'd helped his dad dress wounds in a Siberian gulag. But I dropped my volume to be safe. "Seriously. Why are you here?"

"Let's see." He peered outside again. Jafney and Wyck were small-talking, but she kept craning her neck to look toward the hallway. "From where I'm standing, it looks like I was eating waffles with my girlfriend."

His answer cut straight to the quick. I realized in that moment I'd held out hope that this was all a misunderstanding, but it crashed down around my ears. He wasn't just here with Jafney. He was *with* Jafney.

"Well, mission accomplished," I said through gritted teeth. "But you need to get out of here. Now."

"Here, this hallway? Or here, this century?"

"Both."

"I'm not going anywhere."

Erg! Bree-smash-space-time-continuum.

"You don't understand. You're in danger. I was trying to tell you in the theater. Leto told me your identity has been unlocked and——"

"Is that why I got sucked back to Chincoteague?"

"No, that was a change on the timeline."

"Who changed it?"

It was my turn to take a quick looksee at the table. No way was I discussing Wyck's change with him sitting so close.

"We're not talking about this right now. Just get home."

"Why would someone go to the trouble of unlocking my identity?"

"Clearly not to send you a Christmas card."

"But Quigley erased all my files."

"Somebody un-erased them."

"So she can re-erase them."

"No, she can't." I stomped my foot. "Shut up and listen. When she erased them, you were some blip in history, a nobody who hadn't done anything notable."

"Wow. You really know how to charm a guy."

"Let me finish. You are now a Level Five Chronofugitive. You're in every high order government database in the world."

"I'm a what? Oh . . . this is not good." He clenched his hair. At least I'd gotten a reaction.

"You think?"

"Blark." He bit his fist and looked back out at the dining area. "Don't let Jafney know."

Seriously? That was what he was worried about? Jafney's reaction? I just told him he's wanted by law enforcement, and he's worried about what Jafney will think?

"What am I accused of doing?" he asked.

"That information can't be entered until the crime has actually been committed. One of those chicken-egg things."

"Wait. So I'm accused of something I haven't even done yet?" He shook his head. "The future is so screwed up."

I couldn't argue with him on that point.

"Chronofugitive status is reserved for Shifters who violate laws outside of their own time. The crime could be anything. But the fact that it's Level Five means it's . . . bad."

"How bad?"

"Bad like murder, arson, or kidnapping bad."

"Okay, that's bad."

"What's bad?" Jafney popped her head around the corner of the hallway and caused both Finn and me to jump.

Neither of us answered.

"What's bad, Finny Finn?" She wiggled her fingers at him.

Yet another appendage I wanted to yank out by its roots.

"Uhh, nothing, Jaf." He smiled at her.

Jaf? I mouthed.

He ignored me.

"Come back to the table," she said. "Wyck's telling the most hilarious story about the time he got caught sleeping in his grav-belt at the top of the gym. Come, come."

She made a little grabby hand at Finn. Before I had a chance to tell Jaf exactly where she could shove that hand, Wyck rounded the corner.

"Hey!" he said. "Looks like a party. Did my invitation get lost?"

"No!" I practically shouted.

"Oh." Wyck took a step back. "I, uhh, I was just kidding."

"I know," I said. "What I mean is, I think I'm ready for a proper celebration of your Shift clearance." I walked my fingers up his chest until my left hand rested on his shoulder. If making this look natural was difficult before, doing it in front of Finn crossed into torture territory. "You and I should take this party somewhere more private."

"I like that idea." Wyck waggled his eyebrows. He drew me in for a kiss, and I had no choice but to comply. I could feel my cheeks flare. When he pulled away, he brushed his hand against my face.

"You're all flushed. You really are ready to go celebrate, aren't you?"

Fake Bree lapped it up. Real Bree threw up in her mouth a little bit.

When I turned to bid Finn and Jafney farewell, he'd already swung a loose but possessive arm around her. She reeled him in for a smooch, and when she released him, he had a starry-eyed grin on his face. The knife dug deeper.

"Go home," I mouthed to Finn when Jafney and Wyck had their attention turned away.

He pulled Jafney in closer. The message was clear. He wasn't going anywhere.

As I nestled into Wyck's grip, I'd never hated Future Bree more than now.

>——<

I had Wyck take me back to my house rather than the Institute. I gave him the excuse that Mom and I had plans that evening, but it was really because of its closer proximity. As soon as we reached my front stoop, I—wouldn't you know it—exploded into a coughing fit.

"Sorry." *Hack, hack, wheeze.* "I'd kiss you goodnight, but I don't want to get you sick."

Or touch your lips again.

I wished Future Bree had told me how far up the timeline she was from because I didn't see how I'd be able to pull off this charade for two more hours, much less two more weeks. Or months. Or . . .

No. Couldn't go there.

Wyck squeezed my upper arm affectionately.

Then . . . not so affectionately.

I pulled away slightly, but enough to make the message clear. Let go. The corner of Wyck's mouth ticked up, like we were playing a game. A little tug-of-war. I jerked back. He grasped tighter, then the smirk disappeared. He stared down at his hand as if it were detached from his body. He yanked it away, gripping his wrist with his other hand.

"I want to . . ." He squeezed his eyes shut and gritted his teeth. "I don't want to . . ."

Wyck's eyes popped open and immediately he looked horrified with himself. "I have to go," he said, his voice low and urgent.

I couldn't believe it, but a wave of compassion swept over me. Bizarre as it seemed, Wyck didn't know what was happening to him. He was experiencing a flash of another timeline.

Once, in Finn's time, I ordered us a pizza using his cellular phone. There was a weird echo thing every time I spoke. Finn called it feedback and said I should hang up and try again. It drove me utterly bonks for the couple minutes I experienced it.

Sometimes, I wondered if that's what Neos' flashes were like. Feedback from a timeline they'd tried to change, an echo from a future that didn't exist.

Wyck dug his hands into his pockets and backed away.

"Wait," I said. It wasn't fair. So many people were using him as a pawn. Including, now, me. The fact was, he wasn't Evil Wyck, not yet. And I didn't even know if that was his fate now, with this change to the timeline.

Wyck didn't wait, though. The sun hugged the horizon, and he disappeared into its weak orange rays. He had enough sense to run from his demons. And at least for the moment, I had enough sense not to follow him.

chapter 12

"MOM?" HER BED was unmade, but she wasn't home.

I settled in at my desk and pulled up everything I could find on ICE's Medical Director. Dr. Jenxa Lafferty. Twin sister of Xander Lafferty. Charles' and Xenthia's only children. I scanned the booklist for my Quantum Bio class, and sure enough, the author of my textbook had changed to someone else. I tried to think back to the last time that I had noticed the cover of the textbook, and it had been over a year.

So what change to the timeline had turned Xander from a re-spected Quantum Biologist to a not-so-glorified errand boy?

As I read up on him, I circled my pinky around my wrist absent-mindedly. One of the things that had been driving me crazy these last few days was not being able to wear my heart bracelet that Finn had given me. Since the bracelet had been given to me out of this timeline loop, I thought it would still exist, but I hadn't found it yet.

A news article on Xander Lafferty popped up from around the time of his parents' deaths. He had been on track to following in his parents' footsteps and becoming one of the youngest Quan-tum Bio specialists in the country . . . experimental research on tendril activity in vitro. So basically, how tendrils act outside the human body.

I looked down. I'd scratched a spot on my wrist, right where the heart locket should have been.

Focus, Bree.

So, according to this article, right after his parents' death in a sub-Atlantic commuter train crash—I grimaced as I remembered seeing pictures from that gruesome accident in one of my history classes—Xander was accused of stealing research results . . . from his parents.

Oh, how horrible.

I kept reading. Someone had turned him in anonymously, shown proof that he had taken his parents' research journals. He claimed that his parents had entrusted the journals to him for safe-keeping, that they had feared that in the wrong hands the results of their research could have grave consequences, that he'd been studying their work but had no intentions of claiming credit for it. Or even of making it public. But by that point, his reputation as a researcher had been destroyed. His career was over before it had ever begun.

I scanned through a few more articles, to see what had become of the journals, but they'd never been recovered, except for the few pages that someone had turned in to discredit him.

I had more than a sneaking suspicion exactly who had taken those journals. But I couldn't find any solid proof against his sister. That could easily be what she had changed in the timeline.

Clutching my pillow to my chest, I curled up on my bed. Something hard pressed into my chin. I dug around in the pillowcase.

My locket.

I slipped it on but then took it back off. I couldn't risk Wyck seeing it and asking questions. Not that Finn would even want me to wear it now.

I put it back in the pillow and opened more news articles. Back to work.

Oh, who was I kidding?

Screw it. I pulled the bracelet back out and clasped it around my wrist. I didn't care if Wyck did ask questions. I wasn't going to lose it again.

I closed the articles. Until I got some answers of a more

personal nature, there was no way I'd be able to concentrate on ICE. So I pulled on a sweater and headed to the lair of the eel-faced lamprey who had stolen the (apparently ex) love of my life.

Jafney had set up a sunspot on her back patio. Its beams warmed and brightened a twenty-foot radius, fighting off the chill of early spring. She wore what appeared to be a swimsuit sewn for a six-year-old. Her legs, which were so long they warranted their own Zip Code, stretched out over the side of a hammock hanging between two floating orbs. Finn lay in a hammock next to her, his old Yankees cap pulled low over his eyes.

There was one more person on the patio, scrunched up in a chaise in the corner. And her presence didn't make me happy one bit. Jafney had brought Finn's sassmouth sister along for the ride. Georgie was camped out under a tent of a hat, nose-deep in a book.

I'd been observing—not stalking, mind you, observing—them for a solid hour. From the top of a tree. Across the street. With omnoculars.

Fine. I was Stalky McStalkerson. But it was for good reasons.

Jafney tossed her arms up in the air and laughed at some unheard joke that Finn must have told. Georgie didn't even look up from her book. When Jafney brought her hand down, it landed at an awkward angle on—was that?—did she just? Get your hand off his knee, you spider-limbed Angel of Lovedeath! I shifted my weight forward in the tree to get a better view, and the branch I was perched on bent down precariously and let out an ominous *crack*. Georgie looked up from her book.

Blark.

Through the omnoculars, I could see Georgie's eyes narrow. She'd seen me. Dang it. I shimmied down the trunk, my hair snagging on a chunk of bark ten feet up in my haste. Oww. I paused to try to work it free. Georgie swiveled around to see if her companions had noticed. Jafney had turned to her side and began rubbing oil all over her chest. Finn's eyes were still closed. Georgie hopped up, and I lip-read her make some excuse to go inside.

I turned my attention back to my predicament. It wasn't like I could yank my hair out and leave it there. Ripping a single strand out would be agony, one of the downsides of genetically modified shed-free hair. Besides, it was my secure form of identification. One by one, I worked the follicles free. Finally, I dropped to the ground.

"Hey, there, Double-O-Seven." Georgie was already waiting in the shadow of an adjacent tree, arms crossed.

I wiped a splotch of sap off my cheek as I pulled her into an alley.

"Georgie, why are you here?"

"Just a little temporal sightseeing."

"Finn's in danger. He won't listen to reason. I need you to get a message to him for me," I said. "Can you do that?"

"Shoot."

"Shoot what?"

"That means, 'tell me.'"

"Oh. Here's the message: Go the blark home. And that message goes for you, too."

"I'm staying as long as he is, and he's not straying from Jafney's side anytime soon. Seriously, they're like an amorphous blob. He won't be apart from her for more than two minutes."

Georgie might as well have slapped me full across the check. Finn and I always made fun of those couples. I thought he didn't want that. He just didn't want it with me.

"George? Where are you?" Finn stood at the edge of the shaded alley.

The air felt like it dropped ten degrees. I pulled my sweater tight around my shoulders, but shivers still tickled my spine. Goose bumps prickled the hairs on my arm, and I couldn't help but think of the contrast with Jafney's perfectly smooth, perfectly mocha, perfectly perfect skin.

Finn leaned the top of his body against the red brick, worn almost as smooth as stucco by time. He dug his hands in his pockets, which to the casual observer might appear relaxed, but I knew him well enough not to trust it. His posture was stiff. And he wouldn't look straight at me.

Every urge I'd ever felt toward him crashed over me at once.

Kiss him.

Yell at him.

Hug him.

Shake him and demand how he could do this to me. How could he brush me aside so quickly and move on—was I really that forgettable?

I reserved the more violent inclinations for my future self. And Wyck, for making the change. Well, and I wouldn't mind taking a swipe at Jafney.

Finn spoke just above a whisper. "You shouldn't have come here right now." He peered back at Jafney's house.

"You shouldn't have come here, period," I said.

"Can you give us a minute, Georgie?" he said.

"Are you sure you don't need me to chaperone?" she said.

He rolled his eyes. "I don't think you need to worry about Bree and me."

Georgie wandered off.

"Why are you with Jafney?" I said.

"What did you expect me to do?" It came out in a growl of frustration.

Wait for me. Trust me. Not hop over to the first floozy who tickled your tendrils.

"I don't know what I expected, but not this." Not with her. I gestured back to the patio, where Jafney was presumably getting restless after the three angst-filled minutes he'd been out of her presence. "Have you considered the danger you're putting Jafney in?"

If he wouldn't leave for my sake, maybe he'd leave for hers.

"I'm not going to let anything happen to her," he said.

"You're a chronofugitive, Finn. That's a serious charge. And she brought you here."

"I hadn't thought of that." A tone of real panic filled his voice. Of course it did. Anything to protect precious Jaf.

"But I could always just Shift away, right?" he said. "They can't arrest me if they can't catch me."

"You can't think of any way they could keep you here?"

Blank stare.

"Any way at all?"

More blank stare.

"Any device . . . say, an implant . . . or, I don't know, a *microchip*?"

"They'd chip me?" His cheeks blanched as I nodded.

Must not have thought of that with his hormones all revved up.

"I still don't understand how they could accuse me of a crime I haven't committed yet. It's like a sci-fi movie. Wait." He put his hand over his mouth. "It *is* a sci-fi movie! I saw it a couple years ago. I think the guy got killed at the end."

"Finn . . ."

"Or he killed someone? Someone got killed."

"Finn."

"Oh, my gosh. I'm a walking sci-fi movie."

"Finn!" I waved in his face.

"Huh?" He looked up. It was like he'd forgotten I was even there.

"Go home," I said. "They can't detain you until you're accused of actually committing the crime. If you just stay there, you'll be safe."

Or at least that's what I kept telling myself. He didn't love me, but I still loved him. Laying low in Chincoteague while I figured this all out was the best plan right now.

"I would need to feel a pull to synch in order to do that." He pinched his temple and took a step forward. And another. He was close enough, he could reach out and touch me.

"And you don't feel . . . anything?" I asked.

The heat of his breath, in and out, teased my cheek. Every air particle between us expanded and contracted, pulling me forward. But when I opened my eyes, I saw that he'd stopped inches from me. His hand was held at his side, clenched into a tight fist as if it had hit a force field.

"Nothing," he said and backed away. "Jaf's probably wondering where Georgie and I are."

"Yeah." My eyes filled with tears as I remembered it wasn't my tendrils that held him here anymore. It was hers. "Finn, you know that I—"

"Bree, stop. You don't need to—" He let out a heavy sigh as he looked over his shoulder, back to Jafney-of-the-long-legs' house. "I have a girlfriend. An amazing one. Remember that, okay?"

Another slap. I tried to force my neck into a nod, but it wouldn't budge. How could I forget?

"Finny Finn!" Jafney's voice broke the silence like shards of glass. "Where'd you go?"

Before she spotted us, I shot Finn one final pleading look.

"Go home," I whispered. "Protect yourself. Please."

"If you need me, you know where to find me." He pointed at Jafney's house. "Right here."

"There you are," said Jafney, rounding the corner. "And you're . . . with . . . Bree."

"I happened to be passing by when Finn was out here doing that, umm, thing that he came out here to do," I said.

"Buying me cotton candy," blurted Georgie, trotting after Jafney with a helpless *sorry* look on her face.

Cotton candy. Really, Georgie? Really?

"It's shocking, the way that your history books brush over our raging twenty-first-century cotton candy obsession," said Georgie. "Like an addiction, it is."

"Yes. They can't get enough of the pink stuff," I said, but when Jafney turned her head, I mouthed, *What the blark?*

"I panicked," Georgie hissed.

"And, of course," said Finn, "I realized once I was out here that I have no idea where to buy cotton candy, so readily available on every street corner in our time." Finn shot Georgie a look that mirrored mine. "So Bree here pointed me toward . . ."

"The Pentagon." The only place I could think of that might possibly sell the stuff.

"The Pentagon." Finn's gaze locked onto mine, and for one bittersweet moment, it was like we were standing on the roof of the amusement park, just a boy from the past who liked a girl from the future. Well, a future version of a girl from the . . . never mind.

The moment passed.

"The craving's gone," said Georgie.

"Good," said Finn. "It really is a bad habit."

"A dangerous one. Which should never have left the twenty-first century," I added, giving Finn a significant look which he promptly pretended not to see.

"We should go in." Jafney wrapped her arm around him. "It's a little chilly out here."

"Feels like it's heating up to me," said Georgie, but Jafney had already steered Finn back toward her house.

What was Jafney's deal? She acted like I was the one who had stolen the love of her life, not the other way around.

I waited until they were out of earshot and grabbed Georgie by the cuff of her arm before she could follow.

"So you're really not going to go home?" I asked.

"Oh, heck no. This is better than anything on basic cable."

"Then can you at least do me a favor? Keep an eye on Finn for me. Make sure he doesn't get into any trouble."

"Yeah, yeah, yeah. That's kind of why I'm here. Now enough about me. You have to tell me about that kiss."

"What kiss?"

"With Wyck." She fanned herself despite the gust of wind that rushed between us. I swore the temperature dropped another fifteen degrees.

"What are you talking about? Did you see us at the café earlier?"

"No. Oh, come on. It was only a couple days ago." She shook her head. "There's no way you could have forgotten that. I mean, look at the guy."

"What are you talking about? How do you even know what he looks like?"

"The pictures. Jafney had pictures of the two of you making out in front of your school. Your lips . . . locked and loaded with a very fine specimen of Y chromosomes. Ringing any bells?"

I opened my mouth to say something . . . anything. But all that came out was a croak. That photoflash that I had written off as imagined while I was kissing Wyck right after we left the theater. I hadn't imagined it.

Why would Jafney do such a thing? No wonder Finn had run straight into her arms. No wonder mine repelled him. *I* was the cheater. *I* was the eel-faced lamprey. And Jafney had taken photographic proof.

I had to explain. I had to tell him . . .

"Hey, George, come on!" Finn poked out of Jafney's doorway and motioned to his sister.

"I'd better go," she said.

"No, wait," I said. "You have to tell Finn something for me."

"Georgie!" he yelled. "Now!"

One of Jafney's neighbors poked his head out and frowned at Finn. Blark. He was drawing too much attention to himself.

"Sorry," said Georgie. "We'll catch up later, okay?"

"Okay."

As Georgie jogged away to join Finn, gentle prickles built under my skin, tugging me to some other place, some other time, and as I Shifted away all I could think was, "Anywhere but here."

chapter 13

OKAY, NOT HERE EITHER.

I landed across the street from my house. My mom sat on our front stoop, swaying on the porch swing. At first, I almost shouted "hello," but paused when I noticed the fresh coat of paint on the steps. A corn broom was propped against the brick, and our pot of geraniums was gone. The welcome mat on that porch wasn't for me. The front door creaked open, and a tall, bespectacled man emerged with two steaming mugs. One for Mom. One for him.

My father.

When I was little, I'd had this fantasy of what life would be like if my parents hadn't been kept apart by government restrictions. What our life would be like if I didn't have a microchip in my head, controlling my every Shift.

The fantasy always started with breakfast. I don't know why that was the thing I focused on. Probably because Mom makes a mean cinnamon toast, and it's one of those meals that's pretty much the same no matter what century you're in.

My father handed my mom's mug to her and raised his own to his lips. I'd landed in the weak splotch of light put out by a gas lamppost. I slunk backward, aiming for the shadow of the massive oak across the street from my house. Well, not my house. I mean, yes, technically my house, but it wasn't my house yet. I felt around for the tree before remembering it was nothing but a sapling in my father's lifetime.

The first Shift Mom took after being freed from the confines of her coma was to visit him. I knew what she was expecting, or at least hoping. I'd bitten my nails to the nub expecting and hoping the same thing. *I have a daughter? When can I meet her? What is she like?*

Let's just say it didn't go as hoped.

Turns out discovering that the woman you married is a twenty-third-century time traveler who's aged seventeen years seemingly overnight from your perspective can be a bit discombobulating. Then add to that a long-lost teenage daughter when you yourself are turning the ripe old age of twenty-seven. Apparently, it's a bit too much for the average born-in-the-Victorian-era chap to take.

Mom continued to cling to the belief that he'd come around.

Soon.

Someday.

When he's ready.

We both knew the truth, though. I was no nearer breakfast with dear old Dad than before he knew of my existence. The fantasy was still just that. A fantasy.

Trip by trip, he'd learned to tolerate Mom's ability. She'd pointed to this fact over and over to prove that he'd warm to me, too. But there was a basic fallacy in her argument. He'd loved her before he found out about her "abnormalcy," as he phrased it.

I was nothing but an abnormalcy from the start.

The tips of Mom's fingers steepled against each other as she held the mug in a prayer-like caress. She hadn't taken a sip yet, which was weird. Mom hated her hot beverages anything other than scalding. She stretched the cup out to him, as if she was waiting for something. I could hear the tone of their conversation change into something harsh, something reproachful. My father shook his head. No.

Prayerful hands turned to pleading.

He reached into his pocket and pulled something out—a bottle.

She wrestled it out of his clenched fist and poured a bit of what-ever it was into her cup. Then she tucked the bottle into her own pocket. She took a sip. An angry sip.

My father's back stiffened, and they sat there like that, in starched silence, for several minutes. He finally leaned over to say some-thing, but she stood up. I knew my mom well enough to know when she was horked, and over the last six months, I'd learned that when she was mad, she tended to . . . yep. She disappeared. Faded, just like that. Unless I was much mistaken, that was the Shifting equivalent of a furious door slam.

I took a tentative step forward, into the lamplight. My father glanced up. Even from across the road, I could see the lines of worry that engraved his face. He adjusted his spectacles. I wrapped my arm around the lamppost, and I could tell that he'd seen me. He stood there, just staring at me. For a moment I thought he was going to say something. But then he turned and disappeared into the house. His departure may have been less dramatic than Mom's, but it was no less cutting.

My tendrils began to prickle. The pull was strong—probably a synch. I crouched down, ready to leave this place, and my fin-gertips brushed against something smooth yet sticky.

Compufilm.

There was handwriting on it.

Mine again.

And the same message as before.

To save his, destroy yours.

I looked around to see if my future self had stuck around to explain. But like my father, she was long gone.

━━►

"What were you doing back there?" I stomped up the stairs the second I synched home. Tufty roosted on the landing, his rump wiggling in a predatory stance like he was Mom's sole protector from my wrath. And maybe that was a good thing. I was feeling pretty wrathy right now. My father was never going to accept me if Mom went all bonks on him like that.

She didn't answer me.

"Mom?" I walked into her room. She was flopped over on the bed, snoring. My tone softened as I tried to rouse her. "Mom?"

A groggy "Mmm?" was all I received in return.

"Mom." I shook her shoulder. "Poppy!"

She lifted her head off the pillow for half a beat.

"So shleeepy," she slurred then resumed the snores.

That was weird. It wasn't that late. I wondered if she'd somehow gotten off synch in her return, but I checked her Com and the clock. Nope. She'd arrived here just a few minutes before I had. The cup she'd been drinking from at my father's house lay abandoned on the night table, knocked over, its contents oozing into the cracks. I let out a sigh as I sopped it up. Mom wasn't usually so careless as to bring something back with her. In the grand scheme of things, breaking this rule wasn't too terrible as long as she didn't get caught. But it made me wonder what else she'd let slide.

I gave the cup a sniff. Hot cocoa. Nothing unusual there.

"Mom!" She snored on. What on earth? I pinched her arm. Nothing. My hand was on my speakeazy, at the ready to call medics for help.

My mother had curled into a little ball at the head of the bed. Her front pocket was exposed, bulging with whatever it was she'd taken from my father. I fished the contents out. It was a small, glass bottle with a peeling label. Dr. Feelwell's Sleeping Tincture. I scanned the list of complaints it claimed to heal: maladies of the head, nervous constitution, winds or obstructions of the digestive organs. All with stuff like sassafras root and anise. Then my heart plunged at the last ingredient: laudanum.

Opium.

A narcotic.

I released my speakeazy slowly and laid it down on the edge

of the bed. Detox centers could clear this junk out of her system instantly. But she'd brought an illicit substance from the past back with her, it was a serious chronochrime. They'd check her chip and reinstate it against her will when they realized it wasn't functioning. What would ever have possessed her to do such a thing? And my father had given it to her!

"Oh, Mom." I settled into a rocker in the corner. It was going to be a long night.

><

The wood grain of our kitchen table embedded whorls and ridges in my cheek as the sun's morning rays slipped through the window and forced my eyes open. I barely remembered coming down here last night.

Water. I'd wanted a glass of water.

I lifted my head. A teakettle whistled on the stove. Beside it sat two mugs, not unlike the ones that belonged to my father. My mother leaned on the counter next to it, grasping her old French press that she swore made the best coffee this side of the twentieth century.

She looked like she could use some best coffee right about now.

"Why?" I asked. There was no need to finish that question.

She tapped her nails against the side of the press then placed it on the counter and reached for the kettle.

"I know what you're thinking, but it's not Dad's fault," she said.

"Don't call him that."

He hadn't earned "Dad." Dads let their daughters dance on top of their shoes. Dads took their daughters to the park and tucked them into bed at night. Dads *met* their daughters. He had barely earned "sperm donor."

"Your father didn't . . . doesn't approve of me taking that sleep aid." She sighed. "It's been hard maintaining two different schedules, sometimes falling asleep there, sometimes here."

"So your schedule got complicated and you decided to try out narcotics?"

"I didn't realize, not at first, what the ingredients were. All I knew was that it worked."

"It says 'laudanum' right on the bottle."

"Bree, it's been over twenty years since I've studied historical medicine, and I wasn't good at remembering that stuff even at the time." She plunged the coffee grounds down and smashed every last ounce of caffeine out of the dregs at the bottom. "I found an expired bottle in his medicine cabinet. My days and nights seemed so flipped at first that I took it out of desperation. If I could have just stayed a full night there without worrying about you being here alone, I think—"

"Oh, so this is my fault?"

"No. Of course not."

"Well, if it's not his fault and it's not your fault, then it sounds an awful lot like it's my fault."

"It's no one's fault."

"Ha!" I threw my hands up in the air without realizing that I was still clutching the bottle of Dr. Feelwhatever's Magical Life-ruiner. It slipped from my grip, and I just barely caught it and stopped it from shattering on the floor.

Mom lunged for it, too, and the look of terror on her face—that her precious drug might be lost—made something in me snap even further.

"You're not getting this back." I held the bottle up. "You realize that, don't you? You're lucky you didn't seriously hurt yourself."

"Watch your tone. And, obviously, I'm not going to take any more of it."

"Good." I pocketed it. "You won't mind that I keep—"

"No." She didn't even wait to let me get the last word out. "That's too risky. Leave it here. I'll dispose of it the next time I go to see your father."

Like blark was I giving this back to her.

"I'll toss it in the incinerators at the Institute. Students get rid of junk that way all the time."

"That's not necessary."

"That's not up to you." I was left to imagine what hurt etched Mom's face as I slammed the back door on it.

⤙⤚

I got to my dorm room just as Mimi was heading out, which seemed to have become our modus operandi these last six months. My frequent unexplained absences had stolen a spark from our friendship. It was like a glass wall had shot up between us. But of course, I still loved her more than Finn loved chocolate chip waffles.

"Hey," I said. "Where are you headed?"

"Date with Charlie," she said, snapping a jeweled cuff over her earlobe. I wasn't sure why, but it was a relief to me that the alterations in my timeline hadn't somehow prevented her from getting together with Charlie. They'd still found each other no matter what changed. Their love went down to the roots.

"Where are you going?" I asked.

"It's not the most romantic, but it was his turn to choose. We're going to grab breakfast burritos from a food truck on the way to the tour. So, y'know, I'll call it brunch, I guess."

"Tour?" I'd sat down at my desk and was rifling through messages. One from Wyck popped up right as I had started sorting them. It read: "Approved for first Shift tomorrow. How does it feel to be dating the hottest Neo in D.C.?"

"Tour of ICE, silly," said Mimi. "Oh, I forgot to tell you. Charlie got the official acceptance this morning."

"He what?"

"Bree." There was a tinge of chiding in Mimi's tone. "I told you he had applied to become a Neo last week. Why are you acting surprised?"

"I just . . . I didn't think . . ."

"Did you not think he'd get in?" She laughed. Kind of.

The truth was, I was acting surprised because I *was* surprised. Shocked. I had no idea Charlie had even been interested in becoming a Neo. On the timeline I remembered, he wasn't. (Or at least, he hadn't admitted it.)

"No, that's not it. It's only . . ." Blark it all. I had to navigate this carefully. If I let on that ICE was up to something shady, Mimi would take that info straight to Charlie who would either tell Wyck or ask ICE about it. Either way, it jeopardized my plan to sneak into that black tube during Wyck's first Shift. I was so close. But the thought of Charlie getting snarled up in all this was unbearable. I'd seen firsthand the toll that NeoShifting could eventually take on someone. I couldn't let that happen to him. Not if I could prevent it.

"I'm not sure Charlie is the best fit for the Neo program is all," I said.

"Why not?"

"It just doesn't seem like it would be his thing."

"So no qualms about your boyfriend Shifting? Just mine."

"That's not what I meant."

"So then what?" Mimi said through gritted teeth. "Wyck is better than Charlie?"

She clutched her forehead and winced.

"No! Of course not," I said.

"Well, which is it?" She rubbed her forehead and reached for her Buzztabs, but the bottle was once again running low. She began to root around in her desk for another. "Either my boyfriend's not good enough to become a Neo, or there's something you're not telling me."

"Neither." I handed over a few Buzztabs without her even asking. "But, Mimi—"

"Y'know what, Bree, I'm getting kind of sick of your moodiness. Ever since you were Anchored, you've been . . . you've been . . ."

"I've been what?"

"You haven't been the easiest person to live with."

If anyone else had said that, I would have laughed, but for Mimi, that was the equivalent of a vicious verbal thrashing.

"I know." It was all I could say.

She popped the Buzztabs into her mouth. Immediately, her wince eased.

"It's Charlie's dream to Shift someday," she said. "If you can give me one good reason why I should crush that dream, then go ahead."

"I . . . can't. But—"

"I have to go."

"Wait."

But she didn't wait. And she didn't turn around. There was no point in chasing her down. There was nothing I could say that wouldn't threaten my mission with Wyck.

I laid down on my bed and pulled Wyck's message back up. Tomorrow. That would give me only twenty-four hours to prepare. This was too soon. I needed more time to set a plan into motion. I hadn't even figured out how to break into that Cryostorage Room. Yes, Wyck was my link to ICE, but I still needed a way around the building once I was in.

I headed toward the incinerator room to destroy the rest of Mom's laudanum, but the reverter went off on the way. I was tempted to dump the drug first, but after the previous change that had affected me, it didn't seem prudent.

It ended up being a simple fix, nothing that involved me personally. A middle-aged woman stood outside a wedding chapel, staring at the open door as whispering guests filtered out. A man atop a hovercycle kissed a younger version of her passionately, situating her frothy no-longer-wedding dress around the seat. It didn't take me long to put together the "what-if" that had plagued this woman for the last twenty-odd years. She had just stopped her own wedding to run off with some other guy.

I walked up next to her wordlessly.

In one hand, she clutched her IcePick. In the other, a photo of two teenagers. Both hands trembled.

I touched the picture, and she flinched.

"I don't think you want to do this," I said.

The tremor continued in her limbs. I couldn't tell if it was from the physical pain of NeoShifting or the emotional pain of realizing what she had just set into motion. Probably both.

"Who are you?" she asked.

"It doesn't matter." Once I reverted the change, she wouldn't remember me, only disjointed bits of a life that never was.

"If you go through with this, your children won't exist when you get back," was all I had to say for her to dissolve into sobs.

"I can fix this," I said. "Do you want me to?"

Usually I didn't ask permission to perform a reversion, but something about this woman's brokenness made me voice the question. She gasped and nodded. I pressed the reverter against her skin and activated it. She dissolved before my eyes, but as she was disappearing, she whispered, "Thank you."

She'd be haunted by this. Flashes of what-ifs. I hoped that in the crevices of this woman's soul, comfort would nestle in with those what-ifs. Comfort that, ultimately, she'd chosen well.

I felt a rush of sympathy for my mother. She wasn't trying to hurt me or my father—or herself. She'd lived with seventeen years of big what-ifs, and now she was faced with the reality of what-now. She wanted everything to be like it should have been—she wanted the fantasy—but that wasn't possible. It was what it was.

I still needed to dump this useless drug as soon as I could. I debated leaving it here in the past, but I worried about somebody getting ahold of it. Seriously. What was my mother thinking? This stuff had put her to sleep within minutes, and she probably didn't even remember me yelling in her face trying to wake her up. She'd been totally knocked out.

Knocked out.

I clutched the bottle and smiled.

Maybe it wasn't completely useless.

chapter 14

"HEY! I STILL OWE YOU that celebration." I stood outside Wyck's door holding up two soda bottles like champagne flutes. That amount of sugar had used up every discretionary eating point I had for the month, but it was the only thing I could think of that would mask the bitter aftertaste of the laudanum. Twenty-two drops of it, to be precise. I peered around him and smiled. His roommate was gone, which simplified things greatly for me. "I'm here to give you Shifting pointers for tomorrow."

"Wow. A Blitzenberry Bomb. I don't think I've had one of those since I was a kid. They're really sweet."

"You're . . . really sweet."

He gave me a funny look.

Hold it together, woman. I took a sip of my Bomb and had to hold back a retch. Maybe I should have gone with strong coffee instead. This stuff was nasty, but it was the best thing I could come up with on short notice.

He took a polite sip and winced.

"I don't remember them having this much of an aftertaste."

Distract, distract, distract.

I thrust my lips against his and forced them to move in a close approximation to a passionate kiss. I sang the alphabet backward in my head to stop myself from screaming. My heart started racing but not the good kind. The I'm-cheating-on-Finn kind. Although I wasn't sure it was cheating when he was already with Jafney. At least she wasn't anywhere nearby with her blarking camera this time.

I checked to make sure Wyck's eyes were closed and swished the contents around his bottle to keep them from settling at the bottom.

"Does that help?" As I pulled my lips away from his, I quickly replaced them with the bottle. He took another gulp, laughing.

"Mmm. More aftertaste." He pulled me close.

Kiss. Sip. Kiss. Sip. Kiss. Sip.

What a fun game this . . . wasn't.

After I drained the last dregs into him, I snatched it away and tossed it down the recycle chute. There was no way I'd leave that thing lying around as evidence. When I turned back around, he reached out to embrace me again but veered off course and stumbled toward the couch.

"Whoa, there." I barely managed to catch him and lower all his heft down to the couch.

"M'sorry. Room feels duzzy." He clasped his hand to his mouth. "Dizzy." Then he looked around like I'd said something. "What?"

"I didn't say anything."

"You're pretty."

"And you're pretty tired."

"No. No! I'm going to give you"—his eyes wandered around the room before settling back on me with a startle—"poinkers. No. You give me . . . pointers. Ha! Poinkers."

"Yes. Pointers. For Shifting. Well, first thing is to relax. How about you start by telling me things that you find really relaxing? Maybe something like deep breathing or meditation or singing lullabies to yourself . . . or . . ."

But he was already zonked. I tapped his shoulder, and he let out a snuffling snore.

Score one for the Gilded Age.

"Wy-yck," I crooned in his ear. Nothing.

"Wyck!" I yelled. Still nothing.

Okay, now to really test it out. I pulled out a pair of hair pincers, the kind I'd used to remove my own hair last year for Finn.

The kind that hurt like a fireball of a dickens. I chose a spot at the crown. Seemed like it might be a little less sensitive than right at the hairline. And yanked.

"Wassuh? Huh?" Wyck sat up and rubbed the top of his head. My muscles clenched, ready to prattle off an excuse as to what I was doing, but his eyes slid out of focus, and he slumped back down.

"Aww, kitty cat," he mumbled. "Rurr, rurr, rurr."

His purring sounds receded into light snores, and my lungs released the sharp intake of breath they'd been storing this whole time. So twenty-two drops . . . definitely enough. And, bonus, I didn't accidentally kill him. Yay.

I had the hair, that was the important part. There was no telling what I'd encounter, security-wise at the end of that black tube, but Wyck's access upped my chances considerably of getting past it.

Now for my second task. I used the hair to access his personal database. What exactly I was looking for, I had no clue. I hoped to recognize it when I saw it. *How To Infiltrate An Evil Organization 101*?

Okay, maybe not.

Most of the files were school-related: notes from class, transporter duty schedules, bytes and bytes of Shifter logs. He really was a kick-arse transporter. I marveled at Wyck's meticulousness, down to his notation that my friend Pennedy had accidentally broken a nail off in tsarist Russia. And, hmm, I scrolled through the last few weeks of log entries. It looked like Mimi wasn't the only one with increased Buzz levels. Wonder what was causing it.

But that wasn't why I was here. ICE.

"Give me all the files pertaining to the Neo program." A handful hovered in front of me. I sifted through the top ones. The first was just the notification from Lafferty that Wyck had been approved. Nothing new there. There was a pamphlet of FAQs.

Will NeoShifting hurt? Some people experience minor discomfort. (Ha!) Should I worry about creating temporal paradoxes? NeoShifting is perfectly safe for all involved. (What the what, you liary liars?) How much does it cost? Payment plans are available. (Price: one soul.)

Nope. I needed the real information, the fine print. I wasn't going to find it here, though.

As I closed all the files, a message popped up for Wyck. I glanced at the soligraphic envelope and did a double take.

Jafney.

She'd wreaked enough havoc as it was. What was she up to now? I dragged the message over to where Wyck laid on the couch and used his finger to break the seal on the envelope.

It was an invitation. She and Finn would just lurrrv it if Wyck and I could join them for dinner tonight. Yeah, and I would just lurrrv to tell her where precisely she could shove said invitation. I started my response but stopped mid-sentence. Why was she doing this? If she wanted to torment me with her relationship with Finn, she could do that a lot more easily than through a double date. She didn't need to parade my relationship with Wyck around Finn. He'd already made his choice. And it was odd that she'd contact Wyck rather than me about this. So again, back to "Why?"

I drummed my fingers against Wyck's couch until I realized it wasn't his couch but his head. Jafney's appearance had coincided so perfectly with the change to my timeline. And it actually wasn't my fake relationship with Wyck that had kept me from Finn. It was her. She was the one who had convinced Finn that I had cheated on him. Her word. Well, her word and a photo that I still shuddered at the thought of Finn seeing. But even that was proof she'd continued to follow me.

Why?

She was up to something. And I wanted to find out what.

I changed my response to sound like Wyck. "Sounds plinky! Where and when?"

Her reply came almost instantly. Like she'd been waiting by her message box. "Tonight. 6:00. Virtual Vacay."

That would give Wyck the whole day to sleep this off. Hopefully, that would be enough time.

"See you there." I sent the message then trashed it with a frown. I stared at the snoozing lump on the couch.

This was going to be a long day.

>———◄

"So fuzzy." Wyck stuck his tongue out for the umpteenth time. "I can't believe I slept all day."

Another thing he'd said umpteen times in a scratchy, groggy voice since I'd woken him up an hour ago to tell him of our double date plans.

"It's a good thing," I said. "You'll be rested for your Shift tomorrow."

"The weird thing is that I still feel tired."

"Hmm." I flipped the settings menu around. "What sounds good?"

Virtual Vacay was one of those places that had surged in popularity a few decades ago after Shifters came out of hiding. The place was (in theory) supposed to mimic the experience of Shifting. You picked a virtual destination and time period and then spent a few hours holo-recreating there. Shifters had always kind of rolled our eyes at it, and now that ICE was offering the real thing, I wondered how long it would take them to put this place out of business.

"How about a French bistro?" Wyck didn't even bother looking at the menu. "Ever been to France?"

"Which century?" I asked. The country had lost its charm for me after a pigeon poop incident in the nineteenth century. Plus, I wanted to avoid anything that could be construed as romantic in any era.

"Doesn't say," he said.

"How about—?"

"Ooh, a beach in the Maldives!" squealed a voice in my left ear, peering over my shoulder at the "destination" options.

"Hello, Jafney." I purposefully selected another choice before she sat down. Any other choice. Finn didn't need to be reminded of her dolphinesque swim moves and cute bikini bod. "What about a meadow picnic?"

Finn pulled Jafney's chair out for her and started to sit down next to her.

"Y'know what?" she stopped him. "Let's shake things up. I'll sit next to Wyck. Finn, you sit next to Bree."

I slouched back in my seat as Wyck switched seats with Finn. What was Jafney playing at?

The table transformed to a floating checkered tablecloth. Wildflowers and trees sprouted around us, and a litter of baby bunnies skittered past a chipmunk that was acting a little too friendly and personable to be real.

"Oh, pout," said Jafney. "I love the beach."

Every time I saw her and Finn together, I felt like an amputee, pushing down a spasm of phantom limb pain. All the while being forced to watch someone else walk around with her leg.

Jafney brushed her hand against the order screen. "Whoops," she said as if it had been by accident. The pastoral green around us was replaced with a wide, white stretch of sand. Turquoise, rolling waves lapped at our toes. I could feel the wet through my shoes as if I wasn't even wearing any.

"No beach," I said. The beach belonged to Finn and me. She might have his time right now. She might even have his heart. She even took the waffles. She couldn't have the beach. That was mine. I slapped the order screen, and the meadow reappeared.

"Meadows are so overdone." Slap. The beach.

"I'm scared of the water." Slap. Welcome back, bunnies.

"I hate the—"

"How about"—Wyck placed his hand gently around Jafney's wrist and pulled it away—"a French bistro?"

All signs of wildlife disappeared as he pressed the order screen. La Vie en Rose began playing in the background, and we found ourselves at a candlelit table with a fabulous view of the Eiffel Tower. Fine. As long as there were no pigeons.

"Ooh, I love France," Jafney said.

"Ahh, the Francais." Finn pulled up the food menu and buried his nose in it.

As if Jafney and I hadn't just had the arm-wrestling match of the millennium under his very nose.

"Finn, you must not see stuff like this in your ti—" Jafney slapped her hand over her mouth when she realized what she'd almost said.

"Yes." I rushed in to cover Jafney's blunder. "You must not have Virtual Vacays in your *town*. From what I hear, there aren't a lot of modern conveniences. In your town of, uhh . . ." I found myself at a sudden loss.

"Old New Mexico." Finn took a calm sip of his drink. I ignored the chuckle hiding behind his glass.

I was too busy fighting back my own.

"What's Old New Mex—?" Jafney started to ask, but I kicked her so hard under the table that I jammed my toe. Old New Mexico was the fake place Finn and I had created as an excuse for his somewhat anachronistic behaviors.

But come on, Jafney. No one could be that dense.

"Yeah, I'm not familiar with that area either." Wyck just seemed to be making small talk, but I still wanted to change the subject as quickly as possible. The last thing I needed was a fistfight to erupt at the table between him and Finn. Until I reminded myself yet again that Wyck had no reason to fight Finn. In Wyck's current world, Finn was nothing to me.

Finn looked up from his menu at Jafney and scrunched up his nose. "Wonder if their crepes are as good as Mom's."

Apparently, in Finn's world, I was nothing to him either.

"No one's crepes could be as good as your mom's, Muffin Wuffin," said Jafney.

"You're the Muffin Wuffin," he said.

"No, you are." She tickled him under the chin. "You're the Muffin Wuffin."

"You're the—"

"I think we can all agree that everyone at this table is a Muffin Wuffin!" I practically yelled, not bothering to look away from my menu.

When I finally did glance up, every eye was glued to me.

"Are you okay?" asked Wyck.

Arghhh. So sick of that question. No, I was not okay. I wasn't okay watching Finn canoodle with Jafney. I wasn't okay pressing my lips to Wyck's as if it didn't make my blood curdle, much less liked it. I wasn't okay with the fact that at any moment my reverter could glow green and I could find out that someone had planted a bomb in my dorm room six months ago and all of this was for naught.

"I'm fine," I said. Or at least I would be. I grabbed my fake, holigraphic cloth napkin from my lap and threw it on my plate as I stood up. "I need some air."

"We're surrounded by air," said Jafney, a smirk spreading across her face.

"The non-pixelated kind." I stomped away from the table. As soon as I was around the corner, I kicked myself. Real Bree had yet again screwed up. Fake Bree had to fix this. I had to be the perfect girlfriend. And the perfect ex-girlfriend. Too many lives depended on it. Wyck was my ticket into ICE. Jafney's gaping blabberhole proved a threat to that. I had to guard that ticket at all costs. And I had to protect Finn from himself if he still refused to leave. I should never have come here tonight. My heart had sucker-punched my brain. No more.

I took a deep breath and was about to return to the table when Jafney popped her head around the corner.

"Hi-ey," she said.

"Hi."

"I . . . I'm sorry about that back there," she said. "I almost blew Finn's cover, didn't I? It's just that this has been a really intense few days."

"That's one word for it."

"I know you two were pretty close," she added. "You and Finn."

"In the past," I choked out. All three days of it. Finn's betrayal stabbed afresh.

"Exactly." She turned to head back to the table.

"Out of curiosity"—I gripped her upper arm—"why tonight's double date?"

Her expression darkened.

"Sometimes the best way to get past former feelings is to plow through them."

Unbelievable. In her twisted mind, she actually thought she was helping me. I had no choice but to follow her back to the table. I froze as soon as we entered the space. The setting had changed. It was the same picnic table as before, now covered with the food we'd ordered. But there was no way I'd be able to stomach a single bite.

Gone was the French bistro. In its place was a vast expanse of grass. Familiar buildings dotted the modern scene. But that wasn't what drew my lunch into my throat.

Jutting directly over us, looming like a blunt blade, was the Washington Monument.

"I don't like this spot," I said, glaring at Finn, whose jaw had set into a steel trap. "At all."

"I didn't choose it," Finn said slowly.

"I did," said Wyck with an icy smile, calculated and controlled.

He was experiencing a flash. I could tell. And it was the worst possible one. The last time I had been this close to the Washington Monument with him, he'd been busy trying to throw Finn and me off it.

I slid into my seat and stole a side-glance at Finn. He was still unreadable, but his posture was even stiffer than before if that was possible.

"What, umm, what made you pick this spot?" I asked Wyck. He didn't answer, and I looked over to see why. He was slouched over, and when he sat back up he was his same jovial self as before. Whatever flash of the other timeline that had prompted his choice, it was gone now.

"I know it's not very exotic," Wyck said, "but it popped out at me for some reason. You have to admit, it's a plinky spot for a picnic. I wonder if they have a view from the top."

He pulled the menu back up.

I held my breath. I was having my own flashback. My knee shook under the table. The same knee Wyck had shattered. I waited for him to snap again. But he just stared at the white marble above us, munching away on a breadstick.

"Reminds me of something," Wyck said.

Jafney giggled. I couldn't believe it, but I was actually thankful for her presence in that moment.

"Not that." Wyck laughed.

My tension faded as we all joined in the laughter—Finn's and mine both fake. Jafney asked Wyck how he was feeling about his Shift the next day. While they chatted, Finn brushed his hand against the order screen, and the Monument faded away.

In its place, the ocean materialized.

"*Thank you,*" I mouthed to him, but his only reply was a terse nod.

Jafney was placated by the waves and as soon as we'd finished eating, she bounded up.

"Where to now?" she said.

"Oh, do you have to leave early?" Wyck asked. He looked genuinely disappointed, and Jafney seemed positively delighted at the extra dose of attention.

"No, silly," she said. "I meant where should we go for the next part?"

Finn engrossed himself in the activity menu, the real reason people came to this place. I'm not sure where exactly nonShifters got their ideas about what we did on missions, but apparently, they thought it was all hiking past waterfalls and scaling rocky crags. Jafney joined Finn, and I sat there silently praying they didn't choose something that involved heights or water. My stomach was already set to go into revolt.

Wyck stood off to the side, quiet. I wondered if he was replaying any fragmented memories of the Washington Monument, if this was the first time they'd flashed in his mind. I walked over to him.

"Are you happy, Bree?" he finally said quietly. "With me?"

"What? Of course I am."

"It's just that . . . we used to be like that." He gestured to Finn and Jafney. She glanced our way then wrapped her arms around Finn and yammered on about a Virtual Vacay trip she'd taken to the Amazon.

"You used to be like that," said Wyck.

In that moment, I was jealous of Finn and Jafney, too. But not for the same reasons as Wyck. Their relationship may have been fast and intense. I may have hated everything about it because Finn had chosen her over me, but it was simple. It was Muffin Wuffin and beach dates. Finn and I had never been Muffin Wuffins. Our entire relationship had been built on mortal danger and giant space-time conundrums. Our two most memorable beach dates had involved me wrecking his car and him saving me from drowning.

Finn and Jafney's relationship seemed so easy. So natural. Finn deserved simple. He deserved natural.

Finn deserved Jafney. Well, no, he deserved better than Jafney. But Finn deserved someone like Jafney, someone who wasn't as chronologically complicated as me. Even before this change had happened to place me with Wyck, I'd worried that at any moment, Finn would look at me and say, "Not worth it."

Maybe that's exactly what he did.

Enough. I needed to focus on keeping my ticket to ICE in my pocket and convincing Finn to go home.

"What activity do you want to do, Muffin Wuffin?" I asked Wyck with a flirtatious bat of my eyelashes.

He laughed. A true Wyck laugh, deep and hearty, and I wished I could have my friend back. If it wasn't for the whole killer-waiting-to-be-unleashed thing, it would be exactly like old times.

"Maybe not that much like them," he said, then raised his voice. "Hey, why don't we tromp around Santa Fe? Finn can show us the sights."

"Heh."

"How about swimming?" Jafney said.

No.

"Why don't we go spelunking?" It was the first opinion Finn had expressed that evening.

"Perfect," said Wyck, punching in our choice.

The simulator gave us the all-ready after a few moments, and the mouth of a cave yawned black and hollow before us. Wyck led. I crawled in behind Jafney, and Finn trailed our party. There was no equipment to put on because it was a simulation, but an adjustable beam of light shone out of each of our foreheads as if we wore headlamps.

At first we all kept up a loose version of a conversation, but as the terrain became more challenging, everyone focused their comments on what was coming next or warnings about sharp drop-offs or tricky handholds. The deeper we delved, the farther ahead Wyck's and Jafney's lamps disappeared. Jafney turned a corner, and I lost sight of her completely. Her voice faded away as well. I knew that with these holosims, she could actually be just a few feet away but they created the illusions of height, depth, and distance according to everyone's exact retinal angle.

I was about to call out to her to wait when Finn's hand slipped over my mouth. He wrapped his arm around my waist and tugged me into a side passage.

"What are you—?" I leaned my head back so I wouldn't blind Finn with my headlamp.

"Shh." He fiddled with my light until it flickered off. Then he did the same with his own, dimming it to nothing but a dull glow between our two faces.

I strained to hear any sound but the *drip-drip-drip* of the stalactites. At first, I thought I heard a tinkle of laughter that might have been Jafney, but it faded into the dripping.

"We need to catch up with them," I whispered.

"We need to talk."

"Now?" I certainly didn't want to hear the details of his relationship with Jafney, and I wasn't about to bring up my plans with ICE while Wyck was actually only ten feet away.

"Yes, now," said Finn. "Don't think I missed that stunt Wyck was pulling with the Washington Monument."

I checked the tunnel again to make sure that Jafney and Wyck were still out of the vicinity.

"Fine," I said. "I've got it under control. But you want to talk? Let's talk. Why have you not gone home? What part of chronofugitive does not scare the blark out of you?"

"That's why you think I'm still here? To prove something?"

"No, I think you're still here because your tendrils are all snuggled up with Jafney's."

"Well, obviously," said Finn.

Un-blarking-lievable. He had the sheer nerve to rub it in my face?

"Look," I said. "I know what you *think* you saw in that picture Jafney showed you, but—"

"I think I saw Wyck kissing you."

Oh, you do not get to judge me, Finnigan J. Masterson.

"Tell me," I said, "how long did it take you to throw yourself into Jafney's arms after she showed you that picture?"

Finn's voice grew as dark as our surroundings. "About two seconds."

"That's what I thought." I had nothing more to say to him. "Look, Muffin Wuffin, I have a big day tomorrow, and the last thing I need is you horking it for me." If Wyck suspected me of anything but total devotion, there was no way he'd bring me along to cheer him on for his First Shift.

"What are you doing tomorrow?" asked Finn.

I glanced out of the passage, but Finn and Jafney were still out of eye- and earshot.

"I'm going to ICE's headquarters with Wyck," I whispered.

"You're . . . what?" Finn let go of me and gripped the walls of the simulated cave. The pixels sparked and blinked where he dug his fingers into the crevices. "Why didn't you tell me. . . . ?"

"Why didn't I? Why would I?"

"Because it's dangerous. You saw him back there."

"Oh, *you're* going to lecture me about dangerous? And I told you, I have it under control. Besides, I'm not your concern anymore." I gave him a pointed look. "Remember?"

Finn looked at the mouth of the crevice where we'd crawled in. A sliver of light had started to grow in the distance even though we couldn't hear Jafney or Wyck yet.

"Bree, I may be with Jafney, but you're still my—"

"Enough." I couldn't bear to hear the word "friend" come off his lips. It was like the final insult. This conversation was over as far as I was concerned.

"Come on," I said, tugging at his sleeve to continue down the serpentine tunnels.

Finn, however, pulled me back and cupped my cheeks in his hands. He brushed my hair back with his thumb and leaned down like he was going to kiss me.

"Blark it," he said. Then I realized . . . he was going to kiss me.

I shoved him back as hard as I could. He may have chosen Jafney over me, but surely he didn't think I was the type of girl who would be the object of his wandering eye. Finn tumbled back, a bemused expression on his face, and I realized, yeah. That's exactly what he thought.

No sooner had his bum hit the ground than a bright beam shone in the crevice where we were. Jafney's light wobbled as she tilted her head to the ceiling.

"What are you two doing?" she asked.

"Nothing," we both said.

"Bree tripped, and I was helping her get set back up," said Finn.

"In a hole?" Jafney eyed the crevice we were still tucked in.

Finn and I both made burbling noises that sounded something like "P'buh."

Thankfully, Jafney seemed no more the suspicious than the intuitive type.

"At least you're okay," she murmured.

"Yes, that was close." Wyck spoke for the first time, and only then did I notice his light shining behind hers. He tapped something on his belt, and the cave melted away.

Finn and I were still in the amount of space that the crevice occupied, about a square yard, so our knees were entwined like the teeth of one of Finn's zippers. Jafney and Wyck were crouched a few feet from us. It was bizarre to me how these simcubes worked, how you could be so near your fellow participants without detecting them at all. Finn and I were tangled at such an odd angle that there was no way for me to stand up without assistance.

"Too close," added Wyck, reaching his hand out to me.

Jafney glanced over at Wyck, then back at me, a look of fury now on her face. She reached down and pulled Finn up then nestled herself under his shoulder. He pulled her in even closer.

"It was lucky you were there to help," I said brightly to Finn, my cheeks coloring.

Indignation battled with shame in my stomach. Shame that Finn thought my affection was so transferable—him to Wyck, Wyck to him. But indignant that Finn had given up on me so easily, given up on us. Indignation won out. My motives were pure. His, on the other hand. . . . Apparently, there was only one body part he was thinking with right now. Maybe he thought he had the moral upper ground by chasing after Jafney to prove something. Heck, maybe he even liked the hagfish. But he should have believed in me more. Should have believed in me longer. He should have believed in us.

After an awkward parting as two couples, I fought the urge to look over my shoulder and watch Finn and Jafney as they traipsed down the sidewalk, hand in hand and lovey-smoosh-faced.

Wyck took my hand after a block, and I let him. He had this annoying habit of squeezing it multiple times during a conversation, but only while he was talking. I barely said a word, to the point that I was about to lose circulation in my fingers.

"Sorry you had such a hard time in the caves. Usually you're so nimble in gym class. And you're so much shorter than Jafney. I would have thought . . ."

"Yep, it was weird. Must have been slippery pixels."

"Slippery pixels?"

"Yeah." I wiggled my fingers to loosen them from his grasp. "Slippery pixels."

We reached the steps of the Institute.

"I guess this is good-night," Wyck said. "I'm going to sleep at home tonight. Big day tomorrow." He leaned in for a kiss, and I reciprocated with one that would have bored my dead grandmother.

"You should get to bed," I said when he pulled away.

"You're probably right." He looked up at the stars and hummed.

The tune was familiar. He started to sing the words in a garbled, froggy-sounding voice. " 'It's not easy being green. . . .' "

"Where did you hear that song?" I cut him off. That was Finn's song. *Our* song.

"Hm?" Wyck looked back down at me. "What song?"

"The song you were just singing." Had Wyck gone back to spy on Finn again? But why? On this timeline, Finn wasn't his enemy.

"I was singing a—?" Wyck's brow furrowed. "It was on a show I used to watch when I was a little kid."

"Which one?"

"I . . . hmm. . . ." He dug his hands in his pocket. "That's weird. I can picture it. There were puppets. They taught letters and numbers and stuff. But I don't remember the name of the show." Because that show hadn't been broadcast in 150 years.

What was going on?

"Wow. I must still be groggy from that long nap today," he said.

"Yeah. You should get a good night's sleep. Tomorrow will be hectic."

Gentle as if he were holding a kitten, Wyck reached for my face and planted a soft kiss on the top of my forehead.

He backed away slowly, and I gave into a sudden odd urge to hug him.

He hugged me back, and for a split second, his arms felt like Finn's.

chapter 15

I'D LIED TO WYCK.

Okay, there were a lot of things I'd lied to Wyck about. But this one, I kind of wished I'd told the truth.

The trick to a successful Shift, especially when you have no idea what's on the other end of the space-time continuum, is to look nonchalant and relaxed even if your insides have vomited on themselves in terror. Fear is the fastest way to stick out. Not your clothes. Not your accent. People pick up on fear without even realizing what they're detecting. They're more likely to ask if you need help or directions or a tonic for your weak constitution and color. (Dang you, snooty French Impressionists.)

I shifted my weight from one foot to the other, maintaining a casual stance, as I waited for Wyck at the entrance of ICE's Headquarters. Red-clothed workers gave me hasty but not unfriendly nods as they shuffled past me. I mentally ran over the checklist of objects stowed in my pocket one last time.

Flashlight, check. Stunner, check. Wyck's hair, magno-grappling hook, black mask, invisible paint sprayer. Checkity-check-check.

Also a decent props list for a long-overdue Batman reboot.

There was no telling what waited for me at the end of that black tube (other than creepy, frozen bodies) but I wanted to be prepared, no matter what. I tightened the anti-grav belt cinched under my shirt for good measure.

I checked my Com. Wyck was three minutes late. Not a big

deal, but it didn't help my uneasiness over how much this plan depended on him. My thumb was on my speakeazy when Wyck came up behind me and tapped my shoulder.

"Hey." He looked back at the Pod from which he must have just emerged.

"Hey." I tried to make eye contact to gauge how he was feeling about the Shift, but he kept his gaze trained away from me.

"Sorry I'm late," he said. "Were you, umm"—he watched the Pod as it zoomed away—"were you waiting long?"

"Not at all." My eyelid twitched as I lied. My tell. But Wyck wasn't even looking at me.

"We should probably go inside." Wyck flipped his newly assigned Com open and shut a few times. This wasn't like him to be scared of, well, anything.

"Are you feeling okay?" I asked.

"Fine." He finally looked directly at me. "Let's get this over with."

"Are you having second thoughts?" Not good.

Six months ago, I would have welcomed the news that he no longer wanted to Shift. But today? Today, I needed him to get his butt out of this time so I could get mine down that black tube.

"No," he said. "It's just . . . never mind."

"Don't be nervous," I said. "You're going to be a—"

"Natural. Yeah."

"It's going to be great. I'll be right there waiting for you the whole time." My eyelid twitched again.

"If you're gonna lie to me, Bree"—Wyck let out a chuckle—"you need to do a better job of hiding your tell."

Heat rushed to my face. "How do you know my tell?"

Finn was the only one who had ever noticed or called me on it before.

"I . . ." Wyck blinked and bent away. "It just is. The twitch. It's your tell."

This was the second time in less than twelve hours that Wyck knew information only Finn should know. Something told me this was not a coincidence. But something also told me I didn't want Wyck dwelling on it.

I carefully kept both eyes pried open. "Well, today, it was just a bug that flew near my eye. I'll be right there when you get back."

"Thanks." Wyck gave the top of my arm a little squeeze.

And then a little harder squeeze. Rougher.

"Wyck." I tried to tug it away, but his fingernails dug in. "You're hurting me."

He immediately released it, staring at his arm like it had turned to a hot poker.

"I'm . . . sorry. I didn't realize I was holding it that tight."

I rubbed my palm against the trail of half-moon indentations left by his nails, but didn't say anything. It had been a flash, that was all. The last thing I needed was Evil Wyck poking his head out right now, though.

We entered the building. Lafferty, wearing what was apparently her signature white outfit with red heels, bustled past me, pulling Wyck through the front doors. I trailed behind, trying to stay as unobtrusive as possible.

"My apologies again for the short notice," she said. "As I explained earlier, our scholarship students have to be flexible, scheduling-wise. But tick-tock. Wouldn't want you to miss your window."

What was the hurry? At the Institute, Shifters stumbled in for launches sleep-slogged and ten minutes late all the time. It wasn't like the seventeenth century was going anywhere.

Lafferty led us to a cheery yellow transport tube. She gestured that she'd follow us. Wyck waited for me to step inside, and again the sensation of soaring swept over me.

When I whished into the landing chamber, it was almost identical to the one from the other day. Except this one only had a single porthole leading out of it rather than multiple options.

Without waiting for Lafferty, Wyck and I pushed ourselves through the hole and emerged in ICE's Launch Room.

I had expected it to be like the Student Launch Room at the Institute—cold and sleek and shiny and modern. I couldn't have been more off base. This room very closely resembled a comfy viewing gallery at an art museum. There were paintings lining the walls of the oblong room dating back from recent pop art to centuries old.

"Are we in the right spot?" I asked Wyck.

"Yep." He pointed at what I now recognized to be Launch Pads that stood in front of the paintings in the place where viewing benches would normally be. "I think they're trying to make people feel like they're hopping back into history as if they were stepping into a painting."

"That's ridiculous," I said.

"What's ridiculous?" Lafferty pushed herself primly through the hole behind us.

"Nothing," I mumbled. And that was when I noticed there was an observation balcony situated above us. A herd of onlookers peered over the edge. Most were older, the youngest of them were at least in their forties. It was a diverse group, but they had one thing in common. Not a single person wore an outfit that cost less than a new Pod.

They were all focused on a spot on the far side of the room where a person wearing knee-breeches and a powdered wig stepped onto the metal disk of the Launch Pad. His transporter pressed the IcePick to the back of his neck then adjusted the transport controls. When the man disappeared, the crowd above broke into applause like they'd witnessed a mildly impressive magic trick.

I swiveled back to face Lafferty, unable to wipe the scowl from my face. ICE had turned my existence into a spectator sport for the rich and bored.

Because that was the other thing all those observers had in common. They all looked bored. All I saw when I looked from discontented face to discontented face was a prospective change to the timeline. I counted the number of people up in the balcony but lost track at fifty. My mind spun. I didn't know who all ICE was allowing to go back within their lifetime to make changes, what criteria they had to meet. After my experience with Dr. Canavan and the capuchin fever, though, I was pretty sure that some people were sneaking through the cracks. But if even a fraction of these people attempted to make changes, I would be very busy with that reverter. And this was only one day. One viewing.

"Where have you decided to go, Wyck?" Lafferty asked. Her question threw me off again. Shifters didn't choose where to go. They were told. Either by their instructor at the Institute or by their bosses at work. Even free Shifters didn't have a choice. My tendrils didn't ask me where I wanted to go. They simply took me where I was supposed to be.

"We have several wonderful options, depending on your interests." She handed him a brochure. The images on it swirled through groundbreaking moments in history. The works of art on the wall changed accordingly. "I know in your application you mentioned an interest in the California Gold Rush. We have era-appropriate clothing ready and waiting."

"Yeah." He gave the brochure half a glance. "Now that I've had a chance to think it over, I think maybe something a little closer to home."

Uh oh. No cold feet now.

"You okay?" I asked Wyck.

"Yeah. Y'know, first time out and all. I'll just go back to something pretty recent and poke around."

"What? No. You should go see something more exotic," I said.

"Nah, let's keep things simple."

He smiled, and I forced one in return, trying to keep myself calm. On this timeline, he didn't know he could change his past. On this timeline, he'd just been introduced to NeoShifting.

Wyck lowered his voice as he solidified his plans with his

transporter. I meandered around the room, searching for anything suspicious or out of place. Nothing. Well, nothing if you ignored the fact that people who were never meant to leave their time period were zipping around the continuum as if they had any business doing so. But there was no evidence that suggested that ICE was anything other than what they claimed—a temporal travel agency. I walked past the porthole entrance right as a woman in red scrubs emerged.

"Careful," she said, her voice as stiff as her posture.

I'd almost knocked over the tray she was holding. On it lay what I immediately recognized as an IcePick. A bluish substance sloshed in the bulb stuck on the end of it.

"Excellent." Lafferty pushed past me and took the tray from the red-scrubbed woman. In a loud voice that seemed more for the benefit of those in the balcony than for Wyck, she said, "Are you ready? The procedure is completely painless."

As the techs gave Wyck last-minute instructions, Lafferty positioned him on the Launch Pad. She took final readings of his vitals.

"How are you feeling?" she asked him. "Anxious? Tense?"

"I'm all right," said Wyck, but he didn't look it. He glanced my way, and I tried to reassure him with a simpering Fake Bree smile.

"You're sure you wouldn't like to go further back?" Lafferty was the one who seemed tense as she looked at the woman who had brought the IcePick in.

"You'll be fine," said Wyck's transporter, though it seemed like it was Lafferty he was trying to put at ease. "You remember your training, don't you, Wyck? Observe only. Avoid contact with anyone you know in the past."

"What would happen if he interacted with himself in the past?" I asked, testing them.

"Nothing," said Lafferty quickly. "It's just standard policy. Like Wyck said, it's best to keep things simple."

As Lafferty finished up with Wyck, I stared at her turned back. Liar or lax, she was one or the other, and dangerous either way.

"How long will he be gone?" I tried to make the question sound casual.

"One hour," said Wyck's transporter.

One hour. I had one hour to sneak out, get into that Cryostorage Lab, poke around to figure out what's going on, and get back here without anyone missing me.

I watched Wyck's launch carefully, hoping to spot anything different or unusual. Again, nothing. The only difference between a Neo's and a chipped Shifter's Shift was that right before they began the countdown, Lafferty held the Pick to the nape of Wyck's neck and clicked the end. The blue stuff from the bulb oozed under his flesh. She then handed him the Pick to hold.

"Guard this closely," she said. "You'll need to hold it against your bare skin once again, right where I did, and click the end to return."

The countdown proceeded, and when Wyck disappeared from the Launch Pad, the people in the observation deck broke into applause again. I set the timer on my Com to one hour.

I waited a minute then wandered over to Lafferty, who was deep in conversation with Wyck's transporter and the woman who had delivered the Pick.

". . . and was that a wise move?" asked the woman.

"He probably just got the last-minute jitters. It's not like he even knows he can change anything," said his transporter.

"True, but—" Lafferty stopped when she saw me sidle up behind her. "Yes?"

"Umm." Dang it. "Do you mind if I use the restroom?"

"It's in the lobby." She waved me off like I was an irksome insect.

"Thanks." I scurried off like a tru-ant and practically leaped back through the porthole. Once in the lobby, I pulled a baseball cap out of my pocket and tugged it down as a disguise. I waited for some red scrubs to clear out then strode across the room to the black tube like I knew what I was doing.

I pulled Wyck's hair from my pinky, praying it would unlock whatever was before me. But the black tube activated on its own when I stepped inside. I actually found myself a little disappointed. Maybe the area wasn't as restricted as I'd thought. Maybe there was a justifiable explanation behind the people frozen in that Lab.

The weightless chamber I shot into at the end of the seemingly endless black tube was smaller than the others, the size of my closet at the Institute, only large enough for one person at a time. There was one porthole in and out of it. The only lights in the chamber were the ones lining the hole. I pushed myself toward it, expecting to float forward as I had in the other landing areas but didn't budge. I tried again, but still didn't move. A heavy sensation dragged at my limbs, at my every pore. Any movement I tried to make was counterproductive. In the other tanks, I'd felt thin and weightless. It had been like slipping through silken sheets. But not here. This felt as if someone had dumped a wet velvet blanket over me. I strained to move, but it would have been easier to swim through gelatin.

The fabric of my clothes floated freely around me, so the sluggish effect seemed to be restricted to my skin. There weren't any alarms or locks, and I realized they didn't need any. Only a few select people must be authorized to enter this area. The gel must be programmed to not affect them.

Which was interesting and all, but it didn't change the end result. I was caught in the dead center of a spiderweb.

"All right," I said, but nothing came out. The invisible gel must have absorbed sound as well. No one to hear my cries for help.

The entrance port behind me glowed yellow. Blark. Someone was coming. I had to get out of this chamber. I wriggled my hand down to my waist and grasped my grappling hook. The gel dispersed around it, so I was able to maneuver my hand through its invisible wake. I'd only have one shot for the target to find a mark through that porthole. When I released it, I heard the faint ping that it had found something solid even though I couldn't see what that something was. I activated the handle, locking my hand into place, and with a *chuh-chuh-chuh-chuh,* it dragged me toward the hole. My body fought each tug like a cat battling a bathtub. When my hand reached the hole, I was able to slide it through and quicken the pace by pushing against the sides.

Shlup. I slid through. As soon as I was free, I didn't pause, didn't look behind me. I yanked the target off the wall, reinserting it into its firing chamber as I raced down a brightly lit hallway. It was narrow, only a few feet across, but the ceiling above soared thirty feet high. It gave the feeling of being squished between two metal slices of bread. There was a lone door, closed, at the very end of the hallway. I tried it, but it was locked. Tried Wyck's hair. Nothing.

Nowhere to hide.

Nowhere to hide.

Nowhere . . . but up.

I had one chance at this. My forearm shook as I aimed the grappling hook at the ceiling directly above the entrance to the tube, back at the other end of the hallway. The ceiling was so high, it should be out of their line of sight. I reached out my other hand to steady it. *Ping.*

Perfect hit.

The trajectory was near horizontal, like flying. My thigh slammed into the wall when I reached the target, and I winced but kept silent. Right as the person's torso emerged from the porthole, I flicked on my anti-grav belt and floated upward. My arms and legs were pressed as flat to the ceiling as I could get them.

It was Lafferty. She didn't look up, down, or sideways as she hopped into the hall, and she walked at a decent clip toward the door. I followed, noiselessly, above her.

The trickiest part would come when she reached the door. I'd have to dip down right behind her as she went inside and squeeze through before the door shut again. And if this was indeed the

Cryostorage Room, the walls would be domed on the other side. But I'd made it this far. I wasn't about to give up now.

I waited until the last possible second to follow her to give her a head start. I'd guessed right. It was the Cryostorage Room.

The door clipped my pants as it shut, and I had to yank them free then skitter up the curved wall like a spider. Lafferty must have heard the sound because she whirled around. I held my breath. I was directly above her now, but she didn't look up. She shrugged it off, and when she turned back around, I kicked off toward the highest point of the dome and curled into a tight ball at the center. A bird's-eye view of everything.

The room was unchanged in the fifty years my last visit. Or almost. Along the sidewall, several more of the bubbles were lit up and active. I counted. Nearly a fourth of the cryostorage units had now been filled. Lafferty stood directly below me in front of the giant tank. I could have spit on the top of her head if I'd wanted to. Well . . . I did want to. I should say, if I'd gone temporarily crazy.

"Foxtrot-Juliet-Mike-20-1-6. Access code L5N21KRA983FJ."

I fumbled to activate the sound recorder on my Com and managed to get the last set of numbers and letters of the code as she rattled them off. The movement rustled my shirt. Lafferty froze and looked around. I could tell she was vaguely aware of something off, but again thankfully she didn't look straight up.

I craned my neck to try to see what was going on in the tank below, but the fluid in it had turned smoky and dark. The contents—no, not contents, I reminded myself, *person*—was nothing but a hazy outline in the mire.

"Deterioration rate stable at .02 percent," said a pert voice from above me. It startled me so much my Com slipped from my fingers. I managed to snatch up the very end of the chain before it clattered to the floor below.

"Compatibility rate continues to exceed minimal requirements." The voice droned on with more numbers that didn't mean anything to me, and I realized that it was only the computer. De-

terioration . . . compatibility. I'd heard Lafferty discussing the same
topics with Raspy during Wyck's prep visit. The same sour sensation returned to my stomach as before.

The person in the tank started thrashing around. I still couldn't
see distinct arms and legs through the haze, but I could tell they
were in pain.

"Hang tight." Lafferty patted the edge of the tank jovially, like
she was slapping the haunches of a skittish horse. "Almost done."

The woman who had delivered Wyck's IcePick to the Launch
Room walked in.

"Ahh," said Lafferty. "Everything going well with Mr. Malone
and that transporter student?"

"Mr. Malone is already back," said the woman, tying her hair
up into a knot. "Didn't surprise me. Witnessing the French Revolution sounds downright morbid to me."

"To each his own." Lafferty adjusted some of the controls on
the tank.

"I'm still not sure if it was a good plan approving the kid," said
the woman. "He could be trouble."

"He could also be useful."

"It still makes me nervous, him Shifting back within his own
lifetime."

"He probably just got skittish," said Lafferty. "Besides, what
would he change? It's not like a seventeen-year-old has a lifetime
of regrets."

"I still don't like it. Then again, I suppose it doesn't matter.
Even if he did change something, it's not like we would even
know."

"I would," said Lafferty. "My source keeps me well-informed."

"Your source." The woman snorted. "You're trusting the word
of an unchipped Shifter. Not the most reliable source, if you ask
me."

"I didn't ask you," said Lafferty.

The woman went quiet. She tapped the edge of the tank.

"A productive session, I'd say."

Something along the wall at the far end of the room grabbed my attention. Lafferty and the woman were oblivious, their view blocked by the tank in the middle. There it was again—a movement—behind the metal screen where I'd hidden the last time I was here.

I squinted. It was a person.

So help me. If my future self had come here to screw things up again . . . .

But no.

It was . . .

A sharp lump snagged in my throat.

It was Finn.

chapter 16

FINN RAISED HIS HEAD above the screen like a gopher peeking out of its hole.

From the stunned expression on his face, it was clear that he was as shocked to find himself in his current predicament as I was. I looked around but didn't see Jafney or Georgie with him. He must have Shifted here from the near future. Natural-born Shifter that he was, he immediately lowered into a crouch to assess his surroundings, which included the ceiling. He spied me a moment later, stood up, and opened his mouth to say something. I put my finger against my lips then pointed at Lafferty and motioned for him to hide again. He nodded and ducked back down.

Lafferty finished gathering whatever data readings she was after. She and the other woman marched toward the exit without a backward glance. The door they took was the same one my future self had used fifty years ago. After counting to ten, I tapped the descent button on my anti-grav belt and rushed over to Finn. Even after the way things had crumbled, my first instinct was still to throw my arms around him, but I refrained.

"What are you doing here?" I was getting tired of asking him that.

"Bree, I have no idea where 'here' even is. Last thing I knew, I was in the middle of dinner with Jafney, then, bam, I couldn't fight this overwhelming urge to Shift. Where are we?"

"ICE's headquarters," I said. "Their Cryostorage."

"Storage? What are they storing?"

"Kidnapped Shifters."

"Oh, good. At least it's not anything unsavory." He moved out into the center of the room, gazing at all the equipment. "So how far into the future are you from?"

"Future?"

"When you Shifted here?" He gave me an inquisitive look. "Just now?"

"Oh, I . . . ummm."

"You did Shift here, didn't you?"

"Funny story."

"Wait a minute." His eyes narrowed then flew wide. "Wyck had his Shift scheduled for today. You snuck away by yourself! Bree, if they catch you—"

"They're not going to catch me. I have everything under control."

He glanced up to the spot on the ceiling where I'd been dangling.

"You keep saying that, but kinda seems like you don't."

"Kinda seems like it's none of your business."

"All right. *What* is going on?"

Before I had a chance to respond, Finn dropped his voice to a hush and whispered directly into my ear. "Wait. Does he have you bugged?"

"Bugged? Who? What are you talking about?" I tried to pull away, but Finn clutched me to him and pressed his lips into a silent kiss on my forehead. At first, I melted into it, melted into him, before I came to my senses. "Save it for your lady friend."

"Rawrr," he growled in my ear.

"What is wrong with you?" I shoved myself away from him.

"Well, I'm pretty confused. If that's what you mean."

"I'm not your floozy."

"Yeahhhh. You're not helping the confusion."

"And you're not helping your case."

"My case? Bree, what is going on?"

"I don't know. Why don't you go ask your girlfriend?" I knew I sounded like a toddler. I didn't care.

"I . . . thought I just did."

"Huh?"

"Huh?"

We stood there blinking at each other like two blind cavefish dumped into a sunny stream.

"Say that again," I said.

"Say what again?"

"The part where I'm your girlfriend."

"In which part were you not my girlfriend?"

"But you think I'm with Wyck."

"I think you're doing what with Wyck?"

"No. *With* Wyck."

"I do?"

"You don't?"

More blinking. The realization bobbed there on the surface of my brain until comprehension sank down to my heart.

Finn knew I wasn't with Wyck.

I launched myself at his lips, my kisses hungry and demanding. It was like a dam had kept a roaring river held back, the pressure building and building. It crumbled the moment Finn said those words. Of course he hadn't believed I was with Wyck.

Wait.

I broke away.

"You knew I wasn't with Wyck and yet you still latched up with Jafney?"

"Okay. Back to confused."

"Two days, Finn. You were my boyfriend, and then two days later, you were catching grapes in your mouth from Miss Mushy-face."

"Two days?"

"Two. Days."

"Eight months," he said.

"What?"

"Eight months in my time, Bree. You and I were at the movies. Then suddenly, I was back home in Chincoteague. Without you. And I didn't hear from you. For eight months." Finn ran his fingers through his hair and stared off into space. "I didn't know if you were injured or captured or . . ."

Dead. Finn couldn't say it. His breath came out in shaky little puffs.

"Eight months, Bree. What did you expect me to do? Just wait around in Chincoteague forever?"

"But you waited for me. Before." A hot tear stung the corner of my eye. Technically, I hadn't taken the last visit to Past Finn yet, the one where I asked him to protect me then lied to him and said that I'd never see him again. But in Finn's experience, there had been a year-long gap between that visit and when I showed back up at his house six months ago. He'd waited a year for me then. Why not now?

"Then Jafney of all people shows up one day." He marched straight on in his rant like he hadn't even heard me. "Jafney. All flirty and hair-flippy. Who I hadn't seen since the last day I saw you. Does that sound like coincidence to you?"

Again, he didn't seem to expect an answer.

"And Jafney has a picture of you kissing Wyck. Wearing the clothes I left you in at the theater. Coincidence?"

"Umm, I . . ."

"It was obvious that Wyck had changed something in the past to force you to pretend to be in a relationship with him."

"It was?" Finn got it. Without me having to explain a word. He'd known this whole time. "I mean, yeah. It was."

"So," he went on, "after I kissed Jafney—"

"That . . ." Mmmm. "That is not the response I personally think you should have chosen."

"Really?" He had the gall to look genuinely shocked. "I thought it was a stroke of brilliance."

"It was a stroke of something, all right."

"It was the most direct route."

"What are you talking about? Route to what?"

"To you."

"To me?"

"I just told you, Bree. There was no freaking way I was going to wait around in Chincoteague. Not with Wyck O'Banion's paws all over you. Her tendrils are like yours, sticky or whatever you call it. Her dad was born in the 1940s. It was the only way I could think of to get here to your time. I was . . . hitching a ride."

"But you said she's your girlfriend."

"When did I say that?"

"At the café. You told me you were having breakfast with your girlfriend. And outside her house." I strained to recall his exact words. "You said, 'Remember I have a girlfriend. An amazing one.'"

"Yeah." He nodded. "You. I was having breakfast with you. And you were acting weird in the alley, so I was just like, 'Hey. No matter what happens, remember you're my girl.'"

The last few days tumbled upside down, a snow globe of misunderstanding. It was like rewatching a movie with a massive twist at the end. Every clue in every scene stuck out like a throbbing thumb.

"But then why have you been so standoffish this whole time?"

"We've been around Wyck or Jafney this whole time. We almost got caught the two times I nearly gave in and kissed you. In the alley and—"

"The cave," I said. "So this whole time that I've thought you moved on . . ."

"You thought I'd give up on us after only eight months? Good gracious, woman. It would take at least nine."

I lunged to kind of wrestle-kiss-strangle him.

"Poor Jafney," I said as I came up for air. I couldn't believe those words were coming out of my mouth.

"So now it's *poor Jafney*?"

"You were using her."

"To get to you. Because I thought you were in trouble." He waved his arms around at the cryostorage units. "Which you are."

"Why didn't you sneak off to tell me all this the moment you got here?"

"My pull to Jafney isn't as strong as it is to you. I've had to stay in close proximity to her because I worried that if I didn't I'd accidentally synch. And then when I've been around you in public, I've been scared she or Wyck could overhear us. Besides, I thought you knew."

"So you've been kissing her this whole time?" I knew I didn't have a lot of space to judge, but still. The thought of his lips on anyone else's, but especially Jafney's. The very thought of it made my innards churn.

"That's the weird thing," he said. "After that first time, she hasn't really been affectionate except in public. You've actually seen the extent of our kissing."

"What do you mean?"

"When I've been around you, well, you've seen her. She's all over me. That was the reason I brought Georgie along. To kind of chaperone and help me deflect if Jafney got too handsy, but it hasn't even been an issue. In private, she's friendly and all, but she hasn't tried anything."

"Are you saying Jafney thinks you're a bad kisser?" I asked.

Finn raised an eyebrow. He scooped me up with one arm and laid into my lips smooth and slow until my toes tingled and my knees went weak.

"Not to be braggy," he said while I was still a pile of mush in his arms, "but you've trained me well."

"You'd better not have kissed her like that."

"Well, not like *that,* but my point is, don't you think it's odd? Her affection all seems to be for show, and it all seems to be for your benefit."

"Mine?"

"Who else? You're the only one she's done it around. And then the fact that she even took that picture of you kissing Wyck. What was that about? Why did she even care?"

"So then why were you so upset at the thought of her getting into trouble for bringing you here?"

"Part of it was that I was scared if I got busted I'd have no choice but to synch to Chincoteague. And the other part, well, I really do feel kind of guilty about using her. She's not that bad. I think you guys could even be friends."

I gave him a withering look.

"Okay, maybe friends in an alternate universe." Finn grinned, and his dimple took a dive into his cheek. Adorable. And yet delusional.

Maybe Jafney wasn't the spiny-hulled sea urchin of a man-thief that I thought. But no way in blark did that mean we would ever be friends.

"Well, you're sticking to me now." I wrapped my arms around him.

He kissed the top of my head. "Always."

We stood there, resting in each other's embrace for a beat longer than was probably safe. "So." Finn's shoes squeaked against the cold metal floor as he pulled away to survey our surroundings. He rubbed his hands together and blew on them. "You've clearly been busy. What do we know?"

I only had time to give him the stunner-zap version.

ICE had been kidnapping Shifters. No clue why.

Wyck changed my past. No clue why.

My future self stopped me from reverting that change. *Really* no clue why.

"And you're sure it was Future You that stopped you from reverting the change that Wyck made?" Finn asked.

"I think I know what I look like."

"No, I mean, it couldn't have been some evil clone of you?"

"That's the thing. She didn't seem evil. She seemed . . ." My voice trailed off as I realized the first word that came to mind.

"Seemed what?" His brow knit together in the middle. "Confused? Angry?"

"She seemed desperate."

"That's not good."

"I know."

"Well, what did she say when you asked her about the clue?"

"What clue?"

"The clue." More brow knittage. "*To save his, destroy yours* and all those numbers and letters?"

"Oh, umm. I didn't really pin her down on details about—"

"You *did* ask her?"

"I may not have gotten around to it, per se." I squinched up my face. "As in, I didn't."

"What the huh, Bree?"

"Everything happened so fast!"

"You receive an ominous-sounding message from your ominous-acting future self in ominous conditions, and then you don't bother to question that same future self about it when you run into her?"

"I was preoccupied."

"You had the note in your pocket!"

"I had Wyck's tongue down my throat!"

Wrong. Thing. To. Say.

Finn's face turned purple. He clutched the edge of the soligram in front of him until the pixels fell apart like confetti. One by one, I unclenched his fingers.

"I should have been there to protect you," he said.

"There was nothing you could have done. It was Future Me

that stopped the timeline reversion. He hasn't hurt me. I don't know exactly why she wants me hanging around Wyck, but she does. She hasn't been wrong yet, has she?" I hooked my pinky around his, and it relaxed. "She was right about you. About us."

"I am rather fond of her."

"I heard a rumor she has a crush on you."

"What can I say?" He kissed the bridge of my nose. "We're compatible."

Compatible.

The word snapped me back to the task at hand.

"That's what she said."

"Is that joke still around?" Finn chuckled.

"What joke?"

"That's what she . . . never mind."

"Compatibility," I said. "That's the word Lafferty used the other day when she was talking to Raspy."

"Raspy?"

"The guy in the silver suit." I'd already explained to Finn that Raspy was the kidnapper. "Lafferty said an unchipped Shifter has been feeding her information. I think she means him."

"Why would he do that?"

"No idea."

"And compatible with what?" Finn asked.

"Or who," I said, almost without thought. But once it was out there, it seemed plausible. "Lafferty said they have to trick Neos' tendrils to allow them to Shift. Maybe ICE is kidnapping Shifters to study their tendrils, figure out how to force the Neos' tendrils to act the same way."

"Well—"

"It makes so much sense." I was on to something here. "That could be why they've been kidnapping Shifters from the past rather than the present. They know that after Shifters came out of hiding, people would notice if large numbers of them went missing. But in the past . . ."

"I don't know. It seems like—"

"No one would know the difference." I held up a finger to Finn. I didn't want to lose my train of thought. "Even the kidnapped Shifters' families probably think that they were killed in another era. As an unchipped Shifter, Raspy would know where to find Havens, and then he burns them down to keep other Shifters from the future from putting the pieces together. They'd just think it was a normal fire. And it's not like their families could go to a chronocrime investigator like they could now. The Shifters just—poof—disappeared. No one to miss them."

"*No one* misses them? As a pastling, I find that a little—"

"No. That's wrong."

"Exactly."

I pushed past Finn toward the cryochambers that lined the wall.

"Nava's from the present. Why would they have taken her?" I thought back on all my time spent at Resthaven. She didn't have a lot of visitors. The woman was 107 years old. I couldn't recall any outside friends. Then again, she'd been in Resthaven a long time. Longer than anyone else there, probably. It's not like she could disappear with nobody noticing. Nurse Granderson loved her like she was his own mother. And nothing got past Quigley.

Maybe ICE took her as a not-so-silent threat to the Haven. Just to prove that they could.

"Knock, knock," said Finn.

"Who's there?" I answered automatically.

"Ahh. You remember I'm here."

"Sorry," I said. "It's like I've slipped into lone wolf mode the last few days, trying to figure out a way into this place."

"Rawrr." He slipped behind me and put his hands on my shoulders.

"Yeah, that growling thing is going to need to stop."

"My point is"—he took my hands in his—"you're not alone. But I would like to get out of this creeptastic place as quickly as possible."

"Agreed."

"What were you hoping to find?"

"I don't know." I traced my index finger along the smooth bubbles. About twenty of them were lit up now, the top of each kidnapped Shifter's head visible through the front glass. "An off switch?"

I paused at one of the middle bubbles, counted the ones to the top and bottom of it. It was the one that had held Nava the last time I was here. It was empty now.

"Nava's gone."

"The old lady from Resthaven?"

"She was right here."

"Maybe they moved her."

I went and looked in all the other compartments for her shock of white hair.

"No."

"Maybe she's . . ." Finn gestured toward the center tank, the body inside twitching as the cloudy substance swirled around it.

I'd avoided looking closely at it until now. But, no, the person in that tank was too big to be frail Nava.

"Or she might be . . ." Finn gulped rather than finish pointing out the most probable outcome. I mean, she was 107 years old. There was no telling what was involved in ICE's experiments. And it had been fifty years since I'd seen her here.

"How far back do you think some of these victims go?" Finn was trying to change the subject, I could tell. And I was grateful for it.

I shrugged. "They could be from any time period. And just because they were taken from a Haven in a particular year doesn't mean they actually live in that era."

I moved over to sift through a pile of personal effects that were stacked off to the side. None of it looked like it was from the recent past. Clothing that stank of smoke, a leather satchel with a singed strap, a waterproof wallet with any identification removed.

"I know this man." Finn held up an engraved silver pocket-watch. "Alonso Ontiveros. My dad is friends with him. He was born forty-something years into my future. He's a historian, I think. Specialized in the Renaissance, maybe? He came over for dinner a few times, and I met him once when I Shifted with my father to—" Finn snapped his fingers as he tried to recall where he'd seen Alonso. His face fell.

"At the Haven from the 1666 fire. He stayed there a lot," he said. "He's a good guy. He didn't deserve this."

"No one deserves this." I gestured to the bubbles where row upon row of Shifters were now frozen. "Whatever exactly *this* even is."

"But how did the kidnapper bring them here?" Finn dropped the watch back into the pile of goods. "I'm only able to Shift into my future because of your wonky tendrils."

"I prefer 'exceptional brain,' thank you very much." But he made a good point. "There's only one way that I can see. We already know that Raspy is an unchipped Shifter. But he must be like me. Conceived in one time and born in another."

"How often does that happen?" asked Finn. "I mean, I know you and Jafney have that in common. Are there many others?"

"No, it's rare. Not unheard of, but rare. There might be more than we know. Most people keep it quiet."

I shuddered. The thought of another Shifter willingly doing this sickened me. My Com gave a beep to let me know that forty minutes had passed. It felt like it had been so much shorter than that.

"We'd better go," I said. We'd need to find an alternate way out. I couldn't go back through the transportation tubes. There'd been a few portholes lining the hall outside this room. Hopefully, one of them was an exit to the outside.

As we walked past the center tank, the cloudy fluid still sloshing, I pressed my hand to the glass. The jerking movements inside had whimpered to occasional twitches. A tear leaked from the corner of my eye.

"I wish we could get them out of there," I said.

"I know, but we don't know how this equipment works. We could end up hurting them worse."

"How did it come to this?" I said.

"What do you mean?"

"Where did we go wrong?" I wiped the smudge of my fingerprints away. "In your time, being a Shifter is so uncomplicated."

"Less complicated, but I wouldn't say it's uncomplicated. It's hard hiding. And Mom has serious angst over how many plates to put out each night."

"But she's not single-handedly fighting an evil organization which doesn't give a flying blark about screwing up the space-time continuum."

"Hey," he said, stopping me in my tracks. He tilted my chin up. "You're not doing anything single-handed. You are never going to face this alone."

I wanted it to be true. But we both knew he couldn't make that promise. No one could. There were plenty of things I had to face alone. There was only one reverter, and it was mine. If there was any good from this timeline change, it was that ICE didn't seem to know about the reverter's existence now. They didn't know I was a threat. But if we got caught here, that could all change.

I didn't let any of my fears splash onto him, though. He didn't need that. Instead, I gave a resolute little nod and walked with him to the exit that led to the hallway I'd entered from. We crouched to the edge of the doorway as it slid open just in case there was someone on the other side. We were fine. No one there.

My spirits boosted as we made our way down the hall. Each porthole was marked with a small icon at the bottom signifying its destination. Fork for cafeteria. Leaf for outside . . . or greenhouse? Couldn't risk it. And then there it was, the last one, about ten feet away from the opening to the transport tube. Emergency exit.

I put my foot through the exit hatch and immediately knew something was wrong. My foot stuck like it had been locked into concrete. A red warning light began to flash in the hallway. Apparently, they were more concerned with preventing escape than entry.

Finn grabbed me by the armpits and tried to pull me out. No luck. "What now?"

"Don't panic." I shot my magno-grappling hook at the ceiling, latched my palms onto the handle, and triggered the device. It jerked my arms to the edge of their sockets and my Com slipped from my grasp and fell to the floor, but it was no good. I didn't move an inch.

"Okay, panic a little," I said.

"We'll just tell them we got lost." Finn picked my Com up.

"Finn, that might work for me, but the second they ID you, they'll discover that you're a chronofugitive."

"I haven't done anything wrong yet," he said. "Surely getting lost won't count as a crime."

"Doesn't matter," I said. "They could chip you just to make sure you don't flee to another century after you commit the crime."

"But what if it turns out to be something simple? Like a parking ticket?"

"We already know it isn't some minor infraction, Finn. Level Five means kidnapping, murder, or arson."

Before I could think of any way out of our (literally) sticky situation, burly men in red scrubs slipped through the porthole closest to the entrance to the Lab. One of them was a Shavie, whom I recognized from our altercation in Bergin's office last year. I'd nicknamed him Baldy. Even though I knew he hadn't done it on this timeline, and therefore had no memory of it, I bristled at the cruelty he was capable of. The guy had tried to decapitate me.

Finn yanked on my torso as hard as he could.

"Oww." All it served to do was pop three of my joints.

"Sorry, sweetie," he whispered.

As his stubble scratched against my cheek, a ripple of energy zipped through me. Finn was gearing up for a synch. He must have felt it at the same moment because his breathing calmed.

Phew.

But also . . . dang. There was no way I could explain just disappearing. My cover would be blown.

Finn curled himself around me protectively.

How anyone could ever accuse him of some heinous crime was laughable. I mean, come on. Finn? Killing someone? Or kidnapping . . .

Kidnapping.

There was no way to explain Finn's presence here. But there might be a way to explain mine. That is, if he had forced me up into the Cryostorage Unit against my will.

"Please!" I grabbed Finn's arm and pushed it up so it was around my neck. "Let me go."

"Huh?" Finn tried to pull his arm away, but I gripped it to me tighter and acted like I was choking.

"Help me," I croaked at the scrubs. They looked at each other, at a temporary loss of what to do. Clearly, they hadn't prepared for this scenario. They probably thought they were being sent up here to take care of a lookie-loo, not a deranged criminal and his hostage.

"Ohh . . ." Finn had finally caught on.

"Halt!" Baldy yelled, advancing toward us.

"No, you halt!" Finn flicked my Com open to the stunner.

Nice.

"I have a gun!" he yelled.

"Stunner," I said under my breath.

"A stunner," said Finn. "And I'm not afraid to use it."

From the looks on the scrubs' faces, they didn't give a flying chunk o' blark what Finn was holding. There were three of them. One of him.

But Finn didn't turn the stunner on them. He jabbed the metal into the flesh on my neck. It poked my jugular and made me catch my breath.

"Take one more step and I zap her into oblivion," said Finn.

That's right. My boyfriend's a badass.

"Everyone, just calm down." The nearest red scrub lowered his own stunner. Baldy, however, was apparently not willing to take orders from anyone. He advanced down the hall.

"Scream a little," Finn whispered in my ear as he clutched me hard to his chest, maintaining his death grip on the Com pressed to my neck.

Not hard to fake that one. If his thumb slipped, I really would be in a heckapain. I yelped and pretended to try to wrench myself free.

"Stay where you are." A voice, eerily calm, came from right behind us. Lafferty had emerged from the gravity chamber and was straightening her skirt. I wasn't sure if she was talking to the scrubs, to Finn, or to me. We all froze.

Finn's head whipped back and forth like he was at Wimbledon. We were surrounded. Genuine alarm tightened his grip on the Com.

Then I felt it. A whirring in my pocket. The reverter.

Blark it to Blarkville. This couldn't have come at a worse time. There was no way that I could click it in front of a room full of ICEers.

"Bree," Finn breathed into my ear. His grip loosened, and I had to clutch his arm around me to remind him that he was kidnapping me.

"Look at yourself," he said.

One glance at my reflection in the shiny metal that lined the hall revealed the reason for his shock. My hair had suddenly become disheveled. I was wearing a different set of clothes than before. I recognized them as the same ones I had been wearing two days ago, only now they were rumpled and filthy. A darkness that ran deeper than skin now circled my eyes.

I was at the bull's-eye of whatever change had just taken place on the timeline.

"I'm afraid this section isn't part of the tour." Lafferty spoke calmly, addressing Finn. Lafferty was a nonShifter. She was oblivious to the change in my appearance. As unchipped Shifters, Finn and I were the only ones who could detect there had even been a change.

"Stay back," said Finn. "I mean it."

"What exactly do you hope to accomplish here, young man?" She gestured up the hall. "There's nowhere to go."

The whirring of the reverter had already begun to slow. I pulled it from my pocket. Lafferty narrowed her eyes at the glowing contraption.

"Where did you get that?" she said. "That's a Pick. What have you done to it?"

This was now one change I *had* to fix. If I didn't, my one advantage—of being just another anonymous Shifter, a devoted girlfriend of one of their Neos—would disappear with the other timeline.

She tried to grab the reverter, her greedy fingers aimed at my only hope of repairing whatever had been broken.

"No!" I shrieked, pushing her away. But Lafferty caught the edge of the reverter, and it clattered to the ground between us.

I dove for it at the same moment as she did. But with one foot still stuck in the emergency exit and Finn's arm wrapped around me, I was like a sled dog jolting at the end of its tether. I only managed to brush the tips of my fingers against it. The reverter rolled down the hall toward the open porthole. It teetered on the edge.

"Finn!" I yelled.

He locked gazes with Lafferty, then they both sprinted at it like a starter pistol had fired. Finn reached it first. Lafferty lunged at the same moment, but instead of grabbing the reverter, she grabbed at Finn's hair.

"Oww," he yelled, and from the satisfied grin on her face, I knew Lafferty had gotten a few strands.

Finn ran back to me and pressed the reverter into my hand. The whirring had dulled to a hum. I only had a minute or two left. He grabbed me around the waist, and I pushed the heart-shaped button. Before I had depressed it all the way in, though, I felt a familiar sensation of tingles work their way up my arms to my shoulders until they met at the top of my spine and shivered all the way down.

"No, Finn, wait!" I said. But it was too late. The hallway faded before me.

We landed in a heap on his deck.

chapter 17

"I'M SO SORRY," Finn repeated over and over as we made our way up to his house.

I still clutched the reverter, useless and unmoving, in my fist. I knew I had no right to be mad at him. He had acted on protective instinct. Still, as I sniffed a stain on my sleeve (Ugh, what was that, puke?), it was hard not to be miffed. Whatever had changed in my life, it was permanent. And now, I was back to Public Enemy #1 at ICE. They knew about the reverter.

"I promise next time I'll be more careful," he said.

"Next time?" I whirled around. "No, no, no. There is no next time. You aren't going anywhere."

"Wait. You would have me stay in Chincoteague while you head back there?"

"Uhh, I would have you locked up in your family's safe if I could."

"Those people after you are monsters."

"You're not coming back with me," I said. "It's not safe for you in the future."

"It's not safe for *you* in the future!"

"It's not safe for me anywhere!"

I pinched the bridge of my nose. Arguing with Finn was pointless. I just wouldn't bring him back with me. That was that. And I'd threaten Jafney with her ever-lovin' life if she even thought about it. Not that I imagined she wanted anything to do with Finn Masterson at this point. I started back up to his house.

"That's my point," he said, trailing behind me. "You have no idea what those eight months were like for me, not knowing what had happened to you, if you were even alive or dead. It was torture. I can't do that again."

I'd only experienced a sliver of what he had. A few days of separation. A few days of not knowing how he was, where he was.

He'd nailed it.

Torture.

But only one thing would be even more torturous—knowing that I had had a hand in his capture. I'd return safely, feed the authorities some trumped-up story that he was drunk, tell them that he didn't hurt me and had let me go freely. Surely chronoinvestigators wouldn't track him across the centuries.

But he could never return to mine.

We'd reached the back entrance to his house. I leaned against him and took a deep breath before we faced the impending onslaught. He looked down and gave me a "Shall we?" look. I heaved a sigh and pushed the door open.

Charlotte walked in from the kitchen. When she saw me, her face lit up. Before I had a chance to say "hello," though . . .

Pop, pop, pop.

Quigley, John, and Georgie materialized in front of us and blocked Finn's mom from view. John looked confused. Georgie looked like Christmas had come early. Quigley looked, well . . .

"What in the name of all the Grecian gods and god-ettes put together have you done?" she yelled.

"I can explain," I said.

"Please do." A vein in the middle of Quigley's forehead throbbed. "Because for the life of me, I'm having a difficult time coming up with your rationale behind breaking into ICE's headquarters. After I expressly forbid you from doing anything that might draw attention to Resthaven. I've had chronoinvestigators crawling all over the place for the last twelve hours."

"You did what?" Charlotte rushed to Quigley's side.

"With Finn in tow," said Georgie gleefully. "It's been all over the news. Bree and her mystery attacker."

"I wasn't 'in tow,'" said Finn. "I Shifted to ICE's headquarters from Jafney's house."

"A house that I expressly forbade you from going to," screeched Charlotte. "That poor girl's been through enough as it is."

Oh, yes. Poor Jafney.

"And you." Charlotte turned on her daughter.

"What'd I do?" said Georgie.

"You've known about this for half a day and you didn't think to come and tell us what was going on?"

"And miss the excitement?"

"Georgiana Joyce Masterson!" Charlotte was really getting her shriek on now. "This is not a game, young lady."

I had to agree with Charlotte on this one.

"Georgie, you were supposed to be keeping an eye on Finn," I said.

"Uhh, she was supposed to be my chaperone to stop Jafney from acting like an amorous octopus," said Finn.

"She was *supposed to* keep her feet firmly planted in the twenty-first century!" yelled Charlotte.

"How bad is it?" John turned to Quigley, frowning.

"Finn's wanted on armed kidnapping charges," said Quigley. "Not to mention breaking and entering. Congratulations, Finnigan, you are now officially classified a Level Five Chronofugitive."

Charlotte collapsed to the sofa, fanning herself.

"Mercy," she said. "I'd say you were going to be the death of me if your sister hadn't tapped the last nail into that coffin years ago."

"But Finn was already classified a fugitive," I pointed out. "Now we just know what he's accused of. Besides, he saved my butt back there. If he hadn't shown up, I would have been caught anyway, and then I wouldn't have had a good excuse. Now, I just look like a victim, and he looks like some deranged psychopath."

"Thank you, sweetie," said Finn.

"You're very welcome." I smiled.

"And what if Finn hadn't shown up, Bree?" John was calmer than his wife, but there was an anxiety in his voice not usually there.

"But he did. I'll return safe and sound. As long as Finn lays low, I doubt they'll track him down here." I looked to Quigley to back me up, which she did reluctantly.

"It is unlikely they'd escalate it to a temporal manhunt," she said.

Charlotte began to whimper.

"How did you get past their security?" asked John. "Or did you Shift there like Finn?"

"Ah ha!" I yelled. "See. That could have happened. Then it wouldn't have been my fault."

"Well?" asked Quigley. "Did you?"

"No. I, ummm . . ." Oh, this part was going to go over like a lead balloon. "I may have slipped Wyck some opium and taken his hair. Then I snuck out during his Shift to poke around."

I said it in a rat-a-tat cadence, hoping the faster it came out, the faster they would get over their collective anger.

No such luck.

"You what?" Finn took a giant step back, but at least he didn't let go of my hand. That had to be a good sign.

The rest of their responses kind of blurred together. I distinctly heard the words reckless, dangerous, foolhardy, rechip you myself, aftermath, and better than a telenovela (pretty sure that one was Georgie).

"Look, it's not like Wyck's some blushing innocent in all this," I said. "He deserved what he got. He's already made one change, and . . ." I looked down at my grungy outfit. Great shades of blark.

"He was the one who changed my past this time, too," I said.

"Do you have proof of that?" said Quigley.

"Wyck was the only NeoShifting at the time. It had to be

him. And at the last minute, he decided to go to the recent past. He's trying to destroy me!"

"What motivation does he have to ruin your life?" asked John.

"Vendetta," I said. "For getting him expelled from the Institute."

"You're thinking on the wrong timeline," said Quigley. "He hasn't been expelled on this timeline. Why would he have a vendetta against you now?"

"Maybe he was trying to get ahold of the reverter again." Finn snapped his fingers. "Make her so desperate she just hands it over."

"No," I said. "Even their medical director didn't recognize the reverter for what it was. She just realized it was a Pick that had been tampered with."

"Besides," said Georgie, "if Wyck was trying to get the reverter back, wouldn't it make more sense for him to be the one to drug Bree and take it that way?"

"Yeah, but it's not like he has opium just lying around," I said.

"And you do?" Charlotte asked.

"It's not mine. It's my—"

I froze and stared at the wall of admonishment and concern in front of me. A wall that was missing one key parental unit.

"Where's my mom?" I asked.

"I haven't seen her," said Charlotte.

I looked at Quigley.

"I've been busy at Resthaven cleaning up this mess." Quigley frowned. "She hasn't been in."

"That would have been the first place she would have gone when she heard I'd supposedly been kidnapped." Panic stirred in my stomach. There was no way she would have waited twelve hours, not with it all over the news.

"I'm sure she's okay." Finn tried to put a reassuring arm around me, but I pulled away.

"She's not. I can feel it. Look at me. Whatever the change was,

I'm a mess now. I have to get back to her." I willed my tendrils to take me back, right then and there, but they didn't budge.

Quigley was trying unsuccessfully to hide her own concern.

"Check in with me as soon as you're able," she said. And with that she disappeared.

"I'm going back with you." Finn pulled me closer to his side, and what I would have done to sink into those arms forever, to keep him with me.

"You can't."

"I just got you back," he said. "I can't lose you again."

"You never lost me," I said, even as my tendrils started to prickle. "And you never will."

"I know." He kissed the top of my head. The rest of the Mastersons had the decency to turn away and pretend to talk amongst themselves.

"Promise me if Jafney comes here, you won't use her to go back to my time," I said. "She doesn't need to be pulled any further into this."

"I promise." Finn looked stricken but resigned. "If you run into her, would you apologize for me? I know it was for a good cause, but I still hate that I put her in danger."

"I will."

"And for me, too," said Georgie.

"What did you do?" Finn narrowed his eyes at her.

"There might be the tiniest stink bomb planted beneath her bed."

"You did that for me?" I said.

"For you." Georgie gave me a big hug. "And for my own entertainment."

"Aww."

"Could we have a moment alone?" Finn asked his family.

Charlotte gave me a kiss on the cheek. "You be careful, dear."

John patted my shoulder.

When they left, Finn pulled me into an embrace. I knew full

well that every minute I was gone was another minute I'd need to explain away to the authorities to keep Finn safe. A minute I didn't know if my mother was all right, if she was even alive. But it was also a minute I wouldn't have to wonder when I'd see him next.

"Hey," he said, tilting my chin up. "This is temporary. Your mom's going to be fine."

"Yeah." I tried to force a smile but couldn't muster one. Finn's optimism was usually more contagious than capuchin fever.

Not this time.

"I love you," he said.

"I love you, too." There was so much feeling pressed into those words, it physically hurt to say them.

"I'll see you soon," he whispered. His kiss lingered on my lips as the familiar tug pulled on my every cell. When I opened my eyes, that's exactly where I was. A cell.

A jail cell.

chapter 18

WHEN I WAS TWELVE, my mom got sick on a work assignment. Yellow fever. The virus somehow slipped past the decon-
tamination chamber after she got back, and she ended up
quarantined for a week while the Office of Temporal Health back-
tracked her movements to contain any potential outbreak.

After I'd been immunized, they let me stay with her at the hospital. I remember curling up next to her on the narrow hospital
bed and running my fingers through her thick mane of hair that
was so her—a little wild, a little untamed, always a bit of a mess,
so much fun. Beautiful.

"Someday," I had said, "I'm going to invent a medicine that
protects everyone against every sickness ever."

"Hmm. What about heartache?" She snuggled me up close.

"Especially heartache," I remember saying. "It's the one that
hurts the worst."

➤──

"Mom?" I recognized her profile immediately. She sat in the corner of the six-by-six feet holding cell, a hoodie pulled around
her face. Her posture spoke defeat. I rushed over and threw my
arms around her. "You're alive. I was so scared."

"Bree?" She peeled me away. "What are you doing? You can't
be here."

"What happened?" I asked. "Why are *you* here?"

"Bree . . ."

"Never mind. It doesn't matter. I'm going to get you out."

"It's not that simple." She pulled back her hoodie, and that's when I actually saw her. In all her bald glory.

The thing about hair is that you don't think about how it defines your appearance until it's gone. But in our society, where your hair is your identity, it doesn't just define your appearance, it defines *you*. It allows you to buy groceries. It gets you from point *A* to point *B*. It opens doors. Literally.

I ran a shaking hand over my mother's bald scalp. She was a Shavie now. It was like staring down some alien that had taken over her body.

"What happened?" I let out a choked gasp.

Mom twisted away from me, all twitchy and fidgety. She peered around the corner of the force field that held her captive. We were alone, but she chewed on the tiny sliver that was left of her thumbnail. The rest were bloody stumps.

"You can't be here," she said again.

"Tell me why you're here."

"I got caught." Her voice trembled.

"Caught? What are you talking about?"

"With the sleeping medicine."

"What sleeping medicine? Wait. The narcotics? Mom! That's impossible. I threw those in the incinerator."

Mom stood and paced the tiny cell.

"The chronocrime unit arrived the morning after you took the vial."

"That was yesterday. That's when I was drugging Wyck."

"It was Wyck who went to the police."

"What?"

"He told them he'd caught me trying to throw it into the incinerator at the Institute. He had the bottle as proof," she said.

"That doesn't make sense," I said. "I was the one who threw it in the incinerator. How did he even get ahold of it?"

"I don't know, but my fingerprints were all over it."

"Well, so were mine."

"No. Yours had been wiped clean."

"What does it matter? They're fingerprints! Everyone knows they're completely unreliable." Again though, it didn't make sense. If Wyck was out to destroy me, the most direct route was to put *me* in this cell. And if he was after the reverter, the most direct route was to drug *me,* like Georgie had said. "At least it was only fingerprints. That evidence will never hold in court."

My mother glanced away.

"Mom?"

She swallowed and blew out a slow breath. I could tell she was fighting back a deluge of tears.

"What aren't you telling me?" I asked, holding back my own.

"When they searched our house, they found . . . the others."

"The other whats?"

"The other bottles."

"What other bottles?"

"I had more of the sleeping elixir that I'd bought in your father's time," she said. "And . . . other medicine, too. Pills to help me stay awake."

"*More* drugs?"

"I didn't think—"

"Yeah. You didn't think! You didn't think about me. You didn't think about Dad." It was the first time I'd ever called him that instead of "my father," not that these were the circumstances in which I wanted to suddenly feel a kinship with him. Then something occurred to me.

"How do you even remember any of this?" I asked. As an unchipped Shifter, she should have been as clueless to the events leading up to the change as I was. She should have been trying to piece together her last few days like I would have to piece together mine.

"When the police showed up, the first thing they did was check my chip. One more damning piece of evidence." She twisted her hands in unending knots. "They assumed I tampered with it to get the drugs. I couldn't argue otherwise or it would have exposed the Haven. The police turned my chip back on."

"They what?'

"I'm Anchored, Bree. Permanently."

"Mom, I can't . . . I'll fix this."

"Bree . . ."

"No. I'll fix this. I'll, umm, I'll blackmail Wyck to go and change it back or . . . or . . . Charlie! Charlie got accepted into the Neo program. I can talk him into going back and stopping Wyck or . . . something."

"Bree, stop." A single tear slid down her cheek and splashed to the floor. "When the doctors checked my system, they said that if I had taken any more, I would have overdosed."

"What are you saying?"

"I think this may have saved my life."

I couldn't lose her again. But this wasn't a life. This wasn't *her* life.

We held each other, sobbing. With her hair gone, it was like she'd shrunken three sizes.

Her hair.

"Why are you a Shavie?" I asked.

"They, umm"—her shoulders shook—"they had one of your hairs with them. Wyck told them that he had caught me using it to get to the incinerator."

I let loose a wide swath of swears, every word I'd come up with for that snerfwad for six months.

"Wyck won't get away with this."

"The thing is," my mom choked out, and it was the most pitiful sound, like someone had stepped on a bleating lamb, "he didn't do anything I hadn't already . . . considered."

"What do you mean? What are you talking about?"

"I mean, when you took the laudanum to school to dispose of it, it gave me the idea. I knew I needed some way to dispose of the bottles in a pinch. I hadn't done it yet. I hadn't stolen your hair, but . . ."

"But you were going to?"

She nodded and tried to look at me but couldn't meet my eyes.

"I should have taken you to a detox center when I found out about the drugs," I said. "This is all my fault."

"No." She finally met my gaze full on. "I did this. I'm done blaming anyone else."

There was this saying my grandpa always used to toss around. There's nothing as inevitable as inevitability. Grams said she heard it so much she should cross-stitch it onto a pillow so he could just point to it. But the thought of it sitting on their couch, staring at her, was too depressing.

I wondered how depressed she'd be to see her only child trapped in prison with no hair and no hope.

Mom slumped over, curled into herself, like the very act of existing was too much. I tried to muster more fury at Wyck, but the truth was that he hadn't forced her to take those drugs. He hadn't turned her into an addict or made her so desperate she had considered using her only child to keep that addiction going. He'd peeled away the façade to expose the inevitable.

But maybe it wasn't inevitable. I thought about Quigley's Point Zero theory. I didn't believe that Mom had always been destined to be some sort of drugster junkie. Mom had never used so much as an aspirin before all this mess with ICE started.

My pocket let out a low whir. I yanked out the glowing reverter and yelled, "Not now!" as if the person meddling with his past could hear me. Mom was still in jail, and I still had all my teeth, so apparently it wasn't a change that had too direct an impact on me.

"Aren't you going to get that?" Mom asked.

"I'm not leaving you."

"Bree, you can't stay here. You know that. And you're the only hope that unchipped Shifters have right now of maintaining any semblance of sanity."

No pressure or anything.

"You have to focus on ICE." She held my hands in hers. "You have to go back to the Institute and pretend that everything is normal, that you knew nothing of my drug use."

"No." I squeezed her hands. "I can't do that."

Mom let go and instead gripped me by the shoulders. Gone was the whimpering waif.

"You will." She positioned my thumb on the end of the reverter. "Now go."

"But I—"

"Go."

"I love you so much," I said.

"And I love you." She kissed my forehead and pressed my thumb down before pulling herself away. "More than all the minutes of my life."

This change couldn't have come at a worse moment. I needed more time with her. I needed to know she'd be okay, that somehow I'd fix this.

I closed my eyes as I faded and tried to conjure a mental picture of Mom—my real mom—to cling to, but it was no use. This shrunken Shavie had rooted itself in my mind like a weed.

When I opened them, I was inches away from another weed in my life.

"Leto Malone."

I pulled back my fist and slammed it into his face as hard as I could.

chapter 19

I'D GIVE THIS TO LETO. The man knew how to take a punch. He smeared the drip of blood away from his nose with the back of his hand and spit another trickle out of his mouth. I didn't think I'd hit him that hard, but whatever. We were tucked away in a dark back corner of a nearly deserted convenience store.

"What was that for?" he asked.

"For treating the space-time continuum like your personal playground." I got another little shove in and pulled my fist back again, but he caught it midair.

"Do we know each other?" He gripped his forehead as if it was throbbing.

"Oh, I know you. And stop being so dramatic." I hadn't hit him *that* hard.

"Look, kiddo, I never met you before in my life." He winced and shook his head, his eyes slipping out of focus.

"Let me guess what you're going to change." I tapped the reverter against my chin, thinking back on all his many changes I'd had to revert. "You have another parking ticket that needs fixing. No? A new slimy scheme to shirk innocent people out of a few thousand quiddies? Or maybe just going back to pick some winning lottery numbers."

We were in a convenience store after all. I peered over the aisle and ahh, yes. There was his past self, up at the store counter at the front purchasing lottery tickets.

"How'd you know—?" He probably wasn't used to being addressed this way, especially by a seventeen-year-old girl. His eyelids slipped into their usual snaky slits. "Who are you?"

"It doesn't matter. You won't remember any of this anyway." I was wasting time as it was. The sooner I got back to my mom, the better. I tapped the reverter to the bare skin at the nape of Leto's neck and clicked the end.

Before he began to fade, he reeled to the side and doubled over, clutching his stomach. Leto tried to hold himself upright by grabbing a display of scoop-your-own Blinky Beans. He pulled on it so hard that the side snapped off. An avalanche of candy littered the floor.

"Leto?"

He clasped his hands over his ears and shuddered. When he pulled them away, the palms were covered in blood. He stared at me, his mouth a gaping maw.

And then he disappeared.

"What. The. Blark." I stared at the spot where he'd just been. A small puddle of his hemorrhaged blood reflected the look of horror on my face.

My tendrils prickled. My whole spine felt like it was vibrating.

Something was very, very wrong.

The store clerk rushed over to see what had fallen, and I didn't even bother trying to hide before I faded back to my time. I landed in the sloped basin of a drainage culvert. My foot skidded across a slick of mud. But when I lifted my shoe, I realized it was scarlet with what was actually congealing blood. I fought back a retch then followed the drips like a demented Gretel.

There'd be no candy at the end of this trail.

At the top of a spillway, the trail stopped. I looked over the edge. Leto lay in a heap at the bottom, moaning. I scrambled down to reach him.

"What's happening to me?" he said between gasps of pain. Blood continued to ooze from his ears.

"I don't know." I grabbed my speakeazy. "Stay calm, Leto. I'll get help."

"How do you know my name?"

"I . . . it doesn't matter." I started to call for medical assistance, but he reached up and covered my speakeazy.

"Don't." His voice was hoarse and strained.

"Huh?" I turned his face toward me, expecting his usual sneer, but there was something else entirely. Something I'd never seen on him before.

Affection.

Not just affection. Adoration. Like I was the biggest pile of cash he'd ever seen, walking around on two legs.

"Leto, you're really hurt. I need to call—"

And then he said the one thing I least expected to come out of his mouth.

"Do you think Ed would like the sea grass in Chincoteague?"

"What?"

He didn't remember my name. He didn't remember he'd once blackmailed me. But he knew the name of my pet pegamoo and my boyfriend's hometown?

"Aigh!" Leto crumpled over again, each breath a struggle.

"I have to call for help," I said. He was in really bad shape.

"No." He coughed and blood splattered the ground.

That's when I realized. He wasn't just hurt. He was . . . dying.

I was a free Shifter whose boyfriend was a Level Five Chronofugitive and whose mother was in jail for smuggling narcotics. And I was sitting next to the world's shadiest Neo. Who I'd just punched. And who was dying. I put away my speakeazy.

"You're so beautiful," he said. The look was back, like a devoted puppy.

"Look, Leto, I don't know what's happening to you or what you're playing at or how you know those things but—"

"Have you solved it yet?" He tried to sit up, but it was too hard for him. "Have you solved the clue? It has to be the key to all this."

"What clue? Key to what? Leto, what are you talking about?" Blark it. I had to get help, no matter what the consequences were. I pulled the speakeazy back out, but he wrenched it out of my hands.

"No. It will . . . complicate . . . things," he said between gasps.

"I don't think this can get much more complicated."

"No, focus on the clue. Focus on—" His eyes slipped out of focus, and for a moment, I thought he was gone. But then he started laughing. "Don't you see, Bree? To save his. To save *his*. I believe in you."

His laughter turned to a peaceful smile.

"Just let me look at you," he said.

"Finn?" I wasn't quite sure why I said it. It was ridiculous. This was Leto. But Leto was acting like *Finn*.

His only response was a cough. His coughs turned to gagging. His gagging turned to silence.

Leto's eyes drifted open, unblinking, and I knew he was gone.

I barely remembered standing up.

Barely remembered climbing out of that drainage ditch and running from the scene.

All I truly remembered was thinking, He knows my name. He knows my clue. No one can find me here. Honestly, I was probably in full-on shock at that point.

I was twenty yards away from the culvert slope when I heard the first scream.

"There's a body down there!"

I drew a deep breath and bobbed my bowed head like a buoy in the sea of lookie-loos who rushed past me to the spot where Leto lay.

"He's dead!"

Blend in. Blend in.

That's when I felt it. The reverter went off in my pocket.

I was surrounded by witnesses. There was no way to escape the crowd's notice and Shift. I started to walk more quickly to get out of the thick.

"Did you see anything?" A woman caught me by the shoulder. "You were walking from that direction, weren't you?"

"I . . . no. I mean, yes, I was walking from that direction. But I didn't see anything."

She peered at me like she was taking a mental snapshot, but she let me leave.

I kept my gait calm and even, trying to make my way out of eyeshot so I could click the reverter, but every time I looked back, the lady was still watching me.

The reverter began to slow. Ugh! Time was running out. I felt so trapped—that same feeling I'd had when this had happened at the movie with Wyck, and then again at ICE with Finn.

Wyck had chosen his timing well both times. It was like he'd somehow known when I'd be trapped and unable to get away and perform the reversion in time to stop the change. Like he'd chosen those specific moments to take away the people I love most in the world.

Wait. What if that was exactly what he'd done?

But there was no one in my life left to hurt. Well, no one but . . .

Mimi.

I gave up all pretense of calmness and broke into a run. I sprinted into a clothing boutique and ran back to the restrooms, but they were all locked.

"Ahem." The store attendant wore a pink suit and lifted a pert leg. She looked like a blarking flamingo. "May I help you?"

"I need your bathroom."

"Our facilities are reserved for customers only."

"Fine." I grabbed the first shirt in arm's reach, a hideous green feather and foil number. "I'll take this."

"Very well." She shuffled forward. Faster, lady! She brushed her hair against the lock. "Green is this season's freshest—"

I'd already slammed the door in her face. I yanked out the reverter and clicked the end.

Just as it stopped glowing.

"No!"

"Another size?"

I threw the door open, dumping the shirt on the ground as I raced out. This couldn't be happening. All the way to the Institute, I tried to think of some way to check if Mimi was all right other than simply calling her and asking her if she was all right. That would just freak her out if she was all right and freak her out worse if she wasn't all right.

No. She was all right.

She had to be all right.

I made it to the Institute in record time. As I ran through the school's halls, students shuffled out of the way.

"Are you okay, Bree?" asked Molly Hayashi.

"Fine!" I called without stopping. Molly knew who I was, so I was still a student here. I hoped that was a good sign.

I reached our room, and as I bent over to scan my hair, the door whished open. Mimi stood on the other side. She was startled but definitely alive.

"Thank goodness you're all right." I gave her a huge hug.

"Hi there . . . Bree?" She gave me a tentative pat-pat-pat on the back, and I pulled myself together. She didn't realize anything had changed or might be wrong. Again with the don't-freak-her-out.

"Sorry." I wiped the mists of relief from my eyes before she had a chance to notice. "I've had a really hard day. I'm just glad to see you."

"Oh. Well, I'm glad to see you, too."

That's when the overwhelming muchness of the day hit me, really hit me. Part of me wanted to go straight back to the jail and talk to my mom again, try to figure out a way to get her released. But I wouldn't be much help to anyone without some sleep.

"Are you headed out?" I squeezed past her and flopped onto my bed.

It wasn't until I hit the pillow that I realized something was different. Namely, my side of the room looked like the glitter fairy had vomited all over it.

"What the—?" But I bit back my words so fast that I chomped down on my tongue. This change had apparently affected me after all. It had made me . . . girly?

"Uhh, Bree." Mimi fidgeted at the doorway, glancing down the hall like she was expecting something.

"It's okay," I said. "You can leave. I'll just . . ." My voice trailed as I finally took the time to really look at my side of the room. The frames that usually held pictures of Mimi and I laughing throughout the years were different. Most were filled with Pennedy Addington and various people. Mimi was in a lot.

I wasn't in any of them.

A swell grew in my throat.

"Mimi, can I ask you a weird question?"

"Umm. Sure." The look on her face told me I didn't even need to ask.

Mimi wasn't my roommate on this timeline, much less my best friend. I couldn't let her see my confusion. She might turn me in for suspected Madness.

"I wanted to see if"—I searched the room for something to justify my barging in as I peeled myself off the bed—"if you'd finished your French assignment."

"Oh." She looked relieved although still confused. We must not even be study partners on this timeline. "Yes. Did you want to discuss it?"

"I did," I said, backing toward the door, "but I think I figured it out just now. Sorry to disturb you."

"No problem," she said brightly, her usual cheery self. The self she reserved for superficial friends. Acquaintances. Friends who didn't know she snored like a steam locomotive and held an irrational fear of rabbits.

"Well," she said, looking out into the hallway again, my cue to leave, I realized.

"I should go," I said. "You probably have a date with Charlie or something."

"Charlie?" Mimi said. "Charlie *Wu?*"

"Sorry. I thought maybe you and he . . ."

"He's a *transporter,*" she said.

So I guess there was my answer to how Shifter/Non relations were going.

"Yeah," I said. "I'll catch you later."

"Uh huh," Mimi said, but she already seemed to have forgotten I was there. She gritted her teeth and shut her eyes tight, leaning against the door frame to support herself.

The Buzz.

But before I could ask how she was on Buzztabs, she pushed her sleeve up and tapped a small nodule attached to the crook of her arm. Almost instantly, her features relaxed, and I could tell whatever pain she was in had lessened.

"I'll see you around," she said.

No, she wouldn't.

As the door whished shut behind me, I pressed my back against the wall, swallowing my silent scream. Three changes. Three changes that had been aimed squarely at me. I bet this was blarking Wyck again who'd done this.

When I caught up with him, I would . . . I would . . .

I bit back my fury. There was nothing I could do. I couldn't reclaim five lost years of best friendship. I couldn't grow my mom's hair back. I couldn't even force my tendrils back to Finn.

I was thankful Mimi was alive. Didn't give two whiffs of a monkey's butt about me, but alive. That contraption on her arm confirmed my fears, though. The Buzz was getting worse for chipped Shifters. It made sense. The more changes to the timeline, the further Shifters were from where they were supposed to be.

I passed Pennedy, Mimi's roommate now, in the hall, and she gave me a not-overly friendly nod, which I returned. Pennedy and I had always gotten along okay. It's just—well, it wasn't that I'd call Pennedy shallow. . . . No, actually, that's exactly what I'd call her.

My friendship with Pennedy had always been through Mimi. Come to think of it, most of my friendships at the Institute had had a Mimi-portal. She was pretty much the sole reason I hadn't become a full-on recluse my first year. I'd never operated under any pretense that Mimi didn't make me a better person. But I'd never stopped to consider that maybe I had made her a better person in return.

The real Mimi—my Mimi—would never have stared me out of her room just now. My Mimi would have swooped down on someone who was visibly hurting, whether they were friends or not, and held on tight until things were better. Maybe she had honed that through her friendship with me.

But it was pointless to debate. That wasn't my Mimi.

I contacted the correctional facility where my mom was being held, but a guard informed me that visiting hours were done for the day. I walked back to the entrance and pulled up the student directory, scrolling through the names until I found mine. My profile picture smiled back at me. It was like looking at a ghost. I had no idea who that girl was.

Back to watching someone hobble around on my phantom limb. Only now it was a phantom life.

I pulled my shirtsleeve to my nose, hoping for one more whiff of Finn's shampoo or my mom's perfume to linger on the threads. Again, I had the haunting thought from earlier: How did it come to this? I'd watched a man die in a ditch before my very eyes less than an hour ago. Whatever had happened to him, I was almost positive it was a result of NeoShifting. Leto had been one of ICE's most frequent customers, at least judging by the number of reversions I'd had to do on him. That had to have taken its toll.

And then there was the fact that Leto somehow recognized me. Not only recognized me, but he had feelings for me. And he knew things that only Finn and I knew. Then there was that comment Leto had made about the clue—what was that about? I hadn't told anyone but Mom and Quigley about the clue, and I hadn't given it much thought in the meantime. Finn was the one who had been so set on figuring the clue out since the moment we'd found it.

How and why would Leto Malone of all people have insight into it? The only person who could answer that was dead.

I looked back up to the directory. Room 752. Only two doors down from where I'd just come. Made sense, I guess. Room 752 was Pennedy's room on my timeline. I slowed as I approached the door, unsure of who or what I'd find behind it. It might be a casual acquaintance or an insta-bestie. Either way, I didn't really care. Whoever it was, I kind of disliked her already for her non-Miminess.

And when I opened the door, I realized I had a whole other set of reasons to dislike her.

Because my roommate on this timeline was Jafney.

➤━

Whenever I used to whine about someone growing up, my grandpa would look me square in the eyes and say, "You never know someone until you've flown a mile in their jetpack."

Which . . . sure. That was helpful when that one kid bit me in kindergarten. But Grandpa's philosophy failed to take a key thing into consideration.

What if it's someone you wish with every fiber of your being you'd never met?

"Are you blarking kidding me?" I was the first to speak after we'd sat there for a full minute eating eyefuls of each other. "We're *roommates?*"

"Looks like it," Jafney said. She picked up a frame off my desk that contained a picture of Wyck and me stratodiving. She chucked it into the waste chute. "Oops."

"What is your problem?" I asked.

"You are."

"I'm . . . what?" Un-blarking-lievable. "I tried to help you by turning off your chip. After you *asked* me to. And you can't blame me for this. I warned you that your reality could change."

"Yeah, well, you failed to mention you were going to steal the love of my life in the process," said Jafney.

"Steal the—? You should never have brought Finn to this century. He could have been Anchored!" I yelled.

"You forced my hand!" she yelled back.

"I know he kissed you, but Finn's not the love of your life!"

"Of course he isn't!"

"He's—what? Now I'm very confused!" And still yelling!

"You thought I was in love with Finn?"

"Oh, let's see." I tapped my chin. "You've been snogging his face off every time I've seen you. You made up the most atrociously sickeningly sweet pet names for him that I have ever heard. Basically, you've all but sent out engraved wedding invitations. So yeah. Silly me. I thought you were in love with Finn."

"Really?" She looked. . . . The only word for it was ecstatic. "Did it make you jealous?"

"Do pegamoos poop on the street? You were kissing my boyfriend."

"Uhh"—haughty came back—"you were kissing my boyfriend first. Well, I mean, he should be my boyfriend."

"I thought we just cleared this up. Finn was and is *my* boyfriend. Never yours." This didn't seem like it should even be a conversation.

"I'm not talking about Finn."

"Who else have I been—?" Oh. Holy Blark. "You're in love with Wyck?"

"Since we were First Years here at the Institute."

"So this whole time with Finn, you were trying to make *Wyck* jealous?"

"And you, too. I thought if I brought Finn here, maybe you'd remember that you had feelings for him."

I laughed—couldn't help it. "You think that's something I could ever forget?"

I stared at Jafney, trying to figure her out. I had to hand it to her, she was mad plinky at underhanded plotting. Hmm . . . on second thought, she and Wyck might be perfect for each other.

"So here we are, roomie," she said. "Both in love with the same guy."

"We are *not* both in love with the same guy. I love Finn. You apparently love Wyck." For some unfathomable reason.

"But you—"

"I was kissing Wyck to convince him that I'm his girlfriend so I could spy on ICE. That's all."

"You were using him?"

"Are you really in a position to judge? 'Cause last I checked, Finn wasn't delivered to the twenty-third century by trained unicorns."

"Fair enough." Her eyes started to cloud over. "I don't understand how it didn't work."

"What are you talking about? That was literally the worst plan *ever.*"

"But my future self said that turning off my chip was the way I could be with Wyck."

"Don't get me started on future selves," I said.

We relapsed into a simmering silence.

Jafney crossed her arms but uncrossed them quickly. She pulled a small nodule—just like the one Mimi had—from the crook of her elbow.

"What is this?" she asked.

"I'm not sure. It seems to be some kind of medicine pump."

"Hmm." Jafney took a small tool out from her desk and started to disassemble the pump.

"What are you doing?" I asked.

"Figuring out how it works."

"How do you know how to do that?"

"I had planned to study Chronotechnology at the Institute. Looks like I was able to on this timeline." She gestured to an award on her desk. "I like gadgets and stuff."

Sure enough, with deft fingers, she'd taken apart the whole apparatus within a minute.

"Looks like this last change to the timeline actually worked out pretty well for you then."

Jafney shrugged. "I'm still not with Wyck."

"So what was your next step?" I asked.

"What do you mean?"

"In your brilliant plan to make Wyck jealous. What were you going to do next?"

"I hadn't thought that far ahead. I was waiting for my future self to come back and give me more advice."

"And she hasn't?"

"No." Jafney gave me a look that let me know that she didn't want to talk about it.

She held up a pointy part on the device she'd dismantled. It looked like it had been bent to the side. "Injection mechanism has been jammed on this unit, but yeah. It's a medicine pump all right."

I handed her mine, and she was even faster now that she knew what she was doing.

"Yours, too. Nonfunctional. Looks like you and I just wear them for show."

She took out the tube of medicine and handed it to me.

"Same active ingredient as in Buzztabs," I said, reading the label. I calculated the concentration and whistled. "Except this stuff is over ten times more potent."

I had been right. The Buzz was getting worse.

Jafney reassembled the pump and handed it back.

"I guess we should maintain appearances," I said.

Jafney nodded and put hers back on.

As she put up her tool, I noticed that she had a lot of candid snapshots of other students. Every one of them featured Wyck in some way.

That girl had it bad, no matter what timeline she was on.

I stuck my pump back in place and squeezed my arm to make sure it was affixed tightly. As I pressed my thumb into my flesh, it gave me a flashback to when Wyck had squeezed the same spot.

"Jafney," I said, "there's something you need to know about Wyck."

"What?"

I looked back over at the pictures. In all of them, Wyck looked like his normal slightly cocky, secretly caring self. I highly doubted she had crossed paths with the Wyck who was haunted and hunted by glimpses of multiple timelines.

"He's . . . conflicted," I said.

"So?"

"No, I mean, he's not the Wyck you remember. He's not the Wyck *I* remember. Well, that's not entirely true. He's that Wyck some of the time. But there's another side of him now, too."

"He's just misunderstood."

"Misunderstood?"

I yanked my sleeve up to show her the bruises he had left before I remembered they had been erased on this timeline. Nothing could erase them from my memory, though.

"Look, you have to believe me," I said. "He's not himself. All the changes have . . . scrambled him. I'm not saying the real Wyck isn't in there, but—"

"You don't know anything," she said.

Okay, so that horked me off. "I don't know anything? What do you think I've been doing for the last six months of my life? Traipsing off to have fun little adventures? My life has been shredded. All for what? It doesn't matter how many times I stitch this blarking timeline back together. The Neos keep tearing it back open. Neos like Wyck."

"Neos are changing the timeline?" she said.

I'd forgotten I'd left that part out before. Oh, well. It didn't matter now.

"Yes," I said and held up the reverter. "This is the only thing that can stop their changes."

"But it's not like he's trying to hurt anyone," she said.

"He put my mom in jail. And on another timeline, he tried to kill me!" This was ridiculous.

"Why am I even defending myself?" I said. "*He* was the one who changed the past to be with *me,* not the other way around."

"What?

Her face crumpled. This was the arrow that bit through her armor.

"I'm sorry," I said. "I know that must hurt." It was the truth, though.

"Shut up!" she screamed. "Just shut u—"

Gone.

I can't say I was surprised she'd Shifted right out from under my nose. (Well, above my nose—dang, that girl was tall.) The emotional tension in the room was so thick, it would be difficult to slit it with a lightsaber. I looked around and sighed. Staying at the Institute was pointless. Trying to find answers here was like stumbling upon a shed snakeskin, and from that, trying to figure out what the snake had eaten for lunch the week before.

Even if I could glean some answers about my current situation at the Institute, it wasn't safe to stay here.

I scanned my newsfeed while packing a bag, hoping that I'd find Leto's death was confined to the previous timeline. But no.

Leto was still dead. My mother's incarceration was in there, too.

"Oh, Mom." My heart plummeted. On this timeline, she'd shown up to work acting oddly, and they tested her there then searched the house for the drug stash. Again, they mentioned that the amounts in her bloodstream were approaching dangerous overdose levels.

I flipped through a stack of unopened messages and discovered Quigley and Granderson were still at Resthaven. It was like Grandpa had said. There's nothing as inevitable as inevitability.

The best place for me now was Resthaven, too.

I was back at square one, only to find out it had been a circle the whole time.

I took the Metro to save time. I needed to talk to Quigley. Badly. She and Granderson were the only ones left who could help me hash things out.

I hiked my bag up on my shoulder as I hopped off the train and ran down the steps, eager to catch a glimpse of the Haven's familiar green lights. But as I rounded the corner toward the building, a flood of flashing red and blue greeted me instead.

chapter 20

"WHAT'S GOING ON?" I barged through a cluster of chrono-investigators in order to reach Quigley on the opposite side of the common room.

She lifted her gaze momentarily from her Com to look at my bag. "I take it you'll be staying."

I dropped the bag and repeated my question.

"It's happened," said Quigley with a sigh. "Nava's been taken."

"How do you know she was taken and didn't just Shift some-where?"

Quigley handed me her Com. A soligram note hovered above it: *You know what we want. You know who to come to.*

"Umm, no and no," I said, handing the Com back.

"That's not entirely true." She tucked it in her pocket. "We may not know what they want, but we do know it was ICE who took her, thanks to you and your Future Self."

"Yes, but knowing who took her doesn't do us much good un-less we can figure out what they want." I suppressed a shiver, pic-turing the already frail woman, now on a frozen slab. She wouldn't survive long in such a state.

I looked over at a group of Shifters huddled on a nearby couch. One of the younger women was crying, her shoulders shaking with each sob. Tressie. Nava had been teaching her to knit. An older man—Sam, I think his name was—patted her on the back then pulled away. A glimmer of hope lit his face. He walked into the hallway, out of eyeshot of the chronoinvestigators, and Shifted.

Quigley noticed his disappearance as well. "Everyone has been giving in to the slightest pull to Shift, thinking it might take them to her."

"Any luck?"

"No."

Sam appeared again a moment later in the same spot, the hope replaced by disappointment. He sat back down next to Tressie and shook his head.

"Where's Nurse Granderson?" I asked, surprised he wasn't in the thick of it. Nava was one of his favorite residents.

"He was the one who discovered her absence earlier. Even though he knew it was coming, he took it hard. He needed a breather," said Quigley. "Nava was much loved around here."

"Why her?" I asked.

"Hmm?"

"Why Nava?" I thought of the pile of smoke-covered anachronistic possessions in that pile in ICE's Cryostorage Unit. "All the other Shifters who have been taken seem to be from the distant past, so their absence could go unnoticed or at least uninvestigated." Definitely not the case here. She was the outlier. "So why Nava?"

It didn't make sense.

"I don't know," said Quigley. "I assumed because she was an easy target."

"Breaking into Resthaven, surrounded by other Shifters? Hardly the easiest option. If anything, it seems the riskiest."

"Maybe trying to send us a message?" asked Quigley.

"Have we done anything to hork them off recently?"

"Your guess is better than mine. I stopped trying to figure out my own altered history about three unreverted changes ago."

"I'm trying," I said.

"I wasn't trying to criticize, Bree, but it's true. You haven't been able to keep up." She held up a finger when I started to protest. "No one would be able to. But even if you did revert every change, there's still this." She gestured around the room, and I knew what she meant. Some Haven members still bothered to pore over the news, trying to keep a semblance of sanity. Others had clearly given up long ago. It wasn't just the unreverted changes. It wasn't just Nava. Our entire existence felt like it was spiraling out of control. Even chipped Shifters were being impacted now with the increased Buzz.

I motioned to one of the chronoinvestigators by the entrance. "What do they think about Nava's disappearance?"

"No theories yet." She lowered her voice. "I actually haven't decided yet whether or not to tell them about ICE's involvem—"

"Make way!" The front doors flew open. The top of Nurse Granderson's head was visible over the pack of investigators.

"Clear a path!" he yelled and the investigators obeyed. As they parted, I got a full view of Granderson, and my hand flew to my mouth. In his arms, he held Nava's body.

"Is she . . . ?" Quigley rushed over to the couch where he'd laid her.

"She's alive." He leaned in to kiss her forehead. With her downy hair and stem-thin body, it reminded me of someone wishing upon a puff of dandelion.

"Is she going to be all right?" asked a man behind us. At first I thought he was one of the chronoinvestigators, but he wore street clothes and looked utterly shell-shocked. He was young, maybe ten years older than me.

"Who are you?" asked Quigley, blocking him mid-step.

"It's okay," said Granderson. "He found her outside. He was calling for help when I came up."

"Could we have a word?" the head chronoinvestigator asked the man.

"I'm afraid you've already heard all that I know. I was standing there and she"—his face went even paler than it already was—"she landed on the sidewalk in front of me."

Nurse Granderson ran a medical probe down Nava's arm.

Her eyelids fluttered open. "Devvy Arthur Granderson," she murmured. "I've been frozen solid. The last thing I need is that cold probe turning me back into a popsicle." It was like a breeze passed through the room as everyone heaved a sigh of relief. She was okay. Also feisty as ever.

"Is she synched with her real time?" I asked.

"Yes." Granderson helped her prop herself up on some pillows, and another resident brought a glass of water. "Her tendrils are stable with low activity. Just the way we want them."

It reminded me of that note that ICE had left. *You know what we want.* But we hadn't given ICE anything. They took her fifty years into the past and put her into cryostasis. And then they returned her a few hours later?

Something didn't add up.

"What do you remember about your attacker, ma'am?" asked the head chronoinvestigator. Officer Abernathy, his badge said. With his bristly buzzcut and stern expression, the man looked like he could be ex-military no matter what time period he was in.

"My attackers?" said Nava. "I remember red."

"Red?"

"And blue."

"Red . . . and blue?"

Of course, to the investigators, that meant nothing. But I ventured a sidelong glance at Quigley. Red scrubs. Blue . . . well, whatever that blue liquid was in ICE's tank. Maybe Nava's testimony could garner some police support for the Haven after all.

Officer Abernathy, however, looked out the window at the police light still flashing. Red and blue. He sighed.

"Ms. uhh . . ." He glanced at his notes.

"It's Mrs., young man."

"Yes, umm. How long have you lived here at Resthaven?"

So much for police support. They saw us all as loonies.

"I don't recall the exact length of time," said Nava. "Long enough to see my share of changes."

She chuckled at her joke. Officer Abernathy didn't join in.

"I don't know that there's anything more we can do right now." He put away his compufilm pad. "Gotta go deal with a known chronosmuggler who showed up dead in a ditch earlier."

It was Quigley's turn to shoot a sidelong glance in my direction. I astutely ignored it until the investigators had left.

The second the door shut behind them, Quigley turned to me. "My office. Now."

I followed her down the hall. I settled into a stiff wooden chair, and saved her the question balanced on the end of her tongue. "Yes, it was Leto. I was there when he died."

"Is there any way they could pin you to it?"

"Pin me to it? What are you implying? That I killed him?"

"Of course not, but is there any way you could be linked to him? Did he even know who you were on this timeline?"

"He didn't. But . . . he did."

"Glad we cleared that up."

"No, I mean, he had no idea who I was, even after I punched him, but—"

"Punched him? I thought you said you didn't have a part in his death."

"I didn't. It wasn't hard enough to seriously injure him, much less kill him. He was acting strange, though. He started hemorrhaging blood. I had reverted the change he was trying to make. It was nothing. A lottery ticket in the past. I've used the reverter on him plenty of times before for the same kind of dumb stuff."

"How many times?"

Honestly, I'd lost count. I thought through all the money-grubbing changes to the past that Leto had tried to make.

"Twenty, maybe. Thirty?"

Quigley balked.

"Anyway, Leto synched, but not to ICE's headquarters. He

landed in a drainage culvert, and he was bleeding everywhere. By that point, he was acting really strange."

"When you say acting strange, what do you mean by—"

"He was in love with me."

"In love with you?" Up shot the eyebrow of skepticism. I swear, with that dumb mysterious grin, she looked exactly like the *Mona Lisa*. Well, exactly like herself, I guess.

"Quigley, you didn't see him. And the way he was talking, he knew stuff about me. Stuff that . . ."

"That . . . ?"

"Stuff that only Finn knew. And he had this goofy lovestruck expression on his face. I've only seen one other person look at me that way. It was like Leto *was* Finn."

"Oh."

Great. All hail Bree, queen of the crazy people.

"I realize how it sounds," I said.

"I know you miss Finn."

"It was more than that. Leto talked about Chincoteague, and he knew the name of my pet pegamoo." Wait. "A pet pegamoo I don't even have on this timeline. Explain that."

"I . . . can't. But that doesn't mean—"

"What it *means*? I have no blarking idea what it means. Do you?"

"Perhaps you misconstrued what he was saying."

"You don't believe me, do you?" I dug my fingers into the arms of the chair.

"It's not that I don't believe you, it's that we have more pressing matters to attend to. Those chronoinvestigators were the same ones who handled Finn's alleged kidnapping."

"So?"

"So this is now two trips to Resthaven they've made in less than twenty-four hours."

"Again, so? The trips happened on different timelines. Those chronoinvestigators were chipped. They don't remember the change."

"The one thing I've noticed about all these timeline changes is that the Haven members have been steered toward the same eventualities in spite of the changes. I'm still heading up this place. Granderson is still the medical director. Your mother keeps getting incapacitated. And you keep running afoul of the law."

"Yes, but—"

"Bree, if they find even a splash of your DNA on Leto, do you think that will go ignored? They will swarm this place. The Haven has survived as long as it has by going unnoticed. Resthaven is all some of these Shifters have. They can't survive in the outside world anymore. And the more unchecked changes ICE makes, the greater chance we'll lose our home as well as our already tenuous hold on reality."

"I hate them," I said.

"Who?"

"ICE. Neos. All of them. Shifters have devoted their entire existence to studying the past. We study and study to supposedly figure out how to use our ability to help. Like John with his surgery. Like Mom with her art. And yet after all our studying, all our trying to help, Neos figured out a way to use the ability to time travel for nothing but their own gain. I hate them."

"Then they've already won."

"Quigley, all they do is distort and destroy."

It reminded me of the clue. *To save his, destroy yours.*

"I want it to be back to the way it's supposed to be," I said. "The way it was before all this started. If there were only some way we could figure out a way to change the past like them."

"And what would you change?" asked Quigley quietly.

"I'd . . . I'd stop Jafney from bringing Finn here. Then he wouldn't be a chronofugitive."

Maybe," said Quigley. "But then you would."

"Huh?"

"He took the blame for your break-in."

"Oh." That was true. "Well, then, I'd stop Wyck from turn-ing my mom in for those drugs."

"She had more hidden away in your house. What if the next step had been overdose?"

"Fine." I hadn't thought of that. And Quigley was right. Mom had gotten caught on this timeline without Wyck's interference. "Y'know what? I'd go back and stop ICE from ever Shifting the first Neo. I wish I could stop them from ever discovering they could even make changes to the timeline."

I expected Quigley to point out some fallacy in that as well, but she didn't. She sat there, staring at me, for longer than I was comfortable with, a rare look of brokenness on her face.

"I wish that, too," she finally said, pushing away from her desk. "Some what-ifs are harder to take than others. I'll have a room prepared for you, and I'll notify the Institute that you've entered Resthaven for health reasons."

"Thanks." I hiked my bag on my shoulder but stopped Quig-ley before she left. "Wait. There was one more thing. I think"—I hated to even suggest it but it had to be said—"I think there's a mole in the Haven."

"I know."

"You *know*?"

"I mean, I've considered it, too." She pointed at my reverter. "Only a few people know of that thing's existence, and we're all in the Haven. But then again, that's linear thinking. This person could be from the future."

"Well, we know that Raspy is an unchipped Shifter. And Finn and I figured out that Raspy would have to be a Shifter with sticky tendrils, someone born of two centuries like me, in order to kid-nap people in the past and bring them to our time."

"You think the *kidnapper* is a mole in the Haven?"

"No. I mean . . . I don't know what I think."

"No matter what, you make very good points. Whether

they're in the Haven or not, having an unchipped Shifter running around and working for ICE explains a lot. Namely, how they've been kept in the loop so that they know that changes are even happening. Let me give it some more thought while you get settled in. I'll keep my ears open about any suspicious behavior. In the meantime, I really need to go check on Nava."

"Thanks. Are you going to take Nava to the hospital?" I asked.

"I'll defer to Nurse Granderson's judgment, but I'd prefer she stay here."

"We couldn't protect her before," I said.

"True, but she'd be no safer there. She'll be more comfortable here. And they did return her."

"Yeah." But again . . . why?

Quigley left, and I was alone.

Alone.

The word burrowed under my skin, seeped into my pores. I truly felt it in that moment. No Mom. No Mimi. No Finn.

Alone.

My tendrils began to tingle. It was a welcome relief from the void.

I bent into a crouch and closed my eyes as I Shifted. My feet sank into sand. I dragged my fingers through the grit and smiled without bothering to peek. I would know the feel of Chincoteague sand anywhere. As I lifted my face, the back of my eyelids transformed from cool pink to a burning orange. I twisted my head around as I opened my eyes, disoriented.

Sunrise?

Wrong direction.

Heat pressed my torso like a heavy blanket. My nostrils filled with the familiar scent of smoke. A massive firestorm raged in the distance.

"No." I collapsed.

Finn's house was at the center of the storm.

chapter 21

"FINN!" I KNEW THERE WAS NO WAY he'd hear me over the roaring inferno, but I couldn't stop myself from screaming it. I only prayed there was no way he could hear me because he'd already Shifted to safety.

The fire hissed and spit sparks like an angry, caged beast as it gobbled away at the Mastersons' home. Flames had already devoured the top of the deck, blocking the way to the back entrance. The shrill beep of their smoke alarms shrieked into the night. I ran along the side of the house to the front, ducking my face away from the heat. The window to the uppermost guest bedroom burst. Shards of sparkling orange burst like fireworks into the black sky.

I rounded the corner of their property and came to the porch, each step a silent petition for God to spare this boy, spare this family that I loved. The blaze had apparently begun at the back of the house. It wasn't as bad in the front. I wrapped my hand around my shirt to make an impromptu oven mitt and wrenched the front door open. Smoky, but no flames in the entryway yet. The high ceilings left a pocket of relatively breathable air if I crouched down.

"Finn!" I screamed. "Charlotte! Anyone?"

No response. They couldn't have slept through this, not that I could get up to their bedrooms. Surely they'd all Shifted out. And there was no way John would have gone anywhere without Charlotte. That's what I told myself to stay calm.

I asked myself if there was anything irreplaceable that I should try to get out of the fire. Oh, who was I kidding? Their entire art collection was beyond priceless. My mother was always fussing that they didn't keep it in their safe.

Their safe. I had to get the IcePick I'd stolen from Bergin out of it . . . the one that would become the reverter at some point. I pulled my shirt over my mouth and ran into their living room. I pulled the hidden panel off the wall and turned the lock's combination, a mish-mash of their birthdays. *Phew.* The Pick was still there. As I put it in my pocket, a mass of yellow fur hurled itself at me, barking.

"Slug"—I hugged the family's Labrador around the neck—"let's get you out of here."

Bark bark bark bark.

"Come on." I tugged him toward the front door, but he hunkered down and refused to move. He started to whine.

Slug let out a yelp and took off toward the kitchen.

"No, Slug!" Blark. I lowered my face to snatch a mouthful of clearer air and darted after him. The flames were already creeping down the walls of the living room. I pushed open the kitchen door. The room had filled with smoke but only the back wall had caught fire so far.

That's when I heard it. A coarse cough, hacking and hoarse.

The smoke stung my eyes as I searched to find where it was coming from. I spotted a shoe behind the granite island and raced around it. Georgie was sprawled flat on her back—unmoving but awake.

"Georgie!" I bent beside her.

"Brrrrr . . ." Her jaw was locked in a grimace.

"What are you—?" I recognized the stiff posture. "Have you been stunned?"

She blinked twice. I'd take that for a yes.

"Where's Finn?" I asked.

"Gonnnn."

Thank God he'd gotten out.

"And your parents?"

"Notttt . . . hrrr."

"Don't worry. I'll get you out of here." We were actually only ten feet from the garage. But as I pulled her dead weight across the tile inch by inch, I realized it would be a long ten feet. "As soon as you can move anything, let me know."

I shoved the door open. The intake of fresh oxygen made my lungs happy, but it made the fire furious. Flames licked down the walls and danced across the ceiling toward us. Georgie started to wheeze. I had to get her out of here. Now.

I fumbled in my pocket for my magno-grappling hook. I reached up and raised the garage door. The sudden influx of air whipped the fire into a frenzy, but I needed a clear shot. *Ping!* It hit something solid at the end of their driveway. I placed one side of the handle in Georgie's hand and the other side in mine and activated it. Red light.

Dang it. The hook wasn't designed for fully horizontal take-offs. It wouldn't support both our weights. I readjusted our grips and tried again.

Nope.

All right. I took my hand off and wrenched her other fingers around the handle. Green light.

I pushed the center button and away she went. Thirty feet of driveway would scrape her up something bonks, but she'd thank me later.

I was about to stumble out after her when there was a thunderous clank behind me. Part of the ceiling over their stove had collapsed. The large pot rack came tumbling down.

"Slug!" I cried. He cowered by the range as the rack teetered over the edge of the counter. I rushed over to pull him to safety. It was too late. The rack crashed down, right on top of the whimpering dog, pinning him to the floor.

Unhh unhh unhh. He cried from under the copper cage of pots and pans.

I tried to lift the metal jumble, but it was too hot to touch.

"It's okay," I whispered to the shaking animal. I reached into the drawer where Charlotte kept her mitts and found the thickest ones. The rack wasn't all that heavy, especially with adrenaline zipping through my veins, but Slug had a snow-white muzzle and already-creaky hips. I helped him up, and he hobbled out. I got down on all fours to follow.

That's when I heard it, a groaning screech above me. That telltale sound of a roof giving way. Instinctively, I looked up. Ash and sparks rained down. I started to crawl faster toward the door, but the smoke was so thick. I fought to keep my eyes open against the crackling heat and fumes. Every breath was a struggle as I dipped my head as low to the floor as I could, searching for any puff of breathable air. But there was nothing, only soot.

The door . . . I had . . . to reach . . . the . . .

I was so close. Inches. Inches.

I fell flat on my face, sparks nipping the back of my neck, pulling myself forward in an army crawl.

There was no urge to synch, not a prickle. My limbs loosened in defeat.

The next thing I knew, someone was pulling me up by my armpits.

"Come on," said a deep voice. Strong arms cradled my head against a broad shoulder. "Easy now. Try to hold your breath until we get out."

As we cleared the garage, I cracked my eyes and caught the first welcome flicker of street lamp.

I turned my gaze on my rescuer and looked into deep green eyes, a razor-cut jaw. I relaxed.

"Deep breaths," he said. "You're going to be okay."

"Finn?"

"No, it's John." He laid me down on the grass. "Is Finn still inside?"

"No. He already made it out."

"We need to get you to the hospital."

"No." I coughed. "I'll be fine. Help Georgie."

"Georgie?" He flipped back around to the house, his terror palpable. "Is she—?

"No." I shook my head and tried to say something but a ragged, grating hack came out instead. I pointed the direction she'd grappled.

He took off running. I pushed myself up and stumbled after him.

Georgie was lying at the base of the mailbox, curled in a ball, shaking. At least the stun seemed to have worn off. John pulled his jacket off and wrapped her in it. "Focus on me, sweetie. You're going into shock."

John turned to me. "Why didn't Finn Shift her out?"

"I don't know. He must have thought she was right behind him."

"I tried," she said, crying. "I tried."

"It's okay, honey." John stroked her matted hair. "Shh. You're going to be okay. Everyone's fine."

"Where's Charlotte?" I asked.

"We're staying at a bed and breakfast a few hours away. I'm about"—he looked at his watch then Georgie's—"five minutes ahead of you."

"I tried . . . I tried to stop him." Georgie began to cry. The fire reflected off the flow of her tears so they looked like a web of red strings clinging to her cheeks.

"What do you mean?" I sat down next to her and hugged her. "You tried to stop Finn from Shifting?"

"No . . . I . . . Finn didn't Shift out."

John and I both whirled at the same moment to face the inferno behind us.

"He's in there?" Now I was the one shaking.

"No, no." She grabbed her head in her hands. "The guy stunned Finn before me, then he started the fire."

"What guy?" I asked. But I already knew.

"I couldn't see the face. There was a mask. Like some sort of alien suit. It was silver. I don't . . . I don't . . ." The sobs took over.

"Where is Finn now?" I asked.

"He took Finn with him," she said.

"When you say 'took,' do you mean he Shifted Finn out?" asked John.

She nodded. It further confirmed my suspicions. Raspy had to be a natural-born Shifter, and he had sticky tendrils like mine. But who would do such a thing? What Shifter would work for ICE? And why target the Mastersons? I couldn't imagine anyone having a vendetta against them, much less Finn.

Sirens wailed in the distance. We didn't have much time. Once there were witnesses, it would be harder for me to synch. I looked up at John, but his eyes were closed. He had guessed what I had figured out.

ICE had kidnapped Finn. I didn't know for what purpose. But at least I knew where they were keeping him.

"I've gotta go," I said. "I'm going to get Finn back."

Georgie wiped the tears with the back of her hand so that her whole face had a wet glow. "Tell him I'm sorry, okay?"

"Hey." I turned her face toward me. "You and I both know that when I see him, he'll just tell you to stop being stupid."

"You mean if you see him."

"I mean when."

"I have a message, too," said John.

This one was harder. John and Finn had only recently started to get closer. It had been hard for Finn, after so many years of feeling like his dad had lied to him about his very existence, to trust him again. But they'd been working on it.

"You should tell Finn yourself," I said quietly. "When he comes ba—"

"Let him know that I love him?" John said. "Just . . . I love him."

I nodded.

My tendrils began to tingle.

"Tell your mom everything's going to be okay," I said to Georgie. Charlotte didn't yet know that her whole world was ablaze. She'd be beyond hysterical when she awoke to discover her life was cinder and ash.

Everything ICE touched burned, burned, burned.

"Dad, is Finn going to be all right?" Georgie asked.

"Of course he is." John looked over her head at me, and I knew he was trying to convince himself as much as his daughter. "Of course he is. Bree's going to take care of him."

Me. I was the only thing standing between alive and dead. Or tortured lab rat. Or whatever it was they were doing to Shifters in those tanks. I shuddered again, thinking of Leto's violent end. And he was one of ICE's customers.

My tendrils quivered. The sensation roiled within my very veins; it was almost painful. This was beyond a synch. It was as if gravity had combined with every hold of nature and was pulling me to Finn.

"I'll go with you," said John. "Maybe I can help somehow."

"No, Charlotte and Georgie need you here." I gathered my grappling gear and lowered myself into a defensive crouch, not sure of where I'd land. Not sure what would happen when I got there. Absolutely certain of one thing, though.

Whoever took Finn was going to hurt.

chapter 22

FOOL ME ONCE, ICE? Shame on you. Fool me twice? Shame on you again.

I was nobody's fool.

I cinched my anti-grav belt as tight as it would go, my magna-grappling hook already primed and ready to fire as I stepped into the black transportation tube in ICE's lobby.

One of the only nice things about the changes to the timeline (and "nice" was way too strong a word) was it kept ICE in the dark about me. Well, not completely in the dark. Raspy might have made them aware of my existence, that I was an unchipped Shifter, but he didn't seem to have told them details about what I was up to. Maybe he didn't know.

Or maybe he didn't want to be ICE's fool either.

I had used the hair I'd stolen from Wyck to gain entrance to their headquarters, then meandered along with a tour group until they reached the spectators' gallery. It was a simple matter of slipping away unnoticed, then straight up the black tube I went.

And this time, I came even more prepared.

As soon as my body hit the landing area of the transport chamber, I shot the grappling hook out of the porthole. The heightened gravity tugged tightly on my foot as I exited. Like a chronologically challenged Cinderella I wiggled my boot off and went on my way.

Now for the tricky part.

There was a small rectangular air grate above the doorway that

I'd noticed the last time I was in this hallway. It didn't lead directly into the Cryostorage Room, but my guess was the room would be accessible through the same air shaft. I shot the grappling hook through the grate and set my ascent to slow. The cover wasn't too hard to remove. I put it back in place even though I planned to be long gone before anyone noticed its absence.

The vent was tight but passable. It was also surprisingly well-lit. The same glowing blue fluid that I had seen before swirling in that central tank undulated through a tube that ran the length of the tunnel. I followed the flow backward to its source, and as I expected, it was the air vent at the top of the domed ceiling of the Cryostorage Unit. I pried off the cover, activated my gravbelt, and lowered myself until I hovered over the tank. I grabbed ahold of the side, switched off my belt, and swung myself to the ground.

Now to find Finn and get the blark out of this place.

I turned to face the wall of bubbles. My heart sank. They were nearly full now. I raced along the row of lit cases where the bodies were stored, looking for a description that might match Finn, but they were just strings of letters and numbers, like the ones that Lafferty had rattled off when she'd examined the person who was in the main tank.

Alpha–Lima–Oscar–16–6–6

Kilo–Yankee–Alpha–17–3–1

All the same. Three letters. Four numbers.

16–6–6. 1666. The year of the Great Fire of London.

I came to one that wasn't lit.

Foxtrot–Juliet–Mike–20–1–6

FJM.

Finnigan Jonathan Masterson. 2016. A year I'd just come from.

I yanked out my Com and pulled up the snatch of conversation I'd managed to capture the last time I was here.

"-ess code L5N21KRA983FJ." Lafferty's recorded voice filled the room.

The door to the unit opened. The slab inside emerged.

It was empty.

But if he wasn't in this drawer, he must be . . .

I turned slowly to face the center of the room. A dark mass slammed against the inner wall of the tank's glass.

Finn.

I rushed over to the tank and beat against the edge, unsure if Finn was conscious and if he could hear me even if he was. I couldn't see the details of his facial features, but now that I knew what to look for, I could tell it was him floating in there. I pressed my palm against the glass, willing his pain to ease. He stopped thrashing, and the fluid from the tubes lining the walls reversed direction and now flowed back toward him. At first, I wondered if I had somehow done something to cause it, but then I noticed that a warning panel had popped up in front of the tank. Words scrolled through the air as red lights flashed.

"Hippocampal deterioration accelerated to 7.2 percent. Upper limit exceeded. Additional overrides not advisable."

As the blue matter flowed backward, the dark liquid inside the tank started to clear. Finn's eyelids drifted open, and he lifted his head, zeroing in on my profile. I tried to smile, webbing my fingers against the glass, wishing beyond all wishes that I could press them straight through, grab onto him, and pull him out.

His eyes drifted open and fought to focus. If he knew me, he didn't show it. But as the fluid grew lighter and lighter, I could tell that he began to recognize me. I guess I had expected relief on his part or even happiness. But, no. Pure terror. He pointed toward the entrance and pushed his head from side to side in the viscous fluid.

He mouthed, *"Go!"*

Oh, like blark I was going anywhere without him.

I had to get him out of there. There had to be some kind of escape hatch or lever. Oh, who was I kidding? These people had stripped Shifters of their family, their friends, their very existence. They wouldn't give a flying hoot about taking their lives as well.

I scanned the shadows of the room looking for something, anything, with some heft to it. I'd bust him out of there. I was about to give up and run out into the hall, when my eyes fell on the pile of era clothing in the corner, sitting next to an incinerator, likely awaiting destruction for contamination.

If I was from the 1600s and needed to stop a fire from spreading, I'd probably use an—I dove into the pile, flinging corsets and breeches left and right, ah ha!—axe. The rough-hewn wooden handle was charred on the ends, and the entire pile smelled of stale wood smoke. A fresh wave of anger gripped me by the throat as I clutched the handle of the hatchet.

I went back to the center of the room, pulled back my arm, and swung the dull blade of the axe at the tank. A tremendous crack ricocheted around the room, but when I looked down at the glass, only a fleck of a chip appeared. Dang it. I needed more force. I backed up and came at it running, swinging the axe with my final stride. The chip deepened, but this would take forever.

I looked at Finn, who was still twitching from whatever they'd done to him. I had to hurry. I twisted the axe handle around, thinking. Ahh. Turn the axe around. The glass would be weakened where I'd already hit it. Now, I needed to finish it off with more blunt force.

I pulled back a few feet and came at it in a run again. This time, the tool felt awkward in my hand as the weight shifted forward and slammed the glass with a thunk. But when I looked down at the chip, it had turned to a crack, spreading in a spider web. Again. Again. I came at it until my arms could barely lift.

The liquid oozed out the crack. Instead of dribbling down the side of the tank as I expected, though, it floated off as it met the air. Some kind of gaseous plasma. I got close and swished my finger through it. It was like a vapor, only thicker. My finger left a path behind it that didn't knit back together. I lifted my fingers to my nostrils and sniffed. It didn't smell noxious. It smelled like . . .

Sea salt.

I pressed my nose directly to the crack in the glass. Chocolate chip waffles. And . . . floor cleaner? The scents were coming at me faster than I could sift through them. Spun sugar. Sunscreen. Hot tar. Cinnamon rolls. Horse manure.

I gagged. It was overwhelming. And it wasn't just the smells. Each scent elicited a powerful feeling. Joy, fear, excitement and on and on, mixed and melded into one giant ball of unprocessable emotion. And with each feeling came an equally powerful visual in my mind.

Memories.

A zap that felt similar to electricity zipped down my spine, as if my body were revving up for a Shift even though my tendrils weren't pulling me anywhere. Whoa. It was as if the onslaught of memories had short-circuited my hippocampus somehow. I shook my head to clear it and backed away from the glass.

The warning message still flashed in front of the cracking tank. Finn's whole body lolled from side to side.

"What have they done to you?" I whispered.

No wonder his hippocampus had deteriorated. He was trapped in a huge vat of that blue matter. It would be like experiencing every embrace, every fight, every smile, every tear—every moment of his life—all at once.

I had to get him out of there.

I slammed the axe against the side again. A good-sized fissure formed in the middle. I squared off my shoulders and rammed my body against the hole, taking gasps of air as I backed away each time, so that I didn't get lost in his memories. Some so pleasant I wanted to stop and bask in them. Others so painful they threatened to send me crashing to the floor. I backed up to get another running start at it when I looked back at Finn. His bare chest rose and fell. The wisps of plasma surrounding him had grown sparse.

That was when I realized with a dawning horror that he was

actually breathing the blue matter in. He *needed* to breathe it in. A steady stream of vapor puffed out of the tank where the crack now seemed like a canyon. There was no way to retrieve it, no way to get it back into him.

What had I done?

I held my breath and pressed my whole body against the gap as he continued to suck more and more of those memories back in. What all had he lost? Had he lost Charlotte's red velvet cupcakes? Georgie's snorting laughter? Shifts with his dad that saved so many lives and made Finn who he was? Compassionate and strong and funny and kind.

Had he lost us?

I sobbed as I fought to keep every bit of plasmic vapor contained within the chamber, but it still seeped past me in a steady flow. I watched it float away and dissipate across the ceiling. Once the air inside the tank was clear, Finn appeared to be bobbing up and down in weightless gel similar to the type in the transport tube chambers. I backed away, and stared into his eyes, fearing a new vacancy, but instead I found recognition.

He was still Finn.

He nodded his head slowly and curled into a defensive ball. Whatever they were doing to him, it was done for now. I backed away and squared my shoulders again. This was going to hurt something fierce. I braced my body for the impact just as I heard a shrill whistle coming from the doorway.

They'd discovered me.

I couldn't stop my momentum, not that I wanted to.

When my torso slammed into the glass, it caved in with an ear-splitting crunch. I kicked the hole larger, grabbed Finn's arm, and pulled him out.

The entrance to the room flew open.

"Halt!" yelled a red scrub across the room, Baldy. Why was it always Baldy? I didn't bother even pretending to cooperate. No one would mistake me for an innocent victim now.

Finn and I ran to the far exit. Locked. I tried Wyck's hair. Nothing.

There had to be another way out. I looked all around the walls for more security doors like there were in the hallways, but there were none. Then I looked straight up. The air grate I'd come in through. I clicked the float button on my grav-belt and pushed off as hard as I could from the floor, my arms entwined around Finn's chest. We didn't make it far, only fifteen feet or so. Grav-belts weren't designed to support two people. We started to drift down as I fumbled through my pockets for my grappling hook. It was an awkward angle even without having to keep my arms around Finn.

"Front right pocket," I said to him, not bothering to tell him what it was I was trying to reach. He'd know.

He kept one arm slung around my neck but groped through my pocket with the other.

Ten feet. Nine. The red scrub below us jumped up and his fingertips grazed Finn's foot.

"Hurry," I whispered.

Eight feet. The Shavie swung and hit my shin like a piñata.

"Come on," I begged Finn. We weren't going to make it.

I glanced down and saw that one of the idiots had finally thought to stand on something to reach me. I curled into a ball to keep out of their full grasp. Finn did the same, but too late. One of them latched onto his ankle. Finn kicked until he finally managed to free himself and push off from them in the same movement, giving us a few extra feet to spare while he wrenched the grappling hook out of my pocket.

"Got it!" Finn clenched one side, and I barely had my palm around the other end of the handle when he tapped the button to lock us both in place. He curled around me tight as we flew to the ceiling.

I twisted my body around so that I could ram my one booted

foot through the air grate as we approached it. Finn hoisted me up, and I had to fight the urge to look down and yell, "Suckers!"

Finn pulled himself up behind me. I looked down the hollow airshaft. It was darker now, the residual blue matter fading as it flowed down the tubes that lined the cold tunnel. It was so narrow, we had to crawl along one at a time.

"Any urge to synch?" I asked. That would be the easiest escape route. Obviously.

"No." Finn paused behind me. "Nothing."

"Me either."

I tapped him when I realized he hadn't started moving yet. "Just let me know if you start to feel a pull."

"Yeah. Of course."

I had no idea where we were going. The black transport tube that led here sucked you this way and that so it was hard to tell if you were headed up or down. I got the feeling that was intentional. Still, I kept moving forward, the only thing we could do, following that eerie blue essence. Finn lagged again, and when I peeked back, he had an odd look on his face.

"Did they hurt you?" I asked. "Are you in pain?"

"Huh?" He picked up his pace. "I mean, it hurt, but I'm okay now. Stiff, but okay."

"What exactly were they doing to you in that tank?"

"I don't know. I was unconscious except for when they took me out of the freezer and put me in the tank, and even then it was . . . hazy. It was like being dunked in a vat of memories over and over. Like someone holding you underwater until you think you're about to drown, then pulling you up for a gasp of air before they shove you back under."

I shivered.

"How many times did they put you in the tank?"

"I lost count."

"How long did they have you frozen?" I asked.

"No clue."

"But what do you think? Hours? Months? Years? Did you notice if the workers were aging when they took you to the tank?"

"Bree, it was really fast each time they took me out of that bubble. And so overwhelming every time they did. You probably know more than I do."

"We'll get it pieced together," I said. "Don't worry. And once you're back in Chincoteague, your dad can hire security guards."

"Bree . . ." He had that tone. That Bree-is-delusional-and-I'm-humoring-her-so-she-doesn't-stab-someone tone.

"Raspy may be an unchipped Shifter, but he's human," I said. "It's not like he could survive a gun blast. Oh!" Why didn't I think of this before? "Or we could send some weapons from this time back with you."

"I'm not taking any weapons back with me."

"Even a . . . lasersword?"

He'd been obsessed with getting his hands on one since the first time he'd encountered one in Bergin's office last year. Said they looked exactly like lightsabers.

"Bree, I'm not taking anything back with me. Something's wrong."

I stopped and wriggled around to face him.

"Finn, you can't go back to Chincoteague empty-handed. You're going to have to protect yourself and your family."

"What I'm saying is I'm not going back to Chincoteague, period."

"We're not starting this again," I said.

"You don't understand." He gripped me by the shoulders. "I think they chipped me or something."

"What?"

"I can't feel any pull."

I felt along the nape of his neck. "No scar. They didn't chip you."

He rubbed his fingers all over his scalp to double-check.

"Maybe you're just not being called anywhere yet," I said.

"No. It's not like that. I don't feel anything. I feel numb."

"But—"

"You don't notice it," he said. "You don't notice it until it's gone. My tendrils are . . . it's like they're . . ."

His breath sped up. He was starting to hyperventilate.

"It's okay. It's okay." I squeezed into the space beside him, careful not to get too wedged in lest we get stuck here. "Take a deep breath. Everything's going to be all right."

Calm words came out of my mouth, but my insides were screaming. Even if I could figure out a way to recover his lost memories, he could be stuck in my time forever. I mean, I loved him. I wanted to be near him, but he had a life outside of me. He would never see his friends again. He would never see his family. But I needed to keep him calm.

His breathing returned to normal.

"We'll figure this out." I pressed my forehead to his. "Yeah?"

"Yeah."

"You ready to move?" I asked.

He nodded.

"Wait." I undid my gravbelt from my waist and handed it to Finn. "Makes more sense for you to wear it. You're stronger—it would be easier for you to hold on to me rather than vice versa."

"Good point," he said, fastening it around his middle. But I could tell he was still focused on his tendrils.

We came to a fork in the airshaft. One path took us up. Another down, down, down. Cool, bright white lights lined the upward shaft. It practically screamed, "Follow me!" The downward shaft flickered with the blue goop, fading with each pulse. I didn't hesitate for a moment. I followed the goop, praying with each forward lurch that it was the path that led to a whole Finn.

Heck, it wasn't like I was going to find a herd of teddy bears grazing on daisies down either path.

The air staled as we trudged along. The tunnel itself was more worn the deeper we went. Smooth and scratched at the same time. Older.

We reached a dead end. Above me, a ladder steered the tunnel straight up—the only way out of what was beginning to feel more and more like a never-ending snake nest.

"I think we chose the wrong way," I said. Before we had a chance to back up though, a beam of light shone in the curve of the tunnel behind us. They were following us through the vents.

There was only one way out now. Misgivings churned in my stomach, but it was too late. I counted the rungs as we climbed but lost track around seventy-five. Finally, we reached another vent, this one thinner and taller. It was barely wide enough for me to crawl through, and Finn had to scoot sideways.

The metal grew warm under my palms.

Strike that.

Hot.

I curled my hands into fists and ambled along like a gorilla until we reached a grate. I peered through. The room below was small, maybe fifteen feet square. Something about the room struck me as off, but I couldn't put my finger on it. The tube we had followed entered the room next to the grate and branched into three separate skinnier tubes, each no wider than my pinky. These wended to separate reservoirs in three corners of the room. In the fourth corner was a control panel. Not soligraphic—real buttons and levers.

That's when it hit me, why this place seemed odd. Every other piece of technology in ICE's headquarters was on the sharpest cutting edge. But this room was old. Fifty years, at least.

Fifty years. Right when Shifters first came out of hiding. Right when the Madness began. And right when they'd taken Nava back to. It was all tied into that point fifty years back.

This room wasn't for public eyes. This room had no observational deck. And whatever happened in here had been happening for a very long time. Longer than ICE had been advertising their services on splashy billboards and tempting rich, bored housewives with fixing their every regret.

This room scared me.

The plasmic memory danced an azur tango as it entered the reservoirs. Mesmerizing to watch, terrifying when I realized it was what had come out of Finn.

Kneeling there, my knuckles near blisters from the hot metal, I got angry. No, not angry.

Furious.

Whatever that blue stuff was—memories, bits of his brain—it belonged to Finn. ICE had taken it. Even if I had to crack open those tanks and waft the blue stuff back into Finn's head myself, I would. ICE had stolen it, and I was going to steal it back.

I had already pried my fingernails under the air grate to loosen it when Finn put his hand over mine and pointed down. From his angle behind me, he could see what I couldn't. Four people stood near the doorway. I held my breath, hoping they hadn't heard me. From the loud clanks and whooshes coming from below, it appeared that they hadn't. One of the people I recognized immediately as Lafferty, and she didn't look happy. Which, of course, made me exceedingly so.

"This had better not shut down my Neo schedule!" she barked. The three red-clad workers—two women and a man—each took a place at one of the reservoirs. The woman nearest Lafferty mumbled something in return.

"What did you say?" Lafferty asked as she messed with the control panel.

"It shouldn't," the woman repeated, her voice a mousy squeak. "The boy was highly compatible to several clients. We extracted enough to hold us for some time. If the emergency override hadn't kicked in when the intruder smashed the container, we'd have more, but . . ."

They were talking about Finn, about the experiments they were doing on Shifters.

"But the extraction tank is destroyed," Lafferty said.

"We'll have a new one operational within days," said the man.

"We needed a more efficient one anyway," said the mouse woman. "Some of these Shifts burn through blue matter like bonks. I don't understand it."

What? Burn through blue matter? I thought they were just experimenting on the kidnapped Shifters. What was she talking about? What were they using it for?

Lafferty's cheeks bloomed with a crimson that matched her shoes.

"We'll upgrade the tank," she said.

"But that doesn't answer the question of why certain Shifts are using more of the—"

"Never you mind that," said Lafferty. "We have a bigger concern. That Shifter girl could have gotten to this equipment."

"Impossible," said the man.

"Not impossible," said Lafferty. "It's already happened once."

"I know, I know," he said. "But we stopped her. It was a long time ago, and there was no harm done. Besides, that's why we have it divided in three. For an extra safeguard. Only one of these vats is active at any given time. If that one should fail, we have the other two as backup."

"This is half a century's worth of irreplaceable work. This is my parents' legacy."

I followed her gesture to the glowing blue reservoirs. Her parents had studied quantum tendrils in vitro. That must be what the blue matter was. Shifters' tendrils that she was experimenting on. Her brother Xander had claimed that his parents were worried about their research falling into the wrong hands. I wondered if I was looking at the very hands they had worried about.

"If this had been damaged . . ." she said.

"But it wasn't," said the second woman. Her voice was less of a squeak than the mouse woman's, yet still quiet. I think she was trying to placate Lafferty, but it stirred the opposite reaction. Lafferty stomped over to the woman and held something up in her face. I craned my neck to see what it was. An IcePick.

"Do you know what this is?"

"A Neo's Interchron—"

"This is the future."

The woman gulped.

"Not just your future. Not just mine," said Lafferty. "The game has changed. Shifters are no longer the only players. And soon enough, they won't even be the sought-after players. Why would someone pay a Shifter to be a chronocourier when there are Neos lined up out the door willing to make the same delivery for half the price? Why would someone trust the word of a Shifter of how history happened when they can go observe it for themselves? Shifters aren't better than us. They're not special."

Sounded like she had nursed a deep wound. Two celebrated Shifters for parents. A twin brother who had inherited the same genetic mutation and who was on the same track to becoming a respected researcher like them. And then her. A nonShifter with a sharp mind, a bone to pick with her family, and the ability to go back and change her own past.

Lafferty walked over to the man. She held up the Pick. "Do you know what this is?"

"The fut—"

"This is your next paycheck. And mine. The past belongs to Shifters. The future belongs to us."

Money. And power. I know I shouldn't have been surprised. Those two things had motivated more than their share of un-ethical megalomaniacs over the course of history. But this was a megalomaniac who had the ability to change the course of history. I had to hold myself back from jumping down there and clobbering the crapwench.

Lafferty fanned herself. "This room is an oven. Let's get on with this." She held up her palm. "Wait for my mark. Perfect unison. Three-two-one. And, mark."

The three workers inserted their IcePicks into ports at the base of the reservoirs. The blue matter seeped into the empty cylinder on each Pick.

"Display Neo," said Lafferty.

A life-sized soligraphic figure arose in the middle of the room. When I saw who it was, I turned to Finn.

"It's Wyck," I mouthed.

He nodded.

The soligraphic Wyck shuffled his feet and checked his Com. He looked like he was waiting for something.

"He's getting impatient," said the male scrub. "He's been waiting for a while."

"He's a freebie," said Lafferty. "He can wait."

That was a live feed! Wyck was here at ICE's headquarters, about to Shift. Lafferty hit some controls, and the soligraphic Wyck's hippocampus lit up like a glowing seahorse in the very center of his brain.

"Are we calibrated?" asked Lafferty.

At first, I thought she was asking the workers, but they didn't respond.

"Useless old computer," she said. "Are. We. Calibrated?"

"Calibration confirmed." The speaker must have been close to the air vent I was perched near because the noise made me jump. My position on the grate was more precarious than I realized, and it let out an ominous creak before it gave way. The last thought I had before plummeting toward the ground headfirst was, "Wish Future Bree would have left me a clue about this one."

chapter 23

"GOTCHA!" FINN CAUGHT ME by the ankle. He started to heft me back up but shouts sounded from behind him in the vent. The goons had caught up with us.

"I'm gonna jump," Finn said.

He tightened his grip on my wrist and dove out the hole. At the same moment, I jerked my hand up and switched his gravbelt on. It caught us when my head was a foot from the ground.

I dangled there in the center of the room, my body oddly meshed with the soligraphic Wyck's. Blood rushed to my head, but I knew if we didn't get out of here, my blood would be flowing in more outward directions.

For a moment, Lafferty seemed stunned by our sudden appearance, but only a moment.

"Grab them!" she screamed. In any other circumstances, it would have come off as cartoonish, comical even.

Right now, it was pretty blarking terrifying.

I swung my legs away from Finn in a round kick and knocked Lafferty off balance. I didn't hesitate, didn't think about the consequences—I dug my fingers into Lafferty's perfectly formed coif, wrapped them around a few strands of her black hair, and yanked. The hair held tight. I pulled harder and lifted a strand up in triumph.

World, meet Bree Bennis, future Shavie inmate.

I didn't bother to turn off Finn's gravbelt. Instead, I grabbed his hand and ran for the door. He bobbled behind me like some sort of bizarre parade balloon. The entrance slid open with the help of Lafferty's hair, and on the other side, I held the hair against the scanner and screamed, "Lock, lock, lock!"

The clank of boltlocks reverberated behind us. But I knew it would only take Lafferty a few seconds to get free. We were at the base of a spiral staircase. I pulled Finn toward the ground and tapped the gravbelt so he could run up it with me. Plain emergency hatch portals lined the sides of the stairs. There was a single door, a real door, at the top landing. We were halfway to the top when the first red scrub jumped out of one of the hatches. Then another. And another.

Up, up, up we raced. I held out Lafferty's hair in front of me like an offering to the patron saint of getaways. It had barely registered on the scanner when I shoved the door open with all my might. I'd braced myself for a hallway or more stairs.

Hadn't braced myself for the central Atrium, chock full o' people.

I slammed the door shut behind me and shoved Lafferty's hair against the scanner. "Lock."

A guide in a pert little skirt, who looked not much older than me, led a tour group. There was no point trying to blend in. Finn and I crashed through the people like a bull elephant on the rampage. They scattered and yelped in their snooty tones, and I wasn't too gentle in shoving them aside to get to the front doors. It was hard to believe that ICE hadn't gone on full lockdown mode to trap Finn and me in, but at the same time, they had visitors—influential visitors—who they didn't want to alarm.

"Move," I yelled, pushing a middle-aged woman with more diamond rings than fingers out of my way as Finn and I scrambled for the entrance a mere thirty feet away. It shocked me that they'd built that critical room so close to the front atrium, but then again, depending on how long it had been there, this space might not have been an atrium at the time. At the time it was built, the room we just came from might have been the only thing in existence. I ventured a glance over my shoulder to look at the door we'd emerged from, but it blended seamlessly, invisibly, into the wall.

Finn and I rushed the front entrance, but the doors wouldn't budge. I tried Lafferty's hair. Nope.

Dang it.

They must have deactivated her access.

Crap, crap, crap!

A smidge of red flashed in my peripheral vision, and out of a crimson red tube, a fleet of red scrubs began to pour out.

"Can I help you?" The tour guide, utterly bewildered, had stumbled over toward us. She barely looked at us, keeping her plastic smile focused on the group behind her. It was clear that her instructions had been to keep them happy and impressed at all costs.

"I . . ." Okay, there's no point in lying. What happened next was not my finest moment.

I realized there was no way they'd turn off her access as she led the group from impressive location to impressive location. I grabbed her around the neck and dragged her toward the door. I practically gave her a noogie as I rubbed her hair against the sensor.

"Ow," she squealed, but I hadn't really hurt her. And it worked. The door slid open. I dropped her to the floor, and Finn hopped over her body as we sprinted down the steps away from the head-quarters.

"Take a Pod?" he said.

"Too trackable."

"Metro?"

"Snake in a barrel."

"Actually, the phrase is . . ."

I shot him a look, and he said, "Running it is."

I risked another glance behind us when we reached the op-posite side of the street. A fleet of red poured through the ICE headquarters doors, scanning the area for us.

As if on cue, my fingers began to tingle, building up to a Shift. I smiled. So long, twenty-third century. I paused where we were, dragging Finn to a halt with me. I wrapped my arms around him, ready to leave this chase behind. But the usual sensation of our tendrils weaving together didn't meet me. Instead, it was like someone had doused my body with numbness. The urge to Shift simply evaporated. I backed up, shocked.

The urge to Shift returned.

"Finn, did you feel that?"

"I feel nothing."

"But did you feel—?"

"I feel *nothing,* Bree. Usually when I'm on a Shift anywhere—here, the past—I can still feel at least a slight tug home. But right now, it's like . . . it's like they stripped something from me. I feel . . . nothing."

When my chip was still active, and I'd been Anchored as a punishment, I'd felt heavy. Chained. But what he was describing was something else. Whatever they'd done to him, whatever it was that was still floating in those tanks back at ICE's headquarters—memories or tendrils—it was the essence of what made him a Shifter. Without it, he was trapped here.

"Bree, what if I can never get home? What if I never see my family again or—?"

"We'll get you home. I promise. But first, we have to get you somewhere safe." And fast.

Whatever lead we'd gained had evaporated as one of the scrubs spotted us. They turned en masse to chase us like a school of red piranhas.

"Let's go!" I grabbed Finn's hand and sprinted down a side street until we were once again out of eyeshot. We still had the advantage of the gravbelt and grappling hook. The last direction I wanted to head was up, but in a pinch, I'd jump rooftop to rooftop if I had to.

We rounded a sharp corner and almost plowed into a Pod as it swerved to avoid a soakswitch. The two near-impacts must have shorted out its anti-collision mechanism because it shot straight up into the air about twenty feet and hovered there, like it was cowering.

"Crap," I said. "That'll be like a homing beacon for ICE."

I grabbed Finn's hand again and started to run in the opposite direction, but he just stood there, staring at the Pod with a look of utter amazement on his face.

"Is that a . . . a flying bubble?" he said.

"We don't have time for jokes," I said. A snatch of red lit up my peripheral vision. "Come on!"

We reached the end of the block, and I almost ran headlong into a kid on a jet-propelled disk-dasher.

"This is like a movie!" Finn stumbled forward, not even attempting to hide the awe in his voice.

"Yes, yes." A horror movie.

But then that gave me an idea. He'd made me watch this ridiculous (okay, fine, ridiculously awesome) trilogy of movies about time travel from the late twentieth century that he loved. There was a running gag of chase scenes with these archaic versions of disk-dashers that hovered a few inches off the ground that always made me laugh.

But Finn was pretty athletic. And I'd never met a better magno-grappler.

So, yeah. This was happening.

I shoved the kid off his disk-dasher.

"Hey!" the kid yelled.

"I need to borrow this," I said. Steal it. Whatever.

Finn looked at me like I'd gone insane.

"Like those movies you love," I said, praying he hadn't lost that memory, as I pulled the grappling handle from his pocket and aimed it at a passing Pod. I positioned the hovering dasher under his feet, and his face lit up in understanding.

"You are the coolest person ever." He planted a kiss on top of my head.

"And you'd better be the most naturally talented at balancing on a speeding hoverboard."

"Can't be that different from slalom skiing." He wrapped one arm around me and held the other out to keep his balance, tipping the front of the board up to brace for the takeoff. "Guess we'll find out."

Ping. The target activated, and with a jolt, we were pulled forward just as the men in red reached the kid we'd stolen the dasher from.

I screamed, but Finn let out a whoop of elation. A whoop I'd heard many times before. Which made me feel better and worse at the same moment.

All our joyful wanderings, the thrill of visiting a time and a place never before witnessed by human eyes, had he lost any of those moments? Had he lost all of them?

I couldn't worry about that now. That's what new memories were for. The only thing that mattered was getting him to a safe place. Or at least safer. But where? My house was obviously out. The Institute, out. Taking him to Resthaven would put the Shifters there at risk, but I didn't see any other option. And Nurse Granderson might have additional insight into retrieving the memories and repairing Finn's hippocampus.

The Pod turned sharply at a corner, and Finn pulled me down close to the board in a squat to brace for it as we swung behind it in a swaying arc. We narrowly missed a street sign, and Finn had to kick off from a passing Pod to avoid hitting it. I glanced back and watched as the other Pod filled with foam, sensing the impact.

"That was close," said Finn.

At least we'd lost the pursuing scrubs. I started to recognize the neighborhoods. We were only a few blocks away from Resthaven. The Pod that pulled us slowed for a pedestrian, and I took advantage of the pause to detach ourselves from it. Finn and I tumbled to the pavement, scratched and bruised, but alive and uncaptured. Finn shook the grappling handle and pointed at the Pod speeding away.

"There goes our last hook."

"It's okay. We can walk from here. And the longer we stayed attached to that thing, the greater chance ICE could track us."

"So." He twined his fingers through mine. "Catch me up."

As we walked to Resthaven, I filled him in on everything I had experienced, surmised, guessed, or feared in the last twenty-four hours.

"You're sure Mom and Dad and Georgie are okay?" he asked when I'd finished.

"They're all fine. Worried about you, but fine."

"We'll figure out a way to help your mom, too." He squeezed my hand. "She's no drug dealer. They have to realize that."

"All they know is that she had all those drugs. Finn, she could have *died*. I already almost lost her once. If she . . . I can't . . . I . . ."

My voice had turned to spiky squeaks and Finn held me close.

"Shhh. Nobody's losing anyone. Your mom's a fighter. She's going to be okay."

"How do you know that?"

"Hey." He pulled my chin up. "Have a little faith in fate."

"I have faith in a lot of things," I said. "Fate hasn't been one of them lately. I mean, hello. It gave me Jafney as a roommate."

"Told you that you'd be friends," Finn said, but I didn't laugh. I couldn't after losing my friendship with Mimi.

"Well, turns out she's had a thing for Wyck this whole time. She was using you to try to make him jealous."

Finn bristled.

"I didn't say I have a thing for him," I said.

"Nah. It's just that I like Jaf. She's okay."

"Hmm."

"She deserves better than Wyck."

"I wish you could have met the real Wyck."

"What do you mean?" asked Finn.

"Before all this started, he was a good friend. For a while there, he was one of my only friends. ICE has ruined his life as much as mine."

"Yeah. Still don't like him." Finn wrapped his arm around me, and I could see what he meant about feeling nothing. Usually there was a slight flicker between our tendrils. But when he touched my bare skin, it was like dousing a bucket of water on a candle. Finn didn't seem to notice or care. Maybe he'd gotten used to the numb.

I felt around again, all along his neck, searching for a scar line. If it was only that they'd microchipped him, it would have made things so much simpler. Chips could be disabled. No such luck.

"Let's focus on helping your mom for now," Finn said.

"Okay."

Finn was the only person I knew who could be stuck in the wrong century and still think of others first.

"Is there any way to undo what happened?" asked Finn.

"No. Not unless a Neo changed the past back. Or if another Neo made a change that had ripple effects on Mom." Not likely.

"So a nonShifter could fix things. Obviously, Wyck is out," Finn said. "Charlie?"

"I can't do that to Charlie. My mom would never forgive me. And besides, I get the feeling I don't have many close friends, Shifter or Non, on this timeline. Even Mimi's cut off from me. And she's not dating Charlie now. In fact, I got the feeling from talking to her that things are deteriorating between Shifters and Nons."

"From the way Lafferty was talking, it sounds like that's what she wants," he said. "Does your mom need an attorney?"

"Yeah, but the ones who specialize in Temporal Law are bonks bucks. I guess I could sell the house or—wait! The bank account. I never told Leto the last number. You opened the account before all these temporal loop changes. The account should still exist."

"Perfect," he said.

"So what's the last digit?" I asked.

"I have no idea."

"Are you serious?"

"Very." The strain of empty recollection stained his cheeks. "I remember there's a bank account. I remember that I should know the last number. I just don't remember what it is. It's like it was plucked from my brain."

"It must be one of the memories you lost," I said. "Wait. I have an idea. Fast as you can, name a number, one through ten. Actually, zero through nine."

"Seven," he said.

"Let's try seven."

"Really?"

"Better than nothing." Which was precisely how much money I had otherwise. "If we get it wrong, it will lock the account, but it's worth a shot."

"All right. Seven it is."

I stopped at the nearest dollardock and entered the account numbers I knew and then hit seven for the final digit.

The account pulled up. "Woohoo!" Finn's original deposit was right there at the top. I scrolled down through two centuries' worth of interest accumulation down to the current account total.

$0.00

"What?" I scrolled back up to the last transaction. The account had been drained a few days ago. By Leto Malone. "That's impossible. This withdrawal was the day of our movie date. He didn't know the number then."

"Maybe he guessed, too."

I shook my head. "He wouldn't have risked it. One lock-out, and there would have been a mountain of paperwork and explanations."

If I knew anything about Leto Malone, it was that he didn't do paperwork, and he definitely didn't give explanations.

"Maybe he figured it out some other way," said Finn.

"How? You were the only person who knew that number. Even I didn't know it. Heck, *you* didn't know it anymore."

"Do you remember anything dodgy about that conversation with Leto?"

"Hard to remember a conversation with Leto that hasn't been dodgy." I screwed up my nose in concentration. Less than a week ago, and it seemed like years. I'd been so focused on the Finn-as-a-temporal-fugitive part of Leto's news that I hadn't paid much attention to the rest of it. But it had been same-old.

"He asked me about the number. I basically told him to go jump in a Pod's path. He started to harass me about it then . . . stopped. That was unusual. The next time I saw him was at ICE's headquarters where he had clearly come into a windfall. By that point, he didn't know who I was."

"Did you give him a hint somehow?" asked Finn. "At the movie theater?"

"Couldn't have. I didn't know the number. *Only you did.* It was like he was reading your mind. Or—oh my gosh. Finn, when Leto was dying, he was talking about Chincoteague and sea grass and Ed."

"Ed?"

"Ed. My pegamoo?" A feeling of dread set in as Finn shook his head. He didn't remember Ed.

No, no, no.

"That's not all," I said. "Leto was acting so weird, all lovey-dovey. It was like he was channeling you."

"Or stealing my memories."

We stood there, longer than was safe, both speechless. Finn's memories weren't lost.

They were stolen.

"What does this mean?" he asked.

"It means ICE is an even bigger threat to Shifters than we re-alized." And that was saying something. Not just the unchipped

Shifters at Resthaven. Chipped Shifters with their unbearable Buzz. Shifters in the past, too.

"Bree, if Leto somehow stole my memories, does that mean they . . . died with him?"

"I think so."

"But that's just the ones he had. There are still memories in those tanks. I . . . I could still regain those. And after I do, I'll be able to Shift again, right? It's all tied up in the hippocampus. Memories and tendrils and the Shifter mutation. Right?"

"Yeah," I said. "Of course."

In truth, I had no idea how it worked. He didn't respond, but both our steps quickened to get to Resthaven.

As we walked, I realized that Leto wasn't the only Neo who'd taken a piece of Finn. Wyck had Finn's memories, too. That night when he'd sung Finn's green song. Wyck couldn't recall where he knew that song from. That was because it had been taken from Finn's brain. Who knew what else Wyck had in there?

When we were a block away, I dropped my voice to a hush and asked, "What's it like?"

"What's what like?" Finn took my hand and, even though I didn't like the numb sensation, I squeezed tight.

"Having your memories taken from you." I couldn't even begin to imagine the violation.

"Confusing." He shrugged. "Weird. I feel like I still know what's going on but when I stop to concentrate on the details, it's as if they evaporate as I try to pin them down. It's like . . . do you remember when Aunt Lisa let us watch one of her sessions with Leonardo?"

I smiled. Glad he still had that. That was one of my favorite dates ever. We landed in Florence, and I thought maybe we were just there for a good bowl of pasta, but then the Quig showed up, only not grumpy like usual. She was downright giddy as she let me fuss over her hair while Leonardo da Vinci prepared his palette. Scholars may have later claimed Leonardo's apprentices captured a more exact likeness of her face, but he captured her soul.

"Well, you remember how you said that it was interesting that you could look at the rough sketches he did of her and see the finished *Mona Lisa*? You didn't even need the paint over it. It was so familiar that you could swear he'd already completed it even when it was just some black and white marks and . . . that's what it's like. I know there are things that I'm missing—lots—but as long as I know the end, as long as I know you, I feel like I have the whole picture."

"We're going to get your memories back." I think I was promising myself as much as him.

He gave me a sad smile as I touched his cheek.

"And how are we going to do that?"

That hit me harder than anything, his look of defeat. Finn never admitted defeat. He'd fight and fight and fight until the battle had been won or lost a million times over. But he never quit.

Until now. He'd quit.

"I have some ideas," I said. One. I had one idea. And Finn would hate it. As far as I knew, Wyck was still a viable link to ICE. I had to exploit it. If I could get him to sneak me back into that room with the reservoirs. That locked . . . heavily guarded . . . room . . . full of technology I didn't understand.

Blark.

I still couldn't comprehend how my future self didn't mention any of this. I mean, yeah, catch the kidnapper, great. But how could she not have mentioned that ICE would break my boyfriend's brain in the process? And here's a thought. "Hey, Bree, every time you get close to taking a step forward in this muddled mess, brace yourself for two giant leaps back. Get within inches of an answer and everything around you will change. Just to let you know ahead of time."

"If we can't get those memories back," said Finn quietly, "I want you to know that it's okay. You've done everything in your power to help me. To help every Shifter. Bree, you're not God. You can't create a new world, and this one is what it is."

"And what is it?"

Finn grinned, a real one. "Not finished."

He hugged me, and I let myself melt into him.

Whir.

"Is that a reverter in your pocket or am I just really happy to see you?" asked Finn.

I nudged his shoulder then realized . . . dang it.

The moment that my skin brushed his, there it was. The dousing sensation. Finn wouldn't be able to come with me. I stepped away.

"What are you waiting for?" asked Finn.

"Your tendrils are . . . umm. . . ."

"You're shackled to me."

I didn't respond. I didn't have to.

"Go," he said. "Fix it."

"I'm not leaving you here."

"You have to."

"What if they find you while I'm gone?"

"I'll stay right here." He pointed at the pavement.

"No. They could search this area." I glanced down at the reverter, already slowing. Wyck had been getting ready to Shift while we were there at ICE. This was probably his change. I had to fix it. "Get to Resthaven. Tell Quigley what's happened."

He bit his lip.

"What's the matter?" I said.

"I don't, umm . . ."

"You don't remember where Resthaven is?" I said.

"No." Another lost memory.

"We can't risk a Pod." I looked up and down the street. We were so close. Right around the block.

"That's one of those floaty things?"

"You really don't remember what a Pod is? You weren't joking back there."

"I really don't. But they're dang cool, if I do say so myself."

"But you were the one who asked if we should take a Pod. Right outside ICE's headquarters. Twenty minutes ago. You used the word 'Pod.'"

"I did?"

I watched as the full realization of what that meant spread through Finn's brain.

"I haven't just lost memories," he said. "I'm still losing them."

"That must be the hippocampal degradation they were talking about."

I had to make a split decision. The reverter was still going fairly strong. I couldn't leave Finn here by himself. Not with him actively losing memories. He could forget he was hiding while I was gone. I grabbed his hand and started racing toward Resthaven. If there was any hope of getting him back to normal, it was Nurse Granderson.

Normal.

It didn't exist anymore. Not for me. Not for Finn.

A fresh wave of that complex grief I had felt earlier when I believed Finn had chosen Jafney over me struck. Finn was so good. He deserved to be whole and happy. He deserved normal.

We swung around from the rear to Resthaven. I took a short-cut through the neighbor's backyard. Resthaven was a converted Victorian mansion. Back in my father's early years, it had been a hostel. After World War I, it served as a convalescent home for injured soldiers. Most of the Shifters who lived there now were peace-seeking, like Nava. Lately, it seemed we'd all gone to war, though.

The back door was locked. I brushed my hair across the scanner, but it didn't pop open.

Quigley must have tightened security after Nava's abduction. I banged on the door.

"Come on," I whispered under my breath. The reverter had begun to slow. I wouldn't have much time at all to revert this change.

Someone I didn't recognize—a man about fifty years old with hair so pale I couldn't tell if it was blonde or white—opened the door. "Can I help you?"

"Tell Quigley that Finn needs help. He can explain the rest." I practically tossed Finn at the man. "I'll be right back, sweetie."

"Quigley?" the man said.

"Is she out?"

"I'm not sure who you're . . . oh." His face went flat with just a hint of a sneer. "Was she with that group of Shifters that used to live here?"

Oh no. I held the reverter up, its faint emerald glow dimming by the second. That's when I realized it was the only thing glowing green in the vicinity. The ever-present Haven beacons that normally lit up the doorways of Resthaven were missing. I peered around the man, but the insides of the huge old house were now decorated completely differently. Where a Ping-Pong table had been only a few hours ago was now a velvet couch. Whatever change was happening, the Haven was in its crosshairs.

"I have to . . ."

"Go." Finn took a leap back as if being in his very vicinity might prevent me from Shifting.

I didn't have the chance to even worry about what the random blond man was thinking when I clicked the end of the reverter. As I faded away, all I could think was, God help me if something happened to Finn.

And God help whoever had done this when I got my hands on him.

chapter 24

I LANDED MERE FEET from where I'd just been in my time, right outside Resthaven's back door. I yanked out my Com to get my bearings. A little over a year past. The green flames danced merrily above the doorjamb.

". . . And that's when she started making threats."

I immediately recognized the voice that rang out from around the corner of the building. Wyck O'Banion. That blarking crap-weasel. I edged my way over so I could hear him better.

"The woman was confused but saying things like 'The Haven will take all of you out,' and 'We're going to take over the world.'"

What on the purple polka-dotted seas of Neptune? No one in the Haven would ever say anything like that.

I stooped down and ventured a peek to see who he was talking to. There were two men—I recognized one of them as Officer Abernathy, the head chronoinvestigator who had looked into Nava's disappearance. The other had on the same type of badge and was taking notes.

"I don't know what he's talking about." Cassa, one of Rest-haven's residents, stood next to them, wringing her hands.

"Where were you last night?" asked the investigator taking notes.

"Here. I think. I don't quite remember." Of course she didn't. And this being a year ago, she didn't even realize the reason. That was before we knew ICE was changing the timeline. Poor Cassa. She looked stricken. "I would never attack anyone. I'm a botanist!"

"And the last time you had your chip's functioning checked?" Officer Abernathy asked.

"I . . . uhhh . . ." Her confusion turned to stone-cold fear.

"You're sure this is her?" The note-taking investigator turned back to Wyck.

"I'm positive." Wyck stared at the ground.

"Liar!" I wanted to scream, but I didn't want to alert them to my presence. I'd only get one shot to jab the reverter into his neck. For that I'd need the element of surprise. I pulled the device up to my chest. It had never felt more like a weapon than in that moment.

I peered around the corner once more as I got ready to pounce. But this time, Wyck wasn't staring at the pavement. He was staring straight at me. Like he'd known I was there the whole time.

He didn't appear angry, or vengeful or plotting.

He looked utterly exhausted.

But that didn't mean he wouldn't put up a fight. I pulled out my Com and dialed the stunner's setting halfway up. Enough to stop him in his tracks without paralyzing his vocal cords. I needed to wring some answers out of him.

I was about to step out and take him down when arms wrapped around my chest, pinning my elbows to my side.

"Hey!" I tried to wrestle out of the grasp. So help me, if this was my apparently brainwashed future self . . .

"I don't have a choice," whispered a panicked female voice in my ear. She dragged me away from the corner.

I knew that voice.

I wriggled out of her hold and turned to face her.

"Jafney?"

She stared at my hand, clearly upset. I followed her gaze, and we both watched the reverter dull to a blip. My chance was gone.

Jafney had taken it from me.

"How could you?" I asked.

"I'm sorry." She at least had the decency to sound horrified with herself. "I'm just . . . I'm following orders."

I was so tired of hearing that. Even my future self had defended Wyck's actions with that same excuse. But this was indefensible.

"Whose orders?" I asked. "Wyck's?"

"Bree, it's not what you think. He's my boyfriend now. On the timeline I'm on. I'm trying to help him."

Help him? That meant she was in ICE's clutches, too. That sent me back to my original question.

"How could you?"

"You're not allowed to lecture me." A tear licked her lashes, and she wiped it away then laid an angry finger into me. "Not you."

"What's that supposed to mean?" I asked. Wait. "How far into the future are you from?"

"Far enough to know that you need all the help you can get," she said.

"What?"

"Focus on what matters, Bree. *To save his, destroy yours.*"

"How do you know the clue?" I asked.

"You told me," she said. "I've been the one delivering it to the past for you to find. At the fire. At your father's house. I know you don't believe me right now, but we're on the same side."

She glanced around the corner of the building. "We *all* end up on the same side."

"Are you talking about Wyck?"

"Has it not occurred to you that Finn may not be the only one who needs saving? You've seen what Shifting does to Neos."

"Are you talking about *Wyck*?" The same Wyck who had just uprooted the Haven.

"When you run into my future self," she said, "you have to trust me."

I had a hard enough time trusting my own future self. There was no way in Blarking Blarktown I was trusting *hers*.

Before I had a chance to respond, though, she took a step back. And was gone.

"Get back here!" I yelled like she could hear me somehow. I clamped my hand over my mouth when I remembered Wyck and the investigators were still right around the corner. I dashed behind a tree and surrendered to the fade. Not that there was much to go back to.

I landed behind the tool shed in the backyard bordering the now-defunct Resthaven. Finn was already waiting there for me, crouched behind a rain barrel.

He looked over at not-Resthaven and said, "I guess it didn't work."

"It would have if Jafney hadn't stopped me."

"Jafney was there?"

"She was from the future. And she was helping Wyck. He's her boyfriend on whatever timeline she's on. She must have tipped him off, too, because he saw me, but he didn't look surprised."

"Why would she do that? She's an unchipped Shifter. She needs the Haven just as much as you do."

"I don't know. She claimed we were on the same side." But that didn't affect our next course of action. "We have to find Nurse Granderson. He's still the best hope of helping you."

"Well, even if there's no Resthaven, I'd bet anything that unchipped Shifters are still banding together on this timeline."

I nodded and pulled up a directory search on my QuantCom. It gave me an address for Granderson.

At this point, wasting time on foot with Finn still losing memories worried me more than getting caught by ICE, so we took the Metro. When we reached Granderson's place, it was in an area near my house in Old Georgetown. Only this part was a lot younger and trendier than my neighborhood. I rang the buzzer to the brownstone and waited. Footsteps rushed to the door.

Granderson opened it, disheveled but alive, so that was a good starting point.

"Do you know what happened to Resthaven?" He didn't mince words, and I didn't mince any in return.

"Wyck O'Banion went back and filed some bogus charges against Cassa a year ago. It changed the timeline, and Resthaven must have been a casualty."

"Why would he do that?"

"No clue. Honestly, I doubt it had anything to do with Cassa personally." A siren sounded in the distance, and I flinched. "Can we come in?"

I expected him to throw open the door immediately, but he looked at Finn and me and hesitated.

"We have nowhere else to go," I said.

"Sorry." Granderson stepped aside. "Of course."

Some of the pictures and possessions in the entryway looked vaguely familiar. When I saw who was sitting on a chaise in the parlor, I placed where I knew them from and smiled.

"Nava." I walked over and hugged her.

Finn stared unknowingly at her. I turned to him.

"Do you remember Nava? From . . . ?" I didn't finish the question. It wasn't like ICE's Cryostorage had been summer camp. I didn't want to upset the elderly woman.

Finn shook his head. "I don't remember much at all right now. It's nice to meet you."

We walked back to the entryway to talk to Granderson. He'd been absentmindedly dusting some of the framed pictures. I was thankful to see some familiar faces in them. I couldn't remember all the names, and some came and went at Resthaven without living there. Unchipped Shifters may have been scattered on this timeline, but apparently most were still alive.

"I'm glad Nava's with you," I said to Granderson. "Is anyone else from the Haven here?"

"I don't think so," he said. "We've only been here for half an hour. I haven't had time to piece much information together. This really complicates things."

"Did you own this place before you moved to Resthaven?" I asked.

"It was in the family." He wiped a smudge off the frame he was holding, then tucked it behind the others on the shelf. "My father owns it."

"Good," I said. "Maybe we could round up some more Haven members."

"They must be terrified," said Finn.

"I don't think that's a good idea," said Granderson. "This place is deceptively small on the inside. It's just been my father living here by himself for quite a while."

I looked around again. Other than Nava's stuff that was spread around, this place definitely did look like a bachelor pad. But I never would have guessed an old guy lived here.

"We should at least try to get ahold of Aunt Lisa," said Finn.

"First we need to take care of you." I entwined my fingers with Finn's and was reassured by the pulse of his wrist against mine. "Quigley can take care of herself for now."

"What's wrong with Finn?" Nurse Granderson pulled a scanner out of his pocket and began to check Finn's vitals.

I launched into an abbreviated version of the full story: starting with the fire at Finn's house, my break-in at ICE to save him, followed by our escape, and ending with my failed reversion.

"These changes," said Granderson as he circled some instrument around Finn's eye sockets, "they all seem to happen at the worst possible time."

"Worst possible time for me. Best possible for Wyck." It struck me again, the deliberation that had gone into the changes that had the most direct impact on me. Well-planned assaults, more like it. It wasn't horrible timing. It was perfect. Perfectly chosen moments, as if Wyck had done his homework and knew exactly when I wouldn't be able to revert them. And now Jafney was in on it, too. *Trust her.* Ha!

"Why don't you get settled in, Finn?" said Granderson. "There's a spare bedroom at the end of the hall upstairs."

"Thanks," said Finn. "If you're able to Shift back and let my parents know I'm okay but stuck here, I'd appreciate it."

"I'll try. I haven't Shifted since Nava got back." Granderson coughed, his eyes bleary. Didn't look like he'd slept in a few days. "I don't want to leave her alone."

"I understand," I said. "Charlotte's probably hysterical, though. He's their only son."

Granderson gave a weak smile. "You're right. That's an unbreakable bond. I'll try to track down Quigley and have her deliver the message if she can."

"Thanks," said Finn. "And maybe don't mention my memory loss. I don't want them any more worried than they already are."

"Understood."

Granderson left us, and I followed Finn up the stairs. Granderson was right. There wasn't much extra space. Four small bedrooms and three of them were already filled with Nava's, Granderson's, and his father's possessions. We walked into the spare bedroom, unspeaking, and sat side by side on the bed, untouching.

I leaned up and kissed him lightly. He kissed me back, but when I pulled away, he looked disturbed.

"What?" I asked.

"Nothing," he lied.

"No, what?"

"It's just that I can't . . ." He shook his head.

"Can't what?"

"Can't remember . . ." He squinched his eyes tight, pulled his shoulders back like he was straining against a taut fishing line. When he opened his eyes, the strain was replaced with resignation. The one that got away.

"It's okay," I said. I leaned forward to kiss him again, but he flinched.

Why would he quail at my kiss? And then it hit me.

"You've lost our kisses, haven't you?" I tried to keep my voice calm, but it was hard to hide the fear. What else had he lost?

"Not all of them. But our first kiss. Maybe." The strain was back. "I'm not sure. I'm having a hard time piecing together our, umm, kissing history."

"Oh. Well, that's true for me as well." Toss in a few gaps, and I'd be as lost as a malfunctioning Publi-pod. "There are several candidates for the honor of first kiss."

"Doesn't matter." He planted a peck on my forehead. "The important thing is that I'd do it again in half a heartbeat."

I was thankful when he began kissing me in earnest. I couldn't keep that fake wisp of a smile plastered on my face.

Finn was right. And wrong. I was thankful that he'd still choose that first kiss all over again, that he'd still choose me. But the fact that he couldn't remember our first kiss (and who knew how many other kisses after) did matter. Whatever they'd done to him in that tank, it had damaged him. ICE had stolen things that couldn't be replaced. I was beginning to lose hope that he'd ever get them back.

And losing hope was a lot more dangerous than losing memories.

His hands circled my waist and drew me close. I let go of my fears in the sweet scent of his minty breath, the spicy bite of his cologne.

Wait. He'd been in a vat of goop. How was I smelling his cologne?

A new scent joined the other two: new car leather mixed with briny kelp. With it, an inexplicable, sickening wave of fear—no, terror—slammed into me.

I gasped.

I knew what I was smelling.

"Finn. Your car."

"What?"

"The crash."

Blank stare. "What are you talking about?"

"On the beach. We crashed . . . okay, I crashed your car into the ocean. You don't remember that, do you?"

He met me with blank eyes, and that was an answer in itself.

And the minty breath . . .

"The bus ride. When I first met you?"

Blank stare.

His cologne. Oh. The cologne could be anything. No, that wasn't true.

"Our first real date," I said, a tear leaking from the corner of my eye. He'd drowned himself in aftershave after reading this idiotic men's magazine. I made him wash half of it off.

Blank stare.

I had to stop this. I was losing him.

I pressed my lips to his with an urgency I'd never experienced before, like somehow I could re-create those moments that were literally slipping from his mind. Stay with me, stay with me.

Finn turned from me and stared out the window.

"I'd better get home." He patted his pockets. "Do you have my keys?"

"Keys to what?"

"My car."

"There are no cars in the . . ." My voice caught. "Do you know where we are?"

"Mom will be having kittens if I don't get home." He stood up from the bed, ignoring me.

"Oh, Finn." There was no home left to go back to.

I pulled him down next to me on the bed. Tears streamed down my cheeks in earnest. He tried to stand back up, confusion marring his features, but I held him in place.

"Bree?" He mumbled into my shoulder.

I held him close but had to let go after a few moments. It was too much.

The scents swirled together in my nostrils, a maelstrom of reminiscence and misplaced emotions. Sweet, creamy coconut from Jamaica—relaxed. Bitter, coppery blood from his first lost baby tooth—pride. The heady, heavenly whiff of my cherry blossom perfume—lust. The last crisp wisp of spun sugar from the Pentagon—excitement and elation and trepidation and protectiveness.

All of it whirled into one.

All of it gone.

Finn stared at me for a moment. His eyes had a dull haze to them, then they lulled back in their sockets. He tumbled over onto the mattress.

"Finn?" I tapped his chest. I yelled his name again, but the only response was the twitching of his limbs.

I rushed into the hallway and screamed for Granderson. He took the steps two at a time.

"Hold him still," he said, his medical scanner at the ready.

"What's going on?" I asked as Finn thrashed against my constraint.

"His quantum tendrils have been hyperstimulated." Granderson ran so many tests at once that the air above Finn blurred with a haze of soligraphs.

"How do you even know which tests to run?" I asked.

"He's bordering on hippocampal failure," said Granderson, ignoring my question.

"What does that mean? Help him!"

"I have to sedate him." Granderson pulled out some bio-nodes and attached them to Finn's scalp. "Our best shot is to minimize any brain functioning."

"Best shot? You mean you can get his memories back?"

Granderson gave me a pitying look. "Best shot to survive."

He activated the nodes as I looked on in horror. Immediately, Finn relaxed. His eyelids loosened from their spasms. He turned to face me and got one small smile in.

"Hey," said Finn.

"Hey." I stroked his cheek. "You're going to go to sleep for a while."

"I love you," he said. "Since the beginning."

"I love you," I said. "Until the end."

Finn went limp. I wrapped my hand around his and squeezed, neither expecting nor receiving any response. I was going to do everything in my power to make sure that the end didn't come for a very long time. I burrowed into his chest and drank in his scent, claiming each and every memory as my own. His chest settled into a rhythmic rise and fall, and my breathing calmed to match his. Soon, I had drifted off to sleep.

I didn't know how many hours had passed when Nurse Granderson roused me, but I felt relatively refreshed.

Granderson shushed me when I started to speak and motioned me out to the hall.

"The less sensory stimulation Finn has, the better," he said quietly.

"Even lying next to him?" I asked.

"Even lying next to him." Then he added, more quietly, "Especially you."

"Why especially me?"

"Anything or anyone that could trigger a memory could make it worse."

"But"—okay, I was grasping here—"do you think it could help if we figured out a way to get him home? I mean, his father's an incredible surgeon. Maybe if we brought technology from this time, John could—"

"What home?" Granderson shook his head.

I gulped and nodded. The only home Finn had ever known had been burned to the ground.

"Why don't you go get something to eat downstairs?" he said.

"Okay."

I went and made myself a sandwich. As I slathered an extra

scoop of almond butter onto the bread, it reminded me of the first time Georgie introduced me to a fluffer-nutter. It had turned into a funny mock-fight between her and Finn:

You're a fluffer-nutter.

You're the fluffer-nutter.

Your mom's the fluffer-nutter.

I'm going to tell Mom you just called her a fluffer-nutter.

By the end, it was agreed that everyone and everyone's mother was, indeed, a fluffer-nutter.

Finn was never going to fake-bicker with Georgie again. Or taste another marshmallow. Or . . .

No. I gave myself a mental slap. That wasn't going to happen. I wouldn't let it. I was going to save Finn.

Wait. I took out the clue I'd been carrying with me this whole time. I was going to save Finn. Future Bree had already told me so.

To save his, destroy yours.

And then, those numbers and letters and symbols with all the blanks.

Even Jafney had made reference to it, that I'd save Finn. I smoothed the compufilm out on the counter and squinted at it. With the holes placed so sporadically, maybe they made a picture. But nope.

There was shuffling behind me, and Nava walked up next to me, teacup in hand.

"I'm so sorry to hear about your boyfriend, dear." She laid a bony hand on my elbow.

"Thank you," I said.

"I had hoped that by this day and age, cross-temporal love would be accepted, or at least not quite so taboo."

"No such luck," I said. "Look at my parents' Podwreck of a marriage."

"Don't be so hard on them," she said. "Making that kind of relationship work would be hard for anyone. And with your mother chipped like she was for so long, it would be nearly impossible."

"Are you speaking from experience?" I asked.

"His name's Art." She blushed.

"What time period was he from?"

"We're both Shifters," she said. "Time is just another direction."

"But it didn't work out?"

"What can I say? It got complicated."

Complicated. That, I could understand.

"My point is, you shouldn't be ashamed of those sticky tendrils of yours. Promise me you'll be proud of them and proud of your parents for choosing love."

"I promise."

I tried to smile, but it was hard with my taboo love upstairs unconscious and losing memories by the moment.

Nava placed her teacup on the counter right next to the piece of compufilm I'd been studying and peered at it.

"Planning some trips?" she asked.

"Huh?"

She tapped the compufilm. "Are you going somewhere?"

"What do you mean?"

"This list of transport codes. Although"—she picked up the compufilm and held it close for a better look—"you seem to be missing some parts."

"These are transport codes?"

"Well, that's what they're called in the chipped world. We'd probably use different terminology." Nava refilled her tea and sat down at the kitchen table.

I joined her. "You mean, they're temporal coordinates?"

"No, it's more complex than that. Temporal coordinates are nothing more than chronogeological markers. These are more like temporal DNA."

"I don't follow."

"Temporal coordinates only tell Shifters where and when they are, a dot on a map, a date on the calendar. Transport codes tell you much more."

"You mean, what you did?"

"More like what your brain did. How it was responding to things around you. Physical and emotional stimuli."

"Why isn't this taught at the Institute?" I asked.

"Oh, it is. Not to Shifters, but it's standard knowledge for transporters."

I thought back to the mid-term when I'd first met the Mastersons and then encountered them again when I switched assignments with Mimi. Wyck had noticed the strange tendril surges in my readouts. He'd been able to tell I had been around unchipped Shifters. These transport codes must have been what he was referring to.

"How do you know so much about it?"

"I wouldn't say I know much. I picked up tidbits when I was still in the field. Did Devvy not tell you what I did before I ended up at Resthaven?"

"Why do you call Nurse Granderson Devvy?"

"Give an old lady a break. I've known him his whole life." She smiled.

"I know you collected DNA samples to identify victims from mass graves at a concentration camp."

"That was one project. I was a chronogeneticist."

"I thought you were an anthropologist. Could that be why ICE took you?" I still couldn't piece together how it was that Finn was upstairs, practically in a coma, and Nava was here and completely coherent. They'd returned her so quickly, but it didn't seem like they had any intentions of returning him.

"I doubt it. I didn't have a particularly exceptional career. And I've been out of the field for decades. Even their lowliest technician would be more current on research than I am."

"But, in theory, you could look at these codes and tell me things about these particular Shifts."

"Oh, dear. I . . . no. You would need a transporter to help you with any real details." She picked the compufilm back up and smoothed it out. "And I'm afraid that these codes won't tell you anything without the missing parts."

There was no real pattern to the absent symbols. "Where would I even begin to figure that out?"

"I'm sorry. I do hope you find what you're looking for." She enveloped my hand in hers. "Do you know a transporter?"

"Unfortunately, yes."

chapter 25

"HEY, BREE." WYCK OPENED the door to his family's tiny flat. "To what do I owe this pleasu—?"

I had him down to his knees in a fierce nerve pinch before he could finish the question.

"Whah?" he choked out.

With my free hand, I dug my thumb into his windpipe until he gasped in pain and for breath. Maybe you could catch more flies with honey than vinegar, but I was pretty sure you could catch the most with a hair-trigger bear trap.

"That's for my mom," I said. "And Finn. And Mimi. And the Haven Society. I know it was you."

"You know what was me?"

I had to actually think about that for a second. That was the only thing he'd remember, the change he'd made on this particular timeline. *That* was how screwed up everything had gotten.

"You accused Cassa of threatening you."

"Cassa?"

"From Resthaven."

His cheeks burned bright, then went pale.

"Was that her name?"

"You don't even know her name?" I tightened my pinch. "You took away her home, and you don't even know her name."

"Ow. He didn't say you were going to be this mad about it."

"He? Who's *he*?"

"Me," Wyck said. "Future Me. My future NeoShifting self.

He came to me and said that I was supposed to go to the police and claim that woman threatened me."

"Oh, and your future self told you I wasn't going to be angry at you for making all of my friends homeless? What else did your future self tell you about me?"

"He said you would come here, and when you did, I was supposed to help you, no matter what you asked of me."

"Well, isn't that just . . . wait. What?"

Wyck's brother Den walked into the entryway from what I presumed to be the kitchen, munching on a bowl of cereal. When he saw Wyck and me, he lifted his eyebrows and disappeared back into the kitchen.

Wyck didn't seem to notice. He rubbed his throat and stared at me like I was about to attack him again. I lifted my hands to assure him I wouldn't. For now.

"So is that why you're here?" he asked. "You need my help?"

I nodded, unsure where to start.

"Fine way to ask for it," he said.

"Did your future self tell you *why* you were going to help me?"

"What do you mean?"

"Did he mention that you owe me?"

"I owe you?"

"You're the one who's screwed up my life." I didn't care if he was following orders.

"Screwed up your—? Bree, I tell you I'm willing to help you, sight unseen, and you accuse me of screwing up your life? What the blark?"

"My mother. You know what happened to her, right?"

"There was some kind of drug bust."

"Yes. That's your fault."

"*My* fault?"

I nodded. "And you took my best friend away from me."

"Has something happened to Jafney?" That one struck a note of true panic in him.

"No. I'm talking about Mimi."

"Mimi Ellison? You guys barely even say hello in the halls."

"Exactly."

"Anything else you want to pin on me? Any floods . . . earthquakes?" He walked forward, not threatening, per se, but enough to make me back up. "Tell you what, next time a restaurant burns your toast, you can blame that on me, too. Forget whatever my future self told me. You can go help yourself."

By his sheer bulk, he had jostled me halfway onto the porch. He reached for the front door handle. Dang it. I'd botched this. My one chance of figuring out those transport codes was about to slam the door in my face.

I didn't think. I didn't deliberate.

I sang.

In my best frog voice.

" 'It's not easy . . . being green . . .' "

Wyck edged away from me.

And I kept singing.

"Where did you hear that?" He rubbed his forehead like he was trying to scrub the tune out of his brain.

I didn't answer. Just kept singing.

"Why do I know that song?" He thumped on his ear. That's right. Shake out those stolen memories. Good luck with that.

Kept singing.

"Stop it," he said, his voice a snarl. The tone of his voice took him aback. Probably a flash of Evil Wyck. He staggered away from me. "What's happening?"

I stopped.

I'd tried lies, threats, bodily harm.

Maybe it was time to try the truth.

"Can we go sit down?" I asked. "I need to start from the beginning."

The only problem is, how do you start from the beginning when it's all a big circle? So I decided to start with my feet hitting cobblestone. I decided to start with meeting Finn.

He was why I was here.

I left out a few key parts—namely Jafney's involvement (I still didn't know if I could trust her) and Finn's current residence at Nurse Granderson's house.

"Why should I believe any of this?" Wyck asked when I finished.

"I couldn't make this stuff up if I tried."

"Then why should I trust you? You just admitted you turned off your chip. And apparently made me the rickety line of some lopsided love triangle."

"No," I said. "It's always been Finn. Only Finn. It was never a triangle. Always a loop. A vicious, vicious loop."

"Why did my future self tell me to help you?" asked Wyck. "Why would he want me to get all tangled up in this?"

I thought about what Jafney had told me, that Finn wasn't the only one who needed saving. Wyck's muscle clenched on the sofa armrest, but he didn't make a move for me. I was thankful to be dealing with Real Wyck, not Evil Wyck. For now, at least.

"Because I think maybe I'm supposed to help you in return. I've seen what you're capable of," I said, "and somehow I still don't believe that's the real you."

"That's your pitch? Help you so I don't become a monster?"

"Not a monster. A pawn. Even my Future Self said you weren't to blame, that you're just obeying orders."

"Have I ever struck you as a Yes-man, Bree?"

I couldn't help but laugh. That was the very last word I would ever use to describe Wyck O'Banion.

"ICE must have something really smarmy on you," I said. Now that was definitely possible.

He stared at me for a full minute. I could see the scales tipping one way and the other in his mind. Finally, he stuck out his open hand.

"Fine. Show me the codes."

As I passed the compufilm over, I realized this was my official rock bottom. I was handing my only hope of saving Finn over to a person who had attempted to kill me then dismantle my very existence not once, not twice, but every chance he got. Which had been often.

"Meaningless." He handed it straight back.

"What?"

"The missing pieces. Without those, it's useless."

"Look again." I shoved it back at Wyck.

He scanned it, his expression blank. He opened his mouth like he was about to say something but then snapped it back shut.

"What is it?" I asked.

"This short section is intact." He tapped the film and expanded part.

"What can you tell from it?"

"Not much. It was a recent Shift back around six months . . . local. Looks fairly routine. Wait." He zeroed in on a portion of it. "Interesting. There were two unchipped Shifters in the vicinity. Hold it. No. There was one unchipped Shifter . . . who Shifted twice? That can't be right."

"How can you tell?" I peered over his shoulder.

"Do you really want a lesson in transport code right now?"

"Fair enough. What else can you decipher?"

"Not much. The tendrils are really unstable. Poor guy probably had a helluva Buzz the whole time. Like I said, the rest is useless without the missing parts."

"And the gaps could be anything?" I asked.

"Any letter A to Z or number one to ten. Actually"—he shrugged—"zero to nine."

"What did you say?"

"Zero to nine?"

My exact words to Finn just hours before.

"Seven," I said.

"Huh?"

"Try seven."

"Seven?"

"Just try it."

"For all the gaps?"

"Yes. The number seven."

"Oh-kay." He filled in the holes with sevens with the swipe of a finger. It still looked like utter gibberish to me, but I could see something change in the way he sifted through the code.

"Did it work?"

"I need some space to work."

"But does it make sense now?"

"Space, Bree." And indeed, as he separated out a section of the code and shuffled it into a different area, he seemed to take up half the room. His wrists flicked digits this way and that so quickly, he looked like a maestro drawing out a hidden melody from his orchestra. I'd never seen him working like this. It occurred to me that, chips or not, there was a place for nonShifters in the Shifting world. We didn't need anyone to transport us, but we needed minds like Wyck's to help us make heads or tails of the ocean of information we gleaned from the past.

"Is Chincoteague, Virginia, one of the destinations? What about the Great Fire of London? Maybe retracing my steps could lead us to the kidnapper."

"Bree!" My name turned to a snarl on his lips. His fingers curled to claws an inch from my shoulders, and for a flash, Evil Wyck possessed his body. He felt it, too, I could tell. He snapped his hands to his side, and his face relaxed. "I need some room to figure this out. Please."

"Of course. I'll, umm—" I pointed to the kitchen and took off at a trot. When I opened the door, Den gave me a silent nod and dug back into his cereal. I'd never been to Wyck's place outside the Institute. It was tiny. I knew his dad had taken off when he was little, but you could tell his mom had made the best of what they had. The place was bright and cheery. Taking care of two boys by herself had to have been hard. I perused a collage of pictures on the wall before I settled into the seat across the table from Den.

"So," he said.

"So."

"Jafney know you're here?" he asked.

"Jafney? No, why?"

"No reason. She just gets kind of horkface-crazy-jealous-eyes when it comes to Wyck."

"So she's his girlfriend now?"

Den snorted.

"You just now figuring that out? I thought you were her roommate."

"I've been kind of out of it lately."

"Well, so has she." He glanced at the doorway. "Y'know what? Never mind."

"No. What did you mean by that?"

"I don't know. She's just been more *Jafney* than usual." Den let out another snort.

"I don't really know her all that well," I said.

"After living with her all these years?"

"I mean . . . the real her."

"Does anyone?" he said. He got up and grabbed a carton of eggs and a skillet.

"And what does that mean?"

"Nothing. It's only"—he peered at the doorway again and lowered his voice—"okay, promise you won't tell Wyck about this."

"Promise." I leaned in.

"Earlier today, she was over. I walked into Wyck's room to borrow a pair of jeans. He was outside talking to one of our neighbors, and she didn't hear me come in. She was in there talking to herself."

That was all?

"She's had a lot on her mind this week," I said.

"No, I mean she was talking to herself. Her Future Self. Well, arguing more like it. Her Future Self was trying to convince her to do something, and she didn't want to do it."

"What was it?"

"I couldn't hear the details. But it was something about how much stunner power it would take to knock out a six-foot guy without causing permanent damage." He cracked two eggs into the pan.

"What?"

"At first, I thought she might be talking about Wyck, but then the Future one said, 'This is the only way to protect Wyck. We don't have a choice.' And then something about the distant past and making a better future for the two of them, no matter the cost. So . . . sucks to be some other dude that crosses Jaf's path, I guess."

"I'm sure it's nothing." I forced the words out of my mouth to keep Den's suspicions at bay even as every molecule of my being screamed.

"She was probably joking around," I said.

"Who was joking?" Wyck popped his head in the door.

"No one," I said. "Any progress?"

Wyck grabbed a handful of grapes off the counter and tossed them into the air, catching them in his mouth one by one.

"Yeah." Wyck popped another grape in and flicked the compufilm open, raised up the soligraphic numbers into the air between us and rotated them around so they faced me. "What do you know about transport codes?"

"As of a couple hours ago . . . that they exist."

"Right. Well, each code is split into two different parts. Origin and destination. That's one of the interesting things about these codes. All have origins from the same location and within the last week. All the same Shifter."

"All? How many Shifts are we talking about?"

"Four."

"So someone Shifted four times in the last week. Why is that interesting?"

"You said you got these codes last Saturday morning. That's right before the first origin point."

"Oh." Well, time was kind of wiggly that way.

"No, that's not the interesting part. Look at this." He expanded a section and tapped on some of the symbols so they glowed brighter than the others. "This didn't happen."

"You're going to have to talk to me like I just found out what transport codes are. Because I just found out what transport codes are."

"Okay, so transport codes tell you what a person experienced on a Shift, yeah?"

"Yeah."

"Like, if you Shifted back right now, and someone punched you in the face . . . ."

I backed away from him.

"I'm not going to punch you in the face, Bree."

"Could we just use another example?"

"Okay, say you went back and cuddled a bunch of kittens."

"Better."

"Well, these codes would show how your tendrils were firing and processing the fur and the softness and whatever emotions and memories you associate with kittens."

"You can tell all that?" Wow.

"Yeah, that's just Transport Code 101. But *this* code. Well, it's almost like this Shifter left with one set of tendrils and came back with another."

"Can you put that back in kitten terms?"

"This is like the Shifter went back and was petting a kitten . . . that suddenly turned into a puppy. It's like everything's . . ."

"Scrambled," said Den, sticking a fork into his steaming pile of eggs in the pan.

Wyck gave me a shrug that said, yeah, pretty much.

"Each set of codes has the same anomaly," he said. "They're all off."

Changes. It was a Neo.

"Wait. You said that one of the origin points was right after I got the codes." That would be when we were at the movie theater. The day of the first big change to my timeline—when Wyck became my boyfriend.

"Yep."

"Did the destination match up with the date you mentioned before? Six months ago?"

"Yeah. Why?"

"Was the destination at the Institute?"

"How did you know?"

"And there are four Shifts?"

He nodded.

I cringed. These weren't just changes. These were *the* changes. These were Wyck's Shifts that had ruined my life.

Forget him stalking and spying on me to figure out my schedule. I'd just handed them right over.

Wyck continued to manipulate the alphanumerics. He looked puzzled about something.

"There's a sequence I can't get to," he said.

"What do you think it is?" I asked.

"I think it's a sequence I can't get to."

"Very funny." Although there was nothing funny about this whole situation.

Wyck kept at it. Droplets of sweat dotted his brow, and he swiped his forehead against his shoulder, not taking his hands out of the air for a moment. Finally, he gave up and cursed.

"I wish Jafney was here," he said.

"Why?" I shot Den a side-glance.

"I think better when I'm around her," said Wyck. "I dunno. Steadier, somehow."

Den rolled his eyes, but I didn't respond at all.

I looked up at the O'Banions' picture wall again. Jafney was in a bunch of the shots, smiling like the blazes. In one, Wyck had his arms wrapped around her from behind. He was only a smidge taller than her. She was an unchipped Shifter. Almost six feet tall. Born of two centuries with sticky tendrils. Willing to do almost anything to be with Wyck. Talking to her future self about how to stun a guy Finn's size. My knees shook. The weight of the realization of who I was staring at, at what she had done, pressed so heavy on me, my joints ached.

I was staring at Raspy.

I was staring at the kidnapper.

"Bree? Hello, Bree."

"Huh?" I snapped out of my daze. Wyck was waiting for me to answer something, but I'd missed the question. "Sorry. What did you say?"

"I asked if you could think of a three alpha code that might unlock this." He tapped a tiny corner of the message. I squinted at it, and sure enough there was a password-enabled section.

"Umm. Maybe seven, seven . . . seven?"

"Alpha. Not numeric."

"Oh." Think, Bree, think. "I've got nothing."

"How did you think of the sevens?"

"I didn't. It was something that . . . try FJM."

"FJM?"

Finnigan Jonathan Masterson.

Wyck entered Finn's initials, and there was no question as to whether or not it worked. Immediately, the entire room exploded into a giant jumble of glowing letters and numbers. The air was so dense with code, I couldn't make out Den's features, seated directly across the table from me.

"Whoa." Den's chair screeched as he pushed it back from the onslaught.

"What kind of code is this?" I half expected my voice to come out in a glug. The room was so thick with symbols, it felt as if I were swimming through a sea-swarm of plankton.

"I have no idea." Wyck's voice slipped to a hushed awe. "I've never seen anything like it. It's beautiful."

I nodded. It looked like a work of art.

Wyck retracted the code onto the compufilm with a swipe and handed the note back to me.

"I'm sorry. I can't help," he said and walked back into the entryway, leaving Den behind in the kitchen.

"Wait. What?" I trailed after him. "You're not even going to try?"

"Bree, you saw that. It's way beyond me. To even manipulate the data, I'd need access to equipment that's a lot more powerful."

"We can't just give up."

"We?" He cocked an eyebrow.

"I can't give up. And I'm asking you to help. Not forcing you. Not holding you to something your future self told you. I'm asking you. Begging you."

"You don't need to beg." He reached out and his hand drifted down my spine, just the way I liked it. "I made you a promise a long time ago. Anything."

That touch. Those words. I looked up, positive of what I'd see before I even met his eyes. Of *who* I would see. I mean, they were still Wyck's eyes, but it was as if Finn had taken over Wyck's body.

"Finn?" I whispered.

"We'll figure it out." Strong arms lassoed me loosely, and I let myself pretend they were his. "How hard can it be? Easier than scaling the Pentagon, that's for sure."

It was him. It was Finn.

Or it could be a trap. But, honestly, I didn't care. Yes, it could be a hoax, but in that moment, I'd do anything to talk to Finn again, even if it was through Wyck's ears.

My breath clung to the edge of my throat as I said, "How are you here?"

"It certainly can't be harder than finding that bracelet in a whole beach-worth of sand. The look on your face when Slug had it."

"Finn, we need to figure out what's happening to you, I mean . . . to Wyck."

"I don't trust that guy."

"I know but—"

"We can't ask him to transport you. It's too dangerous."

"What? No one's transporting anyone, Finn." And that's when I realized this wasn't Finn standing in front of me. Not his brain, and certainly not his soul. This was a random stew of Finn's memories, sloshing over the edges of a pot. This was an echo.

It snapped me back to reality. I was here for one reason. To save Finn. For that, I needed one person.

"Wyck." I pulled away from his embrace.

"I don't trust that guy."

"Wyck!"

"I don't—" Wyck shuddered like he was shaking away a bad dream. He stared past me, and I knew whatever flicker of Finn was in there had been put out.

"If I help you," he said, "will this stop? The voices?"

"I don't know," I said. "But I do know it's our only chance."

At this point, every other step headed backward. At least this felt like stepping forward, even if it was directly into a trap.

chapter 26

"ARE YOU SURE you're okay with this?" I peeked over at Wyck then checked the transport tube's landing chamber yet again. Still no one coming. No red scrubs. No Lafferty. Didn't make me any less antsy, though.

It was the middle of the night by the time we'd gotten to ICE's headquarters. The only people there had been techs and the cleaning crew. Wyck had made up some excuse about prepping for his next Shift. Apparently, this wasn't the first time he'd worked odd hours. No one questioned him.

"Little late to change my mind now." Numbers and letters from the code waltzed around Wyck in loose formation. They seemed more orderly in this environment, more stable. Wyck did, too.

"I still don't understand why we couldn't use the Institute consoles," I said.

"Their technology is out of date. It would be like using a toothpick to slice a T-bone." He shrank some of the symbols, expanded others. They meant nothing to me, but they seemed to fascinate him.

"Why are you so worried?" he asked. "I thought you said that nonShifters forget about you with each timeline change."

NonShifters might. Jafney wouldn't. And now that I knew that she was behind the arson and the kidnappings, I had the blarkiest feeling ever in my stomach. She knew about me. She knew about Finn. I'd even told her about the reverter. And if this was her future self we were dealing with, she could keep ICE posted to the minute what I was up to. It was a wonder they hadn't stormed the room by now. But they were probably waiting for Wyck to do the hard work of figuring out this temporal code before they pounced. That had been their M.O. in the past. Keep those scrubs spotless until the blood would blend right in.

I jumped with each beep from the console, flinched every time Wyck flung another section of code to a remote corner of the room.

"Can you hurry?" I asked.

"Uncharted territory here, Bennis." He said my last name with no small amount of malice in his voice. He blinked and shook his head. "Don't worry, sweetie. We've got this." He blinked again.

Wyck gritted his teeth. A flash of Evil Wyck. A flash of Finn. Each seemed physically painful to him. I wondered how much longer he'd be able to hold it together. Leto had gone on a lot more Shifts and attempted a lot more changes than Wyck had, with more reversions, which seemed to be especially detrimental to Neos' health, but Wyck was starting to show the strain already. He scratched at his nose, and when he pulled his fingers away, there was a trickle of blood on them.

"Wyck?"

He squeezed his eyes shut, whispered something to himself, and when he opened them, I could tell Real Wyck was completely back. For now.

"Thank you," I said. "I know this isn't easy for you."

"It's hard to tell what's real," he said quietly.

"I know."

"And this code isn't helping."

"What do you mean?"

"It's not . . . it doesn't make sense. The origin point is about a year in the future. Which is . . . well, not really normal, but plausible. The destination is fifty years or so in the past. Normal. But everything in between is wrong."

"Well, all the other codes were for changes. Maybe this is a really big timeline change."

"It's more than that. It's like—"

Whish

Someone had entered the transport tube's landing chamber. The lights in the Launch Room went out, replaced by red emergency flashers.

"Did you tip them off?" I asked.

"You've been with me the whole time."

True. I motioned for Wyck to put away the code and hide. He swiped the air clean and stowed the note in his pocket. I ducked behind the console with him just as someone slid into the room.

Click clack click clack

Stilettos hammered the floor, and I held my breath as Lafferty walked a lap around the circular room. Her voice was like her shoes—hard, pointy, and needed to get knocked down a peg or two.

"Secure the perimeter." Lafferty sounded almost bored as she dipped her head down and started scanning the floor. "Bree-ee!" she called in a singsong voice that made me want to retch all over her gazillion-dollar shoes. "I know you're in here."

She tap-tap-tapped the soles of her shoes a few feet from my face. If Lafferty knew I was in here, she had to know where I was hiding. But maybe not. Raspy, I mean, Jafney, had withheld key information in the past. And if Jafney thought that Wyck was in danger, she'd surely hold her cards even closer. Lafferty and her entourage all seemed to be waiting for something. They certainly weren't trying very hard to capture us.

Lafferty bent down right next to the console we were hiding behind.

"I know what you're going to do," she said in a low voice so that only Wyck and I could hear. "And I know that you're going to fail. Now, go."

Go where?

And then I felt it, a Shift building in my extremities.

I looked over at Wyck. I couldn't leave him here. Especially now that he knew so much. I reached over and put my hand over his, expecting the contact to disrupt my impending Shift, but instead, the urge to Shift only intensified. Normally, touching a nonShifter would Anchor me to my present. But none of this was normal, and Wyck wasn't a typical nonShifter. He was a Neo. A Neo who now had some of Finn's quantum tendrils coursing through his brain.

A Neo who was in this as deep as I was.

"Sorry for the rough ride." I wrapped my arms around him and Shifted us who knew where.

chapter 27

SHIFTING WITH WYCK felt like I was being ripped through time. Certainly not the strange, almost gravitational pull I experienced with Finn. Not even the jostling push of Shifting with the reverter. Like someone had grabbed every one of my limbs, and they'd been yanked out of socket all at once. When I opened my eyes, I was just thankful we weren't surrounded by red—scrubs or lights.

We were, however, in a tight spot. Literally. Metal pressed against me on two sides, and I fought the panicky urge to beat against the walls. We'd landed in some sort of box or cabinet.

At first I thought Wyck was unconscious, but his eyes fluttered open when I squeezed his arm. I was about to say something, but he pressed his hand against my mouth and formed his lips into a *shhhh*. He pointed at his ears and I heard it, too. A voice right outside.

It was Wyck's voice.

"It's you," I whispered.

"But how?"

He motioned for me to check my QuantCom. We were six months in the past at—*gulp*—the Institute.

"We're at the first change." I strained to listen to Past Wyck's conversation with another version of himself, but I didn't recognize what he was saying. We must have arrived earlier than my past self had with the reverter.

"I still don't get it," said . . . Past Wyck? I peered through a slit in the locker. Yeah. It was Past Wyck. "I can change how the future unfolds?"

"Yes, look," said the other Wyck with shaggy hair wearing a ball cap. This was Wyck from five days ago, the Wyck who had made this change. "You have to follow my instructions very precisely."

"And then I'll be Bree Bennis's boyfriend?"

"Kind of."

"Kind of?"

"Think of Bree as a . . . pit stop in the Pod race of love."

I punched Present Wyck on the shoulder and mouthed *"pit stop?"* He shrugged.

"What's that supposed to mean?" asked Past Wyck.

"Just . . . your true love is out there. Waiting."

Oh, save me the sap. He was talking about Jafney.

"So I screw up Bree's mid-term and then we date and eventually I'll meet my soul mate?" asked Past Wyck.

"Yep."

"Who isn't Bree?"

"Nope."

"How do you know all this?"

That was a very good question. The Wyck of five days ago was the one making this change, but the Wyck out there was knowledgeable about things past that time.

"I'm just following orders here," he said.

"Following orders?" Past Wyck bit his fist laughing. "What are you on?"

"Look, apparently, as soon as I make this change, I'm not even going to remember the last six months of my life as they currently are. I'm just going to remember that I stopped Bree from taking her mid-term, and we're going to be dating."

"I don't care," said Past Wyck. "I don't take orders from anyone."

My head was spinning, and the Present Wyck next to me had pressed his body into the corner of the locker and looked like he might pass out.

"So how do you even know that this change happened?" asked Past Wyck.

Yeah, what he said.

"Unchipped Shifters can detect the changes, and they remember how it's supposed to be."

"I won't do it," said Past Wyck. "Bree's one of my closest friends. I won't do anything to hurt her."

"You're not hurting her," said Five-Days-Ago Wyck. "You're helping her. I told you, we're following orders."

"Orders from an unchipped Shifter?"

"Orders from Bree."

What the great shades of blarking pegamoo crapsicles on a stick?

"Why would she have you make this change?" asked Past Wyck.

Yeah. Why? Why, why, why, why, why?

"She could be Anchored," said Past Wyck. "That would devastate her."

"She doesn't care about being Anchored. She's a free Shifter in the future. She can Shift whenever she wants to."

I was trying (unsuccessfully, mind you) to keep myself from keeling over. I racked my brain to recall my future self's exact words when she had told me that Wyck was taking orders from ICE, but that was the thing. She never used the word ICE. I had just assumed, given my run-in last year with Evil Wyck.

But what else would I assume? Never in my most ridiculous of dreams would I intentionally order Wyck to destroy every moment I've ever held dear.

To save his, destroy yours.

Oh my gosh. I cupped my hand over my mouth. What if he was telling the truth? What if my future self was orchestrating these changes? I mean, the shaggy-haired Wyck out there knew that my chip was turned off. How would he know that? I had to have told him.

"But—" said Past Wyck.

"Look," Five-Days-Ago Wyck interrupted him. "I know what

I'm asking of you doesn't make sense, and I know you don't want to do it, but—"

"I'm still trying to figure out how you're even here, man."

Clang.

Past Wyck had leaned against the locker we were in. I remembered this part of the conversation. This was the moment. *The* moment. My Past Self was out there. She was crouched down a few feet away. Wyck had just hit the locker.

"It will all make sense later," said Five-Days-Ago Wyck. "I promise. But you have to do this. It's important."

"She's my friend," said Past Wyck.

"And . . . this way, she'll become more than that."

I elbowed Present Wyck in the ribs, even though there was nothing he could do about it. I hadn't even known he was here in this locker on the last trip. Which was weird because that would mean I wasn't going to Shift him back to our time. I was going to Shift Past Bree out of here. So how was Wyck going to get home?

"But it's a lie," said Past Wyck. "Bree's one of the best students at this school. I haven't seen any signs that would make me question her fitness to Shift."

"I know that." Something slammed into our locker again, and I bit back a gasp before I remembered it was Five-Days-Ago Wyck's fist. He was experiencing a flash. But he had pulled himself together pretty quickly.

"Look," he said, "just go into Quigley's office and report that you've witnessed some instability in Bree lately. She won't get in trouble. Bree won't even be angry at you."

I twisted a chunk of hair around my index finger. I had to piece this together and pronto. The eensy space I shared with the not first, not second, but third Wyck in the vicinity seemed even tinier as I listened to the repeat argument a few inches away.

"But it's her midterm," said Past Wyck.

I was going to stop myself from reverting the change in a few minutes. Why would I do that? It made no sense. If I'd just re-verted Wyck's change in the first place, none of this would have happened. Finn wouldn't be comatose. Mom wouldn't be in prison. Mimi would still be my best friend.

Actually, that wasn't true. Leto knew about Finn's chrono-fugitive status before the change, so that was still inevitable. ICE could already have tracked him down. Mom had already started using drugs. Mimi and I were already growing more distant. And the changes had already started long before I'd heard of a reverter, long before I'd met Finn Masterson. They had started at Point Zero.

"Give me the clue," I whispered to Wyck.

"The what?" he mouthed.

"The note."

He pulled it from his pocket and handed it over. I breathed on it to get it to warm up and lay flat. Before I had a chance to spread it out, though, my body was pressed back hard against the metal. What the what? Another person had popped up in here with us. I spit out a mouthful of bouncy brown curls.

Jafney.

She didn't even look at me. And she definitely didn't seem sur-prised at her current whereabouts.

"Do you have the note?" she asked Wyck in a hush.

"Huh?" He looked as shocked by Jafney's sudden appearance as I felt. At least it didn't appear he was a part of whatever she was doing.

"The code. Do you have the code?"

"I . . . just . . . gave it back to Bree," he whispered.

"What are you doing here?" I asked her.

"Give me the compufilm," she said.

"No!" I whisper-hissed.

"Oh, my gosh," she said. "What part of inevitable do you not understand? Give it to me."

"No, I—"

But she had wrenched it out of my hand and . . . torn it in two.

"Here." She handed the top part to me. "He only needs the code."

"What?"

She didn't answer. Instead she wrapped her arms around Wyck. Over her shoulder, she said, "So help me, Bree, you'd better be right about all this. We're running out of time."

"What's going on, Jaf?" Wyck asked.

"Shh." She stroked his hair. "Everything's going to be okay."

Then she turned back to me. "I know what you still think I did to Finn. And all those other Shifters. You're wrong. Focus on the clue."

And then they disappeared.

I swished my hands around in the space where they'd just been.

Ahhhh. This was not happening. I literally pinched my arm. Wake up. Wake. Up.

Nope. I was living this nightmare. Twice now.

I spread what was left of the note out in my hand.

To save his, destroy yours.

This had to be at the center of it. But I still didn't know what it meant or who the "him" was referring to. Was it Finn?

Had to be.

But save his what?

Think, Bree. What had he lost?

His memories.

To save his memories, destroy my . . . memories.

I traced my finger over where the transport codes had been torn away. Four changes that had destroyed my life. Four changes that had destroyed my memories.

I pulled the torn fragment tight to my chest.

I hadn't left this message to stop the changes. I had left it to start them. Somehow Finn was destined to get his memories back if I altered my past to lose everything that was precious to me.

But how?

"If Bree finds out I did this . . ." Past Wyck was about to walk off.

I pressed my ear against the metal hinge.

"I told you. Don't worry about that," said Five-Days-Ago Wyck.

He already knew what I had just figured out. He didn't need to worry about me finding out about this change because I was the one who had instigated it.

Wyck was telling the truth. He was following my orders.

The two of them set off to Quigley's office.

Which meant Past Bree was about to follow them.

I had assumed that Future Bree (i.e., me) knew what she was doing. She'd seemed so confident. I felt anything but as I silently slipped from the locker to stop Past Me from doing what I so desperately still wanted her to do. As my will sagged, a puff of faith in my Future Self lifted it.

I knew where we were headed next. To ICE's headquarters, where I could get a closer look at that equipment. Maybe that was why I had to do all this, to get back to that point fifty years ago and figure out how to get Finn's memories out of those reservoirs before ICE became the mega-organization that it was in my time.

Why I would need to dismantle my life in order to do that, I still wasn't sure, but for now, it was enough to know that I needed to take one step forward, then fifty years back.

Past Bree slipped out of her hiding spot. I pushed her arms to her side and wrapped my hand over her mouth to keep her from yelling. She put up a good fight, but whenever Finn and I sparred, he pointed out my go-to moves and what he always did to defeat them. But it felt like there was something I wasn't remembering . . .

And then she bit my hand.

"Ow!" I let go of her arm and smacked it. "I forgot I did that."

She spun around, slack-jawed and silent.

chapter 28

"WHAT DO YOU THINK you're doing?" she said.

"Stopping you from reverting this change." Please don't ask me why. Because I definitely can't explain it yet.

"Don't you realize what's about to happen?" she asked.

"More than you can comprehend."

"Well, explain it." She looked so defeated. "Never mind. There's no time."

She whirled around to chase after Wyck. Crapcakes. I just barely managed to grab her wrist.

"Have you gone insane?" she said. "He's about to take everything from me."

Bwaha. I couldn't help but let out a pity-laugh. *Everything.* She had no idea what was coming.

"Don't be angry at him." I couldn't believe those words were actually coming out of my mouth. But they were true. Wyck was as clueless as I was right now. And there was one thing I knew. "He's just following orders."

Mine.

She said something in return, but I wasn't even listening. A school buzzer sounded, and students filled the halls. She tried to wriggle out of my grasp as the reverter wound down.

"What have you done?" She spun around. "How could you?"

I didn't supply an answer because none existed, at least none that made sense to me just yet. My tendrils flared.

Puff of faith.

I didn't know the why yet, but I had to trust that my tendrils called me where I was supposed to be. I enveloped her in an embrace.

"Where are you taking me?"

To save Finn.

＞—＜

I was pure focus when we landed.

"What is this place?" Past Me asked.

"The Cryostorage Facility at ICE's headquarters." I flicked out my QuantCom and double-checked the date even though I knew what it would say. Fifty years back.

Past Me wandered around until she reached Nava's chamber. She scratched a line of frost into it.

"Don't touch anything," I said.

She shot me a nasty look but obeyed.

"Then tell me what's going on," she said.

"No time." I didn't have long before Raspy would show up with that fresh catch. (Sigh. I'd been so sure it was Jafney, but now I was doubting everything.) I had to figure out how this extraction tank worked. The tubes full of blue matter twisted their way up the walls. I knew they ended at the reservoir room. Perhaps disrupting the flow here—no. The other room was older and more hidden. That was the equipment Lafferty was more insistent about protecting. It was the more important of the two.

"We're time travelers," she said. "All we have is time."

And yet I was all out.

"You sound like Finn," I said.

"Is he okay? When can I get back to see him?"

I pictured his lifeless body, lying in the bed at Nurse Granderson's house.

"You're with Wyck now," I said in a dead voice.

"I'm not with—"

"Of course you're not." How could she even think that? How

could I have ever thought that Finn had abandoned me, even for a single moment? A moment we'd never get back and that he would never remember. I pressed my grief away. "But Wyck doesn't realize that. And you won't let him."

"Do you have any concept what you just cost me back there?" she asked. "What you cost us?"

Oblivious.

And in that moment, I pitied this girl of the past who had everything to lose. There's a reckless, twisted freedom in having everything to gain.

"I know none of this makes sense right now," I said. "And, honestly, it's still really . . . it's . . ." A hopeless mission. A fool's errand. A desperate last resort. "It's not going to be an easy path, but I need you to trust me."

I needed to trust myself.

Past Bree turned her attention back to Nava.

"You said this place was ICE's Cryostorage?" she said. "Storage for what?"

Stop. Talking. I needed to concentrate. She tapped on the glass, and I glanced over at her as she waved her hand around the display, trying to get it to go away. Nava's body emerged from the cryounit.

"I said, leave her alone." I walked over to shut the compartment. I hadn't noticed before that Nava's hippocampal degradation was still 0.00%, so at least it looked like they hadn't put her in that tank yet.

"Her?" Past Me appeared properly horror-struck as it hit her what all these storage units were for. Good thing she didn't know one was reserved for Finn.

I brushed Nava's hair back and touched the red button. At least she wouldn't be in there long.

"Who is she?" Past Me asked. "I mean, is she . . . dead?"

"She's alive."

Nava's classification information was still hovering there.

November Bravo Golf and then a bunch of numbers. NBG—
her initials. No. That wasn't right. Her last name was Schwartz. It
should be NBS.

Must have been a mistake.

I started to return my attention to the tubes but swiveled back
around slowly.

ICE didn't make mistakes. Not like that.

She was the first one taken. And they had held her captive less
than a day. It didn't add up.

I looked back over at the tank. I had an urge to smash it, like
I had before. (Or I guess, like I would in the future.) I realized
what it reminded me of. Back when I was little, my grandpa used
to take me fishing on the Anacostia River. He let me use an auto-
snag and perm-worms because I got grossed out by touching
anything slimy. But he always used a genuine antique reel, and
when we trawled out in his skiff, he hooked a trap bucket on the
back of the boat to catch minnows for live bait. He'd sift through
a bucket of those tiny squiggly fish to find the perfect one. They
all looked the same to me, but he swore he could tell the one live
bait that was most likely to attract the biggest fish.

I turned back to Nava.

Live bait.

They hadn't kidnapped her for her tendrils. They would have
plenty of unknown, untrackable Shifters soon enough for that.
But someone had to bring those Shifters here. Raspy. They needed
the kidnapper firmly on their hook. And for that, they needed bait.

They needed someone who cared about her.

Someone who would do anything it took to save her.

Even if that meant taking everything away from anyone else
who crossed their path.

Nava Schwartz. But NBG.

"Oh my gosh," I said. I'd been so blind. Nava had practically
told me. All that talk about how she'd hoped that cross-temporal
relationships wouldn't be taboo by the twenty-third century. And

that I shouldn't be ashamed of my parents' love or my sticky tendrils. Nava wasn't really talking about me. She was talking about
herself. "I know who . . ."

Nava had admitted to a cross-temporal love affair. I had assumed that the man was in the past. But what if he was in her
future? That would mean Raspy was her . . . no. This couldn't
be happening. I thought over the events of the last few days, and
so much plunged into place. Jafney was telling me the truth. She
had nothing to do with these kidnappings.

"Umm, I have to go." I pivoted on my heel and took off toward the exit.

"What? You mean, synch?" Past Me called, but I was barely
listening.

They had laid out the tastiest bait possible to recruit Raspy.
His mother . . . Nava B. Granderson.

All this time, I'd thought that Nurse Granderson took such
good care of Nava—like she was his own mother—because she
had no one else. But that wasn't true. She had him. She had her
son. She really was his mother. I needed to look Dev Granderson
in the face when I confronted him. (Ahh! Nava had even called
him Devvy. She'd said she'd known him his *entire* life. Seriously,
I could not have been more blind.) How could he? Not just kidnapping Shifters from the past, but Finn—the son of one of his
best friends.

I was halfway out the door before I even remembered that my
past self was still in the room.

"You'll hide behind that." I gestured absentmindedly to the
screen where Past Bree would crouch while she puzzled through
the overheard conversation.

The lights didn't turn on as I entered the hallway. When I felt
along the wall, it was exposed dirt, and I realized that the lights
probably hadn't even been installed yet at this point fifty years
back. Exposed circuitry and ductwork dangled from the ceiling.
A musty, loamy scent permeated the air.

The holes for what would eventually be more transport tubes along the edge of the hall had already been dug out and reinforced. I crawled into one and waited, trying to hold on to the rage I'd felt this whole time toward the kidnapper. But now that I knew it was Granderson and the reason he'd done it—to save his mother—I couldn't muster anything but sadness. So much sadness. He was caught in the same vicious, twisting loop that I was, that Finn was, that we all were.

But that didn't excuse it. I set my Com's stunner high enough to really jolt him without knocking him out. I heard the whish of the Cryostorage door and got ready to pounce. I needn't have bothered, though. He walked straight to the porthole where I was crouched and faced me, his hands at his side, defenseless.

"I'm not going anywhere, but if it will make you feel better to stun me, do it," he said through the voice-distorting mask.

"Take that thing off," I said. I needed to see his face to actually believe it was him. And I wanted him to see with his bare eyes one of the lives he was ripping apart.

Granderson pulled the silver headpiece off with a sigh and stroked the hard-worn stubble on his chin. Now that I knew his parentage, I could see the kinship to Nava immediately. The same soft, compassionate eyes with permanent smile crinkles at the corners.

"Why would you do this?" I said.

"They took my mother."

"They took my mother, too," I said. "Last year. They put her in a coma."

"And did you sit idly by and wait for her recovery, Bree? Hmm? Or did you agree to do the dirty work of a known chronosmuggler?"

"You can't compare *this* to my one botched delivery for Leto!"

"I'm not. But she's all that I have. I'm all that she has."

"That note that they left when they took her from Resthaven. That was for you, wasn't it? That's you right now, isn't it? You're giving them what they want."

"I have no choice. It's the only way they'll return her un-harmed."

"Does Nava know you're a part of this?"

"No!"

"She wouldn't approve of this," I said. "I know your mother, and she would never want you to end other people's lives, even to save hers."

"ICE isn't killing anyone. They're just using them for a while."

"Is that what you've told yourself as you've fed ICE information on your fellow Shifters?"

"Some of it false," he pointed out. "I've . . . I've kept them off your track at times. And I've tried to warn them about the danger of the timeline changes."

"Which has kept them doing it. You created that chicken-egg. You! I can't believe this."

"I don't know how to get out." He clutched his head in his hands.

"Has your father been born yet?" I had no intention of listening to him grovel. We didn't have much time before the red-dressed goon came walking through the door, and I didn't have the luxury of wasting a millisecond of it.

"Yes, but he's younger than me in this time," said Granderson with a sigh. "Mom's one hundred and seven. Dad's in his early twenties. They met when he was on a Shift back for work when she was twenty-five."

"When were you born?" I asked.

He gave me the year. It was two years after my own grandpa had been born.

"So there's an eighty-year-old version of you running around somewhere?"

"No," he said. "Apparently, I die of lung disease a couple de-cades back."

"Lung disease?" I scoffed. No one had died of lung disease in forever.

"Effects of smoke inhalation. My theory is I refuse treatment out of guilt for all this."

I thought about how much my lungs had stung in London and then again at Finn's house. And that was just two fires.

"I took up residence in this time period permanently as a young man," he said. "To care for my mother. With both my parents Shifters, I have no idea what my real synch point even is."

If my family situation was jumbled, his was an entire novel written in anagrams.

"But if your dad's a Shifter," I asked, "why couldn't he disable his chip and come back to take care of your mother as he grew older?"

"Chips aren't optional in the future, Bree," he said. "That's why I can't or, at least, don't go to the future."

"But you were chipped yourself," I said. "Until John disabled it."

"John injected me with the vaccine, but there was no chip for it to react to."

"So why did you—?"

"I faked it."

"Is that house even really your father's?" I asked. I knew it seemed too hip and modern for an old man.

"His house?" Granderson's brow furrowed. "How do you know about his house?"

I'd forgotten that Nurse Granderson hadn't reached that point on the timeline yet. I was dealing with the Granderson of . . . was it this morning? In his reality, Resthaven was still waiting for him on his return.

"Never mind," I said.

"Bree, I know this all seems horrible." He gestured back to the Cryostorage Room where the kidnapped Shifters would soon be brought there by him. "But there's no other way."

"*Seems* horrible? You're pronouncing a death sentence to each and every Shifter you bring here!"

"If I didn't bring Shifters from the past, Dr. Lafferty said she'd start plucking us from Resthaven," he said. "But I told you, no one's going to die. She promised they're not going to hurt any of the acquisitions."

I let out a scoff. "And you believe her? Listen to you. Acquisitions? They're *people*! Fifty years from now, most of those bubbles will be full. You seriously think they won't just go take your mom for a hostage again when they need more? You heard them in there. They've already broken their word after you brought them your first 'acquisition.'"

Almost on cue, I could hear the machine inside fire up.

"I'm going to choose my—" Granderson bit his lip, apparently unable to call them what they were . . . victims. "I'm going to choose the Shifters from the past carefully. Loners who are already dying or who are using their abilities for wrongful gain."

"Oh, and who's going to judge which Shifters are using their abilities for the wrong reasons? You?" Forget what I had thought before about losing my rage. It was back full force. "Who are you to decide who ICE gets to study as their little lab rats?"

"Lab rats? Bree." Granderson pinched his temples, and I suddenly realized how utterly worn down he looked. "They're not studying Shifters' tendrils. They're transplanting them."

"What are you talking about?"

"How do you think those IcePicks work? Jenxa Lafferty changed her own timeline. She went back, stole her parents' research, and framed her brother. Her parents were studying Shifters' tendrils, yes. But not how to mimic them. They figured out how they could hyperstimulate them so they could *replace* them. Their work may have begun as a way to help other Shifters with hippocampal damage, but when they realized what it could be used for—to allow nonShifters to Shift—they abandoned it. Their daughter saw other uses for it, though."

That was how Nurse Granderson had known so immediately

what to do with Finn when he was crashing out. He knew exactly what they had done to Finn.

"Why should I believe you? You're as big a liar as she is," I said as if that was his worst offense. "You're going to go and take Finn. And burn down the Mastersons' house, for blark's sake!"

I expected him to deny he would ever do such a thing, but when he remained silent, I realized the look on his face wasn't shock.

It was shame.

I flipped around to face the door. "No."

"They were adamant that Finn be my first procurement," said Granderson. "They told me that, after him, they don't care who I bring them. Bree, I'm sorry."

Fifty years frozen. Fifty years of taking his memories. No wonder Finn had finally broken. "How could you?"

"She's my mother."

"Yeah, I had one, too," I said, "before she landed in prison for a crime she didn't commit."

"I had nothing to do with that." He reached out and touched my shoulder.

"Well, score one for your conscience." I brushed his hand off like it was covered in filth. Blood, more like. "I can't believe you'd—"

I stopped. The faintest of blue lights flickered into the hallway, and the glow grew as the blue matter creeped through the exposed tubes above us. When that material reached the reservoirs in the other room . . .

"You're too late," said Granderson. "They're about to have the inaugural NeoShift. Events were set into motion long before they ever took my mother. You can't change the future."

"No," I said as he gave me one final sad shake of his head and faded away. "You can't change the future."

But I was damn sure going to change the past.

chapter 29

THE PORTHOLE to the landing chamber at the end of the hall was already dug out of the wall. It was only after I was halfway through, feet first, that I realized there was no weightless gel on the other side, no sensation of swimming through silken sheets. Instead, my legs swayed precariously into plain air. I twisted myself around and panicked as my boots scrabbled for a foothold against the bare bedrock inside the tunnel while my hands clawed into the dirt of the hallway. I slid backward, downward, searching for anything solid to grasp.

Clang

My foot had hooked on something metal. I nudged my toe from side to side to make sure it was stable, then I inched the rest of my body through the hole. I shone my flashlight up, then down. I was standing on a thin ladder that ran along the edge of what would someday be their transportation tube path. Tiny emergency lights lit the edges of the ladder. They disappeared into the distance, both up and down.

I stuck my head out the hole for one more quick peek into the hallway. Finn's blue matter was already almost all the way down the hall. ICE was going to use Finn for their own personal Shifting fuel. Unless I stopped them.

My legs began to shake from the surge of adrenaline, climbing the ladder two rungs at a time. I emerged into an open area in the space that would be their lobby at some point. Right now, the only thing aboveground seemed to be a few offices in a humble building. The door to the exterior was glass with a simple etching on the door: "The Initiative for Chronogeological Equality." I peeked down a long hall. At the end was a door marked LAUNCH ROOM. Noiselessly, I felt along the walls, looking for the hidden panel that led to the reservoir room. I was almost ready to give up and climb back in the tunnel when I hit a patch on the tile floor that was warmer than the surrounding area. I felt along the edges of the tile and dug my nails into a crevice to pry it up.

Then I climbed down another, shorter ladder. This was it. The reservoir room was deserted but otherwise unchanged in nearly half a century. The lights were dimmed, but I could see now why it couldn't have been built deep in the subterranean like the rest of their headquarters. The heat from the three reservoirs and the control panel was nearly unbearable. Coolant bars ribbed the walls, but there was no way they could have vented out all the sweltering air if they'd put this equipment much farther underground.

I walked over to the nearest reservoir. At the moment, it just looked like a big empty jar with a slot at the bottom where the scrubs would draw out the blue matter for the IcePicks. I pulled out the reverter to check and see if it would fit. It was a perfect match.

Fuel tanks. They were storing Shifters' tendrils as fuel.

I pocketed the reverter and went to examine the control panel. It looked like a standard transport panel, but out of date. Thinking back to our first year at the Institute, it seemed like there had been some defunct equipment like this that the transporters trained on, but I'd never given it much notice.

"Note to Past Bree," I said. "Next time, pay closer attention to details in case you ever need to fix your boyfriend's brain."

I wished Finn were here. He would have laughed.

My fingers began to tingle as if he were nearby, and I spun around. Had he regained consciousness and somehow Shifted here?

"Finn?"

No one.

I was alone. I had to do this without him.

But the tingles didn't stop. It was like a Shift that was building, but I ignored it. I couldn't leave. I had to stay here and figure this out. There were three reservoirs, plus the control panel. Perhaps I needed to smash them before the first NeoShift. Lafferty had said that two of the reservoirs were backup, so all three seemed to be identical. Unfortunately, there was only one of me. So much for that idea.

I looked up at the air duct overhead right as Finn's blue matter seeped in and split into three paths that inched across the ceiling. Blark. I didn't have much time left. I had to figure this out. It was like if I kept repeating that to myself, something would click.

Click.

I yanked the reverter back out and clicked the end in.

Of course.

I still didn't know exactly how the reverter worked, how it restored the timeline, but it did. It must neutralize the blue matter from the IcePicks. What if it could do the same thing at the source?

But again, I was right back to the initial problem. Three reservoirs. Only one reverter.

And I still didn't see how it would restore Finn's memories back to him.

The tingling in my extremities had worked its way to my core. I rolled my neck side to side like I was kneading out some kinks. I wasn't going anywhere until I had a plan.

Focus, Bree. What was I supposed to do?

The blue matter continued its death march across the sloped ceiling. My hope diminished the farther the three trickles got from each other. Even if I did have three reverters, there was still only one me. It's not like I could be in more than one place at the same time.

Unless . . .

"It's not going to work," said a voice behind me. I spun around.

Wyck.

But which one?

"How did you get in here?" I asked. The panel I'd snuck in through was still sealed.

"I'm on a Shift," he said. "And I'm here to stop you from going through with your pointless plan."

He had that demented expression that let me know whoever I was dealing with, it wasn't Present Wyck. Or even the Five-Days-Ago Wyck I'd just seen at the Institute. This was a Future Wyck from a timeline gone terribly wrong. This was the same guy who had attacked me at the Washington Memorial. This was Evil Wyck.

"You don't know that my plan is pointless," I said. Heck, I didn't even know exactly what my plan was yet. But I needed to stall him and give myself time to think.

"Nah," he said. "It's pointless. You're going to fail."

"You don't know that."

"Don't you see?" he said. "I *do* know that. You . . . are . . . going . . . to . . . fail. And I'm going to be the one to stop you. ICE already knows about this intrusion. That's why there are no red warning lights flashing, no sirens blaring. They don't need them. Look around you, Bree. They didn't even bother to dispatch a single security guard. They knew I'd be enough to stop you."

"But—" Okay, now I was panicking.

"I'm the plinking hero of ICE. They're going to give me a personalized Pick. My own dedicated transporter. Free rein of a Launch Pad to come and go as I please."

This was what Jenxa Lafferty had been talking about when she said that I had already broken into this room . . . and that they'd already stopped me. They were talking about sending Evil Wyck back to prevent me from carrying out my plan.

"Is Jafney in on this?"

"Don't talk about Jaf," he said, his tone biting.

Hmm. Zapped a nerve there.

"Why not?" I asked. "She used Finn to get what she wants. You don't think she'd use you, too?"

"Don't you dare—" He grimaced in pain. When he unscrewed his face, it had softened. "She doesn't know about any of this. She'll just think I got a promotion for hard work."

"Well, she got one thing right. You're going to have a hard time stopping me." I mentally traced how I could get past him. I might not be able to reach all of the reservoirs, but maybe disrupting one would be enough to cause a chain reaction or something. At least enough to keep Finn stable. I could probably reach the nearest one.

"Actually, no," he said, back to smirking. "It's going to be easy. The tendrils will reach that point"—he gestured to a spot halfway up the wall—"when you'll make a move for that reservoir"—he motioned to the one I had planned on disrupting—"and I'll sweep your legs out from under you. You'll break a rib and puncture your lung. But don't worry. ICE will patch you right up.

"You're the one who's always spouting the Doctrine of Inevitability. It's going to happen. The inaugural Neo is going to Shift in"—he flipped open his QuantCom—"seven minutes."

Seven minutes to figure out how to save Finn's blue matter or memories or hyperactivated tendrils or whatever they wanted to call it. Seven minutes to find some way to transplant them back into him. It occurred to me that these were the last seven minutes of the real timeline. The last seven minutes of Truth. After this, ICE's messy vine of branched timelines would begin.

He lunged at me. I dodged to the left but caught my foot on the console and it knocked me off-kilter. I tumbled to the corner but hopped up before Wyck could get ahold of me. We both yanked out our Coms and dialed them up. Wyck and I had been sparring partners for years at the Institute. Even if we weren't friends on this particular branch of the timeline, I knew his every move. I could only assume he had some muscle-memory of mine.

"I don't know what you hope to accomplish," he said as he almost managed to grab me by the wrist. I wrenched it free and shoved him off with a boot to the head. "But it's not going to work. ICE wins."

His voice dropped an octave. "ICE always wins." He sounded disgusted with himself, but I didn't have a chance to feel any pity. He yanked my arm so hard it almost went out of the socket. "Let's get this over with," he said.

"You don't have to do this!" I scrambled away, grabbed onto the console, and tried to shake myself out of his grip.

"Stop being naïve!"

"Stop being evil!"

His right hand strained into a claw, but instead of grabbing me, he grabbed his left hand, and tried to tug it off me. But then he let go of both himself and me, and instead wrenched a coolant bar off the wall.

"You can't live like this, Wyck!" It was like I had a battleside view of an inner civil war. I had no idea which side would win, but I knew either way, Wyck would lose. Leto already had. No matter what ICE claimed, NeoShifting wasn't safe. Those transplanted tendrils would eventually kill him just as they had Leto.

"Let me help you," I said.

The clue popped back into my mind. *To save his, destroy yours.* Jafney had said that Finn wasn't the only one who needed saving. She was talking about Wyck. Maybe I could still help him.

But to do that, I'd need to neutralize him. I whirled around and delivered a nice bootslap to his ear. As I backed up to land another blow, he caught my leg and twisted it. I tumbled to the side, and he slammed his foot into my ribcage. I gasped in pain and only a smidge of air went in. My breath turned shallow and rapid. The blow had punctured my lung. Just like Wyck had said would happen.

"Why didn't you listen to me, Bree?" He wiped a smear of

blood from his nose. "I told you. You're going to fail. And you're going to wreck your life trying."

"No," I said. "You may have your sources, but I . . . I have better ones."

"Your future self?" said Wyck. "She was wrong this time."

"She wouldn't lead me here if I was going to fail. She wouldn't do that. She wouldn't—"

But as I looked around, with three tanks and one of me, with Wyck calling my every move, I realized he was right.

I was going to fail.

A cold rage built within me. ICE had stripped me of everything. Everything! Even faith in my future self. Well, guess what? I might fail, but I was going to go down fighting.

I swept Wyck's leg out from under him and grabbed the coolant bar out of his hand as he fell.

"Bree! What are you doing?" He looked up at me, and for a split moment, I could tell he wasn't Evil Wyck. He wasn't Wyck at all. He was channeling one of Finn's memories.

"I'm sorry." This was going to hurt me worse than it hurt him.

I clubbed him over the head.

Wyck slumped to the side. Okay, that probably actually hurt him worse. I nudged his foot, but he was out cold. When I tried to sigh in relief, pain radiated out from my ribs. I swiveled to face the reservoirs. The blue matter had made another foot of progress toward its destination. I pulled out the reverter.

Lafferty had been so intense about the timing when they inserted the IcePicks into these things. If I inserted the reverter in the same slot at the exact moment that Finn's tendrils reached the reservoir, maybe it would reverse the flow or something like that. Send the memories back into him in that tank, unused.

Maybe that's what I was supposed to do.

I had that fleeting wish again, that I'd admitted to Quigley before. I wished I could change the past. Like a Neo. But, no. Wyck was the Neo. He was the only one here who could change the past.

I turned around to check on him.

He wasn't in the spot where I'd left him. *Blark.*

"Wyck?" I looked up at the spot on the wall where the blue matter crept down. It was right at the point where Wyck had said he'd stop me. "Where are you?"

"Drop it." He jabbed the tip of his stunner into my neck. The energy of the maximum setting vibrated against my bare flesh, like a cobra set to strike. I let go of the pipe, and it fell to the floor with a clang. Wyck pressed his face right up against my ear. "I told you that you'd fail. I told you . . . What the blark are you doing here?"

Wyck loosened his hold on the stunner pressed to my neck. I slammed my elbow into his solar plexus. He doubled over, and I shoved him away.

That's when I realized what he had seen. Or rather who.

My future self was standing on the far side of the control console. She'd lost ten pounds. A scar ran down her cheek. Her hair was grown out and pulled back into a messy braid.

"ICE didn't say there were going to be two of you," Wyck said. "What's going on?"

"I don't know," I said. "Don't ask me. Ask . . . me."

My future self looked haggard, yes. But she also had a smile on her face that could only be described as triumphant.

"Actually," she said, "I think I'll let Wyck explain."

I turned to Wyck. What the blarkiest of blarks was going on?

"Not that Wyck," she said and stepped to the side. "This one."

Another Wyck stood behind her. His hair was shaved down to a buzz. Like Future Me, he was gaunt and haggard—didn't appear to have slept in ages. But he also had the same celebratory grin as Future Me as well as a non-murdery look.

Non-murdery was good.

"They said it was only going to be Bree." Evil Wyck shook

his head in disbelief. "They said I'd beat her without much of a fight."

"Yeah, yeah, yeah," said Future Wyck. "Big man. You did it. You beat her. She failed."

I felt the place on my neck where the stunner had been pressed. If Future Me and Future Wyck hadn't shown up, I'd be knocked out by now. I really had failed. In exactly the way Evil Wyck had predicted, with a punctured lung and a broken rib.

"So why do you look happy?" Evil Wyck asked his future self.

"Glad you asked." Future Me was the one who answered him. She pointed at Evil Wyck. "Because *you* were the reason I failed. Well, you and complete lack of planning. But mostly you."

"What does that have to do with anything?" Evil Wyck asked.

She pointed to my pocket—the reverter was whirring merrily and glowing a bright and dazzling green. I hadn't even noticed in all the tumult going on around me.

Future Wyck was in the process of changing his own past.

"Thought it was about time to rectify some mistakes," Future Wyck said.

"What do you mean?" I asked.

"This." He stepped around me and, without a word, jabbed a stunner right in the center of his past self's forehead. *Berzap.* Evil Wyck collapsed—unconscious for real this time.

"Did you *kill* him?" I dropped to my knees to check his breathing.

"Nah. Jafney's been practicing on me to find a level that would knock me out without permanently messing me up."

That's what Den had overheard.

"Not that it matters." Future Wyck shot Future Me a knowing look. "Permanent is a relative word in a few minutes."

"Can one of you please explain what's going on?" I said.

"Sure," said Future Bree, "but like Wyck said, it won't matter in a few minutes. Oh"—she made a grabby hand at Future Wyck—"I need his Pick."

Future Wyck wrestled the IcePick out of Evil Wyck's clenched fist and handed it to her.

"Thanks," she said then turned back to me. "Where were we? Ahh, yes. Wyck was about to knock you out and drag you back to your time. That was a year ago for me."

I looked at his lifeless form.

"But I was just with him twenty minutes ago," I said. "At the Institute. He was helping me."

"Oh, that's not that Wyck," she said. "This one's further up the line."

"Honestly," said Apparently-No-Longer-Evil-Future-Wyck, "we still haven't figured out what timeline that version is on. Apparently, each change hits me differently. Sometimes, I'm cooperative. Sometimes, I'm . . . not."

Bree pulled a tool from her pocket and took off the cover of the Pick. Wyck leaned over her shoulder.

"Make sure you don't damage the quandragulation coil or the—"

"Wyck." She let out a sigh of exasperation, like they'd already discussed this ad nauseum. "I can do this with my eyes closed now. Jafney's made me practice a hundred times."

"Fine." He backed away.

"Oh." Bree looked up at me. "I need the spare, too."

"The spare?"

"Bergin's Pick. In your pocket. The one that you got out of the Mastersons' safe."

I'd forgotten it was in there.

"What is going on?" I asked as I handed it over.

"Past Wyck was telling you the truth," she said, continuing with her task. "He did stop me. I failed. Plus, no offense, but even if you'd succeeded in preventing this one Shift, it would have just been knocking an ice cube off the glacier." She glanced up at the blue matter trickling through the tubes, only a few feet away from the reservoirs now. She turned her attention back to whatever she was doing to Wyck's IcePick and sped up.

"ICE took the reverter," she said. "They've been making changes to the timeline unchecked for the last year."

"That's why we don't know what timeline he's on." Future Wyck pointed to his past body lying on the ground.

"Most of the changes haven't involved me or Wyck or Jafney directly, but a few have."

"Jafney's helping you?" I said. "She wasn't lying?"

"She's a blarking tech whiz." Bree finished messing with Wyck's reverter. She pulled her bracelet off, kissed it, and snapped it in half. She fit the broken locket into the end like a key, just like with my reverter. "She's the one who's been working out how to reverse the Pick this whole time and turn it into the reverter. So basically the Pick transplants the hyperstimulated tendrils into them, and the reverter inactivates those tendrils.

"When a Neo's on a Shift, using the reverter on them just disables the transplanted tendrils, and the nonShifter's tendrils will snap back to the timeline they were on. But I realized if I was able to inactivate all the hyperstimulated tendrils at the same time, on the very first Neo's Shift—"

"There would only be one timeline left to cling to," I said.

"The True one," we said together.

"This could work," I said.

"This *will* work."

"So is that why Jafney took the codes from me?" I asked.

Bree nodded. "We needed you to keep them safe for us."

"Why didn't you just tell me what they were?"

"Because you would have destroyed them if you knew that they were the changes to your timeline."

The changes that had ripped apart my life.

"How do you know I would have destroyed them?" I said.

"Because I would have destroyed them." She didn't meet my eyes. "I need your bracelet."

"Finn's locket?" I clutched it to my heart.

She stuck her hand out but still didn't look at me. I unclasped it, and as I did, I *knew*.

"He's dead, isn't he?" I didn't have to say his name.

Wyck stared at his shoes.

It was like a fog of grief filled the room. Future Bree didn't turn from her work, but she stopped moving. Wyck opened his mouth like he was going to say something but then closed it again.

"How long did you have with him?" I asked. "When you got back?"

"Not long," Bree said softly. "But I got to say good-bye. Quigley took his body back. I couldn't."

"No." I'd just . . . I'd just touched him. Just kissed him. Where the rage and sadness and fear had been earlier, I was completely numb.

"And . . . and Mom?" I said. There was so much packed into even saying her name. I watched my future self for a reaction, but she betrayed no emotion.

"Some timelines, she's a Shavie. Others, not. But she'll never be Mom again. Not like she was." There was a hardness to this Bree that I never would have imagined in myself.

"What about Granderson?" I asked, my voice flat and lifeless.

"I haven't seen him since I was captured here." Bree had almost finished putting together the reverter made from Bergin's IcePick. "Nava died about six months ago. He'd already done all the damage, though. I figured he found a new synch point, some other time when she was living."

"Then why are we doing this?" I said. "I thought I was saving Finn's memories. *To save his, destroy yours.* To save his memories. Destroy my memories."

I ran my palm down the tube of blue matter.

"Why are you even here?" I asked.

"You know why," she said. "This is bigger than Finn. Bigger than his memories. Bigger than yours."

"I didn't even get to say good-bye."

"I know," she said. "That's the one thing that made me realize I still had a job to finish."

"What do you mean?"

"You haven't taken that last Shift back to see Finn. Your tendrils are calling you back even now. But you haven't gone yet. And I never did."

As she said it, I felt it again, the steady hum of a Shift building within me. Not strong enough to pull me anywhere just yet, but the urge was there.

"At the Institute," I said, "I heard that version of Wyck say that he was following your orders in making those changes. Why would you do that?"

She broke my locket in two and inserted the key onto the end of the newly converted reverter.

"When Finn was crashing out," she said, "at Granderson's house, do you remember thinking that hope is the most dangerous thing to lose?"

"Yes."

"Well, you were wrong. I was wrong. When you're faced with a grave and terrible choice, when you're forced to sacrifice everything, hope isn't the most dangerous thing to lose. Hope is the most dangerous thing to *have*. I knew if I had any sliver of happiness left, I wouldn't be able to do what I have to do right now. You saw how they've kept Granderson dangling on the end of their hook with a tiny shred of hope. They can't do that to me."

Wyck coughed, and when he pulled his hand away, flecks of blood stained his palm.

"We're not here to revert the timeline." Bree lifted up the two additional reverters she'd just created, both of them now glowing green. "We're here to destroy it. Restoring Finn's memories won't protect him. Not from ICE. It's like all those timeline reversions I went on. Pruning, pruning, pruning. A snip here, a snip there, all the while watching ICE's vines choke out reality. The last fifty years have to be pulled up at the root."

"We're at Point Zero," I said.

I didn't need to restore Finn's memories to normal. I needed to restore the space-time continuum to normal. If we could do that, there would be no more chips. No more Madness. No more . . .

No more Finn.

Except that wasn't true. Finn would exist. If this whole crazy loop of an existence hadn't started, I never would have had a reason to go to Chincoteague in the first place. Quigley never would have given him that clue about the enigmatic grin. I never would have asked him to protect me. Even the Haven wouldn't exist. None of it. None of it would have happened. All of this began within this closed loop of the last fifty years. If this first NeoShift never happened, in theory, it would return Finn, whole and unscathed, to where he belonged. To Chincoteague. To a worrywart mother who cherished him and a drama-queen sister who secretly adored him and a father who desperately needed another chance to connect with his son. To cheesy movies and action figures and a dog who could stand to lose ten pounds.

Finn would still exist. He just wouldn't exist for me.

And ICE didn't think I could live with that. They believed that, like Granderson, I'd continue pruning, pruning, pruning, hoping that I could keep the vine just far enough away from Finn for him to survive.

"To save his, destroy yours." I stared at my future self, a shell of who I was. That clue was never about saving Finn's memories. It was about saving his life.

"But if we do this," I whispered, "I'll never see Finn again. We never would have met on the real timeline. I'll lose him forever."

"You've already lost him," she said. "This is your chance to save him. And Wyck. And every other Shifter and Neo and Non."

It was true. But I wouldn't simply be giving up Finn. I'd be giving up the awareness that my soul mate ever even existed.

"The code's entered," Wyck said.

"The code?"

"The last transport code," he said. "It's a big ol' reset button."

I looked back at my reverter, still glowing green, but the whirring had slowed a bit.

"Wyck has to man that console to enter the code?" I asked.

She nodded.

"So three reverters but still only two of us."

Future Bree pulled out her QuantCom and checked the time. "She's late."

"She'll be here," said Wyck.

"She was having second thoughts this morning," said Future Bree.

"She'll be here."

"If she doesn't come—"

"I said I'd be here." Jafney had popped up next to Wyck. She wrapped both her arms around his waist, and he kissed her lightly before lifting his eyebrows in an I-told-you-so at Future Me.

"You're going to help us destroy the timeline?" I asked Jafney. She bobbed her head.

"Why?" I asked her. "There's nothing to stop you and Wyck from being together now."

She didn't address me but instead turned to my future self. "We don't have time for this. Did you not explain things to her already?"

"I can't do this," I said. "This is all going too fast. I can't let him go like this. This is so horked up."

"*You're* horked up," said Wyck with a snarl.

Whoa. There was Evil Wyck.

"Hey." Jafney squeezed his arm but stayed calm. "Come back to me."

Wyck shook his head. Blood had started to ooze down his face in a steady trickle. "Did I hurt anyone?"

"No. We're fine." Jafney tilted her head toward his. "But you've gotta stay with me, okay?"

I looked around and realized the room had grown lighter. Brighter. The blue had crept fully down the walls and was almost to the reservoirs.

Future Me handed the third reverter over to Jafney.

"That's it?" I said. "We just stick the reverters into the reservoirs?"

"You make it sound like any of this has been easy," said Jafney.

"It's okay." Future Me stood between us. "Everything's going to be okay."

"Just tell her to lay off," said Jafney.

"What is your deal?" I asked. "You got your happy ending."

I gestured at Wyck, but when I stopped to really look at him, I could tell something was wrong. Really wrong. Jafney noticed, too. She rushed back over to him.

"Hey." She clasped his hand. "You've gotta focus, sweetie."

"What are we doing here?" He looked around, muddled. "Have I been here before?"

Then Wyck noticed his unconscious self on the ground, and he really started to freak out. He tried to jerk his hand away from Jafney, but she held tight.

"Shhh," she whispered in his ear. "It's going to be okay."

"Don't touch me." He snatched his hand away from her with another snarl. As soon as he was free from her grip, though, he seemed to come back to his senses. He pulled her into a hug, "I'm so sorry, Jaf."

"It's not you," she said. "This isn't you."

She looked over his shoulder at me. "You're not the only one who's lost everything."

"I'm back," Wyck said. He pulled Jafney in for one more tight hug before he kissed her gently on the forehead. I could almost feel Finn's lips on the same spot. I avoided my Future Self's gaze, knowing how keenly she'd felt the same knife. Wyck and Jafney must have already said their good-byes in private, because she retreated to one of the reservoirs in silence.

"All right," Future Me said. "The moment the blue matter touches the tank, we activate the reverters. And, Wyck, you entered the code, but give us your mark. We have to do it in perfect synchronization. Like we practiced."

"Uhh, I didn't practice," I said.

"You're me. You'll be fine," she said. Rather than the blue matter, she stared at me.

The blue matter was inches from the reservoirs. Still Future Bree watched me. What was she waiting for?

That's when I felt it. The pull on my tendrils grew until it was a frenzied throb that blurred the edges of my vision. If Finn could just be here. . . . His presence would strengthen me, push my fear away.

I closed my eyes, and when I let them drift open, I knew exactly where I was even before my tendrils had stopped tingling. I stood on the top plank of Finn's dock in Chincoteague. He sat on the end. His legs dangled off the edge with his toes dipped in the water. The steps creaked beneath me as I walked toward him, tears splashing the wood in my wake.

I'd dreaded this moment, avoided it, and now all I wanted to do was run down the dock and smother myself in his scent. I wanted to hear him say, one more time, that everything was going to be okay, even though he suspected it might be a lie, and I knew for certain that it was.

Finn turned slowly. When he saw it was me, he smiled that devious grin of his and stood up. My pace quickened. My heart quickened. I practically leapt into his arms. *For the last time,* my vicious inner voice hectored. I ignored it. It was for *this* time. That was all that mattered now.

Finn pulled back when he saw my streaked cheeks. "What's wrong?"

My world was about to end.

I didn't answer. My lie wouldn't fool him anyway.

"Hey." He brushed his thumb across my face, dragging away the tears. "What's going on?"

"I need you to do something for me," I said. "But you can't tell anyone about it. Not even me."

"Bree, what's—?"

"Promise me."

"I don't—"

"Promise me!"

"Anything."

"I need you to protect me." A lie. I was the one who was going to protect him—from ever meeting me.

"Protect you?" He looked up to the spot on the stairs where I'd Shifted like some monster would materialize then and there. "From what?"

"I can't explain." I cupped my palms around his face. "I really want to remember this."

In that moment, I knew exactly why ICE had insisted that Finn be the first Shifter kidnapped. Not because there was anything special about his tendrils.

Because they knew how special he was to me.

They thought I was like Nurse Granderson with his mother. They thought I wouldn't give Finn up, no matter the cost.

They'd called my next move before I even knew there was one. They thought I'd keep running and searching, keep scrambling up ladders two rungs at a time to try to restore him.

But ICE didn't realize what I did. That it came to this simple question: did I love Finn enough to let him go?

And the simple answer to that simple question that somehow broke my heart and knit it back together again was . . . yes.

I did.

"You're freaking me out here, Bree," said Finn.

"I need to go," I said. "What did you promise to do?"

"To protect you." His grip grew tighter on my waist. "Stay here. Whatever it is, it can't get you here."

In his arms, that promise almost felt true. Almost. My tendrils began to tingle once again, though, drawing me back to reality.

"I can't stay."

"When are you going to be back?" he asked.

"I'm—" I shook my head. "We're not going to see each other again."

"Bree, that's—no. Why are you saying that?"

The pull ramped up, and a jolt ran up and down my spine. My eyelid twitched as I fought the Shift off for a few more priceless moments. I could see the suspicion on his face. He thought I was lying. He thought that twitch was my tell. Only it wasn't my tell, not right now. It was just a twitch. A twitch of false hope.

I leaned up and planted a kiss in the cleft of his chin. He pulled me to him and kissed me deeply. I wove my fingertips tightly into his hair. If I could only keep this one sweet memory. But I had to let it go with all the rest.

"I love you." I let my lips linger on his. I felt like a traveler trapped in the desert, lapping up the last bit of water in her canteen. When I couldn't fight the fade any longer, I stepped away and whispered, "Until the end."

I kept my eyes open as he disappeared before me, drinking in every last drop.

The sweltering reservoir room came back into focus in scratchy blinks. The blue glow had only moved a millimeter in my absence. I must have Shifted back to nearly the instant I'd left.

Bree took a deep breath. "It's done?"

I nodded, sweat trickling down my collarbone.

"Ready?" she said.

I nodded again.

Jafney nodded.

Wyck's neck shook like he was having a muscle spasm.

Future Bree and Jafney shot each other a panicked look. This wasn't part of the plan. Wyck was having another flash, an episode, a whatever you wanted to call it.

"Stay with me!" yelled Jafney.

"Come on, Wyck," I said. "You have to focus."

"Stop talking," Future Bree hissed at me. "You make it worse when he's like this."

"Oh, can this get worse?" I pointed to the blue matter, now two inches from the console.

"You did this to me!" he shouted at Future Me. She didn't even flinch.

Jafney dropped her reverter on the floor. It rolled toward me as she rushed over to his side. She gripped his face in her hands. "This isn't you!"

His whole body shook now. Blood poured from his nose and ears. He was trying to fight off the flash, but it was beating him.

"All you have to do is hit the button, and the pain will end." Tears coursed down Jafney's cheeks, tributaries of her own grief.

"This is our only chance," said Future Bree in a small, pleading voice.

"Please," I added, helplessly.

He squeezed his eyelids shut and clenched the edges of the console.

When Wyck opened his eyes, they were clear and fresh. He looked at my Future Self and me in turn.

"I love you," he said. "From the beginning."

Finn.

"I love you," I said.

Future Me reached her hand out toward him. "Until the end."

Wyck crumpled over in pain again. When he stood back up, he was panting but in control of himself. My friend was back.

Jafney gave him a final, fierce kiss. "Let's end this."

He nodded.

"Hurry." I stooped to grab Jafney's reverter and tossed it to her. She ran back to the reservoir.

"Ready?" asked Future Me again.

All nods this time.

The blue matter was millimeters from the reservoirs. Future Bree looked to Wyck.

"Now," he said.

There was one loud click as we all three activated our reverters. At first nothing happened—the only thing I felt was terror that it hadn't worked—until the blue matter turned a murky shade of navy. Then black. And then I felt it deep in my marrow, deeper than the normal sensation of a Shift building. Not a tingling. A burning. My instinct was to yank my hand away from the console, but Bree screamed, "Hold on! Keep it activated!"

The reverter warmed in my hand until it grew unbearably hot. The metal seared my flesh, but I held my grip. I glanced over my shoulder to make sure the others were enduring. Jafney had fallen to her knees but kept the reverter in contact with the aperture. Whatever was happening affected Wyck as well. He knotted his free hand around a clump of hair, no doubt still waging battle with a legion of demons.

Future Me appeared to be in the most pain, but the most resolute as well. The tendons strained from her forearms like scalpels that could slice through her skin at any moment. Blood leaked from her nose, too, and I felt a trail of my own dribble to the corner of my mouth. She caught my eye in the reflection of the reservoir and gave me a weak attempt at a smile. The reverter grew hotter and hotter until I screamed. I had to grip the edge of the reservoir to stay upright.

The fire had reached every cell of my body, explosion after explosion after explosion. But even in the midst of the never-ending inferno, a brighter blaze told me this was the right course.

The fire reached the backs of my eyeballs, outshining my surroundings. Before my vision faded completely, I caught one last glance of my Future Self. We were both mouthing the same thing.

"Until the end."

Epilogue

I ALWAYS LOOK at the curtains first.

Purple curtains mean Mom's house. Lacy ones mean Dad's.

Well, Mom-and-Dad's, but Dad is so dang turn-of-the–twentieth-century that it's hard to think of this house as anything but his when I see lace. Which, this morning, I do.

Technically it's the same house, same bedroom, just different centuries. But it always gives me a headache to think about that.

So I don't.

I yawn and stretch my arms in one of those rapturous reach-the-rafters sprawls as my little brother Peter's Boston terrier Toodles dashes into the room barking.

"Out." I toss a pillow at the dog. It would be fun to see what Tufty would make of this mongrel, but Mom has never let me Shift an animal either direction to find out.

I throw on a simple T-shirt and long, cotton, pleated skirt that covers my very non-era sneakers. I'd rather wear a pair of jeans, or waist overalls as Dad calls them, but I'd either get rude stares from strangers or a lecture on discreetness in Shifting from my mom. So a skirt it is.

Dad's eating a bowl of some kind of granola-esque cereal, a jug of milk out on the table next to him. I skip the cereal and chug a mouthful of milk. I'll give the twentieth century this: they do milk right. So fresh and creamy. We really should look into getting a pegamoo, but they're a lot more work than a cat, and

Mom has a point that we never know when one of us will be in the twenty-third century to let it out.

Without looking up from his newsprint, Dad hands me a glass from the sideboard.

"Sorry," I say.

"You were not raised in a barn," he says with a hint of mirthful reproach, but still not looking up from his reading.

"Some of my classmates might quibble with that." I glance out into the street where a Ford Model T narrowly misses a slow-trotting horse.

Dad looks amused, but he changes the subject anyway. "What are you up to today?"

Hmm. A free Saturday. No homework. Mimi and Jaf had wanted to go shopping, but there was this cute guy named Charlie who Mimi met at the café last weekend and something told me she wouldn't mind the excuse of hanging out with him instead. And Jafney . . . well, she never passes on an excuse to spend the day lip-locked with Wyck. Besides, I'm not feeling any pull to the twenty-third century. It's not like there's a way to force our tendrils to go somewhere they're not called. So twentieth century it is.

"I think I'll just go for a walk," I say.

"Take a sweater." Mom appears out of nowhere, my brother Peter at her side. Neither Dad nor I jump, both of us used to her sudden arrivals. I decide Peter's strawberry-blond curls need a good noogie, and he fights it off with a "Bree-ee!"

Dad always says it's good that he was such an avid Jules Verne fan when Mom told him what she was. And it was good that she'd handed him a stiff shot of whiskey when she told him she was pregnant with me. By the time Peter arrived six years ago, her ability was old hat. The only hard thing was her insistence that she keep me with her when I was little, and now Peter, whichever century she's called to. That means some missed family dinners.

It gets a little complicated.

But complicated can also be fun.

Mom kisses Dad on his bald spot and bends her arm at a weird angle. "I think I twisted my elbow."

"Do you want an aspirin?" he asks.

"Are you kidding? Don't you remember that time I took one, and it made me sick to my stomach for an hour? I don't trust any medicine made before the twenty-second century."

"Suit yourself," he says, turning back to his paper

I grab a sweater off the hook and—*mwah, mwah, mwah*—plant a kiss each on Mom and Dad's cheeks, then the top of Peter's head.

"Be careful," says Dad.

A trek through ancient Mongolian warlord camps, I'm careful.

A stroll down the block, I think I should be fine.

But he's my dad. He worries. So all I say is, "I will."

And as I traipse down the street and trip over a pile of dried horse dung, I realize maybe I should have listened to him and been more careful after all. I sail headlong into a mud puddle, then give the puddle a sniff and console myself with the fact that at least the green tinge seems to be from algae rather than manure.

It's not as much consolation as one might think.

Especially as there are witnesses. Well, one witness. There's a guy standing about ten feet away, laughing at me. At first I think his hair is brown, but it glints red in the sun, and I realize the best color to describe it would be fiery auburn.

I hadn't seen him before. It's like he popped out of nowhere.

He's humming a song.

"What are you singing?" I ask.

"It's a song about being green." He gestures to the puddle and starts humming again.

"That song . . ."

"Do you know it?" He suddenly looks worried.

"I . . . no." I don't. But somehow, it feels as if I should. Like when you're listening to an echo fade away, and there's that first sliver of silence after the last faint reverberation. You know there should be *something* there, but, "No."

It's subtle, but he lets out a little puff of relief. That's when I stop and really look at him. He's wearing the male equivalent of my outfit, completely nondescript. His watch is on his wrist. That fashion trend has barely started—none of Dad's friends wear one. I have a hunch about what he is, but I need to be sure.

"Fine morning," I say.

He nods in assent.

"Fancy a stroll toward the Mall?" I ask. "I always love visiting the Lincoln Memorial when the cherry blossoms are in full bloom."

"Me, too," he says.

"Liar!" I stab an accusing finger at his chest. "I knew it."

The color drains from his face in streaks. He looks like a chameleon that can't pick a shade.

"You're a Shifter." I drop my voice down to a whisper, even though there's no one else around, and even if there were, that word would mean nothing to them.

"How did you . . . ? Wait." His lips form a perfect O. Kind of cute that way. "So are you."

"The Memorial isn't even going to open for another few years."

"You were testing me," he says, but I can tell he's impressed rather than angry.

How exactly I know that, I have no idea.

"When are you from?" he asks.

"I asked you first."

"No, you didn't."

"Well, I meant to. It's practically the same thing." I lift myself out of the puddle with his offered hand.

"Do you have plans?" he asks. "I really do love it when the cherry blossoms are out."

"Me, too." I turn away to shield my smile. He's what my father would describe as fetching. He's what I'd describe as blarking gorgeous. "And I'm free."

Our steps fall in line as we walk in the direction of the cranes and scaffolding and piles of marble, which will soon become the Lincoln Memorial.

We talk about movies.

We talk about books.

We talk about how hard it is to get a decent meal in eighteenth-century Bavaria.

I tell him green is my favorite color.

He sings me the song from earlier, about being green.

We reach the Mall, and a tour to the top of the Washington Monument has already started. I haven't been all the way up in it since I was nine. Heights aren't my plink, but something about this boy makes me brave.

"Do you want to join it?" He points to the tour group. "Or do you think we're too late?" Then he shakes his head as if he can't believe he's forgotten something. "My name's Finn by the way."

"I'm Bree. And I think we're fine." I take his offered arm as we join the back of the queue. "It's only beginning."